future tense

Praise for *Future Tense*

'A poignant meditation on young lives caught up in the sweep of history and politics. Nitasha Kaul is a fearless Kashmiri voice.'

– Mirza Waheed, author of *The Collaborator* and *The Book of Gold Leaves*

'*Future Tense* is a tautly written account of love, resistance, militancy and betrayal. It explores the manner in which conflict has crept into every crevice of the lives of the people of Kashmir. Nitasha Kaul's novels, just as much as her non-fiction, demonstrate her profound knowledge of – and her deep compassion for – Kashmir and Kashmiris.'

– Andrew Whitehead, historian of Kashmir and former BBC India correspondent

future tense

A NOVEL

NITASHA KAUL

HarperCollins *Publishers* India

First published in India by
HarperCollins *Publishers* in 2020
Building 10, Tower A, 4th Floor, DLF Cyber City, Phase II,
Gurugram Haryana – 122002, India
www.harpercollins.co.in
2 4 6 8 10 9 7 5 3 1

P-ISBN: 978-93-5357-263-1
E-ISBN: 978-93-5357-264-8

Typeset in 11.5/15.2 Linden Hill at
Manipal Technology Limited, Manipal

Printed and bound at
MicroPrints India, New Delhi

A koan for Kashmir:

If we don't know that we know,
And we don't know that we don't know,
Do we know?

Part One

What Happened After

1

IT WAS AN autumn evening falling over the house in a Kashmiri village that brought the two of them together.

The woman and child were strangers to themselves and to everyone else. Just then, not one of the many people in the household knew how to comfort either of them. Zeenat, for that was her name, had surprised everyone by ringing the doorbell that October evening, having travelled back to her ancestral home by bus. As she stepped off the vehicle at the end of the street, her head was bowed, she held a suitcase in one hand and a purse was slung over her other shoulder. It was a short walk by the orchards to the big house where her parents and other relatives lived. She arrived unannounced and refused to answer any questions, merely going up the stairs to the room that was once hers, where, now, a little stone-faced child sat in the lap of a female relative. At her approach, the woman dislodged the child from her lap, got up from the carpeted floor, and on her way out to get tea, whispered that the child's parents were dead – he was deaf–mute and had been living with them for the past few days.

When Zeenat and the child were alone in the room, they avoided each other's gaze, locked in their silent personal universes. Perhaps they understood each other perfectly. She slumped down in a corner with her back against an embroidered cushion. His small body huddled in an oversized pheran, he sat staring at a wall a few feet away from her.

Bang! Bang! Bang! Gunshots rang out on the TV screen opposite; a famous daredevil south-Indian hero was making mincemeat of the villains. It was then that she realized that the room had been noisy all this while; her cousin must have been watching the subtitled movie. The sound did not bother her, barely penetrating the iron cloak of wretchedness that she wore. The child kept staring at the wall until the woman returned with nun chai[1] and lavas on a tray. Before placing the tray on the floor, she handed the child a piece of the bread, which he accepted with the delayed reactions of a slow automaton. Zeenat too quietly took the tea, cupping her palms around the warm glass tumbler.

Her cousin touched her shoulder in a gentle gesture of sympathy, switched the television off and, pulling the curtains across the door, left the two mute strangers in the gaudy room. The colours around them challenged their grey states of mind. There was a small chair in one corner of the room, but no other furniture. The carpet that covered the entire floor was bright red, with a diamond pattern of yellow flowers threaded through it, while the walls were a light shade of blue. On one side was a glass-fronted display case that held Quranic inscriptions sewed upon an oval, green velvet backdrop, a pair of porcelain dolls, a framed fold-out family picture, and a small copper samovar. The kitsch dolls had once belonged to Zeenat, who had adored the china couple gazing at each other over a patch of colourful flowers. She looked above the rim of her tumbler and her eyes hooked upon the family picture frame. She could not relate to her own image in that glossy photograph taken on a harvest day in the orchard. Her parents stood on either side of her; everyone looked happy. This was when she had first returned home after her marriage to Fayaz in the autumn of 2013. Today, three years later, she had left her husband and her home, and she felt not even nostalgia or regret, just a piercing sensation of inevitability. Despite all her efforts, Fayaz had perhaps never really loved her.

A rasping sound caught her attention and she turned to see that the child was crumbling bits of crusty bread on the carpet. It stood to reason that she should ask him not to do this, but she stared at him doing it without feeling any need to interrupt him. He was too engrossed in the action, and seemingly unafraid of any sanction. She finished her tea and stood up, leaving the glass on the carpet and not back on the tray. Walking over to the window on the back wall, she pulled the curtains aside and listlessly stared from behind the closed windowpanes at the fading light. The calls to prayer in the local mosque were over, and the birds were flying home in erratic formations over the dark mass of trees. She turned back, leaving the curtain as it was, and sat down again – cross-legged and a little closer to the child.

At length, he looked up. Their eyes met with an unyielding silence that had its own caravan of ruinous secrets. These two stones in a room: What had he seen? What had she felt? Before tears could well up in her eyes, she looked away. He too blinked his eyes, stopped crumbling the bread, and lay down. Tonight, there would be no consolation for these souls trapped in their shells.

Downstairs, the family members continued to confer about Zeenat's unexpected arrival. Her aunt – her father's sister – could not refrain from expressing her shock and dismay at the fact that the girl had chosen to travel unaccompanied, by public transport, under the present circumstances. It was intended to be a barb against her mother and the upbringing that Zeenat had received. Her mother suggested that they call her husband Fayaz right away and enquire as to what had happened. Her father was of the opinion that they should wait till the next morning, when she might be more amenable to speaking. The latter course of action was decided to be the wiser, since they would first hear what Zeenat might say. Moreover, they would have the option of going over to her husband's family home during the day.

It was dark now, and venturing out would be tempting fate, given the presence of armed patrols that treated every moving Kashmiri body with a suspicion that could escalate at the slightest hint and translate into the firing of pellets, if not bullets.

Once this consensus was established, food was sent up to Zeenat and the child. Zeenat's mother herself brought it up, exhorting her to eat well even if she didn't feel like it. The old woman fed the child with her own hands. Like a fledgling bird, he hungrily took each morsel of the rice mixed with meat gravy from between the tips of her extended fingers and chewed upon it, taking a long time to finish. He was then led by the hand to wash himself and get ready to sleep. Zeenat's cousin helped the little boy change his clothes, after which he promptly lay down on the mattress and, covering himself with a sheet, closed his eyes. Zeenat, on the other hand, lay awake in the darkened room, staring at the shadows on the walls.

Everything played out in her head – her days of loving Fayaz, her happiness at their marriage being settled, their first months in Srinagar, her excitement at seeing him return from work in the evenings, their nights in that marital bed, and what followed. It was not when the floods of 2014 had submerged much of the city and spread a sheet of watery chaos all around them, but later, once the waters had receded and the rebuilding had begun, that she had felt Fayaz pull away from her, gradually at first, but definitively as time went on. He had never been easy to understand – something that had added to his charm. His serious mystique had drawn her to him; but as the months passed, he became, not un-understandable, but unworthy of understanding, almost; not merely callous, but cruel. She felt as if she were an albatross hung around his neck – a burden that he had to carry, when all she wanted from him was the warmth of care and affection. He refused her the slightest attention without letting her know the cause of his resentment, or explaining whether it was even connected to her. It made her feel unattractive, foolish, older, and the last was particularly harsh since it was truly the case that she was three years older than him.

They were cousins from the same village and, after he got a job in the administrative services, her family had approached them with the proposal. The social mathematics were that while she was older than him, her family was considerably wealthier than theirs. Nonetheless, his family could have refused the alliance, but they hadn't. So, why should she be blamed for loving him if he had himself agreed to the wedding? He had never himself said anything to her about her age, but she could not help wondering. In those months, she had gone through entire lists of possible reasons in her head as to why Fayaz was distancing himself from her. She had even considered enrolling on a further education course by correspondence, in case he felt that she was not educated enough for a man in a respectable job like his. She had spent hours looking for rare ingredients and cooked exquisite meals for him; she had put on newer perfumes and fancier jewellery, but nothing had made a difference.

It was true, her efforts did initially mean that he was more predisposed to reach out for her body at night; but during the harsh light of the day, everything again resumed its usual course. In the first months after their wedding, he had once brought her a pair of earrings that were very dear to her. In those darkening days of winter after the floods, when she tried to repair their bond, she would always wear these earrings and make sure to put on the salwar-kameez sets he had once liked, as she waited for him in the evenings, and on occasion, late into the nights. She had felt abject, as if she was less of a wife, and more of a failed mistress. Still, she wove frail threads of hope from everything she could. At nights, when he got into the bed beside her, he would immediately turn his back to her and seem sleepy. Often, he would really drift into sleep. But, every now and again, after a while, as if unable to resist a pull, he would turn towards her without any warning and slide closer. When this happened, she knew that he was still somehow hers. He would pull away her clothes clumsily, impatient at the bra that wouldn't unhook soon enough or the salwar whose knot he could not immediately untie, and kiss her lips and breasts with a passionate and devouring ferocity, leaving rose-red marks on her skin and turning her body into a shivering instrument of his desires. When this happened, her spirit was unburdened, she felt sated, and seeded with hope. She lay next to him every night, not knowing when he would pierce her body with his want and when she would not even exist for him in the room. This, at last, exhausted her. She cared less about what she wore and sometimes slid into sleep without waiting to find out what he would do. Her lack of effort at seducing him made him want her less, but her body more. During those later days, when he did enter her body furtively, consuming her with a right that he thought he had, she felt she was sacrificing and surrendering herself to a cause she did not know any more. Without a murmur, she let him dominate her drowsy body, feeling not the pleasure of a union, but a painful sucking of her breasts and a wetness that marked the sheets underneath her. Her unresponsive state did not make a difference to him. After many such nights of being raped, she became numb even to the realization of what was happening to her. Then, this fumbling of the bodies stopped too. He was transferred to Ladakh in the spring of 2015, and he chose to go alone.

She spent most of that night knitting dark shrouds of sorrow for herself from the shadows on the wall. The next morning, she answered a few questions, making it clear to her mother that her husband had deserted her physically and emotionally. Her family had not stopped worrying for her for a whole year now. They knew that he was not living with her, were troubled that she wasn't pregnant yet, and fretted about the future of their only daughter. Her mother wept as she heard about the abuse she had suffered at his hands. Zeenat wished she could have made her marriage work, but she had tried every way that she knew how and had ultimately given up.

That entire summer, not a day had gone by when she had not spent hours crying. At times, she was not even sure what the tears were for. She would hear about the young men dying, the little girl blinded by pellets, the man beaten to death. It was as if a dam had been burst with Burhan's killing and another kind of flood – of despair and defiance – had swept the entire Valley. The cries of 'Azadi' were everywhere. During the hours when the curfew was relaxed, when it was possible to go out to buy supplies for the household, everywhere she looked, she saw the slogans of Burhan's martyrdom and immortality. Being a village girl who had seen the worst times in her childhood, she felt the pain of these fighters who braved the police, the army, the collaborators, the world's indifference, to bust their lungs repeating the one word over and over: Freedom! Azadi! She would shed silent tears that whole summer as she sliced the vegetables alone in the kitchen, cooking her thoughts in the pots and pans alongside the meat and vegetables. Her depression related to her misery as a woman, as a wife and daughter, and as an organ of the Kashmiri body that was being besieged, blinded and brutalized.

The next morning, after breakfast, her father went over to Fayaz's family home, returning several hours later with downcast eyes. Everyone understood what this meant. Fayaz had refused to listen to his family. To the indignity of this humiliation at the hands of their own relatives was the added fact of Zeenat's family having contributed financially to their son-in-law's success and having been repaid with such ingratitude. Zeenat's father and Fayaz's mother were first cousins, but the children had not interacted much during their childhood due to Fayaz being away at a foster home in Srinagar. Fayaz was the serious one, the man who had been the first in their village to grow up in Srinagar, to go to Delhi for his graduation, and later pass the KAS administrative services exam. His command over the English language was praised widely and he had a stable future ahead of him as a government bureaucrat. He was the person whom everyone, including the village elders, called when they needed help or advice.

His success had been exceptional given that he had started out with literally nothing. Fayaz's father had joined the militancy in the 1980s, crossing the border over to Pakistan for training. He had not returned home for nearly a decade, having joined the fighting ranks of Hizbul Mujahideen. The circumstances of his eventual return were not clear, and it was not a straightforward return anyway, since he had spent some years in jail, and had an experience of being in torture centres too. Growing up, Fayaz had spent little time with his birth family; his father was in and out of jails, and his elder brother Junaid was raised by his mother. Over the years, the family had gathered again and was now settled back in their village.

When Junaid got married and had a son, Fayaz found a new bond with Imran, his nephew – a cheerful boy who was the light and life of the household. Imran and Fayaz were only a few years apart, and the uncle and nephew had kept in close touch over the years. Having qualified as an officer, when Fayaz finally returned to his village in the spring of 2013, there had been a huge celebration. His father had invited even those he did not know. Fayaz had surpassed everyone's expectations and made his parents proud. When Zeenat's family proposed the alliance between them, Fayaz's father readily agreed. The family owned little land, and had needed to borrow money from Zeenat's family to pay for Fayaz's education and training in Delhi. A match between the two would cancel these debts and add wealth to the prestige that their son now had from his chosen profession. There was the matter of the girl being a few years older than the boy, but it was decided to overlook this fact, and Fayaz had nodded in agreement, sealing the deal.

Three years later, many things had changed. Fayaz's father had passed away from a heart attack in the winter of 2014 and his elder brother Junaid, who ran a contracting business, took over the running of the household. When Imran finished school, he was sent to Srinagar to live with Fayaz and Zeenat, but then Fayaz moved to Leh in 2015 and made arrangements for Imran to stay at the home of his friend Gul Mohammed, a police officer.

Zeenat stared at her reflection in the mirror as she thought of these changes. She had changed too. Towards the front of her forehead where her head was not draped in the black shawl, she saw strands of white hair. How many? Three. What a coincidence; one for each year of her failed marriage.

Zeenat was called to the room where the elders sat deliberating over her life. She was informed that she would not be forced to return to her husband. A wait and see approach had been agreed upon. If their worst fears were realized and no reconciliation was possible, she should not worry – they would find her another groom. She was childless and with an inheritance. A match could be arranged for her in due course, by which they meant, in the next few years. Zeenat heard them in silence and it seemed to her that they were talking of someone else. She was not expected to reply and she didn't. When they had finished, she went out to the garden and whom should she find there again but the mute child stranger.

The beatific child was squatting on his haunches in the garden and counting the autumn leaves. A small grey waddle of pheran topped by a full moon face, he must have possessed a deep reserve of inherited patience, for he picked up the leaves carefully one by one and lay them on the side; brought to him by the wind, they were carried away by the same wind. How many leaves was he counting over and over? It didn't seem to bother him. Occasionally, he would pause, mesmerized by the vein network on the dry rusty surface. These leaves were engraved by nature and, as he ran his fingertip along the central vein, perhaps he was marvelling at the scattered beauty of the leaves. Or was he thinking sadly of how the leaves are separated from the trees?

Zeenat looked up at the thinning foliage on the tree beside him and imagined the branches to be grieving the loss of the leaves that would never hang from their perch again. Saying a farewell to their home, they fly away, dancing in the wind before being crushed underfoot. The indifferent sky above the child paid no heed to his silent melancholy. He went counting on. He must have reached a count of five hundred something, when the loud and continuous barking of a dog from the dirt track beyond the fence scared him. Like him, Zeenat didn't like dogs, though they seemed to be multiplying with each passing day.

As she watched this child, she thought of how she had yearned for Fayaz to give her a child of her own. It was an inward cry that would ring in her as she went about unwrapping and opening the boxes of solitary mornings that she faced after he left for work. Distracting herself with bustle, she would move back and forth between the kitchen and the rooms, arranging the bedcovers, sorting the clothes for washing, emptying his ashtrays, checking the fridge, boiling water for tea, putting on the electric geyser in the bathroom, checking that the taped-up electric plug was working. In the afternoons, she would languidly comb her hair in front of the dressing-table mirror that had been a gift from her in-laws for their wedding. The small wooden tabletop surface attached to the bottom end of the mirror would be cluttered with her colourful plastic clips, shampoo and conditioner sachets, face powder, kohl pencils, nail polish and a precious little bottle of perfume. She would fumble trying to find things, but the one thing she never misplaced was the pair of earrings that Fayaz had given her.

For a whole four weeks during the time of floods, she had been sure that she was pregnant. She had imagined a glow on her cheeks, thought longingly of her belly that would grow over the autumn and winter, and dreamt of the birth of a beautiful child in the spring. She would wrap him warm in covers embroidered in her own hand and cradle him by the window and sing to him of the emerald leaves blazing with a beauty in every fibre of their being. The liquid gold of the rising sun would warm them bit by bit as the five-pointed chinar leaves, uncurling one by one from the tall trees, would carry forth each wish of hers from the deep wet bosom of the earth to the leafy tips reaching the skies. The child would softly open its marbled eyes and she would lovingly gaze for an eternity into the tenderness of that creation. She would love the child so much that her heart would burst its boundaries!

But, a month afterwards, she had woken up with a tremendous pain in her abdomen. Carefully and quietly, so as not to wake him up, she had climbed out of bed clutching her belly and proceeded with the ritual of washing her salwar, and covering the bleeding between her legs with a cotton sanitary pad. She was menstruating again that summer, and it meant that she was not carrying a baby. She wanted so much to be a mother that those manic moments when Fayaz was inside her, she forgot even to ache with passion because she lost herself wishing, oh so deeply wishing, that she might carry him in her as a new person.

She had been told that this deaf-mute child in front of her was a guest in their home. His mother had passed away during childbirth and his father had been shot dead in front of his eyes. His parents had been poor and nobody wanted to take responsibility for the orphan child. The village gravedigger had left him with Zeenat's parents, requesting asylum for him for a few days while he was away. Zeenat wanted to feel the surge of love that she had once nurtured in the depths of her heart, but she was so broken that not even a motherly feminine feeling rose out of her stone-cold heart to comfort this small human being cursed with such a sordid fate.

It was an autumn of suffering and the world had lost an entire layer of enchantment. She had tried to learn a man, a city, a life, but what was she left with? The delicately winged bird of memory had brought back from that time of a hundred thousand eminently coarse dealings and doings with the world and her own body in it, only a realization of the ultimate perils of intimacy. She felt blank and bare.

'You are so emotional. It is good that you weren't the wife of a terrorist, or he could have made you do anything.' Fayaz had said to her that summer, coating his barb with the semblance of bitter wisdom.

'And you aren't a terrorist? An emotional terrorist? Look how you have hijacked these years of my life.'

He had walked away quietly at her response.

When boarding the mini-bus in Srinagar the previous afternoon, only one thought had possessed her: To begin with, she must drop her bags somewhere; it would be a surrender, but also a picking up of life. When the bus had sped away after dropping her, she saw the words stickered on the glass panel at the back of the vehicle: 'Never Trast An Stranger.' She had trusted Fayaz to build a life with her, and he had turned their relationship into a bully school: her intelligence insulted, her convictions questioned, her beliefs scarred, her innermost purities violated. The ribbons of her love and desire had gone twirling themselves around his life, and she had been damned. She had come to hate the constant accounting, the haggling, the arguing, the discussing of what emotion and how much and why not and how much time and wait. Time that coagulated in smelly pools around her ankles. In the end, she had left him wordlessly, without even making the expected insinuations of poor conscience against him. Underneath herself, she felt a strange self of hers. This morning, it exhilarated and terrified her.

A blackbird hopped on the green grass among the scattered leaves, before going back to its perch among the branches that intersected like so many thoughts and lives. She went inside the house and on to the kitchen where she didn't need to ask what she could help with in order to be given things to do. It was a large house and there was food to be cooked, farm animals to be cared for, fields to be managed. If the life in the mountains around them was remote, rarefied, fragile and faithless, then life in a farming household like theirs was profuse and entangled, fragrant with breathing life forms, picking up pace during hot afternoons on the back of sweaty labours.

As time went by, the deaf-mute child was taken away to live with the village gravedigger and no one missed him except Zeenat, who occasionally wished she had been kinder to him. Everyone noticed that Zeenat spoke much less now than at any other time – only a few words when needed – but they figured that this was her process of mourning her broken marriage. In fact, she had thrown herself wholeheartedly into household work, staying busy from morning till night. The exhaustion of the day gifted her a fitful sleep at night, but she was not worn out from work alone. All day, her silence fermented in the cauldron of her being, till it began to solidify into a desire for revenge. This wish to avenge herself upon Fayaz was her secret, and she nourished it with her pain and carried it around inside her, growing it with each passing day.

Autumn deepened its palette outdoors, spreading a chill on the ground and setting fire to the leaves. On windy rainy nights, when sleep would not come to Zeenat, she would turn out the lights and lie down, only to spend hours staring at the droplets threaded through the cobwebs suspended from the wooden eaves alongside the braids of wires and the naked unlit bulb – everything she saw told her the stories of currents in abeyance, the spiderwebs hung from her very soul and she was ever so surely consumed by the woodworms of a wasted life. She wished for silence, to banish all words from all worlds. Sometimes, her thoughts were intruded upon by images she did not invite. The petals as they eventually surrender to the ruin of the rain. She did not want to think of him standing on the other side of a silent room, his lips whistling and his uncertain eyes reminding her of forgotten songs from times long past.

She had wanted to think with, in, and through him. For them to share questions, anguish, despair, timorous hopes, dreams, regard and feelings together. But, she knew now that her husband Fayaz was constantly losing his self because he was made impotent by his life and surroundings. He was a man who could not bear to be human enough and who did not know how to rebel. His cruelty was not just a symptom or affect, but central to his very mode of existence. And he could not be helped or made sense of. At times, she felt a tremendous outrage, blood gushing at the sheer reality, the all-too-easy possibility, and the pedestrian everydayness of this, of such a brutalization occurring. Of course, it was everywhere in this war zone that was their homeland, in extraordinary renditions, in little police cells, in quiet bedrooms, this incredible yet incessant violence of one upon the other. There was perhaps no hope, but she wanted to be redeemed, even if weakly, through some quixotic act of revenge, outrage and its confession. What she knew for certain was that the outrage needed to be preserved, to be nurtured, for anything to matter at all for a human being. That was the rebellion, inside oneself and then outside, but first of all, always inside.

2

FAYAZ WAS NOT heartbroken when he came home in the evening to see that his wife Zeenat had left him. Their last few months of living together had created a menacing atmosphere, made of laconic silences and forced composure on his part, and implied condemnations and endless sobbing on hers. Perhaps it was for the best that she was gone. His life was partitioned into the many masks he had to put on when dealing with work, with the family, with Zeenat. The only people around whom he felt truly comfortable were his small circle of three men. Over the years, he had deliberately lost touch with many other friends, paring down his bonds to the ones that mattered most to him – with Imran, Rehan and Gul.

Rehan and Gul were his friends from the days of schooling in Srinagar. Gul, who had been their senior by a few years, had stayed on in the city when Rehan and Fayaz had gone to Delhi for their graduation. They had continued living there for another year after their degree to attend the cram school for the civil services examination. Fayaz had qualified and returned as an officer, but Rehan had failed and given up, deciding instead to pursue a tricky career as a journalist in Kashmir. The two men were rather different from one another, but numerous years of shared history and experiences together had led them to understand each other well. Rehan often challenged conventions and displayed a scrupulous integrity at work. Somewhat vain, he was quite the charmer, a man who could recite poetry at the drop of a hat to make hearts heave and lashes flutter. In spite of having a long-term girlfriend in Delhi, his court of worshipful admirers was not much less diminished in Srinagar. Fayaz, on the other hand, made up for his lack of frivolity with his intelligence and discretion. He carried a witheringly necessary need to please those who mattered to him, but was not always able to reconcile with what this required of him. This also meant that he could be squeamish when it came to facing up to resolutions and consequences.

Gul, all in all, was a reliable maverick. He defied the expectations of his family by deciding to join the police services. Without a doubt, it was a career that allowed a significant exercise of power over people, but it was also a profession marked by ignominy and profligacy in Kashmir. His father had been a reasonably respected religious activist, and his son's job would bring them a little envy and a lot of shame. For most people living under difficult circumstances, everyday travails grind down cherished principles to fine dust, which soon vaporizes; and so, as Gul became established and well-connected, he was sought after by his friends and neighbours who might scorn him in private but who needed his help to get files moved through dusty offices, permissions signed, permits arranged, and for their sons to be rescued from police stations when in trouble. When Gul's family wanted a daughter-in-law to keep his mother company at home, he dutifully married. A few years later, when the clashes between his wife and her mother-in-law intensified and assumed the nature of a feud, he again did what his mother suggested, and remarried. The first wife had borne him a pair of twin boys and the second one a baby girl in the previous year. He took the changing seasons of life in his stride and focused on simplifying things whenever possible.

Imran was Fayaz's nephew, the child who had grown up in front of him and who had almost been like a younger brother to him. Fayaz felt a special sense of protectiveness towards him, a motherly feeling that he could not fathom at the root. He saw something of an alternate future for himself in Imran's struggles to choose his path in life. Fayaz was sure that his own parents had tried to do their best for him, given the circumstances in which they had lived. His mother, especially, had endured excessive hardship, living with relatives and bringing up his elder brother Junaid during all those years when his father had taken up the jihad for Kashmir with HM and the gun. But, knowing this, he also felt that they had been somehow amiss in what they had done to him and expected of him. As a little boy in that Srinagar seminary, he had reproached them inwardly for letting him be there, far from the open fields of his village, far from their love. He had shackled his life to the fruition of their expectations, done what they wanted at every step.

As Imran was maturing into a young man, Fayaz understood better the complexities of what was involved in letting a young man do what he wanted. Imran, for instance, had from a very early age wanted to be a cricketer. But who would recommend that as an option? He would never have the facilities for the required training or the significant connexions that were necessary to be picked for a team. And would Imran himself want to play for the Indian team? In all his attempts to dissuade Imran from this ambition, this last question had been the clincher. Imran had finally given up, but then he had started to spend too much time with the problematic young men of the village. His father Junaid had become fearful that he might one day run away to join the militants. So, Fayaz was prevailed upon to persuade Imran to see sense and move to Srinagar. For an extra measure of oversight and safety, Imran was later settled into the household of Fayaz's friend, Gul the policeman. Ever since his transfer away from Srinagar last spring, Fayaz had not been able to be as involved with Imran's life as he once was, and he reproached himself for this. He hoped that the young man was studying as expected. However, what did that mean in this city where, due to curfews, hartals and routine outbursts of rebellious unrest, exams were delayed every year, semesters were left incomplete, and young men chose stones or phones to express their anger and anguish!

This evening, as he sat in his empty flat, Fayaz wished he could counterfeit a worry-free life for himself, a different one in another country and continent and time. But there was no escaping the shackles that bound him to this job. How wonderful it must be to do something that one cared about and wanted to do! A sensation that he had once briefly known. He sighed at the thought of his dreams with her ... Otherwise, life had stretched out as a series of compromises he had made, or would make, to accommodate the wishes of his father, his mother, his wife, and perhaps one day, his children.

He had come to Srinagar as a young boy because his mother had wanted him to be safe from the raids by the army, from the unpredictable movements of the militants, from the guns slung on the shoulders of his father and his uncles, and from the burden of a struggle for liberation that had taken on so many fragmented forms, seemingly never to end. She had wanted him to have a future. But, somehow, those dreams of a future had brought him to spending his days surrounded by the miserable loneliness of an inaccessible past in the centre of a city that was more congested and less livable every new day.

And this city had never welcomed him with open arms. Like the woman he had ended up marrying, he mostly didn't know what to make of it. It was occasionally all plain to him and he could love it for the highs and lows of the experiences he had shared with it, but it was resilient and unforgiving too, and harsh, and petulant at times. And at those times, he felt that everything he was, and everything he could ever do, would always be a mistake as long as he was here. The woman, his wife, whom he had brought to this city, she was, also, the city to him. And the city was her. And he didn't know whether she shared any of his fever at all. Like the city, she had not surrendered herself to him.

Tonight, he was so far from everything he loved. The wide open spaces ringed by mountains that were pencilled sharply into the outlines of a blue heaven; the abundant orchards of fruits that would make the harvesters sweat profusely; the numberless smooth round stones that lined the banks of the stream in his village. A small universe where the seasons lingered as they gently merged into each other, the world of his very early boyhood where he could play under the chinar trees, sit for long hours in the courtyards of neighbours' houses where people would gather on the grass-woven mats to exchange stories, cares and concerns. A world that he had lost, perhaps forever.

It was as if a pitiless snowstorm had covered his past and converted everything into a blank white nothingness. This thought of snow in autumn reminded him of that evening of the first snow in late 2013, after he had set up a life with Zeenat in the city. On his way back home late from work, he had asked the driver of the office car to take a detour and stop at a jewellery shop that was still open near the Chowk. He had gone in without knowing the what or the why of the how that he felt, propelled forward as if by an urgent desire to give a concrete shape to the rush of things in his head, where emotions were crisscrossing each other at a faster pace than the flurries of snow outside. Within moments, he had paid the shopkeeper the fairly large sum of money, and climbed back into the car, bemused at the perplexed expression of the driver who held the door open for him. He had blinked his eyes to melt the flakes on his eyelashes and clasped his fingers a little more tightly around the small red velvet box that held the earrings that he had bought for Zeenat.

Zeenat, his wife, who had cooked and cleaned for him. The woman he had tried to possess in a fierce fog of ardour underneath the blankets with an intoxicated delirium that was a mix of arousal and sleep. But had he loved her? He didn't know. His eyes fastened on the glowing orange lamp in front of him, he wondered. He could be truthful with himself, couldn't he? He had sometimes told her that he loved her.

He had missed her terribly when she had gone to her parents' house for a week after their wedding. He liked to see the hesitation and excitement animating her face when watching her choose clothes as she stood in front of the almirah in their room. When they went out to buy anything, just the two of them, he often let her bargain things down to a price below what they could afford because he enjoyed seeing her come up with creative reasons why the set of cups or the cushions were not worth the money being demanded. He had married too soon; she was wiser than him but still had let him break her. He felt ashamed at how he had used her body while spurning her soul. He had loved her breasts and the outline of her lips. Sometimes, he wished they could have been freer. Or rather, he wished that he could have been less inhibited before he married her. Like the teenage boys these days who didn't think twice before going out strolling with their girlfriends, and spent every minute texting and chatting with girls on their phones. Perhaps these young boys had already tasted the fruits of love; at their age, he was almost an ascetic.

His early years in Srinagar had been spent in a seminary where any contact with the opposite sex was forbidden. The institution was run by a charitable Islamic foundation and aimed to inculcate religious education in young boys. The days would begin early with a recital of holy verses, and regular prayers punctuated the set routine. He recalled his eleven-year-old self: what class was he in at the time? Fifth, yes, probably. He must have had a fight with one of the other boys. He couldn't really remember what the tussle had been about, but it had come to blows and he had been punished; unfairly, he was sure. That afternoon, he found himself alone in a locked room, impotent with rage, hot tears streaming down his cheeks. He had felt an electric current of multiple frustrations running through his veins. He missed his home, especially his mother; he was angry at his parents for sending him here; he hated the school and the people in it; he despised this busy and uncaring city; he didn't want to follow any rules; he wanted not to have the recurring nightmares every night: of soldiers firing at him for no reason; he wanted to watch movies; he wanted to exhaust his eyes staring at the gates of the girls' college across the street; he wanted the classmate and the teacher who had hurt him to get what they deserved; maybe he was hungry too. He wanted to grow up very quickly so that he could be free.

I wish I could grow two years with every one – this had been a fervent wish of his during those days. In all honesty, the thought of that wish had first come to him one late morning when he had sneaked out to a window on the topmost floor of the school building, which faced the street. He had cautiously peered out at the scene over the boundary wall of his school and across the street. From behind the distortions of the glass pane, from between the vertical straight lines of the trees on the pavement, across the dusty road piled with vehicles, he had seen the blue metal arch that proclaimed the name of the local girls' college. There they were, these fascinating unknown creatures that caused his spirit to dance with such abundant joy! These young women in their salwar-kameezes and woollen cardigans, their heads covered (oh so beautifully!), their purses slung on their shoulders, books in their hands as they passed by underneath the arch, past the guard at the gate and the barbed wire rolls all around. The way they walked, their grace! How they talked to each other, animatedly, with embarrassed smiles! They would touch each other's hands sometimes as they discussed ... who knows what! Oh, these fabulous beings who were only a few metres away from him every day, and yet he could neither approach them nor talk to them. His schoolboy self, standing there by the window, saw these young women as if they were heavenly marionettes in a dream that only he could see. Being unable to hear them, he gently placed his index finger on the glass in front of him and tried to touch each form as it receded away from him. Her! And her! And look at her! They lingered in his mind long after each of them was gone, and they toyed with every feeling that he had ever had, even much later as he sat in a class where he understood nothing at all. All he could think of was that the entire magic of the universe was beyond the confines of this building and this body – prisons where his youth must be wasted by the sure desiccation of his desires. These girls were much older than him and so he wished that he would grow two years in one, catching up with them, and with his freedom.

'You grew up, and look, how free you are!' His inner voice said with a cruel laugh. 'What have you? Neither the faith of the devout nor the freedom of the irreconcilable!' He could not counter this. That afternoon at school, in that locked room, alone, he had realized that he was fundamentally alone. Everyone was. And yet, people were able to grow out of themselves and take root inside others, and this, he knew, was not something he had achieved yet with anyone, not with his family, not with his friends, and not with Zeenat. He had perhaps once been on the cusp of such a connexion ... with her ... but she had been lost too. Was it a bad thing? He thought about it for a long minute, yes, he was not self-deficient. Maybe that wasn't a bad thing after all?

He had wanted to be an adult who could decide what to do with his life. Surely, all grown-ups could do that. His father had chosen to be a militant, hadn't he? Then, the older man had chosen to leave the struggle and focus on setting up the contracting business that Junaid now managed. These had been his father's choices. Not even his poor mother had had any say in the matter. If Fayaz had control over his own life, he could also do what he wished. And this life was his own ... but could he do what he wished? He sighed softly. He knew the answer. They had wanted him to be trained in a religious school so he would not ruin his life in the company of those illiterates who throw stones at the mighty occupation; then they had expected him to graduate in a subject like physics because he was good at mathematics; later, he had been asked to marry a good girl who had been chosen for him because her family were wealthy. In spite of his reservations, which had multiplied with every passing step, he had gone along with all of that.

He was, he thought, a good son and a reasonably decent man. Now, he was expected to continue working in his permanent government job that brought him influence, status and an official car topped by a red light; in the future, he was expected to impregnate his wife so that they would have a son. And then, what? Everything would be settled, everyone would be happy. Or, rather, he would have successfully made everyone happy. They would love him. But would he love himself? Did he love himself enough to seek out his happiness? Even if it made others unhappy? Would he allow himself to dream of things that others would not approve of? All his life, he had loved himself too much and too little at the same time, being unable to let go in front of anyone else, and yet submitting to everyone else.

Of what use is a reverie? Men dream in their idle hours, of all that they know to be unrealizable and untrue. Yes, if it were possible, gamblers would nightly look at starry skies as a table full of riches and imagine that they owned all of its diamonds. Dressed in their finery, they would, with the slightest dash of their left palm, clear the dark table of its stars, gather them in a gleaming fistful and scatter them at their feet with an insouciance that betrayed a determined innocence of value. And poets would look at a cloud and think upon how that cushiony down was a personal umbrella they could hold up to shield their precious thoughts against the harsh glare of a bright world. Children would, fearless of cold or censure, run in the rain, chasing the trail of water spiders made by the large drops as they crashed upon concrete, splitting into many little legs of water. And who knows, young men, crazed by the desire for freedom and a longing for their rights, would see only trees that flowered stones everywhere. Round smooth stones, weightless when on the branches of willows, but which would suddenly become heavy arsenal when thrown at the shuttered vehicles of the enemy-with-guns, ripping large holes through this enemy's destructive passion for a land it couldn't subdue and couldn't let go. And soldiers, in turn, would dream of stone eyes for those who resist, a vast and prolific blindness that would turn an entire nation into a silent stage where puppets performed pliantly for their political masters.

This last thought brought Fayaz back to sobriety. His entire life had been an indulgence built upon the sacrifices of others – the tens and hundreds he knew, and the many hundreds of thousands he would never know. Had he not lost friends who had fallen to the enemy bullets? Did he not remember how his mother had feared for their lives at those popping sounds of gunfire in the dead of night? Was it not his own father who had been in and out of those horrific torture centres? How could he forget the raw fear that welled up in him, that churning panic in his stomach, that persistent shiver up his spine – the dread of security forces; a feeling so familiar to him now that he had come to disregard it as being a strange sensation he experienced every time he was stopped by anyone in uniform? In an old photograph, long since destroyed, Fayaz can still see himself as a very small child, standing next to his seated father, with an outsized gun slung upon his tiny shoulder. In that picture, he was smiling beatifically, free of any care. But for the burden of those expectations that made his life what it was now, he may have been a militant. Certainly, by now, a slain militant. A martyr. A casualty. A statistic. A staccato voice read out these terms in his head ... If he was lucky, he would be a named dead body in a Kashmiri graveyard.

His long rumination about his life was interrupted by the phone ringing. It was Rehan asking him if he'd like to meet up. Fayaz tossed the thought around in his head for a moment before saying yes. Rehan was finishing a story for his editor and would come to pick him up in his car at Lal Chowk in an hour.

Fayaz stepped out into a relatively mild evening, marked by occasional gusts of cool breeze. Along the way, he observed the multiple construction sites in his neighbourhood. There were accretions of mud everywhere. In spite of the late hour, there was still a fading light outdoors. He decided to walk in the direction of the Abdullah footbridge and, crossing it, walk left through the streets towards Lal Chowk. Oblivious to other pedestrians, he paused in the middle of the bridge and, resting his arms loosely on the metal rails, inspected the sight he beheld. At times like this, he felt he was wrong and harsh in his judgement of this city. It was beautiful! Who could remain unmoved in the presence of this paradise? He had come from the soil of this land, and its perfume was all he knew. His village was also bound to change someday, and Srinagar too, once, would have been smaller and more precious.

He contemplated the poetry of nature's verses in the still, black-and-white calligraphy of the silhouetted trees, their branches silently supplicating the skies. The mountains came into view in the far distance, gently, like a lover, and then momentarily slipped away in a cloudy haze. On the banks of the Jhelum River to his either side, beyond the moored houseboats, were roads stringed with the glittering white moonstones and the blood red rubies of car headlights as they slid up and down the streets. He saw the awkwardly ambling grey elephant of a crowded bus. Soon, the soothing, ascendant sounds of azaans from the surrounding mosques rung in his ears and a moving hieroglyphic appeared in the soul-blue skies. A flock of pigeons, of the kind that daily congregated on the corrugated roofs of shrines and queued together on wiry perches across the city's lampposts, was flying home. An unknown prayer rose from his heart and escaped through his breath at what he saw. It was as if not only his eyes but his heart too could touch every outline in front of him. He reached into his pocket and took out a cigarette. He wanted to light the ember tip of his cigarette against a star in the sky tonight.

Then, just as he was about to move on, he heard a loud racket somewhere beneath him. He noticed for the first time the hole in the walkway where the metal rafters of the bridge pierced down into the flowing waters of the river. It was a place where numerous birds assembled in the evening. A large gathering screeched loudly in a chorus on the underside of the bridge. He had previously heard similar sounds from the birds that formed a dark mass on the neon-lit trees outside Hazratbal or the Shah-i-Hamdan shrines at night. Inexplicably, the noise made him think of funerals of slain protestors, which were marked by thronging crowds chanting slogans of freedom, of Azadi, in this city and elsewhere. What were the birds shouting? Had one of them died? Did they too want freedom from the gut-wrenching limitations of this paradise?

Shaking off these thoughts, he stubbed his cigarette underfoot and hurried onwards. When he checked his mobile phone screen for the time, he noted that tonight there were no missed calls from Zeenat. Rushing past the superbly fortified houses of the wealthy political-business elite and through the narrow lane of congested shops on his left, he realized how he had outgrown – perhaps too quickly after being married – the urge to hear her voice, to ask her what she was cooking, to utter enderments to her. She had become a fixture in his life. And now she was gone, maybe for good.

The roads around the clocktower at the centre of Lal Chowk were busy. Fayaz stopped at the corner where a mutton seller was doing brisk business serving bread and curried meat from the large round aluminum pot on a small stove in front of him. Deciding to wait there, his eyes strayed to the big CRPF bunker across the road. There, behind a periphery formed by rolls of barbed wire, stood the large olive-green army vehicle with a little metal hat on the top, from where a gun permanently poked out, ever ready to shoot at any sign of trouble. Under the camouflage roofing was a small metal cage with a wire mesh window where two security men stood, also with guns. Nobody paid any of this any attention and, had Fayaz not been waiting directly opposite, he would likely not have, either.

Nonetheless, the sight irritated him and scratched his sense of himself. He turned the corner and thought of going up into the park on his right beyond the gazebo where a pair were engaged in what seemed to be a surreptitious rendezvous. Before he could make up his mind, he received a call from Rehan, who had reached there and was trying to spot him at the intersection.

The cars behind him honked impatiently as Rehan reached out to quickly unlock the door for Fayaz, chirping, 'Fayaz, my brother! How are you?' Simultaneously, he turned down the volume of a song slightly and reached for a cigarette packet on the dashboard. Fayaz felt a surge of warmth. Oh, he had missed his friend! Only his friends could understand something of who he really was. They restored him to himself.

The car was soon on its way through the many traffic jams on the icy roads.

'How are you, brother? How is Zeenat Bhabhi? All well at home?' Rehan asked again. He knew that things between Fayaz and Zeenat had not been good for a while, but never failed to ask the perfunctory question, to which he always received the same answer: 'Life goes on. You? How are you?'

Before responding, Rehan lit the cigarette and rolled down the window slightly to blow out the smoke. 'I am, well, I am great. I am on top of the world.'

Without waiting to be asked further, he continued, 'I filed an important story today. What I think is an important angle on what's going on at the LoC. I think it should ruffle some feathers for the right reasons.'

'Of course. Office was hectic today because of all the press releases we had to put out. First the pellets, now these strikes,' Fayaz said.

They could, like all Kashmiris, perfectly convey an amalgam of sensations and worries about their homeland with the briefest of exchanges.

'So, last week Gul told me that you were in Delhi?' Fayaz changed the topic.

'To hell with Delhi. Going to Delhi was a compulsion, it was for a workshop. What is Delhi anyway? Crowded, messy, polluted, full of Indians. I missed Kashmir, my friend.'

There was a sigh.

'Things are pretty chaotic here these days,' said Fayaz, then asked, 'When did you return?'

'On Tuesday. Even there, I was busy with my cousin's admission, and work. Just didn't get any time. Even Saima was complaining that I don't give her attention.'

Fayaz threw him an affectionate curse and commented, 'Saima, the real reason for your Delhi trip!'

'It's not like that,' Rehan broke into a laugh.

At this point, Fayaz extended his fingers in a V to borrow the cigarette from his friend. As he did so, he turned his head to look at Rehan's face, which was lit up by the flickering lights from the busy traffic. At the same moment, Rehan, who had so far been looking directly at the road ahead, turned for the briefest of instants and caught Fayaz's eye.

He immediately understood something was not right with his friend. But before he could open his mouth, Fayaz jumped in with a question of his own: 'Do you love her?'

Rehan was manoeuvring to join Boulevard at that precise second and he didn't reply until he was on the long broad road by the side of the Dal lake.

'We are going to Makai Park to eat,' he announced when he finally spoke up.

'We are going to hell, brother,' replied Fayaz. 'Answer me. Are you in love with her?'

'Maybe,' Rehan replied.

Making a smoke-ring pensively and shredding it to wisps with his finger, Fayaz said, 'Today you remind me of that time in college when you were madly in love with that girl who used to come for tuition classes in our building. I can tell from your nervous energy, your smile, and from the volume of the song you were playing that your heart is aflutter after meeting Saima. I'm happy for you.' He turned the music up just a little.

'I don't know. She's special to me. At times I feel so much for her, but I'm afraid of marriage. Let us see how things turn out. One thing is certain: having her in my life, even if mostly virtually, makes me want to live better every day.'

Fayaz put his hand on Rehan's shoulder. It was unclear whether he meant to temper his friend's exploding emotions or urge care when driving, since they were also turning a shallow curve on the road.

Rehan slowed down a bit. He took the last drag from another cigarette and, when chucking it out of the window, cast a glance at the lights that bejewelled the scene over the lake, intoning with a deep intensity: 'Manzil bhi woh, rah bhi woh/ Doob ja, kehti hai ishq ki inteha/ Ya dard-e-dil le kar jee le ...'[2]

Fayaz thought about his friend. How radiant he was, brimming with love. It made him happy to see this exuberance of spirit, this ability to let go of one's self, to dissolve into whatever came one's way. Why could *he* not let himself experience emotions in their entirety? It was a rare gift, and he was glad to be with someone who reminded him of the vast canvas of a free life.

They drove in silence for some time. Each was absorbed in an enmeshed web of his own, but also aware of the changing seasons of the other's life.

After a while, when they had passed Boulevard and were much further along Foreshore Road, Rehan continued, 'These last few weeks have been such an eye-opener, personally and politically. I want to change things. So many things.'

'What things do you mean?'

'Oh, I'll tell you all about it. Let us eat, first.'

Rehan's was a difficult profession, with tremendous competition from many others like him, no certainty of tenure or pay, long hours, and last-minute assignments; everything made worse by the constant tide of suspicion one had to face about the true nature of one's motives. There was so much mistrust everywhere; everyone had, at times, accused everyone else of being an agent, of being in cahoots with the administration, central or state government, one or another political party, and possibly favouring some particular version or desired future path of the freedom struggle. No matter what article one wrote, it was seen through a lens of it having amplified the voice and served the interests of a particular segment of society at the expense of all others. And so, generally, the interpretation of any perspective happened in a zero-sum game.

If you wrote a human-interest story about the suffering of ordinary people under the strikes and hartals, you were dishonourably trying to challenge the resistance. If you penned the unjust excesses and wilful violence towards Kashmiri Muslim civilians by the security forces, you were likely to find yourself on a government watchlist. If you drew attention to the ill-treatment of women or the inequality in society, you were being unIslamic or had leftist leanings. If you focused on the religious divides and engaged with Kashmiri Pandits, you were in danger of being co-opted by right-wing Hindutva. If you published anything sympathetic to the stone-pelters or militants, you were assumed to be pro-Pakistani. If you spoke of the lack of proper leadership of the anti-India resistance, you had been given incentives to divide the Kashmiri people. If you expressed a concern about the unemployment rate, standard of infrastructure, or other economic issues, you were a tool of a state that thrived on depoliticizing people. If you wrote well-researched pieces about history or geopolitics ... well, hardly anyone read them, and those who did, already agreed with you. All in all, media was treacherous terrain.

Rehan, like some others, had sought to navigate it with a strategy of writing on diverse themes, often alternately, and making good use of social media to clarify his position and counter the smears. It helped that his family were fairly liberal and able to support him financially when he needed their help. Even so, there was no telling what would happen from one month, or even one day, to the next. And because of all these anxieties, he was in no position to arrange his personal life better. The best he could do was continue his mostly long-distance relationship with Saima, who studied at JNU and hoped to appear for the UPSC exams that year. Maybe she would succeed where he could not and, in time, he would find a decent fellowship to take him away for a year or two so that he could return to better prospects and perhaps even make a little difference to the desperate situation around him. Then, he would think ahead.

All this, Rehan had discussed with Fayaz numerous times, over endless cups of nun chai, as they had sat with their backs to the wall on the blue carpeted floor of Rehan's rented room. Long evenings and nights that had faded into dewy mornings. Today, as they finished their meal of tujj kebab rolls, he wanted to speak at length with Fayaz about what was going on. He suggested that they go and sit on one of the wooden jetties by the lake.

There was no one around at this time of night and the two friends went right down to the lower steps of Jetty Number 5 and sat looking at the dark milk of the placid lake, on one end of which the SKICC building lights cast their reflection.

Without any preamble, Rehan spoke up: 'Tell me what's wrong, Fayaz.'

Fayaz could not keep up the guise any longer either.

'Zeenat left me today.' These four words were uttered in a voice that wanted to inscribe them into sound with an indelible finality.

Rehan knew that only his silence would prompt Fayaz to speak further. And, after a long pause, Fayaz did indeed continue: 'I should never have married her. We were not right for each other. I knew it last spring, maybe even before that, and I should have broken it up myself, then.'

'Did anything happen these last few days?'

'The entire summer was a catalogue of misery. She was always weeping. There was nothing I could do.'

Rehan realized that his friend had not understood the hidden import of his words; so he asked out aloud: 'Did she find out about ... I mean ... by any chance...'

Even as he was saying this, Rehan knew that it was inconceivable that Zeenat could have known anything about Fayaz's infidelity, since Rehan was the only one in the city who was privy to the secret.

'No, she did not ask me anything. It would have been better if she had found out at the time. Then it would have given her an understandable reason for why I could not reciprocate her love. You know how women can be. In any case, I didn't love her even before all that ...' his voice trailed off, choked by memories.

'Is it final? Have you spoken to your mother? Or to her parents?'

'It is final as far as I am concerned,' said Fayaz in a voice weary with woe. 'She and I had nothing in common. We are too different as people. She needed me, but did not try to see the world from my point of view. The first few months were alright, but that's hardly a surprise. Then, the floods happened and we were kept busy by the chaos. When dad died, she just could not see what that meant for me. I was lost, and you know how I felt, but she couldn't see how that affected me.'

'Did you try to see the world from her point of view?'

Fayaz shrugged. 'Maybe not. No, I probably didn't. I am sure I was not the best husband. Anyhow, now she is gone. I will speak to mother tomorrow morning and convey my decision. The less drama the better.'

Rehan drew his breath and reached for another cigarette. His presentiments about marriage seemed to be confirmed by all the collapsing unions around him. Someone was always breaking up with someone in this broken up world.

As if reading his mind, Fayaz said, 'Marriage is a terrible idea. I don't think men and women of our generation have got it in us to make things work the way our parents could. There are too many needs, ambitions, freedoms.'

'Too many freedoms,' intoned Rehan with a wry smile, adding, 'too many constraints, too many freedoms. Ultimately comes to the same thing. We fail as people. We've failed as people to love. And who can blame us? Look at the world up in flames. Everything is going to hell in a handcart and everyone is too selfish to care.'

'You're right. These are wicked times.'

Rehan put his arm around his friend's shoulder. 'Don't worry, these times too shall pass. We've seen worse. Tell me, what do you want to do right now? Ask me for the starry heavens and I will bring them down to cheer you up my friend.'

Hearing this made Fayaz loosen up a bit. He answered in a more relaxed voice: 'You can't give me what I want, brother. I want the peace of a quiet afternoon by a flowing river, far away from this city.'

'Wanting an afternoon at night! How like you, Fayaz. Well, we'll see what can be arranged.' Saying this, Rehan got up and took a few steps to shake off the numbness in his legs.

Fayaz continued to stare at the reflection of the lit-up necklace of lampposts around the lake.

Rehan took out his phone and played a song on YouTube. Despite the low volume, a bird flew out in alarm from a tangle of weeds behind a shikara moored nearby.

After a while, Fayaz said, 'I should have had a few girlfriends, like you, before committing to marriage. It's better that way. Experience counts a lot when dealing with women.'

Rehan smiled, 'Maybe, but everyone is different, and the lessons can sometimes be contradictory.'

'You'd say that, wouldn't you?' answered Fayaz, following it up with a more serious, 'I think I have had enough. I want to break free of all this.'

Then he abruptly stood up and said, 'Let's go. It's late, I have to be in the office early tomorrow. This is a busy week, and those I work with and for don't make my life any easier.'

'Driver at your service,' Rehan joked as they climbed back up the steps towards the car parked on the other side of the road. It really was late and the small silver Hyundai was the only one along the long, neon-lit stretch. An army truck came hurtling along at great speed; they let it pass before crossing the road.

On the way back, Rehan could sense that his friend was contemplative again, but knew not to probe. Fayaz had his moods and sometimes it was better to just let him be. He drove through the desolate city where only soldiers and dogs prowled at this hour. The two friends shook hands as Fayaz got off near his home and Rehan sped on, this time with the windows rolled all the way up and the music much louder. He felt pleased that Fayaz had opened up about some of what he must be going through. His friend had seemed sleepy towards the end; at least he would rest well tonight.

But Rehan was wrong. Fayaz had been assailed by a familiar sense of suffocation and had feigned drowsiness to avoid placing Rehan in the difficult situation of trying to distract him from his melancholy. He had been looking out of the car window at the city. This city, Srinagar, had seemed like a giant threatening to swallow him up when he had first arrived here from his village. Stretching from mountain to mountain, the valley was now dense with buildings – the old, the very old, and the many new, all jostling for space. Ramshackle shops lined long streets, rubbing shoulders with each other, bursting onto the pavements like anxious spectators in a procession that never came. The newer three- or four-storey buildings often declared themselves to be coaching and tutorial centres for the many exam aspirants, else became malls with their fake glitter and a world that revolved around branded clothes, shoes and mobile phones. It was rather unoriginal how every city in the world seemed to want the same things; a globalization of the world that was in effect a colonization of the mind.

Fayaz thought of the mountains around him. The houses of the rich and the hotels for tourists had climbed as far up the slopes as they could in their search for a privileged seclusion. But some of the highest vantage points were reserved for other histories. The Hari Parbat castle, the Pari Mahal, the Shankaracharya temple towered over the city; monuments to its ancient legacies. And down below here, on the streets, crossroads invariably hosted the bunkers where, behind rolls of concertina wire, helmeted Indian soldiers stood with guns. Never had he felt more insecure than when passing by one as a child. The stiff metal, the hostile gaze, the weapon at the ready; he was always already suspicious. As an officer now, these memories should be worrying him less, but all the same, his life felt like a guilty reprieve, a parole of some kind from the real Kashmiri life.

The human skull with the brain of infinite possibilities encased in it was the first prison of the mind. Then, any city was a prison. It imprisoned people into spaces where they lived, spaces where they worked and spaces where they enjoyed themselves. Most of life was spent in transiting from one to the other, finding better and faster ways to transit, and trying to make sure that the living spaces could be just a bit bigger, and one could linger in the enjoyment spaces longer ... But this city wasn't just any prison, it was the king of prisons! Like the layers of masks worn by its politicians, its prisons were intersecting, multi-layered and special. There were prisons one could not see, but feel and sense; prisons crafted from the invisible bars of suspicion that everyone carried on their person. There were real prisons in which one could find oneself, without having done much to upset the system. There were prisons for heroes and villains, of course. There were ghosted prisons of disappearances where the sentences were unknown.

There were prisons of memory and pain, which made history difficult to understand. There were prisons for children who threw stones. There were prisons for women, sometimes with mirror-lined walls and open doors. There were prisons of a comfortable life, which apathy and collaboration made possible. There were prisons of a contented life which success and administration made possible. The graves were a prison; the gardens were a prison. One could go mad, and then there would be a prison for the insane. The sense of suffocation was unbearable if one thought about it.

For most of the night, sleep eluded him. Then came the day again. Now that there was no Zeenat, he dressed early for office so as to eat breakfast outside. He worked even longer hours over the next few days, taking on additional responsibilities. When he had a chance, he hired a servant on the recommendation of his driver. The young man he employed was a hard-working fellow from Kupwara who began to attend to his home so he could live in a clean house with cooked food and ironed clothes.

On the Sunday of the following week, it was a fairly cold morning in Srinagar. The city was gently warming up to the embrace of the sun's rays and the languid limbs of its many districts were beginning to show slight signs of movement as the calls to prayer echoed under the vast blue dome of the sky. Fayaz was woken up early by the clangour in the street outside; someone's metal gate was being banged in an argument. As his tea was brought to him, he recalled his dreams, a loosely stitched series of scenes presented themselves in front of his eyelids; a hazy parade of his subterranean self. Something about spring, something about looking for a shoe, someone walking in the dark.

Before he could finish recalling, his phone rang. It was Gul. He had scarcely said 'good morning', when Gul rushed him in a hurried voice: 'Get ready, Fayaz. We are coming to pick you up in an hour.' To his protestations, Gul replied, 'We are taking you to the wide open valleys of the beautiful countryside today. We are all going out together – you, me, Rehan, like the old times.'

The thought of such a journey brought a smile to Fayaz's face and he checked the time on his phone, saying, 'All right, brother. Whatever you say. Come, I'll be ready.'

When the car honked downstairs, Fayaz was surprised to see the large shiny vehicle. Even more surprising when he went downstairs was the presence of an extra member in the group – a young woman he had not met before. He thought it would be poor decorum to ask straightaway, so he climbed into the car and introduced himself to her. She said her name was Ifra. In response to his quizzical look, Rehan was the first to volunteer information: 'Ifra is the younger sister of a close friend of Gul's wife.'

Gul added, 'We are dropping her to her village in north Kashmir. It is on our route and falls half an hour before the place where the cottage is, where we are going for our trip.'

The presence of a woman in the car meant that, initially, the conversation was rather stilted and formal. Predictably, the usual topics of the weather and the encounter killings were exhausted first. Next came the inexhaustible topic of what was latest on Facebook posts and WhatsApp forwards from their mutual acquaintances. Gul sat in front, next to the driver, with his authoritative bearing in full view as he gave instructions to the driver and threw looks of scorn at errant or impatient drivers of other vehicles on the road. Ifra had the rear window seat behind the driver. Fayaz was placed behind Gul, and Rehan was in between – a place most suited to him since he was trying hard to oil the wheels for a smooth conversation.

Once they left the city behind, Gul got into a discussion with the driver about what route they should take and what the best place would be to stop for prayers. Gul usually prayed and the driver, in any case, seemed a very devout adherent. Fayaz checked the signal on his phone and, when it worked, logged into his email to check up on a few things. Sensing that Ifra might feel alienated, Rehan took up the task of speaking to her.

It turned out that she was studying literature at Kashmir University. She was a self-proclaimed feminist. Politically active on the university campus, she had volunteered for social service organizations and took part in student demonstrations. All of this information came through very soon. At her mention of the word 'feminist', an awkward, bristling current ran through the car. Rehan surmised that she was used to such a reaction and did not care anymore. In any case, when she had joined them in the car, he had noticed that the driver had given her uncovered head an intensely disapproving look.

'So what's up at KU these days? How come you are heading home? No classes next week?' Rehan asked.

Her reply was tinged with a dismaying familiarity about the situation, 'It's a students versus teachers standoff, yet again. We had an American as a visiting lecturer and the students all liked her and went to her classes. And obviously, our dear professors didn't appreciate the contrast since quite a few students don't turn up for their classes. And then, last week, there was a heated argument about the syllabus in Valerie Ma'am's class—'

'Valerie is the American prof?' Gul interjected.

'Yes, Valerie Seth. Seth is her surname and initially we thought she was somehow Asian, though she didn't look it. Then we realized that Seth is an American surname too.'

'I didn't know that either,' Gul replied.

'It wasn't her fault, poor woman. But some teachers seized on her popularity as an opportunity to blame her for being careless. And then one of our professors made disparaging remarks in class about her. So, obviously, many of us who liked her complained to the dean. It's so easy for the established ones to whittle down the spirit of anyone who is different around here.'

'And because of that the classes got cancelled? I think it's much the same situation as when I last checked,' Rehan reflected.

'It's sad. Education is no one's priority here. And, still, all of us Kashmiris are made to study so much!' Even Fayaz smiled at this.

There was an anxious collective pause when they crossed a village where stone-pelting was common. They were relieved to find that it was not happening just then, else they might have had to turn back.

Ifra continued, 'Well, what I told you are the bare facts, but other things happened too. The students were threatened by the dean to shut up; it is terrible, the way the political atmosphere of force and menace has pervaded everywhere. And then, those who had been bad-mouthing Valerie Ma'am started to shed crocodile tears to garner sympathy from the students. So the students, especially some girls, felt guilty. All in all, the whole thing became a mess. Finally, today they decided to hold a series of reconciliation meetings for the academics, because of which the classes in our department were cancelled for the next few days.'

Fayaz felt a familiar pang of pain at the way things were.

'Hmm. Well, we got to meet you because of it all,' said Rehan, quickly fastening on an 'I'm joking. It's really quite bad' to his statement in case those around him judged him for speaking in this manner.

Instead of reacting to what he said, Ifra placed a concise and clearly enunciated 'I'm hungry' on the imaginary table in between them all.

'I'm sorry,' Gul immediately sprung into action. 'Let us stop and get some food packed here and then maybe while the driver and I go to pray, you all can find a good place to stop and eat. What do you think? Or would you like to sit in an eatery and have a meal?'

'Oh no,' she said, to everyone's relief. It was best not to be seen eating in public with a 'modern' girl in these conservative village environs.

'Let us get something packed. I haven't been to a picnic in a very long time,' she sounded excited.

'Alright. I think I know a few places further along here. What would you all like to eat?' Gul asked.

'I'm not really hungry,' replied Fayaz. 'I had a heavy cooked meal for breakfast.'

'Anything is fine with me. It doesn't have to be a proper meal. Something dry would be easier to carry and eat,' said Rehan.

Ifra chimed in, 'We could get some fritters, Lays and Coke or something like that.'

'Well, in that case, let us pick some food from here. I'll see what they can pack. Then you three can eat somewhere. We will eat after praying and I'm going to have a sit-down meal somewhere, then come to pick you up,' Gul said, asking the driver to stop the car on the side of the road.

'All good,' said Rehan.

Ifra saw Uncle Gul walk away from the car, wondering if she had been too informal with the men in the car in his presence. Before she could reach a conclusion, a string of green military trucks rolled past in a convoy. They looked like enormous predators roaming in a pack. On top of each was a hatch with camouflage netting within which stood a soldier with a gun pointed on a swivel stand. These beasts – the rakshaks, the CRPF vehicles, the army and military machines – had been a part of the Kashmiri visual landscape for as long as anyone could remember. The routine scene gave rise to a patchwork of thoughts in their minds that went something along these lines: They couldn't imagine how it must be to live somewhere where one didn't see soldiers with guns all the time, at every corner. What did these men think they were doing? On what edifice of hope did they rest their endeavours? Surely they knew they were unloved and unwanted here. It was all such a game, a political game. And rotten from top to bottom.

A man with a child in his arms, walking next to a woman carrying a metal container, walked past Ifra's window. The man's eyes were on the dusty unpaved ground. She realized that the woman was staring at her in an unfriendly manner. Being herself, sitting in a car outside of the city, she knew why.

'I've got some chicken wings, pakoras, Coke, and even remembered to get paper napkins,' said Gul as he handed the food to the men. 'Impressive!' teased Rehan, as they all got out of the car. Fayaz looked at the bags. 'That's a lot of food. I doubt that we'll be able to finish it.' But he was wrong. They were all hungry and, as soon as they settled into a nice spot, the food began to disappear quite fast.

The morning had been cold but the afternoon was reasonably sunny. The trio had taken their time to choose a spot where there were large rocks under the dappled shade of a tree. They were partly obscured from the main road. In the distance were the mountains, with the brown-green land between them, and the horizon was like a Persian carpet woven with the many colours of autumn. The chirping of the birds was occasionally interrupted by the noise of the cars that passed behind them.

In between mouthfuls, they made small conversation, asking about each other's families. Fayaz finished eating much before the other two. Rehan, on the other hand, polished off the last crumbs from the folded newspapers that served as the packaging for the food. Ifra went quiet while drinking her Coke and gazing intently at a blade of grass near her feet. Rehan picked his teeth while checking his phone. Fayaz got up saying he would find the driver to let him know they were ready to leave. As Fayaz receded into the distance, Rehan recited some lines of poetry from Faiz: 'Bol, ke lab azaad hain tere ... Bol, yeh thodaa waqt bahut hai ... Bol, jo kuch kehnaa hai keh-le!'[3] At this rousing exhortation, Ifra slowly drew her gaze up to his and said, 'If only verses could save Kashmir.'

He met her eyes, posing no questions. In a voice that started off as a whisper and gained volume with each word, she said, 'I can say this to you because I have read what you write in the papers. I want Kashmir to change, Rehan. I want it to be what it once was, but only better.

I am tired of seeing the guns, reading the papers, following the same cycles of politics. I want my university to change. I want there to be an air of freedom. Freedom for all. I want the world to be a better place. I want to live in a world where a Donald Trump is not even an option. I want our own ruling dynasties to change. And then I think, who am I? One insignificant person. A woman at that. *What* am I doing with my dreams? What can I *do* with my dreams?' Her voice trailed off.

Rehan didn't answer immediately. A part of him wanted to react in the way he might have done if she had been a close male friend. He would have employed gallows humour, made a dark joke, tried to laugh off the feeling, knowing that the underlying sentiments were shared by both. Unable to take any of this understanding for granted with her, and realizing that she was a serious young woman, he too subsided into his sincere self. When he spoke, he chose his words carefully.

'What you say is true, though most people don't think like you. I know so many people who never spare a thought – and not only because they can't – about anyone other than themselves and their own. You are lucky to be able to know the destination. You want to make a change and, inshallah, one day, you will succeed.' It didn't add up to much, but Ifra felt stronger for hearing it.

After a few moments, Rehan pulled out his wallet and, opening it, held it towards Ifra. When she took it, he told her that it was a picture of his girlfriend. Ifra asked her name. 'Saima,' answered Rehan, 'she studies at JNU.' Since Ifra felt treated on an equal footing, she too volunteered her secret: 'I have a boyfriend too. He's in a college in Srinagar.' Rehan asked her if she would mind him smoking. It was a bad habit and he knew it. His family knew he smoked, but he never smoked in the presence of a woman unless he was sure she would not judge him. When Ifra said she didn't have a problem, he felt slightly relieved and took out his Wills cigarette out of its pack, making a mental note that he had only two left. Puffing on it, he also felt pleased that she wasn't one of those precious women with whom one had to keep up a pretence.

'You know what this scene reminds me of?' she asked.

'What?'

'Once, he asked me to come with him on a day trip, by ourselves. It was a risky endeavour, but since we weren't going far, only for a few hours, I didn't worry too much—' then she interrupted herself, as if to allay his fears: 'he's not that kind of a guy; he's very good.'

'Go on,' said Rehan, 'how were you reminded of something like this?'

'Yes, so we were sitting in a beautiful spot not far from the road, just the two of us, when the moral brigade dropped by!'

'Oh no, did they hurt him?' Rehan blurted out, genuinely curious.

'Thankfully not! But it was a right proper mess. These holier-than-thou religious boys, some even younger than us, started to threaten us with all kinds of things. They said we were immoral because we were sitting and eating together, by ourselves. It made me so angry! I wanted to argue with them, but Imran was calmer and wiser. When his explanations failed to move them, he told them I was his girlfriend but that I was a Hindu girl! They believed him because my head was uncovered and they didn't know my name. And then they left us alone! Because Hindu girls are allowed to do this sort of thing? Or because it was okay for him to do whatever they feared if the girl is not Muslim. Can you believe it?'

'That's terrible. They just can't live and let live. You know, I've lived in Delhi for my graduation, and this sort of thing goes on even in small towns in India. They hate Valentine's Day celebrations. They hate people falling in love, basically.'

'Is Saima from Srinagar too?'

'I wish! That would have made my life much easier. She's from Kargil. A Shia at that. At some point, it'll be more of a problem, but right now our problem is her UPSC exam preparation and my phone bills!'

Ifra laughed.

'Where does your boyfriend, this Imran, live?'

'Oh, I thought you understood. He lives at Uncle Gul's place. He's Mr Fayaz's nephew.'

'Wow,' exhaled Rehan, 'I didn't even—'

'Please don't tell him anything!' Ifra pleaded, suddenly the nervous young lover again.

'Of course not. I can keep secrets. He's my friend; I am not his spy.'

'Thank you! Thank you so much!' Ifra was relieved. She added, 'I met Imran at Uncle Gul's place when I went there with my elder sister who's a very good friend of his second wife ... *wife*, I mean.'

'But you must take care and not do anything foolish.'

'Of course, I am a sensible girl. And Imran may be confused sometimes, but he's a good person. We don't get to meet often; we generally speak online. The trip I told you about was an exception.'

'It's okay. It's none of my business to probe into your personal life,' Rehan said, standing up. His limbs were numb again. All that desk work with poor posture and lack of exercise worried him when he was bedevilled by these backaches.

'We should probably go and find where the others are,' said Ifra, more composed now.

'Yes, I was about to say that too. Great minds think alike, and great minds should not be left abandoned in the forests in a conflict zone!' Rehan said with a mischievous smile.

~

The next hour in the car went by fast. The scenes that slid past them were so beautiful that the eye lingered hungrily, trying to take in every detail. Soon, they had reached Ifra's village, where her aunt insisted that they come in for tea. It took the combined persuasion skills of the three men, plus an assortment of masterful excuses to extricate themselves from the invitation. Still, a bag of dry fruits was pressed into their hands as they left. Kashmiri hospitality knew no bounds.

When it was just the three men in the car, their conversation became easier and more jovial, even bordering on coarse banter. Rehan whispered to Fayaz that the driver would certainly report the two of them in the backseat to the Jamaatis for being such moral renegades. Fayaz shushed him – this kind of humour, more than any other kind, could really get them into trouble. It was a relief to reach the cottage after the long bumpy ride on the uneven dirt track. Gul joked about how Rehan's little car would fare on such a journey. Rehan retorted back that there was no ride like the one in a policeman's car. The driver took his leave for the next few hours and Gul asked the caretaker to send for some tea and bread.

At last, they pulled up a few chairs and settled down in the majestic surroundings of Gul's cottage. 'It was a long drive, but this makes it totally worth the wait,' said Fayaz, inhaling deeply. The mountain air was crisp and fresh, not a trace of smoke or dust. The gushing jade-green stream at their feet made the most soothing babbling sound as the water went over the rounded rocks, forming numerous swirling eddies. On the snow-crowned mountains in front of them, the sun's rays traced a resplendent hammock shape on the curve of the peaks. A little boy shyly accompanied his father – the caretaker – as he brought the men their repast. As the father carefully placed the biscuits and chhot bread on the small table, laying the teacups and saucers, while balancing the thermos flask on one arm, the child stared from one stranger to the other with big, unblinking eyes. Seeing him nibble at a corner of his shirt, Fayaz beckoned him over and gave him a few dry fruits from the bag that they had just received. The child was overjoyed at what lay in his fist, and instantly scampered away, disregarding his father's calls to say thank you to the sir.

That afternoon, the men were boys again. Over endless cups of tea, they summoned their pasts, delighting in every scrap of memory, correcting each other over the finer details, and laughing at their own follies and misdemeanours. They recited verses from famous Urdu poets – Ghalib, Iqbal, Faiz, Faraz, and many others – about life, love, intoxication, humanity, Sufism. Rehan even recited some of his own poetry. Real Life, threaded as it was with responsibilities, parents, spouses, children, illnesses, arrangements, office work, did not leave them altogether, for every now and then, one of them would look at his phone, or get a notification or a text from someone about what was happening in the Valley. But that afternoon, for a few hours, Real Life was demoted from its pre-eminent position to a secondary status for the friends.

They had taken different paths in life, their luck and talent had led them to different roles in their society, but once upon a time they had been raw young boys who had gotten into scrapes together and vacillated between knowing right and wrong, just and unjust, want and need, desire and indifference. That time seemed at once unimaginably distant and yet as clear as yesterday.

Gul, who was elder to the others by a few years, and was today a police officer with three children, a man who had been married twice, had once also been a serial cheat. He tried to defend himself as his friends recalled his humiliations, but his objections were brushed aside with a 'you scoundrel'. Rehan was asked to recall the famous song that he would sing to girls on the phone. Gul and Fayaz high-fived each other as they made fun of Rehan's romantic ambitions: Casanova forever. Rehan was caught between taking the jokes as they came and insisting that he was a reformed rake now. Fayaz could not be teased for his youthful escapades; so he was insulted for his inability to speak to girls and for his nerdiness. Guilty as charged, he quickly accepted, so they made wisecracks about his colleagues and work instead.

When the caretaker came to refill the flask of tea for the second time, Rehan excused himself to take a call. Since Gul too was getting into a detailed discussion with the caretaker about the local fruit harvest that year, Fayaz thought of taking a stroll in peace. Initially, he walked towards the stream, but he went in the other direction when he overheard Rehan utter the words 'meri jaan'[4] over the phone. Poor Rehan did not know that while the gurgle of the water was making it difficult for the person at the other end (Saima, who else?) to hear him, his trying to speak louder made him more audible to those around him. He ought to have chosen a better spot, Fayaz thought. It was good that Gul had not asked him about Zeenat. He had no wish to speak about all that today. How easy life would be, if only you could laugh in the face of every obstacle! It was obvious that Rehan had told Gul something about what had happened. It saved him the trouble. Moreover, the less Gul knew, the better. Imran lived at his place and he wanted to keep the boy as far from family skirmishes as possible.

Lost in his thoughts, Fayaz had been walking aimlessly for some time, near a few shrubs and flowerbeds. Passing through a gap in a fence, he reached the dirt track at the back. Their car was parked there and the driver was fast asleep inside, with the seat reclined to the maximum. Giving in to an urgent need to relieve his bladder, he paced to a bush by a small locked shed. A dandelion seed brushed past his face and he wrinkled his nose to blow it away. As he zipped his trousers somewhat irritably, he was sure he heard some sounds from within the shed.

Curiosity piqued, he tiptoed to the wall at the side of the shed and put his ear to it. There were definitely people inside. Yet, he was sure he had seen a lock on the front door. His heart beating a bit faster, he craned his neck to peer through the bottom end of a low skylight covered by a dirty paint-splattered window. Inside the small concrete room were a few men sitting on a threadbare carpeted floor. Apart from them, there was a long silver antenna of a transistor or a transmitting device of some kind, a little heater or stove, and a couple of guns. A calendar was hung on the wall, prominent because it was the only adornment in that small space. Fayaz instinctively backed down and moved away as noiselessly as he could. He was not sure what to make of what he had seen. Who were these men? Militants? Informers? He shuddered. The more crucial question was what they were doing there. And why the door was locked from the outside. Did Gul even know they were there? That last question struck him again with a different emphasis: Or *did* Gul know?

As he rushed back to where the chairs were placed by the stream, an entirely different kind of past flooded his mind. Not the youthful past of regrets, deeds and misdeeds, but a hollower, more forbidding, more distant past of his childhood. That barely remembered feeling of having held guns, the subsequent lucid memories of hearing the sound of gunshots, witnessing the dispersal of crowds and the falling of bodies.

When he reached the stream, the caretaker was gone and a steaming cup of tea had been poured for him. Gul was showing something on his phone to Rehan, who was now sitting on the chair previously occupied by Fayaz. If he was shaken, they did not notice. Fayaz thought it better not to ask Gul anything right then. There would be a right moment later. He tried to join in the conversation as before, but could not simulate the giddy sense of relief he had a few minutes earlier. He sipped his tea and gazed at the mountains, trying to let the sound of the water and the cries of the birds fill his ears, but to no avail. The scene had been stripped of its gaiety and its grandeur; it could have been a cheap reproduction of a postcard on a silverfish-encrusted page of a tattered book. He wished he were back in his room in Srinagar. But it would be impolitic to insist on returning since his friends had arranged this outing specially for him. Moreover, Rehan informed him that they would eat at Gul's place tonight. Gul's wife had called saying his family had already made preparations for a big meal for them, complete with tabakh maz, goshtaba and kebabs. Gul added that the instructions were to prepare the chicken biryani just the way Fayaz liked it, with lots of onion and a little saffron.

Fayaz smiled weakly, asking, 'Shouldn't we be starting back, then? So it doesn't get too late?'

They guffawed, thinking it was the prospect of his favorite meal that was making him impatient.

'Well, at least finish the tea!' said Gul.

'I knew you ate far too little in the afternoon,' Rehan quipped.

Fayaz let it pass. He didn't speak much for the rest of the afternoon till they reached Srinagar in the evening. The others did not mind, partly because everyone was tired, and partly because they figured that Fayaz, who could be reserved at the best of times, must be gloomy and prone to mood swings in his present situation.

When they were all in the car and about to start the return journey, Fayaz leaned towards Gul and, pointing to the concrete shed, asked him: 'What's that for?'

'It's a shed,' said Gul, stating the obvious. 'The locals use it sometimes.'

It was not a satisfactory answer and Fayaz wanted to probe further, but it would be strange to pry unless he was prepared to divulge what he had seen, and admitting to his lapse of discretion in snooping around would be embarrassing in itself. He held his tongue and decided to forget about it.

Everyone was re-energized as the car neared Srinagar. The city came into view like a beloved, complete with the golden tresses of the wavy clouds, the shimmering dress of the waters, and the passion in the frenetic life of its inhabitants. Though it had been a day trip, Gul felt he had been away too long, Rehan wanted to get to a proper Wi-Fi connection to reply to a defamatory email from an Indian journalist about the story he had filed most recently, and Fayaz was simply looking forward to meeting Imran after a while. However, no sooner had they entered the city than they were plunged into an exasperating traffic jam. The driver turned off the ignition. Rehan groaned. Gul dialled his wife to tell her they would be delayed and then put Imran on the line to speak to Fayaz. Uncle and nephew exchanged a few odd words before Fayaz hung up with an Allah Hafiz.

Prior to his transfer, Fayaz had been in regular touch with Imran, being involved in the many details of the boy's life. However, since the death of his own father and the move to Leh, he had lapsed in his duties to an extent, often relying on the boy to keep in touch. The knowledge that he was staying with Gul had acted as a balm. Suddenly, he was not as sure of this any longer. He leaned back in his seat, closed his eyes and tried to marshal his thoughts, drifting into a deep sleep.

~

The park was a symphony in green. There surely weren't names for all the shades of green that he could see. The broad-shouldered trees along a large arc at the back held out their arms to welcome the tender breeze that made a thousand detours as it threaded its way through the swaying leaves. On the ground in front was a circle set ablaze with scattered crimson and amber petals.

Where this was, he wasn't sure. The scene didn't look like it belonged to his village or any city he had ever lived in. He hadn't even seen such beauty in a painting or on screen. Fayaz took one step after another in the direction of a thicket behind which he could hear the murmuring of a stream. He was barefoot and the soles of his feet felt the bending blades of grass as he walked. There was no one else around. No human beings, that is, for he had already counted a dozen birds that hopped alongside him. It was a strange feeling. As he progressed through the meadow, the birds hopped and skipped behind him. They weren't leading him anywhere as in the stories of miracles he had heard; on the contrary, they were following him. They twittered and chirped and tossed their heads about, but kept moving along with him without taking a break or flying away.

As soon as he reached the thicket, the birds stopped, as if waiting for him to say something. Puzzled, he looked to his left and right; the birds mutely stared back at him. He wondered if he should shoo them away, but realized he didn't want to. Their mysterious escorting had inspired in him a sense of inexplicable joy and worth. He felt like a magician without a cloak. At this thought, he glanced down at his body to see what he was wearing and his jaw dropped open. He was naked as the day he was born!

This was bizarre. Why wasn't he wearing any clothes? How had he come to be in this bewitched, enchanted place? He felt a rush of blood, and a warmth in his limbs and on his face. He felt embarrassed and ashamed to be out here in the open in front of the twelve pairs of eyes. But the birds didn't care. They stood waiting patiently on either side of him. He gradually uncrossed his arms, bringing them down from the defensive position of gripping each shoulder with the opposite palm. His palms slid down his bare arms and went limp at the sides of his thighs. He was naked. That was all. There was no one else around. The birds were naked themselves; so there couldn't be any insinuation of shamelessness.

At this, he went ahead and parted the foliage to make his way through the grove. He had gone just a few steps further when he paused to look around. The birds weren't with him any longer. They stood at the entrance to the thicket, exactly where they were before. Why weren't they following him any more? He beckoned them with his arms, his palms. Twelve small and still furry bodies and twenty-four resolute unblinking eyes outstared him, making it clear that they weren't coming any further. In fact, though only a few steps away, they now looked more like a painting of birds, gathered for a reason best known to them.

So they had deserted him. His sense of magical sublimity had been short-lived indeed. He concentrated once again on clearing the way ahead of him. The low branches above his head filtered little light and the ground was covered in a spread of jaspé brown. Leaves tickled his skin as they brushed it. At last, a clearing came and he closed the curtain of the branches behind him as he stepped out under the open blue skies.

He had been right about the gurgle of water – there was a fast-flowing stream in front of him. It was too shallow to go swimming in, and treacherously fast and wide to cross. In any case, the other side was no different, being a mirror image of where he stood. The earth was strewn all over with innumerable rounded stones; the smallest pebbles resting in the crevices of the bigger egg-like stones which in turn were ensconced in bigger stones the size of skulls. He would have liked to lie down and rest, letting the purl of the waters soothe him with a lullaby, swirling as they did around the many stones in the stream. But the uneven surface made him hesitate and he sat down instead. He scanned the skies once more, hoping that the birds might have chosen to fly over the thicket and join him on this side.

Letting his eyes dwell on the blue of the sky above, he couldn't help but think of how magnificent this divine dome was; the sky was the first and last cause. The stars, the moon, the sun, the clouds, the rain, the snow – all the adornments the sky ever wore were a joy to behold. After this solemn contemplation of eternity in a long moment, he looked down again. To beguile him further in this wondrous scene, two swans had appeared in front of him. He was past being surprised and simply gazed at them to see what they would do. In unison, the birds started to dip their long necks up and down, repeatedly and forcefully. As they thrust their necks upward, they started to sing. Fayaz had never heard swans sing before. If someone had asked him to imagine what they would sound like, he would have guessed that their music was a mellifluous, graceful one, like the elegance of the creatures themselves.

Far from it. The birds made a loud sound that seemed discordant above all else. Fayaz closed his eyes. What did the noise remind him of? It was a door creaking – a rusty wooden door with bad hinges that was being battered by the wind. Or was it a child crying in pain? No, it was an old man groaning from the aching of his bones. And yet it was also a honking. There was something concave and hollow about this sound. It was the insistent honking of a bulbous rubber horn at the front of a goods truck as it was being squeezed unceasingly by an impatient driver. Honkk honkk. The man in the truck was cursing and sweating. Men in uniform with guns in their hands blocked the dusty road ahead of him; masses of young men were refusing to move away. There was chaos, misery and pain radiating outwards in ripples from the centre of that scene, from the core of that sound. Honkk honkk.

~

Fayaz woke up.

'We're almost there,' said Rehan. 'Good you caught a nap and escaped the worst part.'

3

IMRAN WAS TEARING off every bit of mutton from the bone and shoving the rice mixed with roganjosh into his mouth with focused attention. The men were all seated in a row, enjoying the feast spread out on the dastarkhan[5] in front of them. Gul's mother watched them eat with a contentment illuminating her ageing round face framed by her shawl. Periodically, she directed Gul's wife, her daughter-in-law, to serve more gravy and rice.

Imran was a polite young man who knew not to speak too much in the presence of elders. In between morsels, Gul's father and Rehan discussed the news, mostly the latest round of posturing by India and Pakistan on the LoC – that colonial gash on the land that never stopped giving grief. Gul was telling Fayaz about his plans to renovate and extend the upper part of the house next spring. Since the men had been delayed by the traffic jam, Gul's twin boys had already been fed. They had still insisted on dressing up for the dinner and were now squabbling over a toy action figure, each trying to get Imran's attention to intervene and decide in his favour. An elderly woman from next door held Gul's sleeping baby girl in her lap and muttered prayers to herself. The women of the house would eat later.

Imran was caught unawares when the conversation shifted to talk of his future. He was licking his oily fingers after having polished off all the food on his plate. In the corner was a pile of clean bones with not a single scrap of meat left on them. Gul's family was particular about keeping up appearances, and a meal with multiple meat preparations was reserved for special occasions to impress invited guests. On most days, the food was fairly ordinary: rice and curry, combining vegetables like potatoes, beans, brinjals and cauliflower. Facing his uncle's scrutiny about his life, the delicious taste in Imran's mouth soured and he felt as if he had been chewing a mass of pips. The tone of Fayaz's questions to his nephew was mild, but behind them was a dour reminder that he better be doing well.

During his early youth, he had been close to Fayaz but, over the last year and a half, he had become much closer to his friends in the city. Without a doubt, he had a core of warm feeling for his uncle. Fayaz had been the one who had most lovingly tended to him when he had been hurt as a teenager in the village. Imran had been mucking about with other boys at a wedding party. There was music and light and celebration in the air. Then, someone had set off firecrackers at a distance and the armymen had fired in retaliation, thinking that something else was afoot. An acquaintance of Imran's had been hit and left paralyzed for life. Imran himself had been grazed in the cheek and still carried that scar underneath his short stubbly beard. At the time, his father Junaid, his grandfather, and even his mother had joined in reprimanding him for his careless ways. Why had he strayed so far from the wedding venue? Why did he hang out with those feckless young men? In the din of reproach, Fayaz had stood up for him, shielded him from the worst of their remonstrations, bandaged him, and made him feel better.

That was then. Times had changed. Fayaz seemed to have become a different man since he came to the city. People said that Zeenat, his wife, who had appeared rather severe to Imran to begin with, had turned Fayaz into a colder man. When he had been at their home, Imran had felt uncomfortable and out of place, in an atmosphere filled with unstated barbs. He realized that Fayaz was probably paying his friend Gul some money monthly for hosting his nephew, but he did not know how much. Gul's family was generally busy with their endless household affairs and everyday matters, and did not get on his case too much. He went to college when there wasn't a government-imposed curfew or a shutdown hartal[6] decreed by the resistance. Even on some of the days that the classes did run, he could easily bunk college and hang out with his pals. He had often done this in the past year. On a handful of occasions, this had been to spend time with Ifra, the girl he had a crush on for months before he had proposed that she be his girlfriend. But, more often than not, he skipped studies to be with his diverse set of male friends.

As Rchan and Gul began to fill in the family about their trip to the countryside, Gul's wife enquired if Ifra's family were alright. Fayaz, who had been addressing Imran till then, interrupted himself mid-sentence and told her that the girl had been dropped at her home safely and that her family had hospitably forced a bag of nuts, dates and raisins upon them. Gul's wife was happy to hear this, but the subject provided Gul's mother and the woman from the neighbourhood a chance to decry that the girl Ifra didn't know what was good for her. Unlike the women in that room, she didn't cover her head, spoke too much, and was too modern. Gul's mother additionally meant these things as a veiled comment against her own daughter-in-law, who she thought was a decent woman but who obviously had female friends whose family members (in this case, the younger sister of her friend) did not behave with propriety. Imran listened to these statements as if he were a disinterested stranger.

Imran had first met Ifra on the staircase of that very household. It had taken him two entire months of persuasion on text and messenger to get her to agree to meet him for a date. During those weeks, she had dropped by at Gul's place at irregular intervals and pretended as if she had never seen or heard from him in her life.

At last, one afternoon, dripping with nervousness, he had met her in a mall. She had greeted him first, 'Hello! I hope you didn't have to wait too long?'

'Not at all. It's really nice in here,' he had stammered, feeling like a country bumpkin.

He remembered saying 'thank you for coming' and confessing shortly afterwards: 'I am nervous.'

'Me too,' she had laughed, betraying her lie.

Imran was not one of those boys whose life revolved exclusively around an interest in girls, online or otherwise. He had seen many of his city friends go through infernal torture over unrequited love or infidelity, while some others were past masters at seduction and multiple dating. Until being confronted with Ifra, Imran had thought of girls as a distraction and a source of unnecessary drama. They were coy, trivial and petty. But Ifra had inexplicably managed to alter that opinion in that one wordless meeting on the stairs. He had been slackly coming down the narrow stairs of Gul's household and she was making her way up. When he saw her, he dithered about whether he should go up to clear space, pause to let her pass, or say something first. She had not rushed him with any display of discomfiture. Their eyes had met. She hadn't stared back with any hostility or enquiry either, and had just fearlessly, comfortably, met his gaze and continued to wait. It seemed very simple when he thought of it, but it was a revelation to him. Because he wasn't staring at her, he wasn't aiming to get her attention, and yet he had looked at her for a long few seconds. Just that. There she had stood in her blue and gold salwar kameez, in her coat, open at the front, and the scarf around the neck.

It was Ifra's confidence and spirit, as much as her face and body, that had drawn him in. And it was this same ability to understand, to trust and to be honest about what she wanted to do, that had likely made her say yes to his plan for the drive they had once been on. Another girl in her place would have hesitated or said something about seeking permission, or demurely tried to refuse the offer without wanting to hurt his feelings, or asked him to explain further or make some promises. Not Ifra. She had taken her moment and decided to go for what she liked. There was, he had concluded, very little machination or manipulation in this blessed girl. He had needed to beg a friend for the loan of a car for a few hours to go on that drive with her. His eyes shining with delight, he had picked up the USB with his favourite music, brushed the car dashboard with an old flannel cloth, sprayed some car scent in the interior, and set out. At every red traffic light, he had been tempted to look at himself in the car mirror, where he made sure that a strand of his curly hair fell on his forehead, and checked whether his scar showed through his beard. But the day had been a disaster. They had been shamed by a group of orthodox village boys of the kind that he once might have played with, and he had had to lie about Ifra being Hindu to escape a beating. Since then, he had tried to be more casual and less insistent about meeting her, communicating mostly online. She had either not noticed the shift or didn't care to complain about it, and this was how things stood between them just then.

Imran didn't care what Gul's family thought of Ifra. But it did feel strange to hear her name being uttered by Fayaz, knowing that his uncle was not aware of the connexion between him and the girl whose family he was praising. Imran suddenly realized that Fayaz was again asking him about his plans after finishing college. As Imran mumbled something about a year – maybe two, if the exams were postponed again – still remaining to decide that, Gul good-naturedly mentioned that the boy should join the police force like him. An uncertain look passed over Fayaz's face as he neither approved nor disapproved of the suggestion. Misreading Fayaz's silence as tacit agreement, Gul continued, detailing how the profession meant assured employment, definite power, and getting salaries on time. Gul's father contradicted him, saying not everyone is lucky in such a profession. Had it not been for his own reputation as a devout man of religion and his son's kindness towards their friends and neighbours, it would have been impossible for them to live in a locality such as theirs, given what had happened that summer with the pellet blindings. The families of policemen were always in danger, unless the resistance radicals held their deeds in some regard. Gul could not disagree with most of this; in the past months, he had pulled strings to get many boys out of jail. Almost all of them had been arrested as stone-pelters or been pre-emptively detained under the Public Safety Act. When there was a gap in the conversation, Rehan turned to Imran and playfully added that he should think about joining the police only if he didn't care for leisure and getting holidays sanctioned on time. Gul's wife could not agree more with this since her husband hardly ever got days off. But in view of the assembled group, she held her tongue. When Gul joked that he had taken time off today to go on that drive, the others reminded him that it was a Sunday. Seeing Gul's attitude towards his nephew, Fayaz felt at ease. Maybe he had misinterpreted what he had seen in the shed. Gul wasn't the kind of person to invite trouble. If anything, he would prioritize saving his skin over committing to an ideology of any kind.

Imran was grateful when Fayaz and Rehan left that night. Lying on his bed later, he didn't feel like answering any texts from his friends. He cursorily scrolled down the unread messages from that evening, pondering over how he could possibly be interacting with people who were so different from each other. Imran had a group of friends from his village, boys with whom he was now in infrequent contact. These boys whom he had played cricket with in that open space by the side of the village drain, whom every evening he had gone to the masjid with, reminded him of a time when he had dreams of becoming a militant for the Kashmiri struggle. 'Kashmir banega Pakistan! Kashmir banega Pakistan!'[7] they had cheered, sitting with members of the secret Tabligh group that had counselled them on what they must do to liberate Kashmir from Indian zulm.[8] For a whole year, he had nurtured dreams of running away across the border to Pakistan to train in a camp and fight the Indian soldiers upon return. His intentions had not materialized into action, partly as a result of his father Junaid's ever-tightening grip on him, and partly because of having interacted with his grandfather who never had a good word to say about militancy, despite having been a militant himself.

Then came a time when Imran thought cricket would offer him a way out of the confusions of his life. He spent entire seasons playing cricket with an inexhaustible vigour. When he was not holding the solid handle of the willow bat, he was in the grip of visualizing the flourishes of the game in his head. It was Fayaz who had killed his dreams by convincing him to give up thinking of becoming a professional cricketer. Almost playing the role of an elder brother to the young Imran, the boy held his uncle in high esteem. He wanted to play cricket for a living. He thought he was good at it. But Fayaz had crushed his fantasies with an onslaught of logic, logistics and practicalities. Something precious had died in him the day he capitulated to Fayaz. Though he was ashamed to admit it, this had felt like a bigger blow than abandoning his dreams of crossing the LoC. Perhaps it was because he knew that the yearning to become a fighter would not lose its allure in his world where deaths and killings were commonplace, but that once he had sworn off the visions of becoming a cricketer, he would only ever play cricket or watch it being played, but never live for it in the same way.

After he was sent to Srinagar for his studies, Imran's association with his village friends lost its intensity. Initially, he would speak on the phone with them, catch up on the news back home, ask them questions demonstrating a familiarity with their lives. Then, with time, the distance grew. His life speeded up, their lives changed, keeping him abreast of it all became a chore for them; assuring them he was still the same became exasperating for him. As their conversations became shorter and transformed into occasional texts, their customary codes of speech and inflections too diverged. He still communicated with them, but with only traces of the earlier feeling.

In any case, the city had presented him with multiple challenges that took a toll on his faculties. There was the process of adjusting into Gul's household. Then there was college and its burdens. Most crucial, however, was the tough act of trying to find his exact place among the different types of people here. Drawing lines between 'them' and 'us' in the village was easy. Everyone's history and family story, in all details and particulars, was common knowledge, supplemented by gossip. People in the village knew which group they could or could not belong to and why. Here, in the city, everything was slippery. Imran could choose the people to be with and he would still not be excluded from any grouping simply because of who he was. In the city, people seemed to like converting others into their social and ideological groups.

There were young fellows at college, drunk on frivolities, who chased wine and women; some who burrowed like ants into their obsession with careers and, more often than not, ended up in frustrating jobs. There were those who professed pious faith and threw stones or painted slogans; those who rapped the latest tunes as they threw stones or painted slogans. Still others thrived by cultivating favours from patrons using obsequious flattery mixed with a good dose of wheeling and dealing. Those from any and all of these groups that Imran interacted with, played cricket and spoke of resistance. Their ideologies and their family histories were often opaque, so that neither their passionate belief in, nor their cynical condemnation of, where Kashmir and Kashmiris were heading, carried much truth. It seemed trust was the scarcest commodity here in Srinagar.

Imran had friends he had grown disenchanted with in the several social groups that he had been exposed to. The affluent set were useful to know. It was from one of them that he had borrowed the car for his drive out with Ifra. When he spent time with these sons of businessmen traders, tourism company owners and senior officials, they went to trendy cafes where everything cost triple the reasonable amount and everyone was deferential to them. They cut their birthday cakes in scenic lookout cafes of hotels perched high up above the city. Their girlfriends wore clothes that would not be out of place in the Delhi or Dubai that he saw on TV. They discussed the everyday at CCD Sonawar[9] in between sips of cappuccinos and commentary on the pop music talent shows that played on the TVs above their heads. It was the good life. Imran liked being part of the easy swish of such an existence. Yet, he wasn't one of them. Not that they ever made him feel out of place by referring to his village or his not having been to DPS or Tyndale Biscoe.[10] He was with them at college and they were too liberal to pick on his status. Plus, he himself was from a business family with militancy credentials; his uncle was in the administrative services and he lived at the house of a policeman; all this meant that he was fit company for 'New Kashmir' if not for 'New India'.

Imran had his own difficulties with them. He knew he wasn't as wealthy as them, and even if he had been, he could never waste money like that. He couldn't take Ifra to such meetups because she had prejudices about such people being shallow and politically illiterate. He had tried to tell her once that, while this was true in some cases, these people were good at studies and even knew politics inside-out. Imran's background was nowhere near allowing him access to the scions of actual political families, but a few of this set had families that were involved with political dynasties as their primary workers or allies. Later, he had given up on convincing her. She was too outspoken and keenly ideological to be able to have a good time with such a group. What really got to him, though, were the little things about them. The way they had once sniggered at a group of three women – completely veiled in black burqas – who had come to a posh cafe to have pastries. Imran felt that underneath the affectations of their English-speaking liberal welcoming selves lay a supercilious snobbery that saw itself as all-knowing benevolence.

The downtown boys of his locality had been equally welcoming of him, even though he lived in a policeman's house. They knew that he was a guest there and not related to the family. Being themselves from families that had seen bad times, they understood odd accommodations. Imran knew the boys who pelted stones, the ones who did graffiti on the walls and shop shutters, the ones who listened to endless rap on repeat, the ones who stoned themselves into numbness in the basements at night, the ones who were devout worshippers at mosques. He knew the ones who had porn on their phones. And he also knew the ones who couldn't stand the sight of a young girl in jeans or with her head uncovered. Sometimes, but not always, these two could be the same person. Once or twice, he had stood in an alley by the side, watching the stone-pelters in action from a distance. It was a risk, not just because the teargas shells, live ammunition or pellets could hit him, but because if Gul or Fayaz found out, word was sure to reach his father, who would skin him alive.

He admired these young men who were the same age as him but so full of daring. They reminded him of the time when he had almost run away to cross the border with the village boys. Dynamic sharpshooters that they were, their agile bodies in movement and the circular curving action of their arms as they hurled the stones also reminded him of some of the smartest bowlers he had faced when playing cricket over the years. Their faces covered by keffiyehs,[11] stones in their hands, they bowled steady sixes for the resistance at the cost of their lives. More than once, he had found himself confronting the question of why he could not be one of them. He wanted to do something as brave and as reckless as them. When they talked, these boys and men shared his passion for 'Kashmir banega Pakistan'. Between them all, they had a sense of belonging. This identity acted as a balm in the face of a fractured society, but their fight was for freedoms and, apart from being difficult to attain, sometimes these were not straightforwardly ascertainable.

Not far from Gul's house was a lane where there was a butcher's shop, outside which stood haphazard pillars of piled-up chicken coops. The noisy birds cackled in the dirty cages, shedding feathers all around. Opposite this was a blue shop shutter on which was scrawled in large black paint: We Want I⁻. In all likelihood, the person who was painting this had been chased away before he could complete the slogan. The incomplete alphabets of the missing word were certainly not meant to denote India, but could one be sure that it was Pakistan, or was it Freedom? Most of Imran's friends from the locality thought the two words were interchangeable anyway. Freedom meant freedom from India's despotic rule, and Pakistan was a saviour and an ally in the struggle. Imran tended to agree with them, but sometimes the sight of the restlessly moulting caged birds facing the slogan caused him to feel a vexation that he could not put into words.

During the floods, Imran had worked hard day and night, doing his bit with groups of other young men, trying to help those stranded in the rising waters. When rescuing them, he had felt blessed in his striving for Sunnah.[12] Imran was a religious young man, but he could not bring himself to embrace a life of committed orthodox religiosity because he had already seen several examples of how supposedly religious people could be hypocritical in their deeds. He wanted to be more devout, but he didn't want to let religious piety take the place of the anarchy that he felt inside. In the past few years, he had seen Fayaz weighed down by mundane office work; he knew he could not wear the shackles of a job like that. He was, like so many Kashmiri young boys and men, lost. Lost because he was trapped in several interstitial worlds in a place on the map where normalcy was the official euphemism for fragile gasping pauses in an endless conflict ... and yet, normalcy was also an almost pathological ability of the people – to go on living in the face of their absurdly unlivable circumstances.

As for Gul's suggestion earlier that night that he join the police force. Well, it was laughable. Gul and his family clearly had no idea how Imran felt about the policeman's profession. He had been to Gul's office in Fateh Kadal a few times to run errands for the family. The road to it led over the bridge, at one end of which white rakshak vans were permanently parked behind a pavement covered with forbidding tunnels of concertina wire. When passing by, Imran would spot the indistinct faces of the policemen seated within the vehicle, behind the rolled-up glass windows which were doubly reinforced on the outside with a mesh of black metal. These shields were affixed to almost every vehicle – whether belonging to the police, the BSF, the CRPF, or the army[13] – as a guard against stone-pelting, but not once had Imran managed to pass by the uniformed men sitting inside them without thinking of the caged chicken in the piled-up coops in his neighbourhood street.

Turning the corner into an alley, the way to the police station led past a couple of shops and then the charcoal and crayon scrawls came into view over the permanently closed and shuttered doorways sealed with cement. On some days, Imran had found the words 'Pakistan Zindabad', on others, he had seen 'Fock Indians', which had been overwritten another time later to read 'Fojy Indians'.[14] The guards had been told that Imran was a family member of the SHO,[15] and with every visit making him more familiar to the sentries, he could go straight to the police building through the arched doorway that had been cut from a large metal sheet. Like some of the other buildings scattered around town, here too the J&K police were housed in what had once been a home. The courtyard was littered with plastic chairs and used for functional purposes as required. Gul's office was on the ground floor. It was a large room with a glass-sheeted desk and other amenities that the lower-ranked men did not have. Imran felt an aversion to being here – every time he pulled aside a cotton curtain or pushed at a rickety door in that building, he flinched inwardly. Nonetheless, he was polite and cordial, often even cheerful to the policemen, some of whom lived in that building too. In return, they never failed to offer him nun chai made by a cook in the kitchen shed towards one side. The building had several floors and if he had to wait for Gul because he was out, Imran preferred to go up to the first floor where in a small room facing the front, was a lovely little hideout: the room of the wireless transmitter guy. It was a spartan little cubicle with a bed facing the window, technical equipment and a trunk of clothes and basic supplies. Razzaq, the fellow who managed the wireless, was a smiley middle-aged man who could pass for a poet as he sat there on that bed looking out over the city from his perch, a soulful melancholy in his eyes. Imran liked being in that room with the square beautiful painting of the breathing city for a backdrop. If Razzaq was not around and the room was locked, Imran would go up to one of the top-floor rooms where the jaded off-duty constables sat on the carpeted floor in their vests and trousers, playing cards or having discussions over tea. They hailed him with friendly mannerisms and invited him to join them, but he could sense that they changed their behaviour in his presence. He couldn't tell whether this was because he was living with their boss or whether they generally did not trust young men of his kind.

Though he had visited the police office on multiple occasions, Imran had never gone inside the building next door, which stood directly on the riverbank. The boundary wall outside Gul's building led on the right side through a door to another building occupied by the CRPF. In the courtyard of this other building stood a temple that towered over both the other structures. Imran had heard the temple bell ring and, over the brick boundary wall, he could see the red, white and blue painted structure with a dome topped by a golden metal finial. The CRPF men lived in this building overlooking the Jhelum which, like the temple, was only accessible through the police courtyard. One of them had once tried to strike a conversation with Imran, calling him over the dividing door and into their yard. Imran remembered seeing an engraved marble plaque on the walls near the steps leading up to the front door of their building. Surrounded by elaborate multi-coloured floral paisley patterns on the walls, the plaque said something in Hindi, or maybe Sanskrit. Imran could read neither, nor tell the difference, but he saw other boards too, that had Kashmiri Pandit names in English upon them – Rainas and Kouls. He kept the conversation as brief as possible and on his way out noticed that the CRPF men had their own separate kitchen. When he crossed back into the police courtyard, he heaved an inexplicable sigh of relief, as if freed from chasing ghosts, but he felt himself only when he was out of that entire complex altogether.

He would do anything but work for the J&K police, or work near the Indian forces. Over the last year, and especially since Burhan's killing, his abhorrence of the police and the rest of the forces had become ever greater. He had mentioned none of this to Fayaz, or to anyone in Gul's family. Even Ifra only knew the tip of the iceberg as far as his feelings on the subject were concerned. Like every other child in his village, Imran had for years listened to resistance speeches and later watched videos of Kashmiri men being humiliated in torture camps, of Kashmiri women weeping for the killed and disappeared. Boys from his village had gone to join the militants, never to return. Boys he knew in the city had received pellets in their bodies. Imran had seen the arbitrary might of the Indian state; he carried it as a scar on his face. When Burhan had been martyred earlier that year, Imran too had wanted to die in the isolation of his room at night. His own grief was not unwonted, but even members of Gul's family had been morose at the news of the killing. Like a river flowing underwater that suddenly breaks through the earth and emerges overground, Burhan had become the name of a sentiment that had lived in the hearts of the people of the cursed land, and his killing had bestowed a death-wish to every son with a fire in his heart and brought tears even to cynical eyes. The flags of Pakistan and freedom would go on being raised, and the stones would keep flying from the fists of the men, but Burhan was gone, and that, Imran felt, was truly, heartbreakingly, cruel. The summer had brought an epidemic of blindness to Kashmiri young men at the hands of Indian soldiers and their guns. Before the phone and Internet communication was shut down and he himself became a caged and curfewed creature like the chickens, Imran had called his friends in the village. They told him about the young girls who had refused food for days and the young boys who had seen Burhan's image in the moon at night. Together they had cursed the Indian state till they had no more abuses left to hurl at it.

That autumn night, with the taste of meat and misery mingled in his mouth, Imran sat alone in the darkness of Gul's sleeping household, looking at the names of varied groups of people on his phone. He ignored all the messages but one. He sat there for a long time, turning over and over in his head a proposal that he had been obsessing about for weeks now. At last, deciding what he would do with his life, he replied with the one word: 'Yes.'

Part Two

What Happened Before

4

THERE ARE SIXTY Chinese words for death.

Too few, Shireen thought. Because, when someone died, there were a million ways to not be able to express what that death signified. This dawn when the dark autumnal sky was still a shadowy ghost pressing against the window pane of her room – she had searched online for death in Chinese and blinked away the insistent tears in her eyes. On a screen in front of her, blurred by teardrops, she could see death arranged by status or rank (had a king died? had a commoner died?), by age (childhood? middle or old age?), by special reasons for circumstances (died for love? for one's moral integrity?), by religion (only Buddhist and Daoist here), literary terms for death or suicide (ended oneself? or ascended to heaven?), judgmental terms of praise, humour or derogation (a righteous death? or a stretching out of one's legs?).

An hour before, she had received a phone call from her uncle. Yes, he was her uncle even if his wife was not her aunt and his sons were not her brothers, at least not in any meaningful sense of the term in so far as it related to the warmth of human connexions. Since then, she had been stumbling from one place to another in the rather small room.

One moment she sat on the bed, the next moment she leaned against a wall, the next she sat on the floor hugging her knees. He had called her to tell her that her grandmother had died. She had been in the hospital for the last few days; her heart had collapsed. Shireen had not been told any of this, merely informed of the demise. At least when her grandfather had died two years ago, they had kept up the pretence of letting her know when he had suffered the stroke and been admitted to the hospital.

That was a slightly different time – she used to speak to her grandfather almost every day on the phone, and they could not stop him from keeping in touch. The old man was her uncle's father, after all. He was also her father's father, but that was a much longer story. In the two years since he had passed away, they had kept his wife, the poor woman, under literal house arrest in Delhi, not allowing her to meet many people, and certainly discouraging visits from Shireen herself. A frail, illiterate, elderly woman had died, and she had not been permitted to keep in touch with her granddaughter who lived and studied at a university in the same city. Why? Because there was property, wealth and possession involved. The old man's will had never been found and the old woman had been declared mentally unstable. Now that they were both gone, there was no need to fret over the niceties of acknowledging family for fear of potential inheritance claimants.

Her grandfather, a man who'd always been old in her memory, was once a robust young fellow whose life, if not his death, could be much more easily characterized in the language he was superbly fluent in – Chinese. He had lived his life working for his country, or so everyone thought, though no one knew or could know much about the details of his profession. He was what is known as a spy in the old-fashioned sense; of course, his obituary had said something about his being a research officer in RAW (Research and Analysis Wing of the Intelligence Services of the country).

With her grandmother's death, Shireen had lost the last connexion to family. Her family tree did not throw out its branches in the usual sense, where every marriage and offspring led to further connexions, with multiplying branches and subdivisions that expanded into a fine network like that of the blood vessels in a human biology diagram. Hers was not a regular genealogy of genetics; her family tree was more like a tree in the sense of a computer folder with its neatly categorized subfolders, some never to be opened. In her mind, the folder titled Family was partitioned into two – those who were ostensibly family but had never wanted to know her, and those who were family but could not now be known. In the former were subfolders relating to her uncle and his wife and sons, there was also an assortment of other nebulous relatives who only came into focus at funerals. In the latter subfolder of Family that could not now be known, there were the categories of Alive and Dead. At first, there was a balance: there were two people in each, her parents in the Dead folder, and her grandparents in the Alive folder. But in the last two years, one by one, first her grandfather and then her grandmother had been selected by an unknown cursor and dragged into the Dead folder. The Alive folder could now be deleted.

Shireen was not sure what she should be doing at that exact moment. She knew she needed to put a few clothes into a bag, call for a taxi, wake up her friend Saima who was sleeping in the next room and let her know that she would be gone for a few days to attend the rituals following her grandmother's demise. She looked around her, wanting to get up, but was unable to do so, as if she were in one of those nightmarish dreams where the body is pinned to a position by invisible chains, unable to escape the terrors. In her case, the terrors were a deluge of memories that broke every dam and submerged everything in her senses. She managed to drink a glass of water, hoping it would calm her nerves, but it made her more restless. On an impulse, she poured out another glass from the jug and went over to water the lone plant on the windowsill. It was a hardy cactus, a small aggregation of fine thorns that did not need water in this weather, but she watered it anyway.

She thought of her parents. Faded photographs from the early 1990s danced before her eyes. The pictures were from Srinagar. They lived in Kashmir. She lived in Kashmir. They died in Kashmir. Then she didn't live in Kashmir any more. Sentences rapped on the doors of her mind. The little girl is standing small next to her very tall father in a black-and-white picture in which he wears a radiant white kurta–pyjama and she wears a frock that looks black but could have been red. The little girl is sitting on her mother's lap, looking up at her face, one finger touching the chain of her long silver ornament, the dezhor in her ears. The beaming little girl is sitting on the wooden steps of a staircase in a house; the oversized coat that she is swaddled in obscures most of her body.

Her parents were a distant memory. She was blessed not to have seen their corpses after the horrendous accident in which a shootout in Srinagar had caused a bus to overturn, killing several of the passengers on board, including her parents. She was playing house-house in a neighbour's home with other girls of the locality. She played long past her usual time that day, and no one came to fetch her. The lady of the house she was in treated her with a surfeit of love and care every time she cried asking for her parents for the next few days until her uncle came to take her to Delhi and deposited her with her grandparents.

It took her a few years to properly realize that the people in the neighbourhood in Srinagar whom she called Uncles and Aunts and Bobas and Tathis were not her relatives. Her kin were in Delhi. Her grandparents had showered her with love; so much of it that after a while her enquiries about her parents became phrased as 'what happened to the photo-mom and photo-dad?' Her sense of her parents had gone from an unaware early childhood with them to a confused distancing from them, till she was a bit older and was told that they had perished in Kashmir. But that led to other questions in a seven-year-old's head: why did they live in Kashmir? Why wasn't everyone there? Or why wasn't everyone here? These were harder to answer. Over time, she gathered that her father had been the black sheep of the family. He had grown up in Kashmir, was left behind when his brother and parents had moved to Delhi decades ago, and had chosen to stay behind when the rest of his relatives moved to Jammu – and then Delhi – in the exodus of the migrants.

Kashmir was his country. She had only very recently come to understand the special nuances of saying this. Throughout her school years – most of them spent at the Unity International boarding school in the hills of Mussoorie – she believed that patriotism and loyalty to India was the highest virtue a young person could have. And this meant fighting for the right to keep Kashmir 'ours' as a proud 'we' had done in Kargil in 1999 and in many other wars before. Kashmir was an integral part of India. The Kashmiri Pandits were a Hindu minority that had been expelled by the cruel Muslims in Kashmir, and the killings by the army that were reported sometimes in the news were just desserts for what 'they' had done to 'us'.

This is what her grandfather had always said to her. He had been patriotic and loyal to his country India till the end, never sharing information about what he actually did for his work, where he went when he didn't return home for days on end, and how he had come to collect an entire library of Chinese books. When Shireen came home for her summer holidays, she pestered him for stories about his life, about her father's history. It was her way of filling pages in the scrapbook of her life. He was often hesitant to speak about her father, and repeated the same anecdotes about himself till she knew them by heart.

Story Number 1: Her grandfather had been studying in a college in Lahore before the partition happened. He needed to travel on a crammed train, through Punjab. He had a reserved a berth for his ticket, but late at night, a Sikh man in the crowd requested him to cede a little space to let him rest for a while. When her grandfather obliged, the man sat down and in due course invited others to join him. Soon, the berth was taken over completely, and when her grandfather complained, the Sikh man laughed and said, 'Why worry about physical space, it is the heart that should be vast enough to accommodate others.'

Story Number 2: A few people were flying in a helicopter somewhere in a foggy, mountainous terrain. The ride suddenly turned very dangerous and it was certain that there would be a crash and everyone on board would die. People started to get jittery and murmured their prayers aloud. The lurches got worse as the copter fumbled in the air. Somehow, they managed to survive the nerve-wracking episode, and when they finally landed, everyone was amazed at how one man – her grandfather – had not seemed bothered even once during the ghastly ride.

Story Number 3: Once, he had looked at the palm of a colleague and jokingly said that the man would die in a week. This actually transpired and the man passed away after a few days.

Story Number 4: He was at a party with senior army officials, where everyone was happy with intoxication and conversation. A brigadier's wife came up to him and asked him what spirit he would like, in response to which he told her that he did not partake of alcohol. She looked him up and down and wrinkled her nose disdainfully, not speaking to him for the rest of the evening.

Story Number 5: A colleague was once handed a posting in a small, obscure town somewhere near the border (there were never any specific details). This place was far and rather inaccessible, and the man had no wish to go there. He pleaded with his boss, who was not an inconsiderate man, and so, together, they devised a plan. The man would initially take up his post. After a few months, the boss would ask for his transfer back to Delhi. When he was asked to return, the man would try to refuse so it wouldn't seem orchestrated. But the boss would insist that it was absolutely necessary for this man to return.

When the man went to the obscure settlement, he fell in love with a local woman and, for the only time in his life, he wanted to give everything up and stay there forever. But no matter how vehemently he refused, the boss thought he was playing his part and he was forced to return.

Story Number 6: Hong Kong was beautiful.

Shireen wondered if the story about a colleague was actually a veiled reference to his own life or that of his son. She would never know. The last story about Hong Kong was not elaborated upon. Well before she had arrived in his care from Srinagar, Shireen knew that her grandfather had lived in – been posted in? – Hong Kong for a few years. As a young girl, she loved to run her fingers over the tiny taupe freckle labelled 'Hong Kong' on the middle right side of China on the India Book Depot world map that hung on the wall in her room. It was surrounded by Taipei, Manila, Chong-Qing, Hanoi and the South China Sea, all in fine cursive lettering. How exotic it must be to be in Hong Kong, she thought! Of the many things he must have brought back at the time, an old hand-held slide viewer had survived, along with dozens of little maroon-tinted, memory-card–sized, cardboard-framed slides of the kind taken as souvenirs by tourists. She used to insert these small old-world photo-biscuits into the viewer and watch them one by one, unhurriedly. They were marked with titles like 'Kowloon Bay', 'Pearl River' and 'The Peak'. On some were petite women wearing pretty dresses and posing with fancy umbrellas; on others were images of large lanterns the shape of dragons.

When she was a bit older, she came to know that Hong Kong had changed hands while she was growing up. The land of the two resonant sounds had gone from being under British administration to 'One Country, Two Systems' with China. The countries and territories of the world kept changing, but for that to happen without bloodshed, agreements needed to be honoured with grace.

If her grandfather and father had, between them, divided the choice of their country of belonging as India or Kashmir respectively, then her grandmother had no country. She was, as everyone said, not completely sane, and she never bothered about identifying with any country at all. Her country was probably that of dreams, since she spent numerous hours of the day sleeping under the influence of the tranquilizers that were often prescribed for her. A mad person has no country. It takes a collectivity of mad people to create a country to die for.

Her grandmother's life had come to be defined by her intense need for seclusion and sleep. This did not mean that she was unfriendly or indolent. In fact, before her uncle and his family moved into her house following her husband's death, she managed the household by herself. Shireen felt a deep bond of affection with her. The two of them spent entire scorching afternoons indoors at home together in each other's company in the days before she was sent to boarding school or during the times when she would return for her vacations. Her grandmother oiled and combed her hair, cooked the meals she liked, crocheted beautiful patterns on clothes for her. The old woman could not read or write, so Shireen sometimes read stories from children's books to her. Her sense of geography was fabulously strange. Once, when back from school, Shireen gave her a pen and paper and asked her to draw a map of India. She couldn't. Then, Shireen asked her to draw a map of Kashmir. She couldn't. Shireen realized that her grandma didn't even know England and America were different from each other!

What the grandmother did know and tell her little granddaughter nestling close to her in bed was how the harsh winter cold of Chillai Kalan in Kashmir lasted forty days, the small cold of Chillai Khurd would be the following twenty days, till came the baby cold of Chillai Bachh that was ten days long. Hearing this, a white space of memories would be raked up in the child's head like billowing snow, but it would form only photos from books and fail to bring up anything personal to her, so she gently let the names of the cold fall quietly upon what they signified – the calendar days from late December to early March.

She told Shireen that her son, the girl's father, had been a beautiful little boy. That it broke her heart to leave him behind when they moved to Delhi – for which she always used the word Hindustan, as if all India and Hindustan and Delhi were synonyms – but she had to do what her husband wanted and the boy just did not want to leave Kashmir. She told her granddaughter that the girl's father had been prematurely born and was not initially expected to survive; that he was a rebellious child; that he had married a student of his much younger than himself very late in life against the wishes of his family; that however headstrong he had been, she loved him. At times like this, Shireen was certain that there was nothing wrong with her grandmother, she was not mad, never mind what the others said.

Shireen did not like to ask her grandmother to tell her stories because the old woman knew only one story and it was a boring one that had a grim and senseless ending. It was always the same and went something like this: Once upon a time, a wealthy and successful goldsmith lived in a town with his wife. It so happened that one evening, on his way back from his shop, he bought a large quantity of meat at a butcher's counter and, upon returning home, gave it to his wife to cook for their meal the next evening. On the following day, after he left for work, the wife happily started cooking the meat for dinner. As the meat was being cooked, it smelt pleasant. The woman took a sip of some gravy and then bit a piece, which tasted delicious. She thought of eating a little more, and then some more, and before she knew it, she had finished all of it. When the husband returned in the evening and enquired about the meat, there was none. He rightly suspected that she had consumed it all, whereupon he got intensely angry and beat her soundly; so badly, in fact, that he cut off her ear to teach her a lesson. That was it. The first few times that she had heard the story, Shireen's attention was spontaneously drawn to her grandmother's ears – they seemed fine. The earlobes were distended from decades of wearing earrings, but they were intact. She had asked the point of the story, to which her grandmother had replied that the wife had been punished for her misdeeds. Even as a child, Shireen could not see the point – why didn't the wife go and fetch more meat if she had eaten it all? How did such a cruel punishment serve any purpose? There were no further answers from her grandmother to these questions, so she decided to forget about asking her for stories.

Pigeons fluttered at her window and broke into Shireen's reverie. She roused herself, threw some clothes into a shoulder bag, dialled a cab on her phone, and went to knock on Saima's door. There was no answer. Her friend was probably asleep. Shireen knew that Saima stayed up late at night Skyping with her boyfriend Rehan in Srinagar. She decided to leave a note and slid a scribbled sheet under the door before she left.

Later that day, she was standing outside the red slate walls of the Nigambodh Ghat crematorium near Delhi's Kashmere Gate while her uncle had gone inside to collect her grandmother's ashes. She stared broodingly at the grit near her feet, where, in between the pavement slabs, tenacious little weeds battled the onslaught of the city. A dotted line of moving ants was headed somewhere to one side. Behind her was a stream of honking traffic; she heard the hailing cry of a costermonger near the bus stop, praising the fruits piled on his handcart. After what seemed like an eternity, her uncle came out with a sewed-up white gunny sack under his arm. It contained *her*. Shireen had insisted upon accompanying him here to collect her remains. As a female, she was not allowed to be part of the procession that had taken her grandmother's body there earlier to be given over to cinders. But, once the actual body had gone, the many men and women gathered at the large flat in Mayur Vihar got busy with the preparations for the numerous rituals to follow. Picking up the sack of ashes became yet another task that her son, as per ritual, would carry out. Letting Shireen accompany him made no difference to anyone since it only meant the insignificant acquiescence of the wishes of a peripheral witness. Approaching her from a distance, her uncle's face looked drawn and haggard. Maybe the man was not bad after all, she thought.

When he proceeded to return to the car, Shireen baulked inexplicably. 'I want to go inside and see where they burn the bodies,' she said. The man was probably taken aback at this odd wish but was too exhausted to argue. So, they asked the driver to wait while she went inside the crematorium and passed through a corridor to emerge into what looked like a large open space where multiple pillars held up an extended triangular metal canopy. Like hospital or hostel beds, there were rows of neatly delineated and numbered pyre platforms, each a rectangle of space sunk into the ground, some with smouldering ashes in them. Shadows of the pillars traced a wide-toothed comb over the entire area.

When she sat in the car again, she asked her uncle which number her grandmother had been burned in.

'Eight,' he said. The flat tone of a sonorous Bā – 'eight' in Chinese – rang in her head. As a schoolgirl, she had learnt the numbers from one to twenty and a few other words in Mandarin from her grandfather. Repeated twice – Bà Ba – it became a word that meant father. Her father who was the son of the woman who had just died and the brother of the man sitting in the front seat of the car. Aloud she said, 'Eight is a lucky number in Chinese; I hope she gets peace in the afterlife.' Her uncle grunted softly as if to agree. After a pause, he mentioned that in keeping with funeral convention, they had put a copper coin in her mouth for her soul to be assured an easy passage after death.

She asked her uncle why they did not inform her that her grandmother had been ill. Her uncle strung together several contradictory sentences in a fumbling, awkward manner that conveyed to her something about his family being busy, about her being unstable in the last days and eating too much salt in her food, but then being short of sodium because they were fasting for the nine days of Navratra and then wanting oranges at her deathbed. 'Why was she fasting at her age? She didn't fast in previous years, did she?' Shireen asked a straight question. 'All of us fasted this year. The maid was on leave. No food was cooked. It is important. Religious observances are important. Your aunt wouldn't have it otherwise.' That last line explained it. So the old woman had been made to fast in the name of religion. What her uncle said was hardly surprising – the tentacles of Hindutva conformity had been strangling the whole country since the Great Leader had come to power in the summer of 2014 on a promise to purify the country.

'You know I tried so many times to speak to her over the last year, but you never answered the phone,' she stated, secure in the knowledge that she had nothing to lose by holding up the mirror to him.

'I don't want to argue. You know that your aunt did not like your grandmother meeting people. It made her unstable and then we had to live with her muttering to herself all day. She even used to tell the neighbours that we were poisoning her. Why would we do that?'

'I don't know, uncle, but I do know that you all have been unkind to her. She was not mad.'

'That's easy for others to say when they don't have to take the responsibility of dealing with such a person. I bought her medicines. Do you know how much her treatment cost when she broke her arm last year? We even paid the maid extra to serve her. I couldn't go with your aunt and the boys to Pune because I needed to stay here with her. She wouldn't agree to come along and was always complaining. Boba[16] made provisions for your fees and accommodation, but we have two sons to worry about. Nothing one does is good enough. People always find a way to lay blame.'

This made Shireen angry. Her voice choking with rage, she said, 'Some people just don't have care or conscience; all they think about is money. I thought you weren't like the rest of your household, but I was mistaken. I am sorry if you hate me for saying this, but you know in your heart that I am stating the truth.'

He did not reply. She did not speak further.

When they were about to reach Mayur Vihar, Shireen announced, 'I am going to stay over tonight and I am coming to Haridwar with you tomorrow. You can remove me from every legal right but you cannot force me out of attending the rituals. She was my grandmother too. Whatever the relationship between my father and my grandparents, I know that both Boba and Amma loved me with all their heart.'

'Yes, you can come,' was all he said in response.

Sameer, the driver of the car that had been hired for a couple of days, stared at the back of these two figures as they went up the stairs of the three-storey building in a single file. He shook his head in dismay and then turned on an FM station where a radio jockey was praising the launch of the Swachh Bharat Abhiyan[17] earlier that month on Gandhi's birth anniversary. If only chests could be cleaned of pain as easily as that, he thought.

Then came the agreement of the priest's fee, the gathering of sandalwood, rolls of sacred red thread, specified amounts of ghee and rice, barley flour, sesame seeds, flowers, incense, salt, copper vessels, currency notes in exact denominations, and much else. The women and the men had their roles to play and things to do. Those relatives, acquaintances or neighbours not in the kitchen, at the market, or on their phones, gathered together on the floor of the living room, convincing each other of the beloved and pure nature of the departed soul.

The next morning, Shireen, her uncle and aunt, their two sons, the priest and a distant cousin climbed into the large eight-seater vehicle with the driver. The sack containing the ashes was stored carefully in the vehicle, alongside the bag with the materials for the rituals. They set out on the journey that would take about five hours by road. The priest sat in the front and spoke little, except to occasionally enquire whether something had been packed or to emphasize his own longstanding reputation as a man who had extensive experience of such ceremonies. Shireen took the window seat behind the driver; next to her was the cousin from Pune. Her aunt sat with her two sons at the very back; one of them was constantly making work-related phone calls and she spoke privately in low tones with the other. She had not addressed a single word to Shireen since the previous morning, behaving as if she were invisible.

Shireen did not mind since she didn't want to talk to anyone anyhow. On her headphones, a melange of songs created random marks in a scatterplot of grief as she focused on a stray memorable phrase here, a poignant word there. Her grandfather's favourite song had been '*Ajeeb dastan hai yeh*'[18] from the movie *Dil Apna Aur Preet Parai*.[19] He had told her that himself. She realized that she had forgotten to ask her grandmother her favourite song while she was alive. How could she have been so negligent? What else had she forgotten to ask her forebear? She thought of the framelessness of grief, the purity of loss, and the interruptions of life.

Her grandparents had so little in common, yet they had spent over half a century being married to each other. It could not have been a happy time. He was away so often before his retirement, and then there were also those years in Hong Kong. Her grandmother had seemingly suffered a neurological ailment of some kind throughout her adult life. Her grandfather was a quietly accomplished man, fluent in Mandarin, Persian, Kashmiri, Hindi, Urdu and English. He could solve the Rubik's cube and crack mathematical puzzles well into his dim years. He had served the state in its corridors of power and intrigue. When he and Shireen's grandmother had been married, he was a graduate from Lahore and she was an illiterate young village girl. What had their life together been like? In the initial years, they must have lived in a large joint family in Kashmir, but later, when moving to Delhi for his job, how had she managed to leave a child behind, and raise another child she brought along? Was she always as 'mentally disturbed' as they said? How was she as a little girl? Why did Shireen's own father not live with them even during the decades before he married her mother?

She remembered how her grandfather would always send postal New Year greeting cards to people even in the twenty-first century. These square white envelopes were addressed to people in different parts of the country and some were posted abroad. She had heard her grandmother grouse about his sending cards to his female office secretaries after retirement. Was it unfounded jealousy as a result of her nervous disposition or did she have reasons to suspect him of having been unfaithful to her in the past?

The woman was dead, but her granddaughter still did not know what she had suffered from. Shireen knew that everyone thought the old woman 'not normal'. As a child, when she had enquired as to what was wrong with her grandmother, she had been given indefinite answers peppered with the words 'hypochondria' and 'depression'. She had seen her grandmother swallow pills many times, but only once had she accompanied her grandparents to a hospital for the mentally ill. In her head, she had an indistinct picture of a place where, as she was told, her grandmother was given electric shocks to make her better. Shireen remembered a big waiting area, a carrom board, a glass of water being spilt, and then a long wait, after which her grandmother emerged from a corridor, her face drawn and her husband holding her with one hand and carrying a file of papers in the other.

Maintaining the 'dailyness' of lives requires an immense amount of 'tidying up'. A constant and unending stream of tidying, shoving and shuffling things into ad hoc mind cupboards in the vague delusional belief that they will be attended to later, and so the moral facts of little interpersonal disputes, the criteria used for making simple choices, and the bigger questions, go uninterrogated. As a result, for brief interludes, life 'really is "simple"' and the here and now take centrestage, so that someday, one day, 'those' other questions will be resolved. Such beautiful absurdity!

Shireen opened her eyes as the Radiohead song '*Street Spirit (Fade Out)*' came on. The stretched vocals ribboned out like an endless road upon which a tachycardial beat went bounding as the intricate deltas of sound poured into a magnificently joyous lament. '*This machine will, will not, communicate.*' A continuous reel of scenes unspooled on the other side of the glass window. There were two crows at the back of a torn and rusty scaffolding; three men waited by a bike in a paved courtyard; a burqa-clad woman rode pillion on a vespa holding a little girl in her arms; there was an advert for plastic sandals with red and yellow straps. There were misplaced apostrophes everywhere. One said 'Thank's for coming', another 'Best Lodging's'. A precious few green leaves shimmered on the dust-caked trees lining the highway. As they flit past, the signs announced a training venue for 'Central Investigation and Security Services' or invited pupils to learn English, 'angrezi bolna seekhiye', at the 'Howard International School'.

Shireen had been unable to gather herself in the face of the disorientations of time and space that the last twenty-four or so hours had brought. No one who had raised her was alive anymore, and that reality refused to sink in. It cannot be. She shall not allow it, she thought, and then she collapsed into a mortifying despair again. There is something tremendously debilitating about grief: one gives up. Gives up. This tiny speck of a life, so easily lapsed. No more words from her grandparents, no more consolations, no advice, no unconditional love, no lasting constancy. Just the arresting fact of death.

Now, hold back tears. Hold them back. Cry. Or weep. Let it fall. Nothing matters. Nothing. Her inner monologue was unable to hold up, it teetered, unbalanced and uncertain, like the tears that were balanced on the edges of her lids. She acted as if she was arranging her hair, using the back of her palm to wipe the tears just as they slipped over the threshold and past the brim of her lashes. The peeled orange of the sun was hazy in a sky laced with cinereal clouds. Their car went past watery pools that sat like bowls of paint in a green field. Then came a field with bright yellow sunflowers. She tried to calm herself, repeating, 'Good will come soon'.

Not long afterwards, policemen stopped the vehicle as they reached the border of Uttar Pradesh and Uttarakhand. The signs read Khatauli/Muzzaffarnagar and Rana Chowk Bypass Road Phatak. At the barrier, the driver got out to speak to them. Shireen did not pay attention to what was going on until her aunt loudly asked her elder son to get out and see what was holding them up. He was a couple of years younger than Shireen but always assumed the role of a 'big man'. With swagger, he asked his father not to bother; he would 'handle it'. The situation was obviously not straightforward since there were raised voices and the word 'tax' could be heard over and over again. Or was it 'taxi'? The cousin from Pune shuffled restlessly beside Shireen. The two exchanged a vacuous glance. The priest hypothesized that the police must be asking for a bribe and opined that it was better to pay up in order to avoid unnecessary hassle.

'We should not have to pay a bribe to carry the ashes of a dead relative on a public road. I want to get down and see what's happening.'

As soon as she said this, and before her uncle could reply, her aunt addressed her directly for the first time: 'You don't need to get off. Please sit there and don't interfere. We are taking care of things.'

'Why can't I get off?' Shireen persisted.

'Because this is not a situation for women. We are being accommodating to you, at least be grateful and don't add to our troubles,' she replied.

Seared by the irreparable blow of tragedy, Shireen said, 'I am sorry, I forgot, you are being kind by allowing me to accompany my grandmother's ashes to Haridwar. I may even have forgotten to thank you for letting me be at my grandfather's death ceremonies. Alright, do whatever you want, Aunty.' She placed particular stress on the last word that denoted their relationship.

Her aunt could recognize a humiliation aimed at herself better than she could sense one she dished out to others. She turned to her husband and said in a furious voice, 'I told you this would not work. But, obviously, if you didn't bring me along, who would arrange everything? It is my job to slave and suffer.'

'Dad, can everyone please be quiet? I need to make an urgent phone call for work,' piped up the younger son as he dialled a number and asked someone for updates about the progress with a client payment.

'I don't want any arguments,' said Shireen's uncle as he opened the door and got out himself.

The priest maintained a stony silence and the cousin buried his head into a game of Temple Run with the sound muted.

Shireen too went quiet. She re-imagined everything around her as if it was anodyne. They were all part of an unknown and uninteresting reproduction of a still-life painting hanging in a large transit hall.

Once the haggling over the amount of the bribe concluded, they were on their way again. After another half an hour, the question of stopping for a meal arose. The driver was asked if he knew a good place en route, somewhere not too expensive. He suggested an eatery further along. The priest immediately refused to eat there, saying that it was part of a chain owned by a Muslim man.

At this, her uncle expressed surprise, 'I didn't know the chain had a Muslim owner. I have eaten there before.'

'You don't know anything,' snapped his wife. Then, she addressed the priest deferentially in a mellow tone: 'Panditji, why don't you suggest a good place? You must know one.'

Placated, the priest immediately suggested a highway stop another half an hour away. He assured everyone that it was owned by a pious man and they served good food that was pure and wholesome.

Shireen could not help gazing at the back of driver's head. She was not shocked by the bigotry of her relatives but felt sorry for the driver having been snubbed in this manner.

Upon reaching Haridwar, they checked into a guesthouse where the priest and Shireen were given rooms of their own; the others were all sharing. The priest assumed charge, directing the arrangements, giving timings, laying out the preparations. Over the next two days, there was a sequence of rituals in different locations. On the steps of the ghat by the Ganga, there was extended chanting while freshly cooked rice was moulded into balls and dotted with vermilion and sesame seeds, lamps were lit, and at one point the ashes were immersed into the river. The elder son sat with the priest, a handkerchief covering his head and a long red saffron tika mark on his forehead, as he followed the instructions of the holy man. Her aunt handed every required ingredient to her uncle who in turn passed it on to the priest or his son as the ritual required. The cousin looked on with an unfathomable solemnity. The younger son excused himself twice from the ceremonies to take phone calls. Shireen placed herself as close as she could to what was going on. Tears kept streaking down her face and this time she did not try to stop them. The priest made an attempt to include her in the ceremonies wherever possible and Shireen was a little surprised at this kindness on his part.

The next day, a havan ceremony was held under the leafy shade of the guesthouse backyard. Everyone settled on the mats spread around the centre of a continuously burning fire into which the havan samagri was fed, one by one, accompanied by sacred chanting. Shireen was familiar with many of the Sanskrit verses and prayers being uttered, as her school had required all students to attend a havan for spiritual welfare every term-time Sunday until they reached the tenth standard. Now, as she sat on the ground with her legs folded and her back erect, she was again entranced by the furiously flickering tongues of flame. Her grandmother was now particles in the universe, having returned to the stardust of human origin after her time on this earth. Such sanctification ceremonies upon demise did force the mind back to the barest essentials of being. We are. We are not. Shireen's thoughts sharpened themselves on the anvil of the stark realization that everything and everyone is always impermanent. Every next word that will form from speech is both crucial to the essence of renewing a present and yet also a mere restatement of the eternal truth.

Before dawn the following morning, they had to distribute alms to the needy. It was not hard to summon them – the city was crammed with the destitute and the disabled who could be found begging at every corner and alley. When the food was brought out, nearly a hundred people came queueing at the gates of the guesthouse. It took no less than an amnesia of the conscience to disregard the parade of these hollow-eyed shrunken and sun-burnt bodies, some with a limb or two missing, some preceded by a disheveled but smiling child running ahead, others by a hungry dog trailing behind. To live with food in one's belly everyday and with a roof above one's head every night was lucky, and to continue living in the face of the knowledge that so many human bodies will never have food and shelter, required an immunization by indifference or a recalibrated moral compass. When the food ran out, the skeletal people and the dogs both needed to be shooed away by the guard at the gate.

During their journey back, there were no ashes in the car. Shireen could not get past this bare fact. Wherever she looked and whatever she saw, her thoughts spiralled back into the black hole of death and absence.

It was dark by the time they approached Delhi. The cloudy night sky above foretold nothing with clarity. Would it rain soon? Shireen looked up and wondered; she had been unable to sleep even for a few minutes in the car. The deafeningly loud, roaring and gushing Ganga was inside her tonight, absorbing everything, flooding everything. She was not able to separate what she knew from who she was. She felt unlit, uneven, unfinished, as if all her experiences only reinforced her incompleteness in a broken world.

When the car pulled up at the metal gates of the Mayur Vihar block where her grandfather and then her grandmother had once lived, the sentry rushed to unbolt the entrance that was locked to outsiders at night. As everyone got out of the car, all that remained was for the driver to be paid and the priest to be driven back to his home. Shireen suggested to her uncle that they let the driver drop her off at her PG accommodation. It would be the safer alternative compared to taking a cab alone. She offered her uncle the 400 rupees that a cab would have charged at this hour. He took it without a murmur and placed it in his wallet. As the car pulled out again, Shireen saw a baby bat that fluttered by a streetlight. She had not spoken a single spare word to anyone since the incident with her aunt in the car earlier. Now that she and the priest were the only two passengers, the priest spoke directly to her, asking her where she lived and what she studied. When he learnt that she lived in PG accommodation with another girl near JNU and had recently been admitted to a Masters in Philosophy there, he asked her whether it was a good place to study. 'Absolutely,' she replied.

A few moments passed during which she did not ask him anything in return, so he volunteered further information. 'I have a granddaughter – my daughter's eldest – who is graduating from a college in Meerut and she insists on studying further in Delhi. I have heard different things about universities here, and especially about JNU where it seems our national values are openly flouted.'

Shireen did not reply.

'Though, of course, I know that you are a good girl. You really loved your grandmother. I have been doing these ceremonies all my life and can tell who really feels grief at the loss of a loved one. Otherwise, everyone gathers for a show ... I did not bargain with them even though I usually charge more for such elaborate ceremonies ...' He drawled on, seemingly needing no encouragement to continue. He was a wiry old man with a beak nose and short hair, longer strands at the back of his skull signifying his Brahminical claim. His gnarly, veined hands rested loosely on his lap. Shireen thought that for such a loquacious fellow, it must have been a true feat to remain so quiet during the journey to Haridwar and back.

At last, his house neared. Pre-empting his departure, he gave extensive blessings to Shireen for her future education and her marriage. 'Thank you,' she replied. Then, feeling a surge of warmth brought on by the successful conclusion of an engagement over the last three days, he also thanked the driver and asked him if he was married and had children, perhaps with the intention of tailoring his blessings according to the answer.

'Yes, I am married and have two children, Ayesha and Arhaan. They are five and two,' said Sameer, the driver.

'Sorry? I didn't catch the name of your children. It must be that my hearing is affected by age.'

Rolling up the window with one hand to minimize noise, Sameer repeated, 'Ayesha and Arhaan, Panditji,' speaking a little louder this time.

The red indicator lights of a car in front flashed on the priest's face as it registered a fleeting series of reactions in a helpless fury.

Their car was indicating to turn too and, within seconds, came to a stop outside the priest's home.

In all probability, he had choked on several previous drafts of his words. He finally managed to say, 'Sameer is a clever name for a Muslim. It sounds like one of ours. But you should not have driven us. This is an absolute shame. All those rituals to ease the soul of the corpse, and you the very charioteer, being Muslim. This is not good at all.'

'I am just a driver, Panditji. This is my living. I stayed in an inn over there. I did not touch anything,' Sameer tried to explain.

'Even so. Even so,' repeated the priest, picking up his bag and closing the door of the car as he went away with a stumbling gait.

Shireen did not speak to the driver to mollify him. There were people like the priest who could not be explained away.

He asked her if she would mind the radio being on.

'Not at all,' she said.

He switched to an FM station at random which was playing the fast-paced tune '*Patakha Guddi*' from the movie *Highway* released earlier in the year. As the trance-inducing refrain '*Ali, Ali, Ali, Ali*' filled the car, it was as if a different kind of ritual cleansing was taking place so that the powerful currents of sound chased away the accumulated debris of ill feeling.

There was a fine drizzle in the air when she got out of the car.

Sameer said to her: 'Bye and thank you, madam. I am sorry if because of me your grandmother's rituals got affected.'

Shireen looked directly at him. 'Sameer, their irrational hate has no meaning. I don't believe in anything except that we must be good and the world rests on hope. My grandmother will be at peace wherever she is.'

Saying this made her feel calm, her words lowering an anchor of belief into her being. She slowly went up the four flights of stairs to the shared top-floor flat. Saima came rushing to open the door as soon as she heard the bell.

~

'My darling! I was so worried for you!' she exclaimed, giving Shireen an extended hug.

The two girls had met during their first year at university a few years ago. During their Bachelors degree, they had been classmates, living in the same residential block of the O.P. Jindal University campus in the middle of Haryana. However, it was only halfway through their undergraduate days that they had formed a closer friendship. In the first year on campus, Saima had generally hung out with the 'cool' crowd, sneaking out at night to smoke weed and party with the boys.

Later, in their second year, the disciplinary structures on campus were tightened in response to complaints from various parents. Saima's own family saw her results and gave her an ultimatum that if she didn't get better grades, they would call her back home. Upon choosing to reform into a more studious type, she started spending more time in the library where she later became a study buddy with Shireen. Soon after that, she got into a mostly long-distance relationship with Rehan, whom she had first met on Facebook.

After finishing their BA, they had both enrolled in different courses at JNU and it had seemed obvious to rent PG accommodation together in Delhi. Their small rented flat in Vasant Kunj was not far from the JNU campus. Saima had done really well in her final year undergraduate results and was now studying for an MA at the School of International Studies and simultaneously preparing to take the UPSC examinations later. Shireen, on the other hand, had never been a rebellious student with disciplinary problems; she had neither ever failed nor done exceptionally well at her studies. She didn't like reproducing the expected points of view and was often penalized for her bumbling attempts at originality. Her marks were reasonably good, but she had never excelled at her studies. Before college, she had spent several years at the boarding school practising invisibility. She did not volunteer for any positions, wanting above all not to stand out or be conspicuous. She had enrolled for an MA in Philosophy and had little idea what would follow. Unlike students from 'normal' families, there was no one to prod her with anxious questions about her future, and this had allowed her scope for expansive experimentation.

The two women complemented each other. Where Saima was messy, Shireen was organized. When Shireen was inhibited, Saima could be expressive. Yet, in spite of these different attitudes towards their surroundings and interactions, they were both analytical and empathetic. When dealing with a problem that confronted either of them, they engaged with the tangle of ideas in their own ways and then held out what they found for the other to reflect upon, honestly and with warm care. In college, they had connected in the ways young girls did, over shared dreams, lecture notes, food, secrets, jewellery, and much more. But they had another stronger connexion that explained their friendship over multiple years. Stated quite simply, it was that they took each other seriously as thoughtful individuals. If one of them picked up an exploratory thread of an idea, the other would take it up and allow it the space for unfolding. Once, when Saima was back home in Ladakh and Shireen was in Delhi, after a phone call between them lasting several hours, Saima had remarked: 'I have never spoken like this for this long to anyone who was not a guy.' At one point in the conversation, when discussing how their lives might have been easier if they had been men instead of women – Saima had during those days received a hectoring from a neighbour about not wearing the headscarf, and from there their discussion had reached the topic of there being so few female philosophers – the two of them had synchronously sighed at the two ends of the line. When this happened, one of them smiled, and the other, as if able to see all the hidden meanings in that smile, had said, 'Our sighs just now, the best definition of patriarchy.' Other people – Saima's own siblings and boyfriends – had at times caused their circle to widen for a while, but at the end of a quarrel, a breakup, or a betrayal, they had usually come back to seek solace in each other's company.

Shireen needed her friend to comfort her that night. Saima had not disturbed her while she was away, knowing that she would need her time alone with her thoughts. When Saima received Shireen's text before her return, she knew what she needed to do.

On the table were two pizzas with Shireen's favourite topping of olives. After giving her a long hug – Saima always cheerily proclaimed that a hug was no good unless it was at least twenty seconds long, because that's how long it took for a hug to release the feel-good endorphins in the body: so said science! – Saima sat her down and asked how she was feeling.

Slowly, awkwardly, Shireen opened up. Her sentences formed themselves in between her unpacking, her experiences were recounted as if uninterrupted by the shower she took, her loneliness stumbled out in between the morsels of cheesy dough that she chewed. Patiently, Saima listened.

That night, both of them slept in Saima's room where the bed was bigger. Saima kissed her friend's forehead as she lay exhausted and unable to sleep. She ran her fingers through her friend's hair, saying, 'Everything will be alright soon.' Shireen could be inhibited, but she was not incapable of receiving such love with heartfelt warmth and gratitude. She said to Saima, 'You know, at times like this, when the world seems to be too difficult and I don't know why I am here or what I am to do, I feel so frustrated and wish I could express away my pain. But all I can make out in myself are the words: I want to go home! I want to go home!' She spoke these words like a child who yearns for something it has lost and knows that it is hard to have. She looked like a child too. Lying there in her turquoise nightie, her face pale, her eyes slightly swollen, her teeth biting her lip, her fingers digging into her palms, her toes curling. 'It's alright, dear,' said Saima, 'I know what you mean. You will be alright. I am here for you.'

At this, Shireen widened her eyes abstractedly, speaking in a small voice, 'I don't know. Maybe. But, maybe I don't know what that childhood feels like. Maybe when I say I want to go home, it is the expression of a death-wish because I want to lose my consciousness and my memories, and that can only happen when I am dead, isn't it?' As she uttered the question tag, she looked at her friend's face, as if it would give her an answer, the right answer.

Saima kept her belief in the world alive on days like this. She continued, 'I don't know if I ever told you, but when I first came to

Delhi as a child to live with my grandparents, sometimes, at night, I would reach over to both of them to hear their breathing, just to make sure they were alive. I was so strange. I still am, I suppose.' Saima said, 'Really? You darling baby. It must have been so hard. I knew death as a child, but not in such an intimate way. I wish I had met you then, we could have played together and made paper boats...'

'Yes! Paper boats. I loved paper boats. I would not sail them in the water, usually. I used to keep them imprisoned on a table inside a transparent, oval box.' A note of excitement crept into Shireen's voice. 'Oh, the paper boats, and the magnifying glass that Boba had ... he once showed me how to focus sunlight onto paper with it so it would catch fire ... And there was a fabulous Chinese landscape scene made from carved cork. I adored it so much. And the paperweights, their glass bubble worlds with the million fantasies trapped in them. And Amma's embroidered Chinar-leaf cloth. And the green plastic potted plant she loved. How the memory of those objects lives in me. It's as if I can see and touch them just by thinking of them, right now, right here ...' she grew quieter, 'even though both of them are earth and ashes and water now.'

When she finished speaking, Saima placed her hand on Shireen's forehead and rubbed it ever so gently, then said, 'Why don't you ask your uncle for those things? Surely, they are no use to his family. I don't think they would mind giving them to you.'

'Yes,' Shireen echoed, and then said a bit more decisively, 'yes, I will do that. Of course, no one else would care for those things. They can't possibly have any reason to refuse giving them to me. I will call him. Oh, I don't know why I didn't think of that before. I hope tonight I dream of that world I once had...'

'Shall we go to sleep, then? Shall I switch off the lights?' Saima asked.

'Yes, I want to sleep. And you should too,' she paused. 'You don't need to Skype tonight? I can go to my room.'

'Don't be silly. I don't have to Skype. I spoke to him on the phone before you returned. And even if I had to, I wouldn't let my friend go anywhere out of my sight tonight. I want to make sure you rest well.'

'Okay,' said Shireen softly. 'Lights off, and please draw the curtains aside too, let the night filter in.'

As Saima reached the window in the darkness, she caught a glimpse of the humming neon city through the square wire netting of their secure perch. Knowing that Shireen loved the moon, she peered up to see if it was visible. Saima wanted to take a picture of the moon on her phone for her friend, but the moon was nowhere to be seen.

When she climbed into bed and pulled her bed sheet over her shoulders, Shireen turned around and said, 'Thank you, my dear angel.'

Saima replied in a mock-serious voice: 'Forget about thank you. I have to tell you something ... we have to file a missing report for...'

Before she could complete her sentence, Shireen exclaimed, 'What?'

'Relax, it's for the moon. He's been missing for a few days now. I think we ought to worry a little about his whereabouts. Who knows where he is, what state he is in? On behalf of concerned admirers like yourself, I think we should report his absence!'

'You giddy fool, you! I thought you were serious,' Saima got a playful rap.

Then, in a sober voice, Shireen added 'On the other hand, you are right, the fellow is missing with a lot of silver, he must be found!'

In the darkness, a little mirth passed like a firefly over the bed. Some time later, the cellar doors of their subconscious were lifted one by one and they drifted into sleep.

These two women who dreamt of who knows what that night, had changed each other in ways that they could themselves often forget, so usual it was for them to rely on the resonance they shared now. But, it was not always thus. Had their paths not crossed in the way they had, they would probably have grown more intensely into their own previous selves. And what selves were they?

~

Saima was the youngest of three children, a rebellious child whose upbringing had been influenced by the way her family's fortunes had changed over the years. Her father had gone from being religious and vocal about politics in his youth to a disenchanted businessman who managed his affairs and had scant concern for what happened outside the perimeter fence of his household.

Her eldest sister Layla was ten years older than her. Before she had even completed her schooling, Layla was married to an engineer in Bahrain. Saima remembered running around with excitement at her wedding. Layla was so beautiful; Saima could have worshipped her photograph. She stood tall and fair in Saima's mind. Her eyes had the unique quality of taking on the tint of the colour of the clothes she wore. She spoke softly, covered her head and was chaste as freshly fallen snow till the day she was betrothed. Then, soon after the wedding, she went to live abroad with her husband and his family. For a long time after she was gone, Saima used to miss being woken up by her elder sister in the mornings. Layla would lightly pinch her little sister's chubby cheeks and say, 'Get up, my princess.' Struggling to wake, Saima would open her eyes and lay her fingers upon her sister's arm, twirling her gold bangle, saying, 'Just five more minutes,' and Layla would let her sleep for several rounds of five minutes each, without losing patience or complaining. She would even make excuses on behalf of her little sister to her parents. The sisters shared a room and, at nights, Saima would see her sister comb her long hair with an ivory comb that had once belonged to their mother. It was such a special sight. Most people had not seen Layla with her hair open, and Saima loved to glide her palms down the lengths of her sister's hair – how shiny and silky it was! Before going to sleep, Layla would softly sing for her little sister, melodies about spring and the yearnings of maidens. In the silvery timbre of her voice, the songs became a mass of glinting stars like those daylight miracles made by the sun's bright beams on the surface of a flowing river. But then, before Saima had grown tired of adoring her sister or been weaned off her love, one day, she was married and gone. For a long time afterwards, life seemed hard to Layla's 'little princess'. Then, junior school years ended and she herself arrived on the cusp of her teenage years. Life didn't get simpler, but newer technologies made it possible to occasionally spend time speaking to her sister online. In her skype frame, she still looked beautiful, but seemed more of a stranger with every passing season. She had become completely immersed with her four children and her husband and his family. It was as if she had never really been theirs, and had merely spent some of her growing-up years living in their household before she found her real home.

After Layla had gone, things had turned topsy-turvy all around Saima. Her brother Shamil who had always been a more remote presence in her life came back home after finishing his studies. Her city Kargil, spread out like a sheet clinging in between the dips of mountains, became the centre of a war between India and Pakistan. School was disrupted for months on end. All her father and her brother did was watch the television, flipping between the news channels for scraps of information. There was the sound of tanks, the firing of guns, the bravery of soldiers, the cheers of war. Saima had not seen the battle of Tiger Hill, but she felt she had been there, given the number of times she had seen television reports about it. There was the news about mutilated soldiers and later the corruption scams involving coffins too. Saima had no one she could talk to because she did not want to talk about the war, she wanted to talk about Saif, the guy she was madly in love with and the one she thought she could not live without.

Her father grew weary of endless negotiations between his religion and his nation and his region. From the Indian army to the local administration, everyone wanted to modernize Kargil, educate the women, offer employment to the men; even the security forces launched goodwill missions. Then, after dropping a year from college during which he worked in the business with his father, Shamil decided to join the armed forces. This was perhaps not what his father had expected, but no one knew what to expect at the turn of the millennium. India and Pakistan had tested nuclear weapons, attacks had happened in New York, minds were besieged and newer categories of war were created. Somewhere amid all this, time speeded up for teenaged Saima.

Saif, meanwhile, had initially reciprocated her advances but then acted difficult and distant, thus assuring months of drama and turbulence in her emotional landscape. The more Saima dared to make those late night phone calls, turn up for their rendezvous, and slip him love notes, the more taciturn Saif became. At last, she got tired of longing for him. She also wondered if she had let him kiss her too soon. Through endless afternoons of turmoil, she analysed herself, her life and her emotions. She thought of Layla and Shamil too, realizing that they had both chosen their paths in accordance with their temperaments. What was her path to be? She could not imagine living her sister's life. She had no access to her brother's life. Her happiness could not now depend on dreams of eloping with Saif either, since the boy was steering clear of her passions. The lack of focus affected her studies. Saima had been a bright student through her senior school years, and her teachers had confidence in her ability to pass the entrance exams for medicine. When she didn't, she refused to blame herself. She reasoned that it wasn't because of Saif that she was unable to pursue medicine, but because she hadn't been convinced enough about wanting to train as a doctor in the first place. Separately, she also drew some conclusions about the failure of her relationship with Saif. It was not that she had kissed him too soon that had made him withdraw, but that his behaviour after her letting him kiss her too soon had revealed his true intentions towards her. When her parents eventually sent her to college in Haryana, she would make sure that she made the most of her freedoms.

Shireen and Saima were casual acquaintances until the summer of their second year in college. In the middle of that year, on the anniversary of the Kargil war, a massive Indian tricolour was planted right in the middle of the campus. Whereas previously the flag could only be hoisted at specific locations and had to be taken down at sunset, a legal challenge had paved the way for allowing it to be flown more generally and for it to appear on other articles as a symbol of national pride. India was becoming more like the United States of America in many respects, and on the issue of the flag, the inspiration had been avowedly the liberties in the use of the US flag. For months afterwards, the tricolour remained an important topic of conversation on the campus. It ignited a sense of patriotic pride in the campus community that in turn neatly segued into a pride about their institution for pioneering such a use of the symbol.

This was around the time that Saima had started frequenting the library and catching up on her studies after a year of barely getting by. Shireen would also spend her free hours in the library because it offered her a sanctuary away from the bustle. The library was her refuge, allowing her silence and anonymity. Away from people and their conversations, she would read books at random, forgetting even to take along her course reading lists. She delighted in discovering authors and texts serendipitously. She liked the book of abstract stories titled *Others' Paradise* by Paul Leppin. She came to know that the 'father of theoretical cosmonautics' was a man named Konstantin Tsiolkovsky. It was arcane, impractical stuff. If she had been interested in auditioning for the quizzing team, maybe the trivia could have been of some use, but since she had no desire to take part in any such activities, these nuggets of information merely gave her the satisfaction of populating the silence of her personal universe with uniquely curated words and images.

One afternoon, Shireen was sitting with a book of paintings open in front of her. The page was turned to one of the reproductions of the

Doll Series by Bikash Bhattacharjee. A female doll dressed in a white frock was hanging from a clothesline on a balcony against the backdrop of a nondescript grey sky. At least, that's what Shireen could see. But the title was *Subverting the Seen*. On the previous page had been another doll, this time hanging with her head and arms stuck inside the open compartment of a chest of drawers. Near the doll was a red telephone; on top of the dark mahogany chest lay books and papers, and beside it, on the ground, a glass bottle. As she thought of the dilemmas of these dolls, or of those who had left them there, Shireen was interrupted by a man's voice that said, 'You're the Kashmiri girl, isn't it? The extracurricular co-ordinator was looking for you.'

It turned out that the message had been conveyed to the wrong person. It was Saima whom they sought, and she sat on the other side of the room, assiduously labouring away at making notes from the texts set for the course. Shireen went up to Saima and conveyed the message. They sat together at the lunch table a couple of times. The flag obviously came up. In fact, it was the reason Saima had been wanted that afternoon. Being from Kargil, it was suggested that she might want to write a piece on her memories of the war in the college journal.

A few weeks later, one evening, when many students from their residential block had gone on an outing to Murthal nearby for the famed parathas, and possibly to procure alcohol, Shireen sneaked up quietly to the roof. No one was allowed there, but the students knew where the cameras were and how to sneak around without being caught. Her grandfather had passed away that spring and sometimes when she felt particularly melancholic, she went to sit on the open terraced roof after sunset to watch the skies. She would find a corner, put a playlist on her headphones and stare at the hazy canvas of the heavens where the erratic and wonderfully nonsensical trajectories of the birds would restore her faith in life. In the twilight of that day, she had company. Saima was there, hugging her knees, her head limp, eyes tearful, an unextinguished cigarette butt by her side.

Inexplicably, on spotting the girl there, the first thought that Shireen had was of the Doll Series. Saima looked up at her approach and weakly smiled, saying, 'Hello.' Shireen greeted her back and sat down next to her, not asking anything, not saying anything. Gradually, they broke their silence and opened up. For the next two hours, the girls shared their stories. Saima's then boyfriend had cheated on her, she was on the rebound and had fallen in love online with a guy called Rehan, her parents had threatened to suspend her studies and call her back, and she had tried hard to write the Kargil piece for the journal but gone from thinking that she had nothing to say, to thinking that she could not say it in 1200 words, to missing the deadline.

Shireen had no people of her own, no place of her own, nowhere to return. She went back and forth in chronological time as she told Saima about her boarding school days, about her childhood, about her grandparents. She mentioned her grandfather's death, but could not bring herself to tell her newfound friend what he did for a living: it seemed like a secret taint.

From where they sat, they could see the massive tricolour fluttering in the wind. It dwarfed everything around it – buildings, trees, everything in sight. When Saima mentioned how she wasn't sure of her feelings about the flag being there, Shireen could not really understand what Saima meant, but she didn't say it.

The girls had inherited their own Kashmiri histories, tangled into their name, religion and identity. Saima told Shireen that Rehan was from Srinagar and, unlike her, not a Shia. Until his escape to Delhi, Rehan had grown up surrounded by the military, militants and violence. Shireen told Saima that she had not been to Srinagar since her childhood. She had no family there any more. Saima felt a piercing stab of guilt. It was not easy to be uprooted, to have no safe harbour. But she also sensed that there was something of the tricolour and Shireen in each other. Shireen, on her part, had lately begun to see varying shades of saffron and green in her own perception of things since reading about the deaths of young men in Kashmir during the summers of stone-pelting. It was not something she spoke about much, but she had discovered that there wasn't one Kashmir, but many. The two girls on that roof that evening managed to speak to each other past the accumulated histories of resentments, divisions and bloodshed that they had grown up hearing about and experiencing. In the end, when they grew weary of speaking about democracy, they spoke of dolls.

Shireen told Saima about the Doll Series. Saima told Shireen about her new resolve to study hard and not be what her brother had once called 'wasted'. When they grew hungry, they went downstairs to Shireen's room where they continued speaking over bowls of Maggi noodles cooked with cheese and omelette, sprinkled over with red chilli. There were pictures of birds stuck to the walls. Shireen said that she'd read somewhere that the social standing of magpies was determined by the length of their tails. Saima confessed to loving the fancy twisted stems of margarita glasses at the parties she used to go to, but would now shun. They both agreed that it was grotesque and enraging when people who are well off act poor in order to gain sympathy when it suits their purposes. Then, they spoke of films and zodiac signs.

Just before they said goodnight that day, the moon appeared at the window. They sealed their friendship by coming up with a special way of looking at it. Like the title of that painting, their idea was to 'subvert the seen' and focus on the dark side of the moon, the part of the circle that wasn't silver. In doing so, the moon transformed from a shiny tinselly object in the sky into a magical celestial sphere!

Over two years had passed between that evening of moon-gazing and the night in Delhi when the moon had been missing for days on end.

In the days after her return from Haridwar, Shireen took Saima's advice and asked her uncle for the things belonging to her grandparents which could be of no possible value to them but would be invaluable to her. Unsurprisingly, he agreed. He said he would put all such items, including the plastic plant, the magnifying glass, the embroidered chinar leaf, the old cassette tapes, books, and anything similar he found into a suitcase and get it dropped off at her address.

When the suitcase arrived, Shireen spent an entire evening fondly reminiscing over each object and decorating her room with some of them. There were a couple of diaries and some old photographs. She kept these in a large manila envelope to read later. Her idea was to find or borrow a cassette player from somewhere, play an old cassette from her grandfather's collection and then peruse the photographs and diaries. She didn't know what to do with the worn-out Chinese books, so she put them back in the suitcase. In any case, the next few weeks were going to be busy as she had missed several classes at university and really needed to catch up with her studies.

5

FOR THE FIRST time in her life, Shireen found herself in a landscape where the colour green was so scarce. Encircling her view was a chain of dun-coloured, camel-backed rocky mountains that sketched a barren vastness under the pure blue of a sunny summer sky in Ladakh.

As the plane landed at Leh airport, she was confronted with the realization that she was in some kind of a homeland, years after having been taken away from Srinagar. Even the gentle parade of her dim memories told her that the Kashmir she had left was very different to the one she now found herself in. And yet, both Srinagar and Leh were part of the same entity called Jammu and Kashmir. Who could understand the logic of maps that put people into such boundaries? No maps could seem to define Kashmir to the satisfaction of the many Kashmiris anyway. Kashmir was a longing for her, an unaddressed belonging that she had managed to contain by keeping away from it.

All winter, Saima had been insisting that Shireen go with her to Ladakh during their annual break from university. Initially, Shireen had resisted the idea, though she knew that after her grandmother's passing away, there was no reason to stay on in the city in the coming year. It made sense to try and escape the infernal heat of Delhi. She had not wanted to go to Kashmir for years in order to avoid facing up to her history, her childhood and her trauma, but Ladakh was not really Kashmir. Regardless of the maps, everyone knew that. Saima herself had not been there for several years, always preferring to travel to her home in Kargil by road from Srinagar rather than fly up to Leh. When all her gambits failed to convince Shireen about their vacation together to Leh, Saima had an ace up her sleeve to melt her friend's heart.

'It is a beautiful place from what I remember. It would be an escape for you, given everything you've gone through recently, and ...' she paused here to wink mischievously, 'and Rehan said he could join us there. So, I would be able to spend a few days with him without having to explain at home where I was, since I could say I was there with you!'

'So that's the real deal! To recruit my company for your romance with Rehan!' Shireen exclaimed, deciding to say yes to the trip at the same moment.

'Oh come on. You know that's not the main reason!' said Saima, giving Shireen a hug, knowing that the argument had been won.

Over the next few months, Shireen had taken on a school student for tuition classes to save up money for the trip. As the date of their travel had approached, she had found herself looking at pictures of the place online: it truly was breathtaking; a place where people from the world over came to seek a beguiling charm.

Exiting the airport, Shireen and Saima got into a cab and exchanged observations about what they saw. Compared to Delhi, Jammu or even Srinagar, the airport was tiny! And the road ran right beside the small blue-and-yellow airport wall, topped only by rolls of barbed wire. Of course, the women were right. Ladakh was not the Kashmir in the news. Unlike Srinagar, in Leh, there were no slogans proclaiming or demanding freedom on the walls, no reports of bomb blasts, and a mere few birds in the skies and on trees.

On their way to the city, they saw straight roads that rolled out as far as the eye could see, as if a master artist had steadily painted broad brushstrokes in black on the wild rocky terrain. There was a continuity of pylons in the form of tall metal guardians. And it seemed that everywhere they went, they were being welcomed by one or the other unit of the Indian Army – so many signs that said 'Indian Army welcomes you to XYZ'! Behind the wire mesh fences by the roadside were large swathes of army land, where lines of painted stones, like jagged white teeth, led up the path to war memorials made of puny humanoid statues holding a gun or the Indian flag. But in this land of flags, the ones representing the Indian nation were vastly outnumbered by the profusion of Buddhist prayer flags that were hung on buildings, strung across the squares, tied over doorways and draped over the pillars. Each prayer flag had the same repeating pattern of colours – blue, white, red, green, yellow. On some was the mantra 'Om Mani Padme Hum' divided into five characters; others had elaborate text in the Tibetan language, accompanied by fantastically mythical illustrations of dragons, lions and horses. To Saima and Shireen, these were incomprehensible gems of wisdom. They saw little whirlpools of dust drifting across the road in front of their vehicle, limestone-washed walls made of mud brick, stone cairns, white round gompas and fascinating buildings perched on hillsides.

Shireen had seen pictures in books and scenes from movies that depicted the Buddhist environment, but nothing had prepared her for the florid intricacies that were carved into the imposing gate to the city. It was a massive structure with unrelentingly complex patterns of birds, beasts and dragons painted in the most brilliant hues of gold, red, yellow, blue and turquoise. Atop it were three golden bells caged in glass. Wide-eyed and enamoured, Shireen wanted to get out of the car and become a fugitive in an alley, losing herself in this place which seemed so far away from any trouble. Thinking this, she turned to Saima and thanked her for bringing them there. Saima smiled and touched her hand and responded with a groan about feeling hungry. Then, reading the intense expression in her friend's eyes, she said, 'I knew you would love it here. Someday, we should go to Dharamsala too. Years ago, during our first year at college I went with that group I used to hang out with, and it was mesmerizing.' At the mention of Dharamsala, the driver of their car spoke up. He was of Tibetan origin and chimed in to say that Dharamsala was indeed worth visiting soon because it was modernizing fast. Sighing as he finished his point about transformation, he focused on the road again.

By now, they had entered the congested area near the main bazaar where the dangerous driving by many other large road-faring vehicles was nearly as bad as in other Indian cities. The lone valiant traffic policeman was constantly whistling at the tourist cars and the big 4x4 jeeps that flouted rules. Shireen stated a fact she knew in the tone of a question: 'Rehan is coming tomorrow?' Saima, who was checking the signal on her phone, answered with a distracted 'yes', trying to hide her excitement. Shireen had only briefly seen Rehan on a couple of occasions when he was in Delhi. The prospect of socializing with new people at close quarters induced anxiety in her. Moreover, she thought herself to be especially awkward around men. She did not intend to express any of this to Saima for fear that her friend might misunderstand her apprehension, or worse, read her reticence as a reluctance to acknowledge Rehan. Shireen knew that despite their long-distance connexion and their jocular protestations about the seriousness of their relationship, Saima and Rehan saw a future together.

Soon, they reached a picturesque guesthouse in a quiet corner of the town. The owner was a friendly man, his staff were helpful with getting the details right and, best of all, the rooms opened onto a breezy backyard garden with lovely rose beds, where cushioned cane chairs and dark glass-topped tables lay scattered underneath flowering trees. The allure of the scene was exaggerated by idiosyncrasies and happy chances: a mirror placed in the hollow of a small tree; an oar pinned to a lime-washed wall; a bonny child playing with a cocoa-coloured puppy beside a woman tending plants, her wrinkled face full of cheer underneath her ruby-red scarf. As the women checked into their rooms, the scene outside beckoned invitingly to come and explore, but their weary bodies were beseeching them to rest.

That evening, having acclimatized to the altitude, they went wandering about the small town. It was clearly not full-fledged tourist season, for the European bakeries had not started selling the breads and cappuccinos. By happenstance, they stumbled upon a small cafe in a garage where three Ladakhi women cooked and served food and drinks from a little kitchen partitioned off at the back. Plyboard shelves nailed to the walls served as tables, and there were wooden stools for chairs. There was hardly any decoration except for a Buddhist altar and a child's painting of the Taj Mahal that was placed in one corner next to a plate of dried red chillis. Shireen asked for omelette bread – a spicier version of the French toast, and Saima had momos liberally sprinkled over with chilli paste from a plastic bottle. The butter tea was poured from metal thermos flasks that had pictures of Chinese scenes. It was the most satisfying meal they had had in a long time.

While they ate, Lhaki, one of the women who ran the café, chatted to them. She wore a black-and-pink Jack Wolfskin jacket and multiple earrings in her many ear piercings, which glittered as she animatedly spoke of how they were trying to grow their business. This unassuming eatery had a name: 'Ladakhi Girls' Cafe.' Upon hearing their names, one of the younger girls in the cafe asked them: 'Are you Indian? Muslim?' Saima said she was Muslim and from Kargil, Shireen hesitated between Delhi and Srinagar, ultimately saying Srinagar in a hushed tone, only later remembering to add 'not Muslim, Hindu'. At this, Lhaki's eyes lit up. 'I think you are the first Kashmiri Hindu girl I have ever met,' she said excitedly. Shireen found herself feeling embarrassed at this strange remark. As they were leaving, an old woman with a cerise pink scarf and prayer beads around her neck came in. A smile glowed across her face as she greeted Shireen and Saima. They didn't understand the language she spoke and could not respond meaningfully since she didn't understand Hindi, Urdu or English.

The town was spread in a maze of narrow lanes around a built-up bazaar area. Here, one could browse through a large diversity of shops, see a wide variation of facial features and sample a smattering of different languages. It was truly a place where different kingdoms of the Himalayas had once met. Now, the image of the Buddha was the biggest draw here. A plethora of wayside stalls displayed rows upon rows of Buddha faces and prayer wheels cast in bronze. There were miniature metal thunderbolts, small copper samovars, incense burners, turquoise bowls, curved daggers, heavy beaded necklaces, and keychain souvenirs.

In the curious mix that was Leh town, Ladakhi, Tibetan, Kashmiri and Indian meant clearly demarcated things in terms of identity, whether one went by looks or food. To be Ladakhi felt local, Kashmiris from elsewhere felt it was a different place, and Indians saw it as an Indian wonderland that was simultaneously a 'good' part of 'their' Kashmir, with a Tibetan feel and none of the violence or pollution.

Shireen and Saima picked up on these meanings, which they discussed between them, agreeing and disagreeing over the nuances as they sat on a granite bench in the middle of a square. Around them were the shops, a bustle of people and lights; above their heads was a canopy of stringed prayer flags and electricity wires; behind them was a towering silhouette of a mountain holding everything in its broad-shouldered embrace. As the girls finished their coffees and got up to walk back to the guest house, they laughed and agreed on one thing – when it came to two women being able to sit and talk unmolested by men in a busy square at this late hour, this place certainly didn't fit the definition of a standard Indian or Kashmiri experience.

The next morning, Shireen was up early. She knew that Saima, dictated by habit, would get up late. She rang to ask for tea and biscuits, after which she went out to the garden downstairs. She forcefully inhaled the crisp mountain air that reminded her of her schooldays in the hills of Mussoorie. There was no nostalgia in the recall, though. Her life there had been crippled year after year by an exacting discipline, which included a minute accountability of every hour of the day that had to be spent in accordance with a rigorous pre-ordained routine. How wonderful it was to be free of that! She leaned back into a chair, folded up her legs and stared at the world around her. She had left Delhi only yesterday, but after spending a night here, that world with its unceasing struggles in the city and the university, the constant urgency of the news on the television, the blazing heat and loud sounds, seemed like a long time ago.

A different procession of images flashed past. The rock formations of the hills, the colourful clothes and decorations, picture postcards, frilly and faded curtains, distant houses tucked away in the folds of the heaving earth, tin roofs blindingly bright in the sun, soft chanting music, email and Internet booths, plywood furniture, a soaring eagle, a raven's call, the glimmering lights at night, the eerie mingling of cloud and snow at the top of a distant mountain, the still trees in a reticent breeze, the small boy playing with marbles at one of the stalls, the colourful flags strewn everywhere, the cracked glass window, stone walls, mud tracks. As a warming ray of the sun directly fell upon her face, she tilted her head and looked at the blue skies awash with shades of violet, gold, pink, mauve. Just at that moment, she felt she could go back and inhabit one of the russet-coloured photoviewer slides from Hong Kong that she had cherished in her childhood. It would show her smiling in soft focus against a wood-and-gold scene from a Leh sunrise. What else is magic but a world that appears every day after a dark night?

The future always shoulders hope. It should. For everyone? For me too? Should the future even be thought of? Will I unseal an unspoken pact by bringing it up? A few clouds lingered afar. Do clouds ever get lost? she thought. We speak of stray clouds, but are there clouds that drift too far and lose their home and family? The future terrified Shireen. She had no idea where she was headed. She worried that she would end up like those strange dolls, stuck in a difficult place.

Saima called out to her from the window of her room.

'Shireen, look at that!'

As she turned towards the direction that Saima was pointing, Shireen saw a faint silver bracket of the moon in one corner of the sky. As always, she focused on imagining the rest of the unlit celestial sphere. The moon, everywhere, was bewitching.

'So he's been hanging out here with all his riches stolen from Delhi skies,' she murmured, but Saima could not hear her and asked 'What?'

'Never mind, I'll tell you, I'm coming upstairs.'

Unlike the well-organized 118 next door, Saima's room betrayed every sign of careless inhabitation. The suitcase was flung open on the floor, a couple of scarves and a pair of jeans lay on the chair, numerous items of make-up filled up the table surface, the creased blanket was hanging over the edge of the bed, an ashtray held a cigarette stub in it.

'Did you get up early today just to mess up your room?' Shireen teased.

'Oh you! I got up because I need to get ready properly. I'll be seeing Rehan after months and I want to remind him of what he missed.'

'Alright. Fine. Now, go get ready. I'll shower too and come back in a bit and tidy the place.'

'You dear thing!' Saima gave her a hug, 'You're like my mom,' she smiled, handing Shireen the keys. 'I'll take a while, I have to prettify myself ... by the way, do you have the epilator with you? I'll take it from you now; and when you are ready, don't bother knocking in case I can't come to open the door; let yourself in.'

Shireen loved to be in the company of a bright happy soul like Saima. 'I'm not your mom, but I can imagine how much trouble you gave her. You're such a diva!' she said as she handed Saima the gadget.

A couple of hours later, the women sat in the breakfast room, picking over their food.

'I'm not hungry today,' said Saima.

'Me neither. And unlike you, I don't know why,' replied Shireen.

'Stop stereotyping me! Everything is not about a guy, you know. The food here is so ... so boring. What is this? Parathas and curd and pickle. We are not in Punjab! I wish they had something interesting for breakfast ... something Tibetan to try, or something more exotic and European. This food is like being back at a JNU dhaba.'

'Don't forget the legendary chowmein there!' Shireen reminded her.

'Yes, how strange. I wonder if Indian chowmein means anything to Chinese people,' Saima continued.

'Hey, you know what! Let us eat some proper wazwan food at a Kashmiri place here tonight.'

'What about your being on a diet?'

'Well, you see, that's why. I want to eat less but I just can't stop thinking about food. If I eat a good meal today, maybe I'll be a little less fixated on food for a while.'

'Whatever you say,' Shireen shrugged. 'And by the way, you are looking really pretty. Someday, I'm stealing this kurta of yours!'

'You can have it anytime you want, my jigar,'[20] said Saima, as she clicked a selfie of the two of them on her phone.

Saima wore a close-fitting lilac-coloured kurta with a black pattern at the sleeves. Paired with a black salwar, a light touch of makeup, moonstone earrings and a tiny heart-shaped pendant, it gave her a translucent glow. To Shireen, she looked every inch the fine picture of a beautiful and happy beloved.

Shireen wanted to make sure that she would give these two people as much alone-time as she could. So, after breakfast, when Saima was on the phone, she went to browse the bookshelf underneath the staircase, which was meant for the use of guests. There were boxes of several indoor games, lots of travelogues, some bestsellers by authors she had never heard of, and a few coffee-table spreads. Looking at the picturesque covers, she thought of sketching a few scenes while she was here. Paintings, she felt, captured the essence of emotions and the environment in a way that no other art form could. She liked to watch movies, but the best scenes in any movie, if paused, could also be thought of as a painting realized using the technology of a camera. Books were alright, she reasoned, but they often had to labour too hard with words to convey a sensation. And one could never be sure that words did indeed make the imprint upon the eye of the mind in the direct way a painting could. The line 'a picture is worth a thousand words' popped in her head. Of course, cliches came from a repeated observation or a realization. Yesterday, when looking out of the airplane window, she had thought of how the phrase 'rock face' must have originated while regarding the sublime features that could be discerned in the most ordinary rocks. And this morning, in the garden, when the light of dawn had reminded her of her school days in the hills, she had played with the words 'to see things in a different light'. It was true, the slightest change of light, not just in glorious locations, even a fused bulb in a room, could take one back to a place or a time, dredging up the memories of experiences associated with it. Yes, she must buy some paper and sketching pens in the market.

Having decided this, she made her way to Saima's room and informed her that she would be going to the market.

'But, why now? We can all go together later,' Saima objected.

'I want to go by myself. Rehan will be here soon. It will be late afternoon by the time I am back; and if you like, we can all go out together then.'

'What has Rehan's coming got to do with it? He knows you are here, he's going to be staying here with me.'

'I know, I'm not vanishing. I am just seized by the idea of sketching at the moment and I really do want to go out for a bit. You know how stubborn I can be, you can't dissuade me,' Shireen explained, convincing herself too that there was no other reason that she wanted to be away just then.

'Alright, do as you wish,' said Saima, throwing her hands up in the air. 'But don't be too late. The phone signals are poor and I would be worried that my philosopher has just decided to vanish in Ladakh. Also, we should probably do a bit of sightseeing later today.'

'I will be back after lunch, don't worry.' Saying this, Shireen left.

~

Rehan sent a text to Saima – ♥ – before reaching the bottom of the staircase. As soon as her phone beeped, Saima jumped up from the bed, turned off the volume on her YouTube, and opened the door.

He was standing at the foot of the stairs with a charming grin plastered all over his face. She rushed towards the stairs, but after hopping down the first few, suddenly stopped midway to lean against the wooden banister. Standing there with a twinkle in her eye, she was achingly beautiful. Rehan wanted to fly right up to her and hold her close. Instead, he too deliberately slowed down and went up step by step, as if each step needed a bracing effort.

When they finally stood opposite each other, he held out his hand, which she took.

Suppressing every flutter of their bodies, they walked back to the room holding hands. As soon as the door was closed behind them, they clasped each other, overcome with emotions.

Then, Saima pulled away and went to sit on the bed, complaining: 'You're half an hour late, you know. I've been waiting since morning.'

'Merely since morning? I've waited hundreds of days to see my love! Saima, I can't tell you how much I missed you and how much I love you.'

'Yes, yes, you and your words. What kept you? And look at you, not even a rose for me?'

Rehan came up to where she was sitting and sat down cross-legged at her feet. His hands reached up to hold the sides of her legs. She felt a rush of blood at his touch, even as she sensed it through the coarse black salwar.

He looked at her eyes, those brown marbles, as he called them, and said, 'Sorry, I have no rose for my rose, but I am late because I was carried away creating a bouquet of words for her.'

'Bouquet?'

Rehan pulled out a folded sheet of paper from the pocket of his shirt and opened it to read the verses he had composed for her:

Khudai mutthi main band hai teri,
Teri aankhon main hai jannat meri,
Apne dil main panah jo degi tu,
Ho jaunga tammana-e-ishq se rubaru[21]

He read these words in a soft voice, meeting her eyes, one hand still grasping the side of her knee.

'Don't make me cry,' Saima spoke in a voice quivering with sentiment.

'I love you,' replied Rehan.

'Please, don't make me cry now,' she smiled quaintly, 'my eyeliner will come streaking down my face!'

They both laughed at this. He got up to sit beside her and held her palm in his.

She put her head on his shoulder, but it was not comfortable since they were both the same height, sitting on the bed. Sensing this, Rehan lay down and tugged at her arm, indicating that she lie down beside him.

When she did so, for a moment they both stared up at the bare ceiling, lost in their own thoughts, before Rehan asked her, 'Where's your friend Shireen? Should I say hello?'

'She's gone out to get sketching materials. I think she wanted us to get some time together.'

'What a thoughtful person!' Rehan joked. 'Had it been me, I would definitely have hung around to make the pent-up frustration flare up and to fuel resentment in the lovers, making sure they couldn't have a moment alone.'

'Really?' Saima asked.

'Of course not! How gullible are you? Do I seem that mean to you?' said Rehan.

'Oh, you surprised me with that serious tone. Nothing is ever what it seems with you, you know.'

'You're wrong, meri jaan. I am dying to hold you close and I really am. It *is* what it seems,' he teased her.

They moved up the bed. Saima's kurta was getting crumpled underneath her, but before she could move to adjust it, Rehan propped himself on his elbows and slowly sat up a little. He loosened a strand of her hair near her forehead, twirling it airily. Saima felt light-headed and nervous. Their lovemaking was as lavish as it was rare. She remembered every detail of the brief passionate episodes when his body had wordlessly spoken to hers.

Rehan touched the middle of her forehead with his index finger. Then, he let his finger slide down the shape of her nose and pass over her lips, pulling her wet lower lip away as the finger moved down her chin and neck. He paused again for a slight moment at the base of her neck, as if the finger were an explorer gathering courage for what lay ahead. Four other fingers joined that explorer finger as his hand advanced over to the swell of her breasts, and then lingered to touch the plains of her body below. All this time, the two of them were looking into each other's eyes, burning with desire. Saima had been still as a statue till that moment, barely breathing. When his hand moved further down, Saima could not contain herself anymore. She lifted both her arms and with them drew his head towards her face, kissing him on the neck again and again.

They did not know how long their bodies took to madly consume each other, but when they re-emerged from the intoxicating spell of lovemaking, they fell into a gentle sleep. It was a calming sensation of being close by each other knowing that they were close to each other.

At last, Saima reached for her phone. She asked Rehan what song he would like to hear. When Rehan did not acknowledge her words, she turned over to query his silence. The look in his eyes was steely, almost frightening.

'What happened?' she asked.

'What do you think is that?' he pointed to the cigarette butt in the ashtray.

'Oh. I thought I had cleared it. I don't smoke a lot; only sometimes.'

'When were you planning on telling me? How come I never knew this till now? When we met in Delhi, were you smoking then? Or is it someone else's cigarette?'

'Slow down,' said Saima, her eyes flashing, 'I told you I smoke sometimes. I have done so since the college days. And since you smoke yourself, what's your problem?'

'My problem is that you are my girlfriend and I love you. Hell, someday I imagine a future with you. What am I going to tell my parents: here is this smoker I want to marry? You know, my parents are liberal. But they still live in Kashmir.'

'Girls smoke in Kashmir. Secretly. Like me. I never said I'm proud of it. I tried to hide it from you so that you wouldn't feel bad. I'm sorry I forgot to hide it today.'

Rehan kept quiet.

'I went to such lengths rinsing my mouth, did you smell anything when you kissed me? Tell me, why don't you? I tried, okay? I tried. It's hard. Sometimes I give in to the temptation.'

'How about we make a habit of giving in to temptations? Any temptations? Shall I do the same? There are women *I* meet too?'

'What? You *already* smoke! How is the temptation of a smoke the same as other temptations?'

'All right. Do whatever you want. You are a modern, liberated girl.'

'I am not perfect. I never said I was. But I thought you were a modern liberated man for sure. I guess I was wrong about that.'

'You are right. We are wrong about each other. Maybe we are wrong for each other.'

Upon hearing this, Saima stomped out of the room, wrapping the bed sheet around her. She headed to the bathroom, closed the door loudly, turned the taps on full, and wept as she watched the red plastic bucket fill up noisily with water.

Her head was spinning.

When she opened the door, he wasn't there. She washed her face, re-applied her makeup, changed into a pair of blue jeans and a long pistachio-green shirt, and opened the window. She carried out these actions on autopilot, without pausing to involve her thinking. When she was completely ready, she emptied the ashtray into the bin and defiantly pulled out another cigarette from the box that was buried underneath her clothes in a nook of the suitcase. She was about to light it when she heard Rehan's voice in the corridor, telling a guest house employee that he too was staying there now, and had entered his details in the register downstairs. She placed the cigarette and lighter in a desk drawer.

Rehan came in; this time with a suitcase in one hand and two small chocolate milk cartons in the other. She did not move from where she was standing by the table. He kept the suitcase to one side and addressed her with these words: 'Still angry?'

'Why wouldn't I be?' she retorted, though in a mild tone, which took the edge off her words.

He came right up to her, kept the cartons on the table and placed both his hands on her shoulders.

'I'm sorry. I over-reacted. It wasn't just the cigarette, it was the realization that there was something like that which you were hiding from me. I mean we used to speak on Skype, and during all those long conversations you never once said anything about smoking. Not even when you saw me smoke in Delhi at that mall...'

'Listen, Rehan,' she interrupted him, 'I'm sorry too. I don't know why I never told you. I think it was for the exact same reasons you mentioned when you were angry. Without admitting it to myself, I wanted to be the person whom you could own up to, whom you could like.'

'Hey, baby,' he lifted her chin, 'it's a lousy habit, and I'm addicted to it. It's so bad. I'd hate to see *you* be chained to it.'

'Well, for your kind information, I only smoke occasionally. When I'm particularly anxious or something,' she stated.

'Okay, let us be anxious together right now. I got us the chocolate milk you like. Let's sip from those little straws and share a cigarette just this once.'

'What! After that sermon just now!' she giggled.

'Yeah, that's how I roll,' he shrugged his shoulders jocularly. 'You know, for a moment I did think a guy had left it behind, and it blew my mind with anger. I felt a surge of jealousy.'

'I know, you are a mean, mean fellow. We live apart, you know. If I was interested in someone else, I wouldn't have come this far to be with you.'

Rehan was quiet for a bit, then said in a thoughtful register: 'You know, I was thinking of asking Fayaz to join us tomorrow. He's posted just outside Leh these days, and it was good catching up with him here last night. I think it will be good if the four of us went somewhere. Shireen will also have some company.'

'Which Fayaz? Your friend from school, the quiet, mysterious one? I don't think I've met him.'

'Yes, the KAS Fayaz, yaar. The other Fayaz from the newspaper is hardly likely to be here,' he clarified.

Saima thought for a moment, then said, 'Actually, that's a great idea. We could all even go out of Leh somewhere; to the lake, for example.'

'Absolutely. And he's a good fellow to have around. He's not become a snob, like most government servants, and he's a dear buddy; so I'll have the same joy as you, with my friend and my beloved in front of my eyes.'

'Wonderful,' Saima clapped her hands. 'Now what about that chocolate milk?'

Rehan kissed her on her forehead, and then on the tip of her nose, and at last on her lips. 'Oh you kind temptress. I wish I could lock you into my suitcase and never let you get away from my sight.'

'So says the man whose world is locked in my fist and whose heaven is locked in my eyes ... Decide, my dear: do you want to be the jailer or the jailed?' Saima referred to the poem he had written for her.

'For you, the jailer, the jailed. Any ... and all. You're my lock, I'm your key. I'm your lock, you're my key.'

'Spouting such Rumi-esque verses every few minutes, you're not feverish, are you?' she tittered as she touched his forehead with the back of her hand.

He did feel feverish from arousal, but knew this wasn't the time, so they hugged tightly and he only let go when Saima had counted to forty seconds.

'Double the benefit of a twenty-second hug,' she laughed as they pierced the milk cartons.

'I'm going to smoke with you today, you know. I've been in groups where women have smoked, but I never even imagined I could love a girl who smoked,' he said.

'I don't want to any more. Not now,' she replied. 'And by the way, have you forgotten that last time in Delhi when we went to that Agha Shahid Ali poetry event, after which we all smoked weed on that terrace?'

'That! Yes, I had totally forgotten. But that was weed. That's different. That's not a habit with you or me.'

'Anyway, you go ahead, here's the ashtray. I'm going to try calling Shireen,' she said.

When Shireen returned, her face was flushed from the long walk up to the palace. She had bought a large white sketchpad and some colouring pencils.

As the three of them met, she said to Saima: 'Did you both eat anything? I brought back these snacks,' and extended her hand to Rehan: 'Nice to meet you, Rehan.'

She thought of something else to add on to the end of that sentence, but couldn't come up with anything.

'We just had some chocolate milk, but we'll happily relieve you of the chips and sandwiches too,' chirped Saima.

Rehan shook Shireen's hand, saying 'Very nice to finally meet you, Shireen. You look even more beautiful than in the photographs.'

Saima rolled her eyes, smiling.

Shireen felt abashed, responding with 'Shall we all go sightseeing?'

Rehan politely said, 'Whatever you both decide. I've a friend's car with me and we're good to go anytime.'

They set out for the Magnetic Hill, stopping at a gompa and a stupa along the way to take pictures. 'What's the difference between a gompa and a stupa?' asked Saima, as she sat in the front with Rehan, who was driving.

'I don't know. It's my first time here. Didn't you find that out in Dharamsala?' he replied.

'I think a gompa is a Tibetan monastery and a stupa is a white structure like the one we just saw, with Buddhist relics inside it,' said Shireen.

'Is that master Google speaking? Did you check it online?' queried Saima.

'I went to the palace in the afternoon and read it on one of the signs,' said Shireen.

'How is the palace?' asked Rehan, his eyes on the road.

'It's a great viewing point. I didn't go inside ... most of it was closed to visitors due to some renovations ...' Shireen paused to show Saima some photographs from the palace on her phone.

'I really like the colour combination of the structures here. The board there said that the palace was built by a seventeenth-century ruler called King Namgyel. It is intended to look like the Potala Palace in Tibet, in Lhasa.'

'Tibet must be spectacular,' said Saima.

'The Dogras defeated the people here, and they took over our Kashmir too,' said Rehan. 'The very idea of Dogra rule in history makes me so angry. How oppressive it was!'

'I wish they'd teach us Kashmiri history properly in schools, and not just Indian history,' echoed Saima.

Shireen felt somewhat disconnected. She knew about the Dogra rule, but wasn't all autocratic rule oppressive? That's why a democracy made sense. But, who knew what the future of democracy was in the world? Aloud, she said, 'I need to read a lot more history too. Sometimes, I think studying history might have been a better idea instead of philosophy.'

'No, I think philosophy is much better. Either that, or literature. History is a farce. Always told on the terms of the victor,' answered Rehan.

'Or the sciences. That's quite removed from reality too,' said Saima.

'I'm not sure literature or philosophy or science is removed from reality, Saima. I think they're just tributaries that feed into our understanding of reality in subtle and complicated ways, with lots of disagreements that are endlessly debatable.'

'Sorry to play the cynic here, but meanwhile, the dying continues,' said Rehan. 'When did a story ever change a life? Don't get me wrong, I write in the papers for a living, but I wonder if I'm deluding myself into believing that any good comes out of such endeavours. Ultimately, we are the puppets of the politicians and the histories, literatures and sciences they choose to promote.'

'The artists can take a stand, I suppose. Isn't that why the awards are being returned in protest of the government these last few months?' Saima intervened.

'It won't eventually matter; such efforts are a drop in the ocean,' countered Rehan.

'Who knows where the currents carry us, will carry us,' said Shireen, looking out at the Indus River snaking below them between the mountains, the overlapping outlines creating a splendid diorama.

Saima looked at the river too, adding, 'We must swim so long as we can, with or against the currents. What we want, we must work for.'

They were silent for some time. In the course of their uneasy conversation, each of them had been addressing him or herself as much as the others. Palaces and rulers reminded Rehan of the history of revolts that he had inherited; they made Saima think of the power of vision and the hope to continue building something, come what may; and to Shireen, they seemed ever ephemeral despite all their solidity, like paintings on a page that could be turned over by the wind at any time.

When they spoke again, Saima asked Shireen, 'Have you settled upon what you will sketch first?'

'Or whom? It could be a person,' Rehan threw the two of them a quick happy glance.

'I'm not sure,' was all Shireen said at first. Then, after some thought she began, 'So earlier today, when I saw the white-and-red palace and the picture of the Potala Palace it was modeled after, it made me think of the folds of a Bengali saree, white with red borders. As if the structure was merely a fabric frozen in motion...'

'I wonder if the abundance of turquoise in these Himalayan artefacts has anything to do with the colours of the rivers here ... they are the same colour as that stone ... Colours somehow enter the being that we become ... I don't know what I want to sketch,' she halted the stumbling outpouring of her thoughts with this last statement.

'You really are a philosopher,' said Rehan.

'How lucky am I to have a poet for a boyfriend and a philosopher for a friend,' piped up Saima.

'We love you,' said Rehan, taking one arm off the wheel to briefly touch her shoulder.

The Magnetic Hill was not all that magical. They saw a signboard that said, 'The Phenomenon that defies gravity. Park your vehicle in the box marked with paint on the road and experience the wonder.' The straight long road between the dry brown undulating hills was striped on each side with yellow lines and at a point in the middle was a box marked with white chevrons. Rehan parked the car there and it gently rolled backwards. Saima was unimpressed. The two women got out of the car and decided that the incline was probably not uphill anyhow.

On the way back, Rehan put on assorted music from his playlist. They noticed the moving shadows of the evening clouds upon the serrated mountains and the parallel straight lines of the electricity wires that ran in the foreground. The town in the distance looked like a toy set as they approached it.

'Shall we go for dinner somewhere?' asked Rehan.

When Saima did not respond, Shireen spoke up, leaning towards the back of Saima's seat, 'Didn't you say that you would like Kashmiri food tonight?'

'No. Right now, I just want to go home. To the guest house room, I mean,' declared Saima, without any further explanation.

'All right,' said Rehan. 'We can decide about dinner later. Is that okay, Shireen?' he threw a glance back to confirm.

'Of course,' she replied. In Rehan's presence, she was not sure how to ask Saima why she was being taciturn; so she chose to be silent too.

Rehan concentrated on the road, puzzled by Saima's change of mood, concluding that whatever it was could be best dealt with back in the room.

When the two were alone in the room, Rehan asked her what was wrong.

She plonked herself on the chair and almost broke into tears.

'Oh! I hate my body!'

'Why? What?'

'Rehan, I am about to start bleeding any minute. My stomach is churning in pain. My back hurts. I feel like tearing down the walls or scratching at things. It's so irritating!' she sounded truly exasperated. A tear rolled down her eyes.

'Meri jaan, is that all? That's it? Are you weeping because of this? What a baby!'

'Don't *baby* me, okay? You are a man, you won't understand. It isn't even my date. I wasn't supposed to be on my period till next week. Why did it have to happen now? I feel so angry and embarrassed. Here, in this beautiful place where we finally get to spend some time together away from everything, and my stupid body betrays me,' she went on.

Admittedly for Rehan, this was the first time he would have to be at such close quarters with his girlfriend for an extended amount of time while she was on her period. But he was earnest about not wanting to feel daunted at the prospect of the experience.

'Alright, I won't understand. But I know it's hard, I've studied some biology too, you know,' he began, then stopped himself from delivering the speech he was preparing in his head about how she should try to be calm and not get upset. Instead, he pulled her close to him and gave her a long hug, softly whistling a tune he knew she loved.

When he spoke, he uttered that consoling Kashmiri phrase that is a universal balm of reassurance: 'Kehein chuy na parwah.' There's nothing to worry about. And he meant it too; she needn't fret, he was there for her.

'I'm here, meri jaan. How can you be so sad? Come on, smile a little for me, please.'

Saima smiled weakly through her sniffles. 'I feel like I'm ruining the trip, and I can't help it. I feel like a spoilsport. I'll be in pain all day tomorrow, I know. And after all the planning to be here, I feel so terrible.'

'How selfish of you not to want to give me a chance to be with you when you are feeling unwell! How do you know I wouldn't love to be here in this room with you? Who cares about Leh? We can see it later. We'll lie on the bed all day and watch TV and listen to music, okay?' said Rehan, kissing her hands.

'Are you even for real?' said Saima.

'No, madam, I am very unreal. And if you don't pull yourself together, I might even vanish,' he replied.

'I'm sorry,' Saima mumbled as she got up to get sanitary napkins from the suitcase and went to the bathroom. When she returned, she had taken off her makeup and changed into pyjamas and a T-shirt. She had braided her hair in the manner of schoolgirls. She was more composed, but evidently in a lot of pain.

'My periods are just terrible the first two days. I'm sorry you don't have an option but to bear it now.'

She climbed into the bed, put two pillows behind her back and snuggled under the blanket.

'Poor Shireen must be wondering what happened. I bet she thought we had a quarrel.'

'I'll send her to you on my way out. "*I will be your hero, baby*,"' he mimed the Enrique Iglesias song as he got up to get food for everyone. Now tell me what would you like to eat?'

Saima's eyes lit up, 'Food, yes, I wanted something tasty. Can you get rice and rogan josh?'

'Done, baby!'

'I love you!' she said, throwing her arms around him.

'You wicked girlfriend of mine, do you realize that's the first time you've said that today?'

'Is it?' Saima sounded genuinely surprised.

Rehan threw her a sidelong flying kiss, checked that his wallet was in his pocket, and set off.

Shireen knocked on the door soon afterwards.

'What happened? Is everything all right?'

'Yes, I started my damn period. I feel so terrible.'

'Oh no. Do you want me to ask them for a hot water bottle? A cup of tea?'

'Yes and yes, my darling. I don't deserve people like you and Rehan in my life.'

'Don't be silly!' said Shireen matter-of-factly. 'By the way, I've sent a complaint to his bosses about the silver-thieving fellow of the skies. They said he'll show up tonight. I've arranged for him to linger longer at your window,' she added, as if it were all a very serious matter.

'You dear! How you bring a smile to my face ... but ...' she twisted this way and that, 'Ouch ouch, these cramps really hurt! Why does it have to be so effing painful?!'

The tea arrived first, then the hot water bottle, then came Rehan with the packets of food, which they all ate together from plastic plates. Shireen excused herself after dinner, in spite of their protestations. She really was tired and wanted to sleep. Rehan cleared away the leftovers and changed into his shorts and a vest. Saima was watching TV when he got in beside her. In the flickering light of the screen, her face was pale and the brown marbles of her eyes shone bright. When he settled on the bed with his back raised against the pillow, she slid down to nestle her head on his arm. He held her close.

'Shall I switch off the TV?' she asked.

'No, let it be for a while,' he replied.

'I'm sleepy, you take the remote. Don't worry, the sound doesn't bother me,' she closed her eyes and placed one arm on his chest.

He kissed the top of her head, smelling a faint perfume from her skin. Then, he flipped the channels till he reached one showing cricket highlights. All his focus shifted to the screen as he watched the game. It was a while before he was done. When he turned off the TV at last, he realized his arm was numb. He gently extricated it from underneath Saima's head, made space for his pillow and eased his body down. By now, the moon shone right upon the bed and on his face. He pulled up the covers to his chin to shield his eyes.

Saima was fidgeting slightly but was otherwise in deep sleep. He felt a surging wave of affection towards her. Simultaneously, he felt a twinge of worry. Was this it? This was the pinnacle of romantic love, was it? Would he be able to bear it well?

As he drifted into dreams, he remembered wondering if all men felt this way.

6

A WEEK LATER, six human figures sat in a circle at the edge of a vast glassy lake under the star-studded thick black blanket of the night sky. They were all travellers who had come to this remote windswept border region of Ladakh to witness the stunning sorcery of nature.

The Pangong Lake, like clouds, birds, and mountains, did not respect the boundaries of countries; its waters were insouciantly pushed by the wind from India to China and back. Any human being with the tiniest mote of sensibility could not help but be moved by the magical scenes that changed with every hour and shade of light.

These six people, living in the same encampment of tents by the shores, had been awed beyond words. Saima and Rehan were sharing a tent; Fayaz and Shireen were occupying individual ones. The other two people were a couple they had all befriended over the course of the last two days here. Shorn of the baggage of urban living, when people find themselves in raw natural surroundings, there are many reasons for them to connect with each other. It is an ancient connexion, forged from the need to communicate when in relative isolation, to exchange information about best routes for potential exploration, and to express a shared wonder at their environment.

Sridhar and Michael were living in the tent next to them. Every year, the duo drove up from Manali by road to Leh and then to Pangong Tsho in order to spend a few weeks of summer together. Michael lived in Sweden and Sridhar in Bangalore. They loved each other across the continents, their skin colours, languages and histories. And they came here every year to experience their togetherness away from their jobs, cities, and burdensome prejudices.

Tonight, it had been decided that they would all stay up as long as they could. They would gather and spend the night gazing at the marvels around them, sharing the singularity of human life, and if possible, cheer the sunrise in the morning. The possibility of this last happening was rather slim, since they had with them cans of beer and several joints. The question was whether induced sensations could keep them conscious until the morning. Even if they failed, it would be an unforgettable experience.

Three days ago, Fayaz, Rehan, Saima and Shireen had travelled up to the lake, making a treacherous journey across the mountains from Leh to Pangong Lake through the high-altitude Chang La Pass. They had chosen not to hire a professional driver. Fayaz had wanted to drive them through the route: a task that suited a quiet person like him on a long journey with others in a car. Throughout the way, he was silent, and focused all his attention on the road, honking at every approaching blind curve and negotiating passage with other vehicles on narrow, sheer precipices.

Starting out from Leh town in the afternoon, they had passed almost every season imaginable along the way. There had been the long straight roads dotted with prayer flags that had led them up to the mountains under a cloudy grey sky. Then, when they had left the river and the last fuelling station behind, came the winding climb up to the pass. Here, the 'road' was a euphemism for tricky potholed tracks that were lined with fallen rocks and snow. At one point, the visibility had been marred further by lashings of rain and columns of fog. Rehan and Saima had traded sleep in each other's arms in the back seat, with intermissions of good-humoured banter designed to lighten the mood. Shireen had sat the entire journey in the front seat beside Fayaz, speaking little and feeling a shared calm focus. She had watched the hairpin bends of the road below, the pebbles encrusted in the dirty fallen snow, bubbles trapped inside the spear-shaped icicles hanging from ledges of frozen land. It had been a kind of happiness.

When they reached the Chang La pass, the Indian Army logo of the seal of Ashoka and two crossed swords underneath it welcomed them at 17688 feet (5360 metres). On the red-and-green board, she remembered noticing that Srinagar was 526 kilometres away. *A world away*, she thought. Like every other car that made it to this point, they too had stopped at the small Chang La cafeteria and taken photographs beside the bright yellow memorial pillar heavy with Tibetan flags. On one face of the concrete hexagonal obelisk, in capital letters painted in black, it read, 'Nothing Great is Ever Achieved Without Enthusiasm,' on another, in smaller cursive writing, was a quote, 'Greatness is Responsibility,' attributed to Winston Churchill. The four of them had gone, shivering with cold, into the cafeteria constructed in a Buddhist style, and bought teas and coffees, and stocked up on chocolates, chips, and biscuits. Rehan had wanted to take over the driving, but Fayaz had refused to let him; so perhaps in an attempt at bravado, Rehan had smoked a cigarette at an altitude where oxygen was scarce and people often felt dizzy. Saima had been unimpressed, giving him a look that produced stirrings of guilt in him, an emotion that was attenuated only when the old Ladakhi man running the cafeteria had shown profuse gratitude in return for Rehan giving him a cigarette.

Once they had crossed the pass, the road became clearer when descending, offering a marvel of sights that rose from the earth as a dream. The rocky mountains were sculpted with labyrinthine patterns of snow, the visual effect depending on the nature of the rock and water – powdery snow on tall brown slopes produced a continuous grainy pointillist picture, as if it were a city seen from the skies, while thick white snow on smaller rocky hills created an abstract expressionist effect such as that produced by dripping paint on a brown canvas. A providential ray of sunshine bursting through a clear blue patch in the skies blessed a spot of earth here and there, while diffuse halos of light through the clouds sanctified some peaks. As they descended, they travelled through majestic uninhabited valleys where a patch of water stood its ground between the striking slopes, reflecting light like a small oval mirror that a fleeing goddess may have dropped. Throughout the drive through these coppery mountains, there were no trees, not a single one. Much later had they seen small patches of dry wild grass where herdsmen roamed with yaks. Shireen had spotted a limping yak calf that had been separated from the herd they came upon later. She asked Fayaz to stop so that she could tell the herdsman about the stray young one. He did so, feeling that it was a welcome break from the arduous driving that he might otherwise have been loath to take, and also thinking that he had not been wrong in the last few days about his warm opinion of Shireen. Everyone climbed out of the car in the rocky valley, taking smiling photographs beside the unmindful yaks as they complacently nibbled the grass with their eyes and heads fixed on the ground.

Further along, the shadows of moving clouds became clearer on the mountains, framed as they were in the golden light of an impending sunset. Signs of human activity began to appear. They passed by squat-roofed white and green army settlements where once again the electricity wires came into view. In a while, an Army arch announced a welcome to Durbuk, after which the Border Roads Organization signposted Lukung. They were on the last leg of the journey, but they would miss the sunset over the lake that evening. On this stretch, they passed by long marching lines of soldiers dressed in camouflage uniform, hats and boots, with their guns slung on their shoulders. As they passed between the procession of soldiers on either side of the remote valley, they all stiffened slightly. 'Bharat Mata Ki Jai,' said Rehan, with not a little derision. Fayaz did not react, Shireen thought of the tired dark faces of the soldiers in this wilderness. Saima surprised everyone with a jovial series of remarks about how the scene around her was making her feel hungry.

The clouds were candyfloss, she said. They made her think of the pink-hued delicate fluffy masses of sweet confectionery sold on little sticks. The Karakoram mountain range that they were surrounded by made her think of large chocolate and nut brownies dusted with fine powdered sugar. It was true, the others admitted, the large brown undulations of the earth looked like heaps of doughy chocolate and the snow sprinkled on the top was certainly like fine sugar. The vista could seem a mudpie cake. The flaxen evening light was honey dripping all over the feast. Everyone laughed at these merry comparisons of glorious views to such victuals, even Fayaz joined in. However, the feast was soon taken away from them by the enveloping darkness of the night. The last thing Shireen remembered noticing was a charcoal shade extending across the base of a large mountain before everything was engulfed in an anxious gloom. It was late when they reached the lake and the excitement of travel had given way to the bodily dissipations. They found their food and their tents. The shelters were rather comfortable habitations made of layered canvas, and each one contained beds and a washroom with sinks that had running water. All that remained to welcome the coming day was a night of fitful sleep.

The whole of the next day, the group of four had wandered about the lakeside, swapping superlatives about the magnificence they were in the presence of. The Pangong Lake was every conceivable shade of green and blue constantly altering from one to the other. The plashing sound of the gentle waves against a low pebbly shore was an invitation to a transcendence that was both seductive and soporific. A person could just sit for hours by the lake, mesmerized by the brilliant blue skies above and the rolling brown snow-dusted mountains in front. Obscure as this place was, there were not too many people or dwellings; a mere few cottages, traditional homesteads and tent encampments stood by the shore. The four took long walks, occasionally drifting apart to observe a scene at leisure, and at times stopping to speak to the village folk.

Rehan and Fayaz chatted with a couple of young Kashmiri men who had come from villages near Jammu to work during the tourist period. The pay seemed paltry, but the accommodation and meals were taken care of. Later, the two friends disagreed over whether the men were actually Kashmiris or Dogras.

Shireen went in to survey a traditional homestay run by an old Ladakhi family. Constructed recently from grey concrete, it had bright carmine-coloured window-frames and wood-fuelled bukharis for heating the rather bare rooms. Outside were lines of walls made from heaped stones, several scattered straw mats and small water tanks in viridian plastic casing. A cobalt-blue banner flag fluttered loudly on a tall pole, the wind moving in sine waves through its ruched green fabric edges. Saima strolled into the large kitchen of the homestay where the family cooked meals for the guests. It was a circular stone-walled enclosure covered by fabric stretching out from a wood pillar at the centre, around which were multiple stoves, pressure cookers, flasks, pots and pans. A wooden rack held rows of jams and marmalades, powdered milk boxes, and cartons of masalas and spice. A few men and women were busy at cooking-related tasks; potatoes were being peeled, tea was boiling on a gas hob, dough was being kneaded. A small boy played alone with a plastic bat and ball in a corner.

Speaking to each other as they walked in a group, they commented on the absence of any vegetation till they saw a small hardy plant underneath the rocks. The leaves were thick and fleshy like cactus, but it had scant a thorn. Instead, it was shaped into tiny olive-green roses.

Rehan wanted to pick one for Saima, but she refused to let him deprive the earth there of that modest bit of green. Fayaz watched Shireen closely as she bent down to speak to a little girl, handing her a chocolate bar from her bag. The child was unkempt and dressed in threadbare clothes. Shireen drifted a paper boat into a plastic tub of water, which produced an expression of wondrous delight in the child. Later, Fayaz and Shireen spoke about the abundance of colour in people's lives here. Even the little girl with a podgy face, ruddy cheeks and small intense eyes had been wearing every colour from red to orange, to pink, yellow, black, blue and purple. They mused if the adoption of such an array of colours was a way of creating joy in the presence of harsh natural surroundings. Surely, it must be unbearable in the winters here. Fayaz had learnt from the workers earlier that all supplies here had to come in trucks every few weeks. There was nothing that could be cultivated locally.

Later, Saima and Rehan went on a drive together, Fayaz discussed the driving routes with Sridhar and Michael, while Shireen went to sit by the lake shore. At first, she leaned on a rock, slowly taking in nature's tableau, then, as her sunglasses became ineffective against the blazing sunbeams of the dry afternoon, she moved to the gravelly ground, facing the lake while resting her back against the same rock. In this shaded position where she was hidden from view, she felt confident enough to vouchsafe her feelings into form. She took out the sketching pencils and paper, peering intently at what lay in front of her, trying to discern what lay inside her, and hoping to discover affinities. She wasn't sure how to begin, but knew that lines, curves and colours were her allies in subduing the creative agitation that she felt.

As she yielded to expression, a gentle afternoon breeze wove silver threads of waves upon the lake. Those radiant few clouds, ambassadors of the blue heavens, whispered bliss into the hearts of the mountains. An eternity was assembled there, infused in a single mindful moment. Was it the people who had come there to see the piled-up stones and shimmering sands, or was it the stone cairns that watched the marionette people at mortal play? Shireen tried to sketch the poetry of colour, shape and sound in abstract forms – all the ingenuity of human beings paled in comparison to the loving gentleness of a soft wave surrendering to the ironclad shores.

At length, she heard a crunch of feet upon the gravel behind her, and hastily closed the sketchbook. It was Fayaz, who had been looking for her.

'I'm sorry if I disturbed you,' he said, looking at the pencils and sketchpad. 'Rehan and Saima have not returned yet; Michael and Sridhar left on their bike; seems like it has been agreed that tonight we will all stay up and have a bonfire gathering.'

'Really? No one mentioned it to me!' said Shireen, surprised.

'Me neither. It must be the work of those two,' offered Fayaz.

Over the past week, 'those two' had become a phrase Shireen and Fayaz often used to refer to Rehan and Saima. Far from being pejorative, it was meant to be an affectionate encapsulation of the love and life that their friends brimmed with.

Then there was a moment of silence before Fayaz asked if he could sit there too.

'Of course,' replied Shireen.

They heard the call of a lone bird and the whirring noise of two grey patrol vehicles in the distance.

'We are at the border,' said Fayaz.

'Yes,' Shireen sighed.

After some time, he spoke, 'Like you, I don't speak much. It's not because I don't find the people I am with ... interesting ... it's merely hard to express myself.'

'You don't need to explain anything. I totally understand. I'm like that too,' she answered.

'Maybe it's my way of accepting that I am a boring person who has no poetry, no humour, no skills,' he reflected.

'I wouldn't say that, Fayaz. You definitely have the skill of driving through a perilous route with admirable equanimity.'

Fayaz felt a current of joy. Even though they had not spoken much, he had liked spending time with Shireen over the past few days. She had addressed him familiarly with his name and complimented him on his ability. He was emboldened to request if he might see what she had been sketching. This made Shireen feel trepidatious. She did not want to show it, but she did not want to seem brusque by refusing bluntly.

'I'm not a good artist at all. I wish I was,' she replied, evading the question.

He did not press again, but asked her for a sketch pen instead.

Puzzled, she asked him 'Which colour?'

'The colour of your thoughts right now,' Fayaz replied, surprised at himself for having come up with a line like that.

Shireen hesitated, then handed him a black pen, saying 'That would have to be silver, a colour I like, but since there is no silver, here's black, it's good for outlines.'

Fayaz picked up a small pebble and scrawled a smiley face on it, then gave it to her and said 'A gift from Kashmir.'

'From a Kashmiri,' she smiled.

'To a Kashmiri,' he smiled back.

'Thank you,' she said, touched by his simple gesture. Was it peace she had felt?

That evening, Saima came into Shireen's tent to chat about the drive she had been on with Rehan. As they were speaking, Saima noticed the smiley-faced stone on the bedside table and joked, 'All that art material, and *this* is what you sketched, jigar?'

Shireen laughed her comment away – not clear in her head as to why she had omitted any mention of Fayaz having given her that stone – and opened the sketchbook to show Saima her drawings.

After a while, she asked Shireen if they should go for dinner, and learnt the real reason why they were being delayed.

'It turns out that Rehan's friend Mr Fayaz spent the afternoon with those two guys next door and only then realized that they were a couple! Bizarre, isn't it? So right now the two of them are arguing about rectitude, homosexuality and Islam. I said I don't want to be a part of your weird discussion, and came here.'

'Oh!' said Shireen, 'so that gathering planned for tonight ... is that off?'

'I hope not. I am really looking forward to it. When are we going to get such a chance again? Life's too short not to have fun. Rebel, live and let live.'

'Yes,' came the reply, solemn and entire.

When the night came, the six of them gathered in a circle around the lake.

It was only when trying to procure firewood for a bonfire that they had realized that it would not be allowed. Had they not seen and heard the patrol boats in the afternoon? They were at a sensitive border! Moreover, it was a place of natural conservation and they could not have blazing fires near the water, not even small ones!

A trifle disappointed, they agreed to go ahead with the get-together anyhow. Rehan and Fayaz arranged for more blankets. Michael brought along a couple of sturdy portable gas powered heaters. Sridhar supplied the beer and joints. Saima and Shireen came along to give company, bearing water bottles and snacks, even though no one expected them to care for anything.

They had resolved to make it a night to remember.

They peered into the starry heavens, speculating about the infinity of the universe and the insignificance of the human condition. At one point, Michael excused himself to get his laptop and, with the screen light dimmed, began playing an enchanting song that unfurled out into the dark wilderness. Rehan enquired what song it was, and was informed that it was '*Von*', or Hope, by Sigur Rós, an Icelandic band. Shireen knew the name, but only Sridhar knew their songs apart from Michael. When Saima caught Shireen's attention, she pointed to the moon, and Shireen blew her a kiss. Saima was quiet for a while, thinking of how the moon had bled into her body that week, staining her periods silver; a mercurial message that had been the passionate fever on her brow, and Rehan's too.

They passed around the beer cans. Fayaz was the only one to decline, though he shared a smoke with Rehan. While Michael was recounting seeing the aurora borealis one winter in Iceland, Sridhar borrowed a cigarette from Rehan and set about meticulously rolling the joint. Shireen watched in rapt attention as he emptied all the tobacco from the stick onto a sheet of paper and then crushed it between his thumb and forefinger to mix it uniformly with the weed. Then, he rolled a piece of cardboard to make a roach and wrapped a long thin white paper around in a funnel shape before filling the mixture into it, tapping the object from time to time to create a consistency. It was artful to see him prepare the stuff. When Rehan asked him about the extent of his experience with substances, he confessed to having experimented with things ranging from recreational tablets to sniffing gravity from makeshift contraptions of plastic bottles and buckets. As he finished speaking, he brushed aside that past as bygone days of the engineering college hostel. Shireen felt nervous in taking even a drag.

Fayaz broke a silent spell by asking Rehan to recite some of his poetry. Rehan jovially agreed on the proviso that the others would then take turns to entertain as well. Clearing his throat and winking at Saima, he began:

Hamaari yaadon ki yeh imaarat
Jiske saye main kayi raatein beeti ...[22]

Then, he stopped and said, referring to Michael and Sridhar: 'Never mind. That's in Urdu, and the later verses are too complicated to translate, so here is one in English for you both.' As an afterthought, he added: 'I can't remember my English poems by heart, so I'll read the middle part of one from a note on my phone.'

Wear that pain with pride,
That comes from light inside.
Tyrants, puppets, masters hear,
We do not bow, we don't concede.
This fight is ours, it always was,
Unfasten that spirit, let it soar.
Glorious in struggle, raw and real,
The dignity of a beautiful ideal.
For love and good and God are one,
Each day is a harvest of our hopes,
Our human voyage has just begun.

Michael clapped softly, saying that the poem was rousing in spirit. Saima and Fayaz felt proud. Shireen said she was drawn to the line 'For love and good and God are one.' Sridhar looked up from rolling another joint and said, 'Well done, brother. Hats off.' With the exception of Shireen and Fayaz, the rest of the group had been getting high on the drags being passed around.

Saima and Rehan exchanged whispers until Rehan covered his lips with his palm as he purred the words 'Let us go' into her ear, touching the skin of her lobe with his lips and the edge of his teeth. Saima felt convulsed with a thrill that coursed through her every vein. They got up together, admitting defeat in the middle of the night and waved good night to the rest. Zipping up the tent, they found delight together on the bed, silencing their moans for fear that the others might hear them. 'You're my bonfire,' he said to her at the end. 'I'm your only bonfire, remember that,' she corrected him with a titter, as they fell into an exhausted sleep in each other's arms.

Michael lay down after some time, communing with the utter quiet of the night. As Sridhar spoke, Fayaz thought of Rehan and Saima there in that tent. He then thought of Zeenat, but felt none of the desire to kiss and make love and sleep and eat and listen and dream and sing like life was a blessing to be had. She was a grey transaction in a world of colour. A world of colours in which at this point, under the silver stars and the silver moon and the silvery waves, he had a silver sliver of desire for the woman who sat silently across from him, preferring silver too.

In a while, Michael began snoring mildly. Sridhar nudged him, whereupon he sat up and tapped Sridhar's arm, saying, 'Shall we?' 'Maybe,' replied Sridhar. Michael rubbed his eyes and took more gulps of the beer, waiting patiently. Sridhar took out one of the cigarettes from the box that Rehan had left behind for Fayaz and rolled another joint. When he was done, he placed it in front of Shireen, saying, 'In case either of you change your mind.' Then, he got up and said, 'Goodnight, let us know how dawn broke when we meet tomorrow. You both seem quite sober, sanity prevails in such marathon tasks.' Michael sleepily shook hands with Fayaz and Shireen and murmured, 'Tack, Tack.' Sridhar explained, 'That's thanks in Swedish,' and then they ambled towards their tent.

When Fayaz and Shireen were the only ones left, both opened their mouths to say something at the same instant.

'You speak first,' said Shireen.

'I was about to ask if you were going to try that joint,' he said.

'I'm not sure. I had every intention of joining them, but then his mention of those serious drug escapades at college scared me,' she replied.

'And you, what were you going to say?'

'Oh, just that I really do want to stay here till dawn; so if you are sleepy, you don't have to feel obliged to keep me company.'

He was touched at her innocent incomprehension of what he felt towards her just then. Under those skies, on that night, he could never have contemplated anything other than being alone with her.

'I want to see the dawn too,' he replied.

Shireen picked up the joint; Fayaz lit it for her. She felt a scratch in her throat as she inhaled. After a few drags, Fayaz reached out his fingers in the V shape he was used to with Rehan when asking for cigarettes. Shireen passed it carefully.

As he smoked, she drank gulps of water from the bottle beside them.

They shared the joint in silence and said to each other that they did not feel high at all.

She admitted to feeling suddenly chilly, at which he offered his jacket, which she refused.

Then, saying that they ought to have had a kanger[23] and pheran[24] here, he unfolded a spare blanket and draped it around her. Sitting back down, he smiled at the bundled-up parcel that she had taken on the appearance of, saying, 'You look cute, your head is the only thing visible now.'

Time seemed to fall out of place. She thought of the picture from her childhood in her father's coat.

'I have not been cute for a long time,' she answered, telling him of the picture.

He asked about her parents. She gave answers that were as short as she could possibly manage. From the texture of her voice and the look in her eyes, he knew that she was not being curt, merely keeping her stories at an arm's length.

Without waiting for her to ask him about his family, he told her that his father had been a militant and later a businessman, that his brother now managed the family affairs, that his nephew was close to him and lived with a friend in Srinagar, that he had grown up in a strict foster home and a conservative religious boarding school. There he had stopped. He did not tell her about his marriage to Zeenat.

She was taken aback at the mention of his father having been a militant. She had naively not realized until then that, of course, in a place fraught by so much violence over the years, there must be so many people related to militants. Militants were men, and they were also husbands, sons, brothers, fathers who chose to take up the gun for their cause. She dwelt upon this thought for a while.

When she spoke, she told him that she had been to a conservative boarding school too, the difference being that it enforced the dictates of Hinduism rather than Islam. Then she stopped too. She did not tell him that her grandfather had been an intelligence agent.

'From a Kashmiri to a Kashmiri,' he repeated, as if to emphasize the overlapping brokenness of their experiences, but unbeknownst to them, it also indicated the chasm of secret silences between them.

'I was thinking earlier,' she said, 'is a country a concept? A series of resemblances? A historical familiarity?'

He stared at the lake, thinking of its waters crossing into China. 'I don't know. I do know what my country is, has been, and will always be.'

By degrees, the celestial firmament above them was assuming the mantle of a faint rosy light. She let the blanket drop from her shoulders, saying, 'Yes, you were right, there should have been a kanger and pheran here.' Their eyes met and they shared a soulful moment. Maybe they were asking themselves, 'Am I the self that is supposed to tie all these experiences together?'

What could they have said to each other of their memories and histories anyway, in the vast blank silence of that curious space?

He would have said: 'The hills are alive with the sound of fireguns ... What fireguns? What hills? The hills do not reply back. No answers. We stand muted. We stand silenced. We stand forever. Blast? What is it about? This shelling, the sound, this fury in the skies, these cries of agony. It's about saving my own skin. I fight so that I do not die. I fight so that the other may not live.'

She would have said: 'What are you talking of? I do not know. I am a little flower in the grass by the pond. The pond in the glade. The glade in the Valley. The Valley between the hills. Oh! The hills again. What hills? The hills of the pond of the glade of the grass of the flower.'

He would have said: 'I look down, hang my head in shame. I cannot bear to look. They are killing me. I die as I have always died. Always lived. Always died.'

She would have said: 'I love my home. Everyone has a certain feeling for what is or for what they think is their home. They either love-it-enough-to-never-leave-it, or they love-it-so-as-to-return-to-it, or they may wish they didn't have to leave or belong.'

As the sun's first rays painted the waters ultramarine and the hills sepia, it painted their faces too, with a light that seemed to say: pain has its place, but it isn't the only game in town.

Tired, Fayaz stretched his legs. As he got up, he extended his hand to Shireen, who held it for a short moment as she stood up. She took a few pictures of the awe-inspiring scene and then, without needing to say so, they took a picture of themselves together too. As she gathered the things, he asked her to wait a moment. She saw him step away to observe the ground carefully, as if looking for something he had lost.

When he came back, he held out for her a bean-shaped stone in the palm of his hand.

'What's this?' she asked.

'A bakvat shaped stone for a bakvat,' he replied – a kidney-shaped stone that was a reminder of a peculiar Kashmiri term of endearment: kidney.

In the weeks and months to follow after their parting in Leh, Shireen and Fayaz set about creating a shared secret universe of communication.

7

THE TAPE CLICKED to a close abruptly, startling her.

As if she was an unreal being in a room with many phantoms, Shireen felt she could see herself from the outside as she opened the front of the Sony tape recorder. There was a clacket as it disgorged the cassette – it was an instrumental recording from long ago, titled *Erhu Recital: Bird Calls Echo in The Hills*. Those were the only words in English; everything else was in Chinese ideograms. These symbols had at all times seemed perplexing to her whenever she had encountered them anywhere, except that today they seemed calming in their mystifying nature. Like everything else she had read in the old diaries of her grandfather and experienced in her life and read about in books, they didn't make any sense.

She felt an utter disorientation of the senses and tenses.

Words? What were they good for? Could anyone build a life from them? Could anyone keep believing in them? Words were overrated. They failed people at the specific instances when they were needed most. And so distances grow between people, and armies are always at war. Because no one can ever seem to find the right sequence of words when they are most needed.

And yet, she had spent entire hours going through every page of the old journals, jottings and sketches. And what had that given her? A confused state of being where the only consolation came from the characters on the tape which comforted her; her incomprehension letting her know that it was okay, that she was not meant to understand things, that's how the world was.

She looked up at the long rectangular scroll painting on the wall – a Chinese grisaille landscape. In fine strokes of grey monochrome were painted mountains rising out of a grey mist. Mountains that looked like an infinitely old man's flowing beard, or a pile of discarded fluffy angel wings. The grey trees drooped at various heights on the mountain passes. Of all the trees, one was inexplicably bare and leafless, offering a confession of its denuded wretchedness in the foreground. A grey snow fell on the entire scene. The artist must have wilfully sought to create an effect of intense melancholy.

The painting echoed the grey state of her mind. The birdcalls had echoed in the hills in the recording. Words had echoed as tears in her eyes.

How was she to make sense of what she had read?

Scenes from the diary entries mixed with dates from history mixed with smells from her childhood mixed with memories of Kashmir, all let loose into the twilit space of this little room in Delhi where she now sat surrounded by ghosts.

There was a young man who had his trunk stolen on a train near Jallandhar on the way back to his home from Lahore to Srinagar. The man's mother had not let him travel to Lahore again.

No, there was a woman, a woman who had been married to that man. But what of the woman?

No, there wasn't a woman. It was too painful to think of her as a woman. Let us say there was a doll. Dolls weren't real, were they? Dolls could have their heads stuck in chests of drawers; dolls could hang from their sleeves on balcony clotheslines. Yes, she was a doll.

A Kashmiri doll. A Kashmiri doll in the land of Kashmir long ago and far away. Long ago? Was 1947 that long ago? Was Baramulla that far away? The doll was dead now. She had slept through most of her life, trying to live with what had happened to her. Then one day, being made to fast against her wishes, yearning for oranges, the doll had stopped breathing. When that happened, a copper coin was placed in the doll's mouth and the doll's body was burnt to ashes and the ashes immersed in a river. The doll's tragedy was finally over.

The doll had carried her secrets to her grave. She had been the wife of a spy, after all. If the spy was a man who lost a trunk on a train and became a polyglot who was unafraid during dodgy helicopter rides and spent years in Hong Kong, the doll had her own secrets. So what if nobody trusted an illiterate Kashmiri doll with the secrets of the state. Women carry their secrets in their bodies, in their silences and in their sleep, as she had done.

The doll. The doll. The doll.

The doll had been raped.

The doll had been raped.

The doll had been raped.

Have you ever looked at an incandescent light bulb in a small room through tear-filled eyes and moved your head to see the liquid visual patterns of pain? Shireen looked at the bulb hanging from the ceiling.

The land of Kashmir was created from a whirlwind. It had to have been. If this wasn't a legend among the many legends, it ought to be. There was a whirlwind that tossed people who were wise and foolish, of many religions, of many misty histories, of good and bad faith, and this whirlwind had scattered the people into this land. Unable to communicate, they had killed and raped and pillaged and drawn lines on maps, and pushed each other out like puppets on a little stage, and this never could stop.

But what of the doll?

The doll was a young girl once. Had she cowered in a corner of the kitchen as the marauding mobs of invaders had rampaged through her town, looting, ransacking and raping? Had she screamed for help as the assailants had kicked open the old wooden door of her village home seven decades ago? Had they bound and gagged her?

The doll, the old woman, Shireen's grandmother, had been raped by the invaders in 1947.

Since she returned from Ladakh, Shireen had read books, articles, old newspaper reports – anything and everything she could find on Kashmir and its history. The last book that she had been reading lay open facedown on her desk: *Jammu & Kashmir 1949-1964: Select Correspondence between Jawahar Lal Nehru & Karan Singh*. She wished she had continued reading that book and never thought of opening the suitcase with the diaries today. She looked at the fawn-coloured dust jacket and stared long and hard at the two ampersands in the title. How they resonated, those two little chasm-naming symbols. Jammu & Kashmir with that ampersand in the middle. Ampersand: how many places in the world were named with an ampersand? And did they all have similar troubles?

Kashmir was not India, Kashmir was not Pakistan. Kashmir was not even Kashmir. It was a casualty. Like a woman's body in the wars of men. Her body is the land they seek. And when they can't have it, they force themselves. And now and again, here and there, the law lets them. Because the law is of the land, but for the landowners. The little pain of Shireen's own history magnified into the big pain of the big history as a big heavy teardrop, then the big history, collapsed into its grotesque barbarity as the tear slid down her cheek and the little history was all that mattered. But the little history is little cared for, little people and their little pains cannot be seen in words of treaties and letters exchanged between big men.

Big white men going back to their Great Green Island Kingdom, tired eventually of the Indian summers, the Indian mutinies, and their wars of the world. Big king men in Jammu deal with their family feuds while facing rebellion in Poonch over land and taxation. Big statesman in Delhi with supreme self-belief didn't want to upset the big king men of any skin colour. Big men in Pakistani uniform gather tribesmen and send them to invade Kashmir. Big men in Indian uniform promise to help for a signature giving away land. Big men make false promises on every side. Big Hindu men fight for complete integration. Big Kashmiri statesman has everything but loses it all.

Heroism was tragedy, literally.

Then came the age of the small men who want to be big (and sometimes small women who want to be small men). The big men were losing everywhere; small men and big men turned out to be the same, after all. A small man in Kashmir wanted to stay king forever. A small man in Kashmir would stab anyone in the back for power. Small men in Delhi and small men in Kashmir and small men in Islamabad and small men in Beijing played chess with real little people's lives on real land which wasn't divided into neat black and white squares. The checkmate is perpetual.

Little people, meanwhile, are *little* first. Then women. Or men. These little people looked at little things, and when they thought of big things, they wanted to do big things. So, little people fought and fought and fought with each other. Little people were killed, raped, thrown out of their homes, made to vanish, still they go on fighting and fighting and fighting with each other. Being so little, they are kept from the big picture. When they see a bit of the chess, they hate each other more, pushing each other out of the way for little gains. The big picture is for the new big men. The new big men don't make promises. They make deals for profit alone.

In all of this, a young Kashmiri man lost his trunk on a train, wasn't allowed to return and found himself married to the doll who had been raped. The man was once a boy too. And what kind of a boy had he been? He had written about some of that too in his journals. *Had he been a child once*, he had asked himself aloud in writing. Then he had recalled that he had been a timid boy.

The meek boy had been beaten by his domineering father. Beaten because he had tried to be friends with the son of a despised relative. Beaten with a stick on his right forearm, raising angry welts that the crazy father would massage the next day. The meek boy had also been prone to excessive religious devotion, wanting to run away from home and become an ascetic. This he never did manage, but he fasted whenever he could, and when he had fasted one Shravan Purnmashi[25] against his father's wishes, he had been beaten for that too. In his later years, when the weak-kneed child had grown up to be a man, he had fasted on the death anniversary of his mother, but never for his father. In a twist of fate, he had been married to a woman who had not cared much for fasts, and still had met her death through enforced fasting.

Shireen saw her grandmother offering her matschgand[26] and her grandfather asking her to pass the monj achar[27] as the three of them are sitting at a meal. She is a young girl. Perhaps as young as her grandmother was when Kashmir was bartered over the violation of her body.

The man who had been the meek boy had heard Nehru, had seen him as part of a gathered crowd. This he wrote about in his diary. He had worked as a translator; he had intercepted communications. Probably detailing the scandalous affairs of the big Kashmiri men that resulted in the loss of their power. This he didn't write in his diary. Why had he chosen a profession that had not allowed him to talk openly all his life? Was it because he saw a kind of religion of the nation in the devoted service of the state? Was it because he wanted to do whatever he could to keep Kashmir Indian, having known (at what point did he come to know?) what the invaders from Pakistan had done to his wife? Was it because it suited his diffident childhood self? And then he had become proficient at Chinese. He had studied the language for hours and hours over weeks and months and years till he could go to those unknown areas in those dodgy helicopters and save Tibet from China. And wasn't saving Tibet as an Indian spy the same as saving Kashmir for a Pakistani spy? No, it couldn't be.

Could it be? And then what of the waters of that blue blue lake? Well, what of them? Why, didn't you see how they blithely traipsed across the border! And what did that have to do with a timid boy who was married to a doll who was raped in a time when everyone in Kashmir was afraid of the policemen and the foreigners lived at Dalgate and there was no Jawahar Tunnel. No Jawahar Tunnel? The man had to take a bus to Rawalpindi and a bus and a train to Lahore. A train! Was that the train to Jallandhar? Train, compartments, chains of thought, trains of thought that lurched across unknown stations like birds – birds that could only speak the languages of the birds. Why? Because for English speakers the incomprehensible is Latin and Greek, for the Greek it is Chinese, for the Chinese it is the language of birds. What has Chinese got to do with it? Characters for death, that's what, so many dead and so little joy. The room is dark and needs light but am I here? I am buried under the weight of heavy words in that Pangong night. A Pangong night and the son of a militant.

Shireen's mind was a kaleidoscope that threw up the patternless scattered stars of the night sky. The scenes, dates, moments, memories, places, were jumbled, with no regard for any lines of control between what she knew, what she had heard, what she had experienced, what she had read, what she remembered and what she could never know. A big white rubber eraser made up of intergenerational trauma was being wielded by a massive giant, who was hell bent on erasing the Lines of Control in her mind till she could not understand her self, her country, her people, her life or her ability to love someone.

Pain. Difficulty in reconciling. Repetitive questioning. Awareness of limits. Inability to remember everything together. Guilt. Consciousness. Need for closure. Need for sanity. Cannot understand the sequence of events. Cannot rationalize the actions. Rationales at odds with each other. Feel paralyzed. Want to escape into a world where none of this has happened. Feel dirty. Incapable. Unable. Low in spirit. Want to renounce the self.

Shireen continued to sit in the darkness. She had read not a single word about her father and mother in these journals of her grandfather. The couple had left a child behind in Srinagar. The child, her father, who had never been theirs. Whose had he been? Had he been the result of a rape? If her father was the child of a raped woman, no, raped doll, then she herself was ... But she was. She still was.

The old man who had never owned up to his wife's son from a rape, he had been kind and loving to his granddaughter. Why? Because people mellow with age? Because it was charity and the right thing to do? Because it was a chance to redeem himself? Because his wife had spent her life being mad from her trauma? Because she, Shireen, was destined to be loved by her grandparents, if not her parents?

The faded old pictures of her father swam before her eyes again. So, who was he? Half-Pashtun? Half-Afghan? Half Pakistani Muslim? Half the son of a rapist? Why had all these people taken these secrets – that did not belong to the state – to their deaths with them? Why did they not sit her down and tell her that her grandmother had been raped and her father was not her grandfather's son and this was why they had left him behind and this was why his brother's family could not be bothered to care for her as a niece? Why? Because this is not the sort of thing that families want to admit, especially those made up of quiet spies and illiterate crochet-loving madwomen, especially in front of the daughter of a man who had married late and perished with his wife soon thereafter while insisting on living through a strife that should never have been his business?

Still, she must remember that her grandfather had been kind to her.

Shireen thought of what he had written about why he gave up eating brinjal. He had never eaten brinjal in his later life, giving it up because his own mother had loved brinjals and made the tastiest Burzawangan.[28] He had left such a sketchy account of his life. Recording in his diary that he had watched the movie *Mughal-e-Azam* on 14 August 1960, that he had watched nameless movies every evening in Hong Kong, but nothing of what he felt towards his family members.

Shireen thought of what he had written about why he was unfaithful to his wife much later in life – after his return from Hong Kong, in fact. Like many other life-wrecking events, he had mentioned this too in his terse unemotional phrasing. He had not slept with anyone other than his wife for decades after marriage. Not even in Hong Kong. But returning to his life in India after the Hong Kong years had felt drab and life-denying. He had not, after all, slept with his secretaries. He had gone for housemaids. Furtive sex behind his wife's back, paid for by cash under the pillow.

It was a dirty world. Men raped women. Men bought women. Men played with women. Were all men like that? Even the ones who gave you kidney-shaped stones, gazed shyly into your eyes, and sent you emails every few days with the most beautiful and thoughtful words?

Shireen thought of Fayaz.

In the last few months, they had corresponded regularly. She had held herself back much more than he did. She wrote to him of her thoughts after philosophy classes at the university, he had written to her of images from his dreams that he hoped she would sketch someday.

They had often sent thoughts to each other that need not be discussed only between lovers, but perhaps the thinking together of which reflected a connexion as the one between lovers.

She had mused on the fate of failed seekers under the impossible weightlessness of hope: and what is the fate of failed seekers? On which roads do they register their ultimate despair, at which gate does their soul and will shriek in unison – too much, no more, alas! The pain that for an eternity has lived in the historical memory of humankind, the remembered pain of centuries, which the average person feels stabbing them a few times in life, it is this pain that warms itself and sharpens its edges in the hearts of the failed seekers. The seekers failed, not all together, or even for the same reasons, they failed and continue to fail every day for a million reasons. Yet, they have all mistaken, at one point or another, the tolling of temple bells or the calls from a mosque for the crazy orchestra of hope. Their failures must not be held against them. But what absolutely must be held against them are their troubled measures of hope. They know not why they hope, for what, or what it means. The endless return of hope, its ever-renewing perspicacity, is the worst and most bitter kind of condemnation that can be wrecked upon thought. Such hope kills. Immoderate hope is not a blessing but a curse.

Reading her words, he said, he was sure that he was a failed seeker.

He had written to her about the image of a forest where stones grew on trees. What happens when the stones are shed from the trees? Do they vanish like crushed petals of a cherry blossom in the wind, like the bombed out bodies of Hiroshima victims? Stones refuse to disappear, he had written. The moon, her beloved silver sphere, was a stone too. A stone in the sky. In a P.S., he had asked if she still had his bakvat stone.

Yes :) of course, she had the bakvat stone, and the smiley-faced one too (she had deleted the smiley face twice from the email before deciding to let it stay). She was going to take elements from his images and paint a forest where crescent moons grew on trees. Would he like to see such an image?

She had ruminated on what knowing meant. What does the concentrating driver know about the paths that dispersal pods or the migratory birds take? Not much, you might think. But, beware, for the semiotic spread of the universe is such that at every turn and corner of the path, even the snatches of a song hummed quietly, carries traces of consciousness that span half of all time and three-quarters of all space. It is not so much what we know, as the 'know' suggests, it is what is known to us, whether we know it or not.

He had to look up semiotics in the dictionary, he said. He didn't know! And yes, he didn't know what was known to him without his knowing! :)

He had now dreamt for her the image of a plant, like 'our' Kashmiri willow, by a flowing stream. The plant has branches that overhang the waters. Unlike the willow, it has broad leaves that curve upwards at the edges, so that when they touch the water, they turn into tiny green boats that go sailing along the currents.

She liked the image a lot. It made her think of Thumbelina, a fairy tale she had read in school, she said.

She contemplated whether meagre dreams were better than epic ones. The sounds of birds outside her window were very loud. It was as if the more she tried to discern the sounds, the more she could hear. There was an unending pitter-patter of rain, and the honking of cars and bikes. Her window faced the street. The rain was a relief.

He had never heard of Thumbelina. Boys don't read fairy-tales much, he supposed. He had found the story online and saved the link to read later, he said.

He liked the sound of rain. He was sending her the image of a Chinar leaf.

When she did not reply for a few days, he had sent her a message with a question: Did she think 'loving' was an intransitive verb? It was followed by the suggestion to sketch a heart.

This had been the exact point at which Shireen had realized what had been happening to her. She recognized why she had not told Saima about the smiley stone that night, or even mentioned anything to her about emailing Fayaz over these months. She had been keeping it a secret from others in order to keep it a secret from herself. And behind all the facades of serious words had lain the erotic edge of words.

Then they had broken past the barrier of unfamiliarity by speaking on the phone. Even so, writing to each other still remained the way they could best express themselves. They had sent each other music.

And more recently, they had begun to talk about Kashmir too. With undeterred diligence over months, she had read up on Kashmir's contemporary history. He, of course, lived there. If she corrected his facts about something, he could simply say that she ought to come and see for herself. And he did. More than once.

Someone's car alarm went off on the street.

Why did any of it matter now that she had read what she had read in the diaries?

The tears had dried on her cheeks. She got up and switched on the light.

As she had cleared the papers and diaries from her bed that night and stuffed them back into the suitcase, she had torn a sheet of paper from one of the notebooks and taped it to a wall behind her laptop stand.

It was a hand-drawn map.

The sketch was of a Srinagar locality. The handwriting on it was her grandfather's. Maybe it was intended to explain the area to someone, or perhaps it was a walk down memory lane. Jhelum was inked on the middle of the page between two black lines. The governor's office and the king's palace and a temple were marked, along with labels of areas such as 'Muslim neighbourhood', 'Maisuma' and 'Karan Nagar'. In one corner was a small cross, marked in black ink with the word 'house'. On another corner of the page was a rough inset drawing of a house with four floors, the rooms being unlabelled small squares and rectangles.

Was this 'house' her home?

Shireen wished she could be in Srinagar right at that moment and find her way somehow to the building marked on the inexact sketch and find the place to call home.

Pushing aside even the pain of the raped doll, that little black cross was the last thing on her mind as she finally managed to sleep that night. This disorientation of the senses and the tenses could only end when she returned to that city where she had been born and where her parents had died. She would go to Srinagar, she decided.

In her dreams that night, the spinning blue sphere of water and mud entered her insides. She slowly started to ingest the globe, with all its countries, peoples and names. Everything was one in her. Nothing mattered except this touch of the world in her insides. Like the waft and weave of incense spirals, the world entered her and started to diffuse. She saw the shapes of countries in peeling patches of concrete and people were overlapping footprints on pavements beneath rainy skies. The world was inside her body. It was melting into a cosmic city inside her flesh, forming roads and lamps, buildings and trees, through water and earth. She could see this cosmic city from the sky and know that it was inside her body. Then, a giant picked up a soap of light and dark and started rubbing it on her body, on the body of the world in her. When the froth appeared, it was her breath.

8

SHIREEN WAS WOKEN up in the middle of the night by the loud screech of a car tyre on the road outside. She threw aside the duvet and got out of the bed, intending to drink some water and go over to the window. On the polished Srinagar hotel room floor, she saw the moon reflected, a gleaming stray coin of an image.

This was her first night in a city to which she belonged but which did not appear to belong to her.

Upon arriving that evening, Fayaz had received her at the airport. They had exchanged rather artificial pleasantries in a public space, conscious of the fact that they were meeting alone for the first time since that night by the Pangong Lake many months ago. When the two of them were alone in his car, he had nervously handed Shireen a small plastic rose kept on the dashboard, mumbling that in the depth of winter, real flowers were hard to come by. The small red rose was flecked with transparent plastic imitation dewdrops. It looked like something meant for teenagers at Archies stores. She had been touched by his gaucherie.

On the way to her hotel, they had spoken about what she would like to do and where she would like to go in the days that she was here. She had not told him that she was here to try and locate a black X mark on a hand-drawn map that might once have been her home. He appeared happy to see her, talking more than usual. As he drove past, he pointed out to her the watermarks on the walls from the devastating floods a year and a half ago. He alluded to the names of areas, bridges, and locations. She was simultaneously trying to absorb every name he mentioned and also create a catalogue of all that she could see outside the car windows.

Was the city anything like she had imagined it? Was it anything like the pictures she had seen? Did she remember anything from her earliest memories that might resonate? What she saw was grim. Numerous newly built concrete houses with tinted glass windows, roads in a state of disrepair, noisy traffic jams, large hoardings advertising cement and dahi,[29] bare trees, men in uniform overseeing slow-moving pheran-clad bodies crowned by crestfallen faces. When they reached Boulevard Road and the vicinity of the Dal Lake, she let out a sigh. The occult magic of the mountains in the evening light reflected on a lake's surface infused a calm into her troubled mind. She read aloud to Fayaz the names of some houseboats and shikaras, smiling at the sight of 'Facebook Deluxe'. It was all for the tourists, he said. For the tastes of the varied tourists, everything was curated, the display, the costumes, the pure vegetarian eateries, even alcohol. She thought about the deeper significance of the last two things he had mentioned, but didn't say anything.

When she asked him where he lived, he gave an evasive answer, saying that he lived with his nephew Imran whom he was very close to, following it up with an expression of how he would like to spend as much time with her as possible while she was here. He wanted to take her to the ruins of ancient temples outside the city. He would show her stones, nay, rocks – massive, magnificent, ancient carved rocks that lay in these ruins. Then, he turned to her and said that it was cold, would she like a cup of warm tea?

Later, when they reached her hotel and he directed the employee carrying her bags up to her room where they both knew he would not be allowed, she told him that the tea had been special. He waved her off and left. Barely minutes afterwards, once she had closed the door of her room and sat on the bed, her phone had rung. They had then spoken for an entire hour.

'I am sorry, I was unable to say anything in person. I could not tell you how happy I am to see you. I have been thinking of such a time since that night under the stars,' he said.

'How many stars there were in that blessed place! And how few here!' she said, opening up too.

'This place is a desert at night; nobody ventures out. Everything here is a cruel joke; even the stars shun it.'

She had been quiet, thinking of her parents dying here. Then, she spoke, 'But there are trees here, and birds.'

'So many! You should have come during the ... You should come again during spring . Then there are flowers: real roses, and heavily green chinars, and rows of pollarded poplars on the way to my village, and birds...'

'Don't the birds migrate away?'

'Yes, some of them visit, like you, between autumn and spring.'

'I am a migratory bird, yes, but not all migrations are alike.'

He had been silent then.

'A flock of starlings in flight, that's my image for you to sketch someday.'

'I've carried your two stones with me.'

'I wish I could see you now.'

'I'm not leaving tomorrow, Fayaz.'

'Tomorrow, yes, what is your plan for tomorrow?'

'I am not a tourist,' she stated, in a denial brimming with feeling.

'No, baten,[30] you are not a tourist,' he said in an uncharacteristically familiar manner.

She was slightly taken aback at the use of this word. It marked her. She was indeed a Kashmiri Pandit woman, but it was a word with many echoes, coming from his mouth, because didn't saying that make him a Kashmiri Muslim man? Their inherited histories collided in the sound of that word on his lips and in her ears. She had heard her relatives in family gatherings at her grandfather's place talk of slogans during those times when they had left, slogans that had proclaimed, 'We will make a Pakistan here with the Kashmiri Pandit women, and without their men'. Fayaz would have been a child then, and yet, and yet.

'If you call me baten, I will call you mujahid,'[31] she fired back.

'Fine, I am *your* mujahid and you are *my* batni,' he said, seemingly without taking any offense.

'But tell me why do you want to see the innards of this crowded city? Kashmir lives in its villages,' he asked her again.

'When I come again, I will go to the villages. I want to know this city first. I was born here, my parents died here. Once upon a time, my family had a home here,' saying this, she realized she had said 'when' and not 'if' she would return.

After a pause, he only said, 'Yes, we are a tragedy.'

'Do you know what a professor of mine during undergraduate days once said? He told people that Lal Chowk is called "Red Square" because it is full of blood.'

Fayaz laughed.

'And he said that grenades were sold like eggs everywhere in Kashmir.' She continued, 'Saima and I both had to tell everyone later that the man hadn't a clue!.'

'What do the Indians know about Kashmir anyway?' he said tonelessly.

'Not much, I agree,' she replied.

'They come here for honeymoons and to look for their movie scenes. We are their exotic servants...'

'And their most dreaded enemy warriors too, don't forget,' she reminded him.

'Of course, warriors we are, your mujahid excepted. I am merely at war with myself, unable to do anything to make my dreams a reality.'

'What are your dreams? Are they epic or meagre? Remember I had once asked you this before,' she said, referring to their emails over the previous months.

'My dreams? I suppose they are the same as everyone else's. To be able to choose my life myself, to determine for myself what I want to do, who I want to be. But, that was never going to happen. They said study physics, they said get a job, they said—' he stopped. 'Never mind. Inshallah, one day, I will be free.'

'Inshallah,' she said, 'I wish peace for you.'

'Batni, you really are something. I have never been able to unburden my thoughts in front of anyone in this way. Maybe with Rehan, but never with a woman.'

She felt a colour rising to her face. 'Isn't it late?'

'Late for what? Oh, you mean late? Yes, rest. We will speak tomorrow.'

'Just a moment, I forgot something about those two! Saima has sent a parcel for Rehan, so perhaps the three of us can meet.'

'I will call him and let you know so we can coordinate. How is Saima?'

'She's doing well. Her family is in Delhi during the winter weeks; her brother's got a few days' leave and her sister Layla is coming from Bahrain soon with her family, so she's quite busy with them. Otherwise, she would be here.'

'Yes, I haven't seen Rehan for a while too. Maybe we can plan a drive out of this hellish city together on Saturday.'

'That would be good, thank you,' she stiffened a little, unable to fathom why. Was it because he constantly berated the city that she had not even embraced yet?

The next few days, Shireen wanted to let the city find a place in her eyes to match the one she had long tried to erase in her heart. She initially refused the offers of a vehicle and the company of Fayaz and Rehan, wanting to navigate its wintry veins on foot all by herself as she searched for a place called home.

This was easier said than done. On the first couple of days that she ventured out, she realized that she attracted peculiar attention in spite of her salwar kameez and pheran. Her head was uncovered; she was shuffling through snowy streets aimlessly. Men stared at her as she walked alone on the roads, boys on bikes stopped to politely ask her for a telephone number, telling her they would like to be friends with her. Cars slowed down as they passed by, people inside curiously wondering what a single young woman was doing wandering about in what weren't the supposedly scenic sites. Notwithstanding her best efforts, she could not project a native's familiarity with the surroundings, occasionally having to stop and ask for directions. While people were civil, they almost always displayed a mix of bemusement, suspicion and questioning in their responses to her.

At a busy intersection like Lal Chowk, no one paid her any heed. She looked up at the clock tower and around at the winter clothes hanging from the rails, the lodging signs for the 'yatries', the soldiers behind the barbed wire rolls. The 'Lal' of the Lal Chowk was almost invisible now. Inspired by the Russian Revolution and the communist sentiment, Kashmir had once been that progressive hotbed in a Cold War world. She had read this in the history books. From the diaries of her grandfather, she had understood that this is where he had heard Nehru speak. Had her parents walked these same streets? No, how could they have been the same? The fire in 1993 must have destroyed what her parents would have seen here. More than a hundred people had perished then. And, as with everything else in Kashmir, there was never any accounting or investigation for the endless deaths, betrayals and brutalization of the people. Her parents, her own grandmother too, that doll who was raped; it was unimaginable to think of any justice in the face of marauding mobs, uniformed military and militants on missions. Kashmiris were united by their ability to bear the consequences of the political in the personal, living on, year after year, till they were killed, eliminated, buried or burnt.

She walked towards the old town, keeping close to the Jhelum River wherever possible. Periodically, she consulted the folded map in her pocket, but there was no way of locating a specific house based on such a rough drawing. At one point, she paused on a bridge, overwhelmed at the sight of a devastated wooden building on the opposite bank. It was a miracle that the structure still stood without collapsing, so tattered were the carved wooden planks that held it together. It had once been a four-storeyed house with numerous windows perched in rows upon latticed bands of wood. Now, under the grey skies, it was a ruinous dream made of timber. Some casements precariously hung from their hinges, every bit of glass was cracked, and L-shaped, teal-coloured metal sheets in the lower depths reinforced the disjointed thing where it touched the riverbank. This was not the house she was looking for, but maybe it wasn't so different from the house she had hoped to find. Then, further on, towards what she was told was Habbakadal and Zainakadal, she came upon many similar, if smaller, wooden houses in similarly broken-down states. In the downtown streets, she pulled her scarf over her head and felt that doing so tucked her better into a landscape tense with many haggard faces, distressing sights, and furious slogans on the walls.

When an early evening rain started to fall, she hailed an autorickshaw back to her hotel. The last picture she took was of a mound of mud clods, brick segments, wood scraps and remnants of snow beside a dilapidated house in a residential alley. The grim mud, brick, tin and wood house was a strange ghostly presence among the other houses and stores. A few people passing by had stared at her there. The auto driver was a middle-aged man and a devotee of a sufi saint whose picture was taped prominently near the rear-view mirror of his vehicle. He assumed that Shireen was a tourist and told her in Urdu about his exertions to find employment for his son. His son had finished schooling two years ago and was unable to find any jobs that weren't temporary. The driver had queued for hours at the offices of political leaders and submitted applications begging that his son be employed in any capacity, however humble. His story was not unusual, Shireen learnt. The livelihood struggles of the poor Kashmiris did not make the news unless it was for political point-scoring. The option of joining the army or the militancy clearly did not derive their appeal in a vacuum of destitution and suffering.

When Rehan called her that evening, she agreed to his offer of showing her around the city. Unlike Fayaz, Rehan was enthusiastic about the place and brimming with information. During the weekend, they could all go together on a drive to the ruins.

In the morning, about an hour before he was to pick her up at the hotel, Rehan sent Shireen a text asking her if she would mind wearing jeans and a long jacket. Shireen was puzzled by this strange request, but followed his advice. When he turned up downstairs, his first words to her were, 'You are even more beautiful today than how I remember you.' The statement was accompanied by a gleeful smile.

'Oh! Thank you. Saima sent this package for you,' replied Shireen, breezily.

In turn, he handed her a small pouch, 'A gift for you, saffron from Kashmir.'

'That's lovely!' said Shireen. 'I used to love saffron in the kehwa my grandmother made.'

'You should try making it, she'll be happy to see you from the heavens.'

Shireen thought of his pleasant, easy-going manner on the most sombre of topics. She asked him, 'Why the request that I wear jeans?'

He explained to her that he was going to take her to various parts of the city, including the older historic ones, and that some of these were conservative.

'I realized that. I'd covered my head when there yesterday,' Shireen interrupted.

'Well, that's not it, you see. If you looked like a local and I spent the day walking around with you, I would have to deal with more queries. If you wear jeans and a long coat, and we speak in English, then you are clearly a visitor and I am the person showing you around, your guide, if you like,' he laughed. 'Then people don't keep asking me who you are, you don't have to keep giving long explanations and I don't end up giving someone who might know me the impression that I've a new girlfriend!'

'Wow, that's well-anticipated,' she reflected. 'You are the guide, now that I'm wearing the jeans; so please introduce me to the city.'

Time with Rehan went by beautifully and fast. Shireen really did feel like a tourist, since he made painstaking efforts to take her to a diverse range of locations, viewpoints, and monuments. He told her the legends and stories he knew, and in her head she tried constantly to connect them with the histories she had read about. They spent the next days walking around downtown, going to Jama Masjid, Hazratbal Shrine, Pathar Masjid, Zain-ul-Abidin's tomb, Shalimar and Nishat, Pari Mahal, Hari Parbat, Shankaracharya Hill, Kheer Bhawani Temple, Makhdoom Sahib, Eidgah graveyard, and of course, he took her to the newer cafes by the Dal Lake.

When they went to the cafes – frequented by the bright and beautiful youngsters and the upper-middle–class denizens of the city – they would sit and gossip conspiratorially, making observations about the people they saw.

'That man there is a well-known doctor; his son works for the party in power,' he would say.

'An important functionary?'

'Nah, just an oily collaborator. He'd switch sides tomorrow if the opposition won.'

When they went to the monuments and ruins, she would get lost in her thoughts gazing upon the stone domes and the patina on metal. While she thought intensely of the histories, he would find local men to chat with and gather extra information that he would relay to her later.

'I know how everyone loved Zain-ul-Abideen, the Budshah, the learned and tolerant ruler who knew not just Persian, but Sanskrit and Tibetan too,' she remarked at his tomb.

'It is said that the sang-e-bilawar and sang-e-firoz stones that used to be here were from China, but taken by the Dogra king,' he told her.

When they went to Hindu places of worship, she took off her shoes and went in ahead, while he hung back outside the inner sanctum, texting on his phone or speaking to the security guards and policemen.

'Their life isn't easy, the poor pawns,' she said, seeing the men from the plains of north India who hated the mountains and the cold. They sat beside small fires outside their hovels where she could see stoves, rolled-up mattresses and pictures of Hindu gods on calendars.

'If you come in the summers, you will see a lot of poor villagers from Rajasthan and UP who sleep on the pavements, and do odd-jobs. It is said they also bring in the drugs.'

'Drugs?'

'The young of which society do not need to lose consciousness in these crazy times?' he replied with a rhetorical question.

'Here in Kashmir, there isn't the kind of poverty I have seen in India,' he added with a sense of pride.

When they went to the masjids, they went into their separate gendered areas for men and women.

'The guard was lamenting that now there is sometimes just a single saf, the row. He thinks the devout worshippers are dwindling in number. He also minds that women are being given more access due to tourism,' he told her.

Once when walking through a downtown alley, Shireen stopped to observe a metalsmith burnish a samovar in the fire. Rehan was smoking a few steps away. As they set off again, a man came up and began walking alongside him, asking who she was.

'She's a tourist, a friend,' he replied.

'Friend?' queried the fellow.

'Like a sister,' supplemented Rehan, before the man left them.

Shireen looked at Rehan with amusement.

'There are areas where I'd even have to say Saima was my sister if we were questioned,' Rehan laughed, 'though, of course, we wouldn't go to such places!'

On the ascent up to Makhdoom Sahib, they climbed the many broad flights of stairs up the hill, passing by a woman who stopped them to ask Rehan if the woman with him was single. He said no and wished her the best. She had come to pray for a wife for her son who has an MCA, Rehan emphasized, 'in case you're tempted to consider a match'. When he was done joking, he told her that women especially came here to relieve their hearts of their burdens and make wishes. Shireen too made a wish.

In the graveyards and by the ruined houses, all humour left them and they both became melancholy.

'You have nameless houses and we have nameless graves,' he said one afternoon as they were turning back from some graves at Rainawari. At his words, she lifted her gaze from the sight of some poor boys playing with puppies.

She uttered the two words, 'Countless sufferings.'

Later that day, they had sat in a quiet cafe and spoken more seriously, recounting anecdotes and stories.

'You know there's a friend of mine from south Kashmir, he teaches at a college there now. I was talking to him the other day. We recalled how as children they would play games where they buried pebbles and make graves for them.'

'Graves for pebbles? Why?' asked Shireen.

'The pebbles were supposed to represent slain militants. Every time a militant was killed, the people wept. They still do. The children would gather dust in plastic bags and throw them at each other, pretending they were grenades. Every child who has lived in Kashmir through the 1990s has experienced something that is so hard to explain and put into words. We used to get shivers at the sight of Indian soldiers in uniform, even Fayaz and I, when we were at school ... They could literally do anything to anyone, no questions asked.' He sighed long and deep.

'I read about it. I wish the Kashmiri Pandits never had to leave and we were not divided and ruined.'

'A Kashmiri who isn't able to be at home in Kashmir, why that's misery in itself. Those times were awful. The Muslims who worked for the state were targeted too. You'll know that from your reading. Of course, the rural Hindus suffered the most.' He continued after a pause: 'It's all a game; everything was engineered. And it's still a game being played by India, and by Pakistan, and by America and China everywhere... we can make little difference.'

'Perhaps. But many little differences add up to a lot,' she said.

When the waiter came by to check, they placed an order for second helpings.

Shireen said, 'I went to Lal Chowk the very first thing.'

'I read books about the poets who were here then, the visions for a New Kashmir before 1947.'

'Land to the tiller, Quit Kashmir, Naya Kashmir manifesto, yeah, JNU talk; a lot of our old nostalgic columnists also keep bringing that up,' said Rehan cynically, 'but what about what came later – Pakistan, Afghanistan, yeh communiston ka kabristaan.[32] I've heard of hard-core communists having to apologize and retract their ideology in print. Some were imprisoned with hard-core jamaatis. Others were served death-threats by triple-crossing militants who crossed over into government and then joined HM and then the army. As poor communists were dragged to mosques to forcibly make them pray, they didn't even know how! They became depressed, neither able to be communist, nor Muslim.'

'Kashmir is not an exception to what happened everywhere to many people – communists or those just asking for more rights – from Berlin to Kabul to China from 1987 onwards,' she said.

'You are right. But it isn't an Islamists' problem either.'

'Do you mean it isn't a problem of Islamists or that it can't be solved by Islamists?' she asked.

'Both, I think,' he said after giving it a moment's thought. 'You know what Kashmiri people want – freedom, but also hak, batta, kangri, pheran.'[33]

'And the hundred kinds of bread,' she added.

'Hundred kinds of bread as in what we bake, or the hundred things we have to do to earn that bread?' was his riposte.

They were quiet as a smiling young male server placed the sandwiches and coffees in front of them.

'I was saying that the people here are not the fundamentalists that the popular Indian imagination makes them out to be. Their TV channels make my blood boil. I mean, forget about the stray ISIS and Al-Qaeda graffiti, those kids don't even know what all that is. Our so-called terrorists get captured trying to meet their girlfriends and wives, they're young men from the villages in desperate times and no one understands them and their grief,' Rehan spoke up again.

'I know what you're trying to say, but it was a long process of learning,' she paused, 'and unlearning. As for media, it's become especially bad since this government. Kashmiris here should at least not watch those programmes, and instead have their own media.'

'You think! Even alternative news channels that reported things were shut down and banned after 2010. How can we have alternative media programming, plus there are few resources. On every side, funding guns is easier than finding the right pens.'

'You are writing. There will be others,' said Shireen.

'I'm a failed administrative services aspirant. I mean, don't get me wrong, it was my lack of vision that I even sat for those idiotic exams for that job, but I am happy that I didn't qualify. Now, I can't imagine doing anything other than writing.'

'Saima is appearing for that same exam.'

'She's an intelligent person, I know she'll make it,' was all he said.

'And your, I mean our, friend Fayaz does that idiotic job too.'

'I didn't mean it for everyone. It would have been wrong for me. Fayaz is my friend and I've known him a long time. He's not bad, but he's confused. All Kashmiris have a confusion gene in common,' replied Rehan jovially.

Shireen's phone rang just then. It was Fayaz.

After asking about her day, Fayaz asked to pass the phone to Rehan. The two friends spoke for a few minutes. Shireen couldn't hear Fayaz, but Rehan seemed to be amused and, at times, expressing assent. Hanging up, Rehan told her that Fayaz had reminded him not to take her to Char Chinar or to the Buddhist ruins at Harwan.

'Not to take me there? Why?'

'I am forbidden to take you there because he wants to do so himself. Obviously!' said Rehan, turning into his relaxed happy self.

'How is that obvious? I might not want to go there with him,' Shireen smiled.

'That's between the two of you.'

His saying that reminded Shireen of the phrase 'those two' that she and Fayaz had shared about Rehan and Saima.

'Why does Fayaz live by himself with his nephew? Where's the rest of his family?'

'His family is in the village. But who told you that he lives with his nephew?' asked Rehan, slightly puzzled.

'He did. I mean, Fayaz did.'

'I don't know. I don't get personal too much,' replied Rehan, wondering what Fayaz was up to, and making a mental note to ask him about this.

'Anyway, you tell me, if you were, or had been, a tourist, what would you have liked most in the city, of all that you have seen?'

Shireen replaced her coffee cup on the trendy square saucer and looked at the baubles hung from the cafe window. After some thought, she said 'Pari Mahal.'

'I don't know if "like" is the right word, because this city could have been so much to me in my life and I do want to get past the gulfs of distance and pain, but Pari Mahal is where I would like to go and sketch someday. Beneath the remote Zabarwan mountains and above the busy city, it's a half-way house with the brown of stone, the green of leaves, the white of snow. The terraced parapets, the vaulted arches, the birds. And the city looks so gentle from there, like a baby asleep in the lap of its mother.'

'Pari Mahal is literally the palace abode of fairies, after all,' there was a twinkle in his eyes. 'I said it in Leh and I'll say it again: you're beautiful, a charming philosopher and an artist too.'

'Don't! Then, I didn't know you, so I kept quiet, but after these last few days, I think I can tell you to not make me self-conscious!' she beamed.

'All right, then I'll tell you how repellant that place used to be in my childhood. It was swarming with soldiers who had made it their camp. I can still see them all over the place, polishing their big black boots in the sunshine,' Rehan said. 'In any case, didn't you like the view from Shankaracharya Hill?'

'Well, you can't take any pictures there since they don't allow even phones at the crest, and it's perhaps too remote and austere. The city is too distant from that eyrie. It is still beautiful, though.'

'I bet the best views are inaccessible to the public,' Rehan winked.

'Where are those?'

'There's a constellation of lights like the big dipper on the dark mountain facing one side of the city. There's an Indian Army R and R there – Rest and Recuperation resort. I am sure that has the best views.'

'Or maybe just a lovely view of the massive Indian flag on the opposite mountain!' she countered, telling him about the flag on her college campus. He had heard about it from Saima.

'In keeping with our flag talk, tonight, to celebrate the end of our sightseeing adventures, I'm going to take you to dinner to a famous Vaishno dhaba in the city.'

'Okay, but what's special about it?' asked Shireen, realizing that she spoke as much in Rehan's presence, as in Saima's. The two of them radiated a contagious effervescence.

'Fayaz wanted me to take you to Ahdoo's. It's well known, etcetera. But, the last time I was there, I smelt LPG gas in the stairwell and we asked to be seated in the far corner, nervous of being blown up. And it's also rather expensive for a journo like me,' he explained.

'You don't have to pay for me,' she objected.

'I don't have to, though tonight I will,' he declared in a tone of finality.

That night, they ate in Krishna Dhaba. It was a modest eatery bustling with all kinds of people, ranging from Indian tourists to locals. People queued to eat there, even though there were many identical-looking dhabas on either side of it that boasted empty tables. A burly bespectacled man behind a counter at the entrance shouted out the take-away food orders to the waiters who scurried around busily. It reminded Shireen of student canteens in terms of its décor, which was spartan, with chipped white plastic laminated tables and chairs arranged in rows. On the walls were calendars of J&K Bank, and images of Hindu gods and goddesses. Rehan pointed to a table that was being cleared and they took their seats. He said that their butter-fried rajma-rice combination was a speciality; so they ordered two portions – half a plate for her and a full plate for him. Glancing around her, Shireen could not believe that she was in Kashmir. The atmosphere was remarkably alien to anything in the city. As if to emphasize this, the waiters' grey uniform on the back spelt the name of the dhaba and, underneath, broke the word Srinagar into two – Sri Nagar.

As if reading her thoughts, Rehan said, 'It's what Kareem's would be in Delhi.'

'I wonder if Kareem's would be allowed to serve meat in Delhi in a few years,' she wondered aloud.

The food arrived soon and lived up to the name.

'Next time, you must come home and eat with my family,' said Rehan.

'Of course,' she replied. 'I will.'

'They'll cook a lot of dishes, and I'm sure my mother will have varieties of spinach saag on offer. Kashmiri Pandits used to like that, she tells me.'

'I like spinach,' she said.

'You know, she also told me that they would make their children study and not bother if the Muslim children didn't.'

'I wouldn't know,' she said, asking the mustachioed waiter for some water, which he promptly bought in a stainless-steel jug.

A couple of children chased each other, running dangerously close to the legs of the rushing waiters and causing annoyance to others, but there was no consternation or attempt to pacify the kids by their parents who were preoccupied with loudly discussing their plans amid the general din.

'Don't get me wrong,' he said. 'I meant that there is a general impression that they always thought themselves superior.'

'It must be a Brahminical legacy. Caste is India's unique brand of historically resilient racism.'

'On the other hand, my colleagues here often speak in unfair terms about how the children of those who migrated did better because they had found better pastures,' he added.

'I understand. It's the inability to see past our histories. We're locked into them. I hope there will be bridges in the future,' she mused, a trifle sadly, wanting to believe her own words.

'Cheer up. God is a writer too. Maybe the future tense will be a hopeful one.'

She smiled at his words, saying, 'God is a writer. I like that. A writer of fictions for sure.'

'Fiction is all there is. Everything is a fiction if you think about it.'

'Life as a fiction in search of the future tense,' Shireen replied.

As he paid the bill, she continued to think about the words they had just exchanged.

He waved his hand in front of her eyes, saying 'present tense?' in a teasing manner.

She blinked, as if coming back to the there and then, saying, 'I just hope the future is not more tense.'

He gave her an affectionate pat on her shoulder. 'Hope, hope. Remember that song that guy, what was his name ... Michael? ... played that night. That haunting Icelandic song about hope.'

'I wonder what worries Iceland has,' she smiled, 'being an island on the map away from everywhere else.'

'Everyone everywhere has worries. Even Iceland.' He repeated this as they made their way out of the dhaba, past the rush. He had been barely audible the first time.

'Do you know that Mandarin Chinese has no tenses?' she said suddenly.

'Interesting, if rather strange!' he responded. 'How do you know Chinese?'

'I don't. I have a head for trivia, I suppose,' she said, revealing none of her complicated familial disorientations.

In a few moments, they stood beside a pavement spread of wooden souvenirs – cheap keyrings with crudely carved chinar leaves and shikaras, papier-mache ducks and lid boxes, polished stone-eggs. Notwithstanding his efforts to dissuade her from buying a gift for him, she bought him a pair of papier-mache bell-hangings and two wooden birds: 'They are for you and Saima.' At her insistence, he took the bag with gifts, rationalizing to himself that the elderly seller who was out in the cold at this hour trying to make a living, deserved the joy of making a sale.

That night, after dropping her off, Rehan called Fayaz to ask why he had told Shireen that he lived with his nephew. Fayaz swept the question aside as if it were an inconsequential matter, merely saying, 'You know how moody Zeenat is. These days, things are not good between us. If I told Shireen I have a proper home in the city, I'd have to invite her over and so on. So I just kept things simple.' Rehan figured this made sense, unaware as he was of any attachments or the secret communications between the two over the preceding months.

That night, upon reaching her hotel room, Shireen too called Saima in Delhi. Saima had begun by asking, 'So sorry, jigar, I've been busy here and couldn't call. Tell me, how have you been, how has the city been to you, how has my boyfriend been treating you? Has he been a gentleman?'

The women talked for a long time. They spoke about Shireen's encounters with the city, of Saima's parents beginning to think of her marriage, of Layla's naughty children, of the way in which some places on maps are so engraved into the imagination that it is hard to shake off the burdens of the lines and see them not as a territory on a map but as peopled lands with real struggles, blessings and sufferings.

It was almost midnight when Fayaz rang her.

She was surprised but took his call; they usually spoke at night but not past midnight.

'Your phone was busy earlier,' he began. Was there a trace of petulance in his hoarse whisper?

'I was speaking to Saima.' She decided to not be piqued by the interrogative opening remark.

'Sorry, I have no business enquiring whom you were speaking to,' he said, backing down.

'It's all right. Isn't your nephew around?' she asked.

'No, why would he? He's not a child. In any case, he's at the wedding of a relative this weekend.' He was telling her where Zeenat was.

'I want to take you to Char Chinar tomorrow. And then on Sunday we could go to Harwan, the three of us,' he said.

'Rehan told me that you had forbidden him from taking me to these places. Why, may I ask?' she asked, uncertain as to exactly why he would wish to show her these particular places himself.

'Because I couldn't bear to imagine you there without me,' he replied simply.

'Mujahid, you are a dangerous man.'

'Batni, you are a perceptive woman.'

It was a long night they spent talking to each other on the phone in a freewheeling conversation that switched languages from Urdu to Hindi to English to Kashmiri.

He told her that their language Koshur did not have a standard SVO, unlike other South Asian languages.

'What's an SVO?' she asked.

'I thought you were smart, it's the subject-verb-order,' he said.

'So?'

'So, it's our distance from them. We come from the nomads of the Silk Route, the cattle rearers of central Asia, before the Banihal tunnel, we were insulated.'

She thought of the ampersand in the title of that book. 'We're Buddhists and Hindus and Muslims and Sikhs and so many others, aren't we?' she spoke her thoughts aloud in an innocent question tag.

'We are a carpet woven by the Persians, of all the colourful threads that they could find,' he said.

'It's overwhelming to think of all the invasions, expulsions, and barters of people in history,' she confessed.

'It's the pattern, it's the sights of the city, the sounds on our tongues.' 'Kath booz,'[34] he continued, 'do you see how our speech has an abundance of vowels? We have the dental fricatives, the way our tongues touch the domed roofs of our mouths and the edges of our teeth when we speak. How different the sound is to anything that could possibly be Indian?'

'Or Pakistani,' she added, for a fair measure of her conscience.

'Yes, batni, or Pakistani. This is us, Kashmiris, in the shapes that our tongues make inside our mouths, in our sounds.'

She could taste those sounds in her mouth as he spoke. In explaining the sounds, he would ask her to pronounce this word or that, making her affricate and velarize in turn. Sometimes, she would say a word slowly, even as her heartbeat quickened.

He told her about his village house and the many things that grew there, the clusters of white calla lilies, plums, mulberries, peaches. She imagined each of them. He mentioned the green walnuts that become brown much later, the raw pears, lemon buds, cherry and almond trees, tomato beds, grape vines, hazelnut trees, the little Baltistani apricots. And beehives too.

She chronicled to him her love of the moon and the special way she saw it. How the waxing and waning moon had been her companion through her childhood days on the Delhi balcony and the nights in Mussoorie, and how she had seen it the night before, rising through the reeds in Srinagar. A copper moon had risen rust red and then alchemically transformed itself into a honeyed shade of silver.

In their darkened rooms, where shadows scripted the ceilings in streetlight neon and charcoal black, they had lain on their separate beds on two sides of Srinagar that night of chillai kalan, opening up their hearts in the sheltering embrace of the snow. She had carried her phone to a chair by the window, tracing a heart on the dusty glass. It had drifted from one island of memory to another in the archipelago of her mind. In his world too, the night silently returned a grace. A thickly braided cord of feelings made him alive to thoughts and things. In exposing their rawness to each other, they felt just a little less broken by their own selves, a little more free, as if touched by words heard from Sufis that are danced in the rain.

They realized that both of them loved pomegranates. But disagreed over chess. He liked the game and its remorseless ways. She could not stand the thought of the neat black and white squares that allowed for no grey areas.

'We should play it sometime,' he suggested. 'You might learn to love it.'

'No,' she announced. She would play a game of chess where the chessmen could decide to be anyone at any move.

'How do you mean?' he asked.

She imagined a game of chess where there are no pre-determined moves for any piece. You could lift a piece, say, a horse, and it might want to move like a bishop, or the pawn could want to be a queen. If that were possible for every piece on both sides, the results would be truly serendipitous.

Before he could register the quantum of surprise that he felt, she added that the pieces could also decide to share the squares sometimes, instead of edging each other out.

'That's crazy chess. It's not possible,' he said.

'It's possible. You could have a board with sensors, and the pieces could be programmed to declare their random moves when lifted off the board. It's digi-chess.'

'It's still crazy chess,' he laughed.

'It's beautiful, don't you see. There'd be so much less misery on that chessboard.'

'It's a game. You are over-thinking it by connecting it to everything else.'

'No,' she said again. 'Games become real. People learn life from the games they play. And then they play life as a game and people like moves. If Kashmir was a crazy chessboard, fewer people would suffer.'

'Kashmir is a chessboard crazier than any crazy chessboard; crazier than any that anyone could imagine or invent.'

As they spoke, he unlatched the door of a sorrow in his heart and told her about his father's death. He had been a militant who had died worrying about ledgers, having lost all his idealism. What is more, in the bargain, he had turned himself into a terrible patriarch who had forced his will upon his son's life path.

She had consoled him the way she knew, telling him of her grandmother's death that same season, and how her kin didn't belong to her. She hadn't mentioned the doll's story, just that she was forced to leave a son behind who had been alienated from the family.

They spoke of stones, of guns, of crematoriums, lakes and rivers, of memories where soldiers mixed chilli powder or sand into bags of rice as punishment, of memories where there was always a painful leaving and a perpetually deferred return. Their eyes open and their hearts brimming with confessional silences and communion, they asked each other, if they focused on an object-image that lay at their core, what would they be? He is a tall green stalk that reaches up to the heavens, he said. She could not find an image easily, and when she did, it embodied a contradiction. She would be both the magnet and the scattered bed of nails below it. They puzzled together over what made a soul and what made its connexions. What *are* souls? Was love a blue soul of the night, of a night like this, embracing the white body of the earth, where words arise, gather, dissipate?

With their words, for hours at a stretch, they tried to keep a frosty morning at bay. They wished that time would go on a general strike and restore the present to itself forever. But, though the heart is a wonderful imaginary place, it is also a muscle. And, unlike the circularity of its beating rhythms that have no past or future, the clock-face solely indicates an eternal and unidirectional future. Both love and sorrow barefacedly lie, time never stagnates in pools. Dreams hang on lashes, heavy and far, but time moves on.

The sky outside their windows was the colour of a sheet made from crushed crystal sapphires when they realized that they had waited together for another dawn, this time not by a lake, but in a city with a lake. She thought of stars, he thought of caves.

'Sing that song, '*Roshay*', for me before you go,' she said, referring to a Koshur melody of lament and longing.

'Tomorrow, I will sing it for you tomorrow,' he replied. 'But first, I need to reach you today.'

With that, they bid goodbye for a few hours.

He could not fall asleep easily after hanging up. His unpacified longing was restless like the wind over all the mountains of the world, crashing against every solid surface, making waves out of water and pebbles out of land. She immediately dropped into slumber, dreaming of an island of roses in the middle of the ocean.

When he came to meet her, it was past noon. In a sharp contrast to her sprightly demeanour, he was weary and short on sleep.

'You are worn out,' she said.

'I couldn't sleep.'

'Shall we cancel today so you can rest?'

'I have a better idea, why don't we go somewhere else today and to Char Chinar and Harwan tomorrow.'

He asked her if there was anywhere she would like to go. The museum, she said. It was history and she could never have enough of it.

The rather disorganized Sri Pratap Singh Museum, or the SPS Museum as it was commonly known, was in Lal Mandi and it had been affected by the floods. It was in the process of being shifted to a new building nearby, where the construction was incomplete. When they reached, Shireen immediately busied herself with reading the descriptions and taking endless pictures of archaeological artefacts from Burzahom. Fayaz and Shireen were the only visitors on that floor. His phone rang shrill in the empty hallway corridor. Fayaz took a glance at the number calling and pushed the silence button. He decided to sit somewhere warm and rest. Eyeing the place, he noticed a heater, half the size of a person, stationed in the large space towards the end of the glass cabinets on that floor. An employee obligingly brought him a chair and turned it on. The young man was a distance education student from a poor family who felt fortunate to work there for a living. Without much encouragement from Fayaz, he chatted about how slowly time passed in the museum. Hardly any visitors came on most days. They endured a daily power cut. When he left, Fayaz went up to Shireen to let her know that she need not rush, but he would rather wait for her in one place. By now, she was in the section displaying images of Hindu deities. At his words, she gave a nod, continuing to be immersed in the objects.

Returning to his cosy chair, he passed by a row of ninth-century Ardhnarishwar idols which were a depiction of the Hindu deities Shiva and his wife Parvati as one, in a half-male and half-female representation. They disgusted him so much that he made sure to sit out of view of those images. How weird were these bronze statues of dancing human figures that had a breast only on one side and something of a male organ too. It puzzled him to think what kind of artists would make something like that. And how it could be regarded as a form of the divine. The sacred for him was something much more expansive, much more suffused in the directions of word and thought, than could ever be captured in forms cast in metal. He couldn't grasp what he saw, though he understood well why there were so many of these idols in this museum named after kings and rulers who had shared neither his faith nor his conviction.

Warming himself at the electric bukhari, Fayaz dozed off for some time. Upon waking, he went to find the young boy and asked for a cup of tea. Sipping it, he paced the rooms aimlessly, noticing little, save for a four-thousand-year-old stone-sculpted conch shell in a glass table cabinet.

What does it mean to have lived a meagre lifetime when faced with objects that survive over centuries and millennia? Did it matter that long after he was gone, everything would still be as it was? If one could total up the age of everything in that one building alone, it would amount to a large part of the history of the entire humankind. And how many such buildings were there in every city in the world? And perhaps when you added up all those years, the sum might even surpass the age of life on the planet itself. These parallel ages of ancient civilizations, if strung together, would shame the very idea of a clock! How important a person feels in their own life and how we are even less than a mote of dust in a magnificent yet unknowable storm! When he thought like this, he wished he was still credibly religious. Maybe if he could have, with utter faith, as he had once done, kneeled and prayed in front of the divine, he would have an anchor to hold his soul together in the turbulent seas of existence. He didn't go to masjids now. He observed the occasions but did not pray, at least not conspicuously.

'I was beginning to seriously think about the meaning of forever,' he said to Shireen as she finally returned from her explorations.

'I've hardly had enough. So many rooms are closed, and would you believe, they have Buddhist and Hindu artefacts but hardly anything from the Islamic period!'

'I would believe,' he said calmly, 'also, we don't make idols.'

'How would I not know that!' she said. 'I'm sure they have the carvings and the metalwork and textiles somewhere, but it's all disjointed and much is in storage at the moment, I'm told.'

'Shall we now go to a real place?' he asked.

'A real place?'

He meant the temple ruins. 'I am rested and refreshed now. Shall I drive us to the Awantipora Temple? It's not too late.'

They went to the ruins of the temple that evening and took a shikara to Char Chinar the next afternoon. Rehan could not join them for Harwan, so they went there by themselves too.

Shireen had to leave the next afternoon. Fayaz arranged an official car for her so that she would not have too much trouble through the numerous security checkpoints that began almost a kilometre outside the airport. They knew that nobody but the passengers were allowed inside the cordon of the Srinagar airport, so they said their final goodbyes over the phone.

Images flashed in her mind's eye in the manner of the photo-biscuit cards from Hong Kong. Only this time they were not neatly arranged to be viewed in a slider, but fell like the rain in the background of a Magritte painting in one of her college library books. She saw the tiny green clover leaves growing out of the colossal stones of the temple ruins. She saw the yellow pointed edge of a shikara push its way though the frozen lake, framed by the blue mountains on their way to the Char Chinar island on the lake. She saw herself and Fayaz leaning over the wooden balustrade at one end of the island with the four chinar trees, looking at their reflections in the waters below. She heard the singing of the boatman in the background when Fayaz asked her if reflections ever kissed. She saw herself feeling a wild abandon in the stony remains of an apse at the Harwan ruins. She had felt light as a butterfly, sublime like the angel rays of sunshine that are panoramic on the snowy peaks. It had started to drizzle at the ruins. At the same time, numerous azaans had begun; their resounding echo reverberated through the city spread out below them with its sloping roofs, buildings and boats. She saw the wet fingers of the Jhelum River passing over the green land and heard the soothing sound of the wind through the trees.

There is no distance between the past and the present in the recesses of the mind, where all realities live simultaneously, cohabiting the universe of a life lived by the moment, in the unguarded truth of each moment. The aspirations and yearnings of her multiple wishes wove a web in which she had unwittingly found – or was it lost – herself.

On her last night in Srinagar, he had taken her to Gulmarg. Ringing at midnight again, he had said, 'I want to take you to Gulmarg, that valley of roses, right now.'

'Now?' she had said, stunned.

'Yes, now.'

She had held the phone to her ear in the darkness and he had taken her on a journey in words from Srinagar to Gulmarg, slowly and carefully describing the turns of the HMT Road outside Srinagar, going past the intersections at Lawaypora and Kirmani Abad, the long stretch of the Narbal-Tangmarg Road, till they reached the winding paths up from Tangmarg. They had even stopped to buy the vehicle tickets and only then reached the grand open vista of the beautiful sounding Gulmarg. Later, they had held hands in Gulmarg and he had sung a song for her too. It was a magical feeling in the depth of a dark deserted night in a solitary room, a feeling that refused to evanesce in the white obscurity of the morning. Sunbeams lit up every colour inside her marvellous snowglobe of happiness.

As her plane lifted off and she leaned her head on the oval window frame, the white and green valley was a velveteen spread. It was a wet green earth of fertile memories. She observed the scene below. There was the odd red or blue tin roof amid the grey and green. Silted river channels stretched out, gullies of snow were sketched among the pine slopes. She felt that a tableau of heaven was there in the bounteous beauteous green, the meadows, the mountains, and the clouds. The plane climbed further up, penetrating above a thicket of clouds, a white pathless forest of sculpted mist. Light and shade danced on the propeller under her window. She saw a precise shadow of the aeroplane on a screen of clouds. The clouds themselves were a white marble terracotta army in the skies. The fractal edges of the clouds were like her memories, paused and poised.

Sailing out of this valley of love and death, her heart felt unburdened. It had been embroidered with love. The future was always another country, wasn't it? She dared herself to imagine again that it was her home, a place to which she would return. A home in infinite regress, but one that still was hers.

9

SHIREEN SOMETIMES WONDERED if she had really returned from Srinagar that winter. Kashmir had been a seed germinated in her mind and it was all she could think of even when in Delhi over the following months.

The news did not make it easier for her to forget. The chief minister of J&K had died; a new government headed by his daughter was in the process of being sworn in. In her university campus in JNU too, the slogans of 'Azaadi' had resounded loudly and resulted in the detention and arrest of several prominent student leaders. The question of seditious speech played out non-stop in the media, with the right-wing anchors hyperventilating about the audacity of using the words Kashmir and freedom in the same sentence. The media persons took out marches in the city to protest against the curbs on free speech but vigilante goons attacked them in full view of the cameras. The perpetrators of these attacks were not subjected to any stringent application of the law. It was alleged that the student leaders were assaulted in the court premises. Some lawyers, donning their professional black robes, took out a procession through Delhi streets, raising the slogan 'Bharat Mata Ki Jai'.[35] Prominent dissident academics at her university stood up to speak truth to power and were, as a result, roundly vilified in the populist climate of bigotry.

Shireen buried her head in the philosophy books but could no longer insulate herself from what was going on around her. They were talking about Kashmir and India. These were not entities on a map somewhere faraway; they were part of her core. She felt utterly vanquished under the onslaught of a plastic politics of posturing that had no space for understanding real people. Kashmir was an abstraction to Indians, India was an abstraction to Kashmiris. The politicians who successfully traded in these abstractions on either side made a killing.

For the first time in her life, Shireen attended a political event that spring. It was a gathering of human rights activists, journalists, progressive media persons and students. The usual suspects, you might say. But, for her, it was a new and daunting experience. Saima and Rehan, who were articulate and seemingly pro at interacting with people in such an atmosphere, accompanied her. Shireen shrunk into a corner, wanting to say many things, but unable to find the right words. If there were one or two people there, she would have tried to unseal her thoughts, but in the presence of so many people who seemed to have so much to say, she just kept quiet. Rehan recited a poem of his, titled 'Search Me, I'm From Kashmir'. It was met with a thunderous applause, Shireen herself had continued clapping till the end.

Saima's family had been staying on in Delhi long after her brother and sister had departed back to their posting and home. She often lived with them, only returning now and again to her room in the shared flat to pick up books or clothes. Her preparations for the forthcoming exams were in full swing. Rehan had come to Delhi for a few days and had been casually introduced to her parents as a 'friend'. Saima too was planning to go to Srinagar during the summer sometime for their next meeting. They were headed for a period of courtship before they could find their feet and manage to persuade their parents. Shireen knew that they were emotionally strong enough to reconcile to the situation as they found it.

Shireen herself had an unclear grasp of her emotional landscape these days. Fayaz communicated with her on a regular basis, but their exchanges left her feeling oddly uneasy. For one, they never spoke at night anymore. She had once called him late and he had declined the call, texting that he was busy with work. Also, he constantly tried to convince her to return to Srinagar, but never mentioned any plan of coming to Delhi to meet her. On her part, she had been non-committal. Fayaz, perhaps, had been more interesting to her when he was less transparent as an ordinary lover. She missed the early days of their secret exchanges last year when they had opened up to each other about those profound heartfelt things. How he had sent her the images to sketch and she had shared with him her perplexities about life's ways! Now, he sent her pictograms of roses and hearts and asked her how her day was and told her what he was working on and how the food cooked by his servant tasted. When she went too far down this line of thinking, she drew herself back, acknowledging that she was being too harsh on him. They were in something like a relationship and he naturally wanted them to share the details of their lives.

Notwithstanding her dilemmas about her feelings, she was beginning to head towards a much more lucid understanding of what she wanted to do in terms of her life. The answer was simple – Kashmir. Reading about its history, politics, and society had become an idée fixe for her. Words, ideas, scenes rained upon her mind, and with the insatiable appetite of parched earth, she could not stop ingesting them. She wanted to know everything about Kashmir. It was a quixotic wish. Everything could not be known; she would never know if she knew everything, and whatever did everything mean? In her case, it meant reading the accounts of the long-dead British explorers, the retired Indian Army figures, the correspondence between statesmen, the texts of the treaties, the stories of the young men and women online, the stories of the migrants, the songs of the movies, the human rights reports. She was resolved that she would school herself into the many dimensions of her belonging to Kashmir – invasion, occupation, ornithology, linguistics, legend, intrigue, poetry, politics. The names were endless – Abdullah, Abhinavgupta, Ali, Bashir, Bazaz, Bernier, Berreman, Biscoe, Bose, Dhar, Geelani, Gervis, Gigoo, Guru, Kalhana, Kaul, Khan, Koul, Knight, Knowles, Lamb, Lawrence, Manto, Mattoo, Morris, Muhammad, Nehru, Neve, Noorani, Pandita, Parvez, Peer, Rai, Rothfield, Roy, Sapru, Schofield, Shauq, Shah, Stein, Swinburne, Wade, Waheed, Whistler, Whitehead, Younghusband, Zia, Zutshi – and she felt it would take her a long time to imagine a future; understanding the hold of the past often took up all her energies and time. If wishes were horses, she would find one to load with a caravan of texts and artefacts and fly far away to battle her phantoms, a Pegasus to slay her chimeras.

Her studies at the university were not going so well. With the highly charged and uncertain atmosphere outside, she was unable to concentrate in the classes. She wondered over and over again what had led her to philosophy – why had she not chosen history instead? Was it too late? History of Kashmir, that's what she felt she could really immerse herself in. If she read enough, she was sure that she would find a question that no one had asked about that history before, and then she could work towards asking that question of the past in such a way that it would mean a different and better future. It was possible, wasn't it? It could happen, she told herself. At times, trying to think more practically, she had visions of studying for a doctorate on the topic if she could find the right question. And yet, there was only one place that she felt she could allow herself to ask that question. It could not be Kashmir because ... she would be too close, it could not be Delhi because she would be too far; it could only be in Hong Kong, she thought. It didn't make sense. Hong Kong was not midway to anything, Hong Kong had no connexion to Kashmir, Hong Kong certainly didn't make sense. But, somehow, Hong Kong made sense. Hong Kong was the island in her mind where she could lose herself in Kashmir. What was it about Hong Kong other than that child's fascination? It was a little island at the edge of a big landmass, transferred from one governance to the other, beset with its own struggles. Shireen could not answer this question of 'Why Hong Kong?' through logic, and when she failed to do so, she would surrender to an instinct that told her that she could only ask the right question about the history of Kashmir if she was in Hong Kong.

If her waking dreams were puzzling, her dreams at night were no more straightforward. One night, she would dream of herself as a little child being asked how much she loved her parents. She would roll over on a soft bed, opening her arms wide and stretching them out into a big circle that went around the whole earth and say, 'This much!' More than the universe, more than eternity. Then, she would wake up feeling a bittersweet sensation of being an orphan in a room alone in a big city with only memories for company. At these times, the beating red heart in the text from Fayaz would bring a smile to her face. On another night, she would dream of blue skies where the trail of an aeroplane at sunset was fragmenting so that it looked like a delicately constructed anklet floating in the skies. Upon waking, she would look out of the window at the dusty Delhi outside and find herself wanting to paint, wondering why the sky was never green and the land never blue. Sometimes, then, she would send Fayaz a message, saying, 'Perhaps there are, in the post office of hope, small parcels of love that were addressed to me. But here I am, an outline of flesh, an infinitely reflecting mind, yearning.' On still other nights, she saw the sinister sight of an incompletely blown-up yellow-and-white building in the middle of a square. It would be laden with sandbags and surrounded by ominous blue military vehicles and a gamut of uniformed police and army men in camouflage gear with guns pointed at her. She would drift past them as an apparition and go inside the building, which then transformed itself into a cinema hall where she is the only one sitting in the darkness. On the large flickering screen in front of her play out images of herself and Fayaz, now drifting on the lake in a boat, now lying on the wet grass in a ruin. When she opened her eyes, she would realize that the image had been of the crumbling Palladium cinema in Lal Chowk that she had seen when in the city. Then, she would pick up a pen and paper and write a note to herself 'I do not want to know where today is. I want to be in a field in the middle of a dark ocean, a field of water where only the most vulnerable can tread in utter safety.'

The months passed, exams came and went, she finished her final semester. The question of what to do over the summer returned to haunt her. She enrolled on Art Appreciation classes at the National Gallery of Modern Art in Delhi. In addition to painting, she took tuition classes for school children and separately continued with her punishing, self-prescribed syllabus on Kashmir. Delhi had turned into a furnace and, whenever possible, she stayed indoors with the air-conditioning on and a book or a brush in her hands. Although prone to dark moods time and again, she was beginning to relish the idea of a solitary life where the only people she had any meaningful interaction with were voices on the phone or display profiles on digital media.

Then, one afternoon at the start of July, she got a call from Saima. Alongside completing the university exams, Saima had already finished her coaching classes for the civil services entrance and gone to her parents' home in Kargil to focus and finalize her preparations for her UPSC prelims that were coming up in August. When Shireen asked her how she was, she merely said, 'Exhausted from fasting.' Shireen then remembered that it was Ramzan. It was going to be Eid in a few days and then it would be over, she told Saima. It had been a hard time, being away from the city, having to study all the time, and not even being able to express herself to Rehan, who was fasting too. During these days, they both stayed chaste, forswearing any love-talk. This made no sense to Shireen. Rehan drank alcohol; Saima and Rehan had been intimate; so why all the fuss over purity? But she kept her questions to herself, trying to be the compassionate listener that her tired and frustrated friend needed at that time. She tried to cheer up an uncharacteristically depressed Saima by bringing up a picture of how she would feel after she had cleared her exams and achieved her goals. Judging by her voice, it helped lift her spirits somewhat, but was no substitute for the in-person twenty-second hug. Shireen and Saima both knew that their paths were now on the cusp of diverging. The university days had drawn to a close and their career ambitions would tug and propel them in different directions. Reflecting upon these matters, they cooked up a plan. Why didn't they try to meet up once over the summer, all four of them, as a way of revisiting the memories of Ladakh? As soon as this came up, Saima's brain went into overdrive thinking of the possibilities. Shireen too was keen because it would be an escape from her long stint of isolation. It wasn't that she didn't like being by herself, but it would be a change to meet Saima and Rehan and, she admitted to herself, Fayaz. Where should they arrange to meet? While Saima was thinking of options, Shireen said the one word: 'Gulmarg?' The place had been on her mind since that night in Srinagar when Fayaz had taken her there on a journey over the phone. Saima jumped at the idea, forgetting all her blues. 'Wonderful! Yes, that would be perfect!.'

Later that night, she called back to relay the results of her coaxing. They would all meet in Gulmarg on the day after Eid, which was to fall this time on a Wednesday in the middle of the week. Indeed, it would have to be after Eid for 'those two', flashed through Shireen's mind as she smiled into the phone. Saima would find an excuse for her parents to arrange for her to be there on the Thursday afternoon or early evening. The drive would take a few hours even if she started early.

'Would you be allowed away?' asked Shireen, to which Saima replied with the bravado of a gangster: 'Jaani, I know how to make things happen. I'll find a way. If I don't, I'll make a way.'

Shireen loved the bubbly Saima and realized how she had missed her over the last few months. Saima continued to gush about the other details. Shireen would have to find a ticket to get to Srinagar on or before the morning of the day after Eid. Then, Rehan and Fayaz would go with her by car to Gulmarg and they would all spend the night there. On Friday night, they could return to Srinagar, where Saima and Shireen could stay on until the Sunday. With the phone tucked between her shoulder and neck, Shireen was already checking websites for tickets on the laptop screen in front of her. However far Kashmir might be for Indians and vice versa, the flights to Srinagar were certainly aplenty and often inexpensive. Yes, it was all eminently doable. Upon hanging up, she let herself imagine that next week at this time she would be in Gulmarg with her friends and ... Fayaz.

The next day when she spoke to Fayaz, she could not contain her excitement. While he sounded happy, she could also sense a tinge of resentment in his voice.

'Is anything bothering you?'

'No,' he said, 'not particularly.'

'Tell me,' she insisted.

'Why did you decide on Gulmarg for our get-together? I thought Gulmarg was special, it was ours.'

'Well, it is, isn't it? We're going to be there,' she said.

'Yes, but those two will be there too. It won't be just the two of us. And I won't be able to take you there by myself as I had planned.'

'I hope I am coming to Kashmir again, we can go another time. And maybe before that, you could drop by Delhi someday.'

'Anyway, leave it. I'm really looking forward to seeing you again.'

A week passed by in the wink of an eye. Saima and Rehan counted the days to their next rendezvous, fasted and prayed, sending each other not texts with kisses, but photos of their sehri[36] dates and nuts, their iftaar[37] spreads, their glasses of babritresh.[38] Then, at last, came Eid. The cacophony of traffic queues, decorations, and fireworks outdoors was matched by the joyous eruption of colourful dresses, lavish meals and laughter indoors.

When Shireen landed at the airport the next morning, it was Rehan who was waiting for her. She tried to sound as casual as she could when asking 'Isn't Fayaz here?' No, said Rehan, telling her that he had gone to his village, but would reach Gulmarg later that day. She felt sullen and upset that he had not bothered to let her know that he wouldn't be here. It was an anticlimax to what she had envisioned as the plane had taken off from Delhi that dawn. Spectating upon the capital city that had grown more miniscule with every bit of the ascent upward, she had felt a familiar hope sing in her heart. Now, as she sat in the car beside Rehan, she thought of the plastic rose that Fayaz had given her that wintry day. As if to heighten the poignancy of the moment, she seemed to spot crimson roses bursting over the barbed wires wherever she looked when they made their way through the city and out onto the highway towards Gulmarg.

It was a while before she remembered to wish Rehan 'Eid Mubarak'.

He was chatty in spite of her laconic responses, which he put down to her being tired from having got up so early to take the plane.

When she caught herself repeatedly drifting away from what he was saying, she tried to bring herself back into the present and be attentive.

'The things one does for a girlfriend!' he was joking, referring to the effort he was making to meet Saima.

'Yes,' she said, with an inaudible sigh.

In a couple of hours, they had reached Gulmarg.

The way there had been beautiful, especially once they reached Tangmarg. Rehan drove expertly along the curving roads, emphasizing that he would have been an equally good driver had Fayaz let him drive any part of the route from Leh to Pangong.

As they paid the entry toll into the area and the meadow came into view, some of her gloom lifted.

It was a vast expanse of undulating land, surrounded by breathtaking mountain scenery. Within that fenced green bowl stood a few dainty structures. The red roof of a temple with gable windows and the green sloping roof of a church built from grey stone distinctly announced themselves. Ponies grazed beside little green bridges that arched over gentle rivulets. There was a scattered profusion of flowers: clusters of daisies, poppies and daffodils vied with each other for splendor. What made the scene even more special was the way in which everything inessential had been shoved into the corners, leaving the charming meadow in the exclusive spotlight of the heavens. The hotels were grouped into specific regions, as were the shops and eateries that did brisk business in the bustling main market. On their way to the hotel, they stopped by the market, where Indian tourists, ponies and guides jostled with each other. They went into a small dhaba where an expert fellow furiously chopped onions, tomatoes and chillis behind large aluminium boilers, while another stood by fires emanating from wok cooking-pots, frying gravy for wazwan. Rehan ate a large amount of rice with goshtaba and rogan josh. Shireen had chicken chowmein brought over from the eatery next door. At the sight of her plate, Rehan shook his head in disapproval. 'Batta Djinn,'[39] she replied, cheerfully.

Later, the two of them checked into their rooms to rest before Fayaz and Saima's arrival. The hotel had been arranged by Fayaz. Shireen and Saima were to share one room and the two men would have the adjoining one on the top floor. When alone, Shireen realized that she was indeed sleepy from having an early start. She glanced outside the windows before drawing the curtains close and promptly went to take a nap. Rehan switched on the television next door and got busy on his phone, texting his Khair Mubarak replies to his relatives and friends and asking Saima and Fayaz for updates on their respective journeys.

Fayaz had arrived with a bagful of excuses to explain his delay. He had been preoccupied with the post-Eid family rituals of meeting and greeting people, sending and receiving gifts. There had been an accident on the road, causing delay. His car had developed a minor fault.

When Shireen had opened the door at his knock, she almost failed to recognize him, so different did he look with a beard and new glasses. He had brought her another plastic rose. 'Why? Is it winter without flowers still?' she had asked, miffed at his lack of communication about the travel plans for the day. 'It is always winter in my soul,' he had said, completely bypassing the intent of her question. Shireen did not press further, deciding to let things take their own course. After a while, when he was in the other room with Rehan, her phone had beeped with a message from him. 'Sorry,' it said. Shireen and Fayaz weren't sure if they were the strangers who had met in Ladakh, or the lovers treading over a distance with words on a screen and sounds over the phone. They had known themselves in the past as a couple that might really have been soulfully together in a snowglobe city once. But, what relationship could a batni have with a mujahid when both of them were trapped within their own secret shells and unable to acknowledge each other in the company of even friends?

When Saima came, she brought in trains of excitement and stories to share. Apart from her curiosity about how their lives had been, she had something to show them. Her sister had sent her a large and fancy camera that cost an enormous amount of money. A Canon with a single-digit suffix that could take incredibly crisp pictures of almost everything. As they talked to each other, sharing personal snippets, anecdotes, and news of people they knew, Saima pointed the lens from one to the other, capturing hundreds of digital pictures of the flutter of a lash, the grip of an arm, the way they gestured or looked away in abstraction. Rehan borrowed the gadget from time to time, taking group photos or closeups of patterns on the bedsheet and the grain of wood in the panelled walls.

Gulmarg was outside at their doorstep, but did they care to rush out to it? They sat in a circle in a room, upon the chairs and beds, catching up on their friendship, reminiscing about the past, sharing anticipations of the future, passing packets of chips, interrupting each other to make their points, winking, giving high-fives or rolling their eyes. Shireen and Fayaz were part of this whirlpool, and though the other two thought of them as friends, they knew they had an undercurrent that could only be silently experienced through an odd glance or a word with an exclusive shared meaning.

Hours later, they had all sat around a table with white tablecloth and silver cutlery, taking second and third helpings of the biryani and the four other dishes they had ordered. Not one of them had cared for etiquette as they urged each other to eat, transferring food from one plate to the other, talking of the restaurant as if the waiters could not hear them, laughing as if they were inebriated. Saima fed Rehan with her hand, Fayaz pushed his glass towards Shireen when hers had no water left. They made plans for the next morning when they would go out and embrace all of Gulmarg. They would take a gondola ride, said Fayaz. She would run through the meadow dancing, said Saima. They would stay another night, suggested Rehan. They would go climbing up the hills, stated Shireen.

It was the last time the four would be blissfully laughing together in such a way.

Upstairs, Saima went to Rehan's room. Shireen looked out of the window and saw Fayaz downstairs, waving at her, asking if she would like to go out for a drive. The two of them were alone for the first time together since the winter. In the quiet of the Gulmarg roads at night, Fayaz drove through forests and past the brooks and the army camps that shone a flashlight but didn't bother further. Shireen let loose her long hair and rolled down the window. His eyes were on the road, but Shireen could feel them upon her as he stopped the car by a desolate stretch on the upper reaches by a little green bridge that was black in the darkness. They turned off the lights and let the moon rain silver upon the windscreen.

'His silver orchestra of the skies, those stars beside him,' said Shireen.

'Did you see it yesterday?' he asked.

'The crescent moon of Eid,' she said, without giving a direct answer.

He put his hand upon hers as if to lift it, saying, 'Come, let us go outside.'

They went up to the picturesque little bridge. 'Wait,' he said, and knelt to pick daffodils for her from the clusters flowering beside the water.

The sound of the water was silver too, she thought, before saying it aloud.

He held out the daffodils, five of them, towards her with an outstretched arm, without getting up. When she took them, touching his fingers gently, he pulled her beside him and said, 'See.'

He had filled water from the stream into a gowpen between his cupped hands and angled it so that the moon shivered in its reflection on the surface.

'The restless moon on a miniature lake,' she said, moving closer.

He let the moon slip between his fingers and put his wet palm in hers. She clasped it close.

'Batni,' he said, 'I think I love you.'

'Call me Shireen.' She wasn't sure why she said that, but she wanted him to know everything about her at that moment.

'Shireen, look at me.' His voice was shaking.

When their eyes met, their lips followed. For the briefest of instances, they had both been sure of who they were – two people who might allow themselves to love each other in a world that they had never known.

For a while afterwards, they had sat wordlessly on the wooden edge of the bridge, holding each other.

'Why?' she asked, as they got up to go.

'Because,' he replied, knowing that she would understand.

~

Saima came out of the shower with a towel draped around her body. Rehan held her, inhaling the perfume of her skin that he had missed for so long. They had made love passionately at first, and then languidly, and at last been willing to let go of each other's bodies in the bed.

'No TV tonight,' said Saima, drying her hair.

'Nothing but you tonight,' replied Rehan as he put the kettle on boil to make warm cups of tea for them. As he tore open the pouches of sugar and pulled the lids off the small milk cases, Saima turned towards him from where she was standing in front of the full-length mirror and said, 'Rehan...'

'What?'

'Rehan, you don't think that Fayaz and Shireen are up to something?'

'Up to what?' he said, still busy with the sachets and the cups.

'I mean, it just occurred to me ... what if they ... I mean, what if they become more than friends, you know, fall in love and all that.'

'I hope not,' said Rehan matter-of-factly, stirring the tea in the cups.

By now, Saima was on her back, lying horizontally across the bed, furiously flipping through the photos from the afternoon on the digital screen of her camera. She was counting on the keen eye of the camera lens to give her clues about the possibly restrained feelings of her friends.

'Here,' said Rehan, handing her a cup and stroking the wet nape of her neck.

'What's worrying my darling?' he cooed.

'Rehan, I'm serious. That would be quite something if they quietly withheld it from us!.'

'How is it our business if they don't want to tell us?' he said, straightening up to lean against the headboard.

'Look— No, wait, tell me, why did you say earlier that you hoped there was nothing between them?'

Rehan paused, balancing his thoughts on a knife-edge of rival answers.

'Because Fayaz is married and someone always gets hurt in such cases.'

'What?' cried Saima. 'Why didn't you tell me that? Why didn't you tell her that?'

'Can you be calm for a second?' he said. 'Firstly, I believe in a policy of live and let live. If I'm not asked for an opinion, I don't offer it. Other people's lives, even my friends' is not my business.'

'But—'

'Wait, let me finish. Also, Fayaz is not happily married, from what I know. He doesn't share much, but I know that he and his wife have been having problems for quite a while. Moreover, don't you think Shireen would have asked him that if she was interested in him? And lastly, where do you think they have been for the last few hours? Why should we interfere in what isn't our concern?'

Rehan made sense in a way, but Saima repeated the one thing over and over again, 'She's my friend, Rehan. I know her; she's not very experienced in all this. If she gets involved with a married man, she will suffer.'

'Come on. We are all adults here. She may have her reasons too, like him, to keep her feelings secret,' he said, adding, 'Shama ke jalte dil mein bhi / parvanon ki bekhudi hai ... yun hi rishtey nahin bante / raaton ki tanhaiyon mein.'[40]

The thought crossed his mind that Fayaz had lied to Shireen about living with his nephew and not with his wife. But he had at the time been convinced by the reason his friend had given and there was no need to cause additional complications at the moment by confessing that to Saima now.

Saima was continuing to think aloud: 'On the other hand, Shireen did not tell me about any of this, if indeed something is going on. So how could I have kept her safe from such an involvement...'

'Exactly,' agreed Rehan.

'Not quite. You could at least have told me that he was married. Why did you never mention it to me?'

'There wasn't any occasion to do so. I didn't, and don't, know either if there's anything going on between the two of them,' he stole a quick look at the clock on the wall and added, 'though, at this point, I am tempted to think that something might be afoot since they are not back yet.'

'So what do we do now? Call them?'

'Are you crazy? They're the ones who either want to be left alone, or need their respective rooms. Either way, they ought to call us. We don't need to do anything except turn the lights off, lie in each other's arms and tell each other about our missings over the weeks and months.' Saying this, he softened his voice and blinked slowly, drawing her in.

She snuggled up to him, 'You might be right. I'll try not to worry. But if he does anything to hurt her, I'll never see his face or speak to him again.'

'Now can we be *us* once again?' He kissed her forehead and then, turning off the lights, sucked at the sides of her neck as she bit his ears, moaning, 'I missed you!'

They had fallen asleep when Shireen and Fayaz came up the stairs and went into the other room together. Neither told anyone else what transpired between them that night. Was it pleasure or bloody pain? Did they unseal their lips and let it all out, sparing no secrets from each other? Or had they receded into their furthest selves, separated by the chasm of darkness between their bodies?

Saima and Rehan continued to maintain their different views on this. Shireen must have wept, said Saima. He did not pretend to care for her anymore once he had prised open the secrets of her body. Nothing must have happened between the two, said Rehan. One of them had probably refused the other, and the rest had been plain to see.

Morning brought the curse of inclement weather. Rain lashed against the windowpanes with its unrelenting beat. The four of them had breakfast together. It was a drab affair, marred by long silent internal monologues that weighed heavy on each of them. They discussed the provision of windcheaters, umbrellas and the checkout timings between hurried mouthfuls of buttered toast dipped in runny egg yolk, gulped down with strong cups of tea.

Saima and Rehan were decidedly unsure about how to react to Shireen and Fayaz, and their discomfort bounced back off their quieter friends with an amplified magnitude. Saima tried to disguise her feeling of being nonplussed with bouts of pointless chatter, but there weren't many takers. Shireen said she didn't feel restored by her sleep but still expressed hopes of ascending a hill. Fayaz mentioned that a gondola ride in such weather was not only inadvisable but also impossible since the service would have been shut down. Rehan wanted the sun to come out, positive that the sunshine would liven everything up.

But, light, alas was nowhere to be found. They waited in their rooms for the merest glimpse of sunshine, ultimately extending their checkout and having a meal delivered upstairs. Outside the windows, they saw Indian tourists braving the weather in soggy wet jackets covered with plastic sheets as they sat atop ponies that slowly plodded along the dirt tracks led by the local men. It was a dismal sight. When the rain abated, they decided to go on a drive. Fayaz insisted that his car would fare better since it was a 4x4 and bigger than Rehan's. On their way out, the manager jovially remarked that they were having a taste of the English weather in Gulmarg.

Saima sat in the front seat beside Fayaz since she was enthusiastic about taking pictures from the window. Shireen and Rehan silently looked out at the misty scenes beneath the overcast skies. Here were the saddled horses resting underneath the trees on the periphery, there was a raven perched philosophically at the tip of a green gazebo ceiling. At one turning on the long road that circumnavigated the meadow, they passed by a man wearing a loose check-pattern pheran and blue sports shoes, who sold boiled eggs and coconut slices underneath an enormous multicoloured umbrella. Saima took several pictures of the contrasting colours and Shireen thought that she might sketch such a scene someday. As they passed one of the little green bridges, Shireen asked if they could stop there for a while. She wasn't sure if it was the same bridge from last night, but it was a reasonably similar location and she wanted to revisit it. Fayaz instantly parked the car to one side and they all got out.

The valley was unfurled wet green in front of them. Saima handed Rehan the camera and excitedly ran ahead for a few steps, twirling around. As the two of them took pictures of each other, Fayaz told Shireen that there was an echo at this location. He cupped his mouth and shouted 'Fayaz' loudly in order to demonstrate. True enough, 'Fayaz ... Fayaz ... yaz ... az ...' reiterated the mountains. Rehan too climbed a small rock above the bridge and shouted 'Saima!' first, and then 'Shireen'. 'Saima ... aima ... Shireen ... reen ... een ... een,' the sounds fell back in a confused jumble. Saima hoisted herself on the same rock with Rehan's help and burst her lungs with 'Gulmarg! Gulmarg! Gulmarg!', not giving the echo enough time to be clearly repeated. Rehan chided her for her impatience as she came down into his embrace. Shireen was eyeing the gentle sloping ascent of the hill behind them. She too wanted to scream. She knew what she would have wanted to hear echoed: 'Kashmir'. Kashmir, in its many sounds and spellings and accents. Kashmir, she wanted to proclaim with all her might, and hear it over and over again. She did not know why she felt unable to do so. The word rolled back on her tongue, subject to a peculiar linguistics of repressed emotion. She looked at the three of them sounding out the names and she just couldn't bring herself to shout the one word that was in her heart and mind and soul. Somehow, the word formed a shadow inside her and quietly slunk in a corner, unable to be forgotten, impossible to utter.

The others were too preoccupied to notice that she hadn't said anything. They were telling each other things about the place and the weather. Saima's camera was being passed around as they marvelled at the scenes, discussing how a particular picture would look on a Facebook profile. Shireen called out to Saima, saying that she was going to climb the hill. 'Go ahead, jigar,' she replied, 'I'll be here, prancing for the pictures.' Rehan waved at her and Fayaz looked at her uncertainly, wondering what she had in mind. She wished she could say to Fayaz, 'Come, let us walk this incline together, let us go to the very top where the forests begin; it's not that far. We can make it side by side. It will be a struggle but the dreamy view at the end will be worth it.' But she didn't say anything. Going up step by step, she realized that the summit of the hill was farther than it looked and it would probably take her a quarter of an hour to get there. The grassy earth was wet all around her feet; the only vegetation was at the top, where the forests began. Lost in her thoughts, looking down one moment, looking ahead and up the next, she managed to get as far as possible. Then, she could not go on any more. There were brambly bushes and the ground was strewn with sharp pointed branches and fallen tree trunks. To one side was a collapsed roof of curving terracota tiles from a burned-down structure that had once stood there. She finally turned around. The scene she surveyed was beyond words in its melancholic symphony of undulating green and grey. In the distance, islands of mist drifted between the pines on the mountains. A bus plied on a far road beyond the roofs. Down below were three figures near a green wooden bridge. Saima was taking pictures of Rehan who, Shireen narrowed her eyes to perceive, was smoking now. Fayaz was oblivious to everything around him. His head was bent to the ground and he was speaking on his phone, pacing up and down a green carpeted patch of earth as if it were an office corridor. She couldn't know it, but it had been Zeenat on the phone. She continued to look, zooming on him alone, hoping that he might lift his head and see her here. It must have been a minute before she thought to herself that telepathy was nonsense and began her slow descent downwards. Feeling spent and dejected, she saw a crushed daffodil on the ground. Who had left it here, stemless and forlorn? She unfastened the velcro straps of her sandals and went barefoot, holding her shoes in her hand, walking with a stamping gait that betrayed her sour mood.

The wet blades of grass and small leafy weeds touched the soles of her feet. It was a crenulated sensation that carried her into the folds of her memory. She had felt this uneven and irregular caress against her skin in her fingertips as a child touching her grandmother's serrated gold earrings and in her hands when stroking the chinar leaves carved into a wooden board. She was simultaneously in many places as she reached the bridge but she felt she was certainly not in Gulmarg, not with the people in front of her.

'How was it?' asked Saima, referring to her climb.

Before she could answer, Rehan looked at her wet feet on the mulch and said, 'You're walking barefoot?'

Fayaz, who had finished his phone conversation by now, came up to where they were and hearing Rehan's remark, shook his head, saying, 'You're not from Kashmir, are you?'

'Sorry? What?' She turned to him.

Fayaz chuckled and said, 'You can't be Kashmiri, walking around on the wet ground like that.'

That was all. Fayaz didn't think he had said anything significant or profound, but Shireen's reaction left everyone floundering.

'No, I am not,' she said emphatically. 'How could I be? I could not possibly be Kashmiri, could I? You would know, Fayaz, having driven me out, my people out. I could be born here and my parents could have died here, and it could be all I ever yearned for, but you, with your militant mind can decide for me whether I am Kashmiri or not. No, I am not, I am a Kashmiri Pandit, a batni. We come from the stock of spies and Indians, don't you know? Yes, you do know. How could I be Kashmiri? I am a Palestinian, probably. No, wait! You think *you* are Palestinians, or is it Israelis? Are you Palestinians or Israelis then? My grandmother was not a Kashmiri either; we just lived and died here. You are the real Kashmiris. You have Kashmir now. Why ever did you ask me to come here? I am not Kashmiri, of course, I am not Kashmiri. I have no home. You have a place to call home. I have nothing, not even Kashmir. I have nothing. Kashmir is not mine. I am not Kashmiri.'

Tears were flowing down her face and dripping on to the black frock that she wore over black jeans. She was repeating herself, sobbing hysterically, unable to make sense of her anger, her reaction or the words that were flying out of her mouth as if a catch had been released, a dam had burst.

Saima stepped forward and put her arms around Shireen's shoulder, telling her to stop crying, to gather herself. Rehan was explaining that Fayaz was only joking, he didn't mean anything by his statement. Fayaz was looking at her, his stare fixed on a crumbling Shireen, glowering with rage. He did not utter a single word. He was the first one to return to the car, slamming the door behind him.

Shortly afterwards, Rehan fetched a bottle of water from the car for Shireen. Fayaz sat stony-faced. Saima held Shireen as they walked back to the car. Rehan took the wheel and Saima sat with Shireen in the back, holding her hand, patting her head, rubbing her shoulders, saying, 'I love you, jigar. Please try to be calm.' Shireen could not stop weeping as her eyes met Saima's. She felt terribly guilty now and wanted not to know that she was here or that any of this had been real. She had no idea why she had reacted like that, but it was a million things, it was everything that she knew and could feel. Fayaz? How could Fayaz not see how she would feel at those words? Fayaz of all people, the Fayaz who had said 'From a Kashmiri to a Kashmiri' to her in Ladakh, the Fayaz who had sung for her, the Fayaz who had made it possible for her to dream again. And what of Kashmir? What good did knowing about its history do? There was the badaamwaari festival and its twelve days of singing and dancing common to Hindus and Muslims. There were once the bonfires that were radiantly lit in spring across the Valley by its people. The other name of Pari Mahal was Koont-Lyun. The migratory birds came to Khunhalsar near the old town. Pindych came from Siberia. The legend of the Krael Sagar, the zoonthkol, the kuttukol, the Zero Bridge. Nothing mattered. How could it? There were people, different people, some were spies and officers and rulers, others were the potters and the peasants. Guns were all that mattered. Their guns, our guns, their flags, our flags. All statements had become worthy of suspicion, and the truth had shifted around everyone. But what of her and Fayaz? The batni and the mujahid? How they had chosen their names, as if rehearsing a past, foreshadowing a future! And still, and still. She had been cruel to him. She had used the word 'militant', knowing that his father had been one. She had said his people had driven her people out. As if they were all on a chessboard. How could she have said all that? Chess was for cruel people. The two of them had wanted to be people of love, people who were people before anything else. Her head was spinning and she broke into another round of sobs. This time, when she lifted her head, she wiped her tears and looking at Fayaz who sat diagonally across from her in the front seat, said, 'Fayaz, I'm sorry.' He did not reply.

Sensing an opening in the tension, Rehan stopped the car close to the meadow and said, 'Let us go out and breathe the fresh air for a bit. Let us not stay angry at each other.' Saima seconded him immediately.

Shireen got out, feeling her legs weak under her.

Fayaz refused to leave the car.

After taking a few steps together, Shireen said to Saima, 'I'm sorry, I don't know what happened to me. It was as if something ancient was triggered in me, something that wasn't even all mine.'

'It's alright,' she replied, holding her hand. 'I know you didn't mean to be like that. But you should understand that it really was a joke; he didn't intend to hurt you, I am sure.' As she said this, the conversation with Rehan the previous night surfaced in Saima's head. She didn't know whether Shireen was aware of his being married. In any case, this was not the moment to trouble her further.

Walking along, the two of them came upon the church.

'I want to go in,' said Shireen, decisively.

'The gate is locked,' replied Saima.

'I want to go in,' persisted Shireen. At the same instance, she gripped the metal frame of the gate and started to climb up, placing her feet on the narrow horizontal ledge spaces between the metal bars. It looked to be a risky venture in the slippery wet weather, but Shireen put one leg over the spikes at the top and hoisted herself to the other side and then jumped down. She was being a crazy child who could not be reasoned with. Saima followed suit. When they were inside the fence, they made their way to the main door, which was locked too.

'We can't break in!' said Saima, humorously warning her friend.

'Of course not. I am going to pick a flower from here, turn off that tap running full in the yard there. It must have wasted gallons of water by now. Then, we will go back to the car and I will sanely apologize and we will all be better again.'

She spoke like a programmed toy. Saima knew that her friend was battling her emotions and trying to create peace inside herself.

Shireen picked a daffodil. 'I will give it to Fayaz,' she said, once they were back over the gate.

'That's wonderful, dear. But please don't take it to heart if he rejects it,' Saima cautioned wisely.

In the car, Rehan had been trying to make Fayaz see why Shireen had blown up. He also hinted that Fayaz had been insensitive in not realizing the import of his words. 'She's Hindu. Their history and their memory isn't the same as ours. Plus, she's a woman. They are sensitive creatures, you know. You can't joke with them like that. Not on such topics anyway.'

Then he lit a cigarette for Fayaz and took a puff before passing it to his friend in their customary manner.

Fayaz felt an agitation inside that he could not explain to anyone, not even to Rehan. He decided to mask it for now with tact and sustained silence.

When Shireen and Saima settled back into their seats, Shireen leaned over and held out the daffodil for Fayaz. To everyone's surprise, he took it. What is more, he reached out his hand for hers across the seats and pressed it gently. He didn't say anything in words, but his eyes were eloquent.

Saima and Rehan wished they weren't there so their friends could open up and communicate. Rehan suggested that since they had two cars anyway, why didn't Fayaz and Shireen drop them at the hotel and return to Srinagar in Fayaz's car? To stem any potential refusals, Saima coyly added that the two of them would like to stay here another night. Shireen and Fayaz knew that they were being set up for a reconciliation but since there were two cars, the plan did make sense.

Half an hour later, Shireen was sitting beside Fayaz as they started the drive back to Srinagar. Perhaps both of them were waiting for the other to speak first or maybe they wanted to remain boxed in their selves. In any case, much of the journey was wordless. As they wound down the roads in Tangmarg, Shireen felt condemned to recognize the pathos of their real Gulmarg trip. Maybe Fayaz had been right. She ought to have saved Gulmarg for a time when he could have taken her there. At last, she spoke, and when she did, she realized that she was still stuck in the moment of her breakdown. 'Fayaz, if two people, if you and I, who care for each other, cannot get past these things ...' she hesitated, '... these histories of ours, then what hope is there for anyone, for anything, for Kashmir?'

He did not reply. All his words were hardening inside the flames that consumed him. He was beset by an anger that convulsed his being.

He could have said so much, he thought. But, he forced himself to stay quiet.

When he responded, he merely said, 'It was a mistake. I'm sorry too.'

At his words, she could feel herself sliding down an immense spiral caracole stairway, while simultaneously standing at the bottom of it, watching herself unstoppably slide down that structure shaped like a shell.

He was not prepared to let it go. She was not prepared to let go.

The wretched impasse could not be wished away.

Except ... except it could be, if they tried hard enough.

She realized that she may never hear him sing again. That she had never shown him her sketches. That she would never be able to lovingly refer to him as her mujahid. That Kashmir had divided them.

He felt chained to his self, unable to be the person that he could have tried to be in that moment. His emotions towards her, which had arisen unbidden and afforded him a feeling of being unshackled for the first time in his life, had shrivelled back into the cold deserts of his frustrated core. Kashmir was not a place for dreamers.

As they neared Srinagar, she asked if they could stop by at a cafe before he dropped her at her hotel. The weather here was clear and pleasant. He agreed. Sitting in the lawns of a cafe, she ordered a coffee and a cake, he asked for a cup of tea and a glass of water.

He cast a glance around at the others there, reassuring himself that no one he knew was around. She drew a smiley on a paper napkin and slid it towards him on the granite tabletop. He folded it and kept it in his pocket, giving her a smile for the first time since the previous day. An angel of tenderness sprinkled silvery dust over their heads and for a few moments it seemed as if they might recover themselves, their previous selves.

Without any context, he suddenly asked her if she had remembered to pick the plastic rose he had given her yesterday.

'Yes, that and the five daffodils too. Don't forget the daffodil I gave you that's in the car, okay?'

She spoke softly. The afternoon had made them angry at each other, but they were gentler now that they were about to part.

He wanted to gather himself, she wanted them to forgive each other everything of the past and the present, for the love of a future.

Her hotel was across the road from the cafe. It was getting to be late evening when they crossed the street together. He quickly brushed his hand against hers, saying, 'Goodbye.'

'Goodbye, Fayaz ... I think reflections can kiss,' she said, answering the question he had asked her when they had leant over the balustrade at Char Chinar on a wintry afternoon.

'Let them kiss each other in our eyes, then,' he said. 'A lake of our reflections for you.'

She sensed a sorrow in his words. Their parting felt incomplete, but she consoled herself with the thought that she was here for a while and they could always speak over the phone. If anything, they had been more devoted to each other in the disembodied voice and the written word.

He crossed back to where his car was parked. At the wheel, he looked impatient, delayed by the toll attendant who was being tardy. Then, from up the road came a flock of bleating rams and sheep. The gujjar shepherds were known to drive their flock across that thoroughfare, causing chaos on the road for a few minutes. The people on the street were used to it and were threading their way through the herd, honking and navigating carefully. Shireen wanted to run across the road again; she wanted to look into his eyes and say, 'You are Mujahida, I am Batni, and we can be Kashmiris who are equal and who are allowed to love, in spite of everything that we have been told in our lives and everything that we have inherited from our histories.' Shireen took a step forward, but was thwarted by the animals that blocked every inch of the road. Fayaz waved at her and started out.

That night, Fayaz had a bizarre dream.

~

They were two large stones that guarded the entrance to his kingdom. One on either side, the huge bulk of these stones seemed like a couple of squares framing the skies. They were actually two large black books in stone, and within every stone page of these books, there are stone words and each of these stone words is in a language unknown to anyone but him. He has spent nearly half of his life mastering the language of the stones.

Once inside the threshold of the kingdom, he is an old man of history and logic. There is nothing in the kingdom that bends or adapts. It is full of truth-like things – rigid, hard and painful to rub against. Everything inside is along the lines of the jagged edges of splintered raw wood. There is nothing fluid here.

His head is full of love for this kingdom that was handed to him by his father and brother, and to them by their elders. It is a wise kingdom and especially rare for its honesty. Love here is expressed in the rhythms of clocks, feelings are marked on large maps that can engulf an army or two. It is an orderly kingdom where it is forbidden to be cryptic or figurative; everything must always be spelt out fully and completely. And then whenever anyone finishes speaking, an animal pops out of thin air (a bird, a cat or a rabbit, sometimes a tiger or, on rare occasions, a snake) and immediately starts to spell out in great and painstaking detail the consequences of what has just been said by the human. Every human has their own animal that comes up from nowhere to spell out consequences every time they speak.

In the absence of humans, these consequence-detailing animals find it hard to interact amongst themselves, because the interacting animals just spell out the consequences of consequences. Thus, it is not advisable for, say, a cat and a squirrel to entangle themselves verbally into each other's consequences to produce an endless chain of meaningful yet incomprehensible analytics.

Every once in a while it rains in the kingdom. This is a most trying experience because rain brings fluidity and change, the wood becomes soggy, the clocks start to rust and the maps begin to dissolve. Around the time of the rain, the humans also suffer terribly, for they cannot speak to each other or convey anything because the animals play truant when it rains. They hesitate to do their work or don't appear at all. Under such conditions, speech is pointless as no human understands anything unless the animals pop up to spell out the consequences of what has just been said. People look at each other when it rains in the kingdom and wonder whether they should risk speaking.

At such times, he goes up to the gates and re-memorizes the stone words in the large stone books in a language unknown to anyone but him. When he thinks inwardly, the animal consequence-detailer, in his case a mynah bird, is not required.

He sometimes wonders what would happen if the kingdom was invaded. How would he deal with an onslaught of strangeness in the form of mirrors and smoke and fire and cloud? What if the vanishing animals rebelled? What if the rain never stopped? The people would then never be able to understand each other, ever. What if the animals were bribed into purposely detailing the wrong consequences of every speech? He shuddered and looked up at the skies. Such things were not to be contemplated.

He would not forgive himself any disaster if he could not stop it. He must keep intact this rule of order and sanity in his kingdom. The kingdom must be protected from the mirrors and smoke and fire and cloud, and the animals must never deliberately misinterpret anything.

As he was pacing up and down by the stones, the mynah sprung up from nowhere, eagerly interpreting the consequences of his speech. He realized with terror that he might have been speaking aloud while being caught up in his thoughts. The animal listed all the consequences of his words and then looked up, keen to lap up more of the verbal soup. A bead of perspiration rolled off his forehead and deposited itself on a shingly wood surface that dampened just one bit, the clock slowed down for a second while the map rolled over in curiosity.

~

When he awoke from this absurd dream, he was covered in sweat. Upon waking, he became aware that his parting with Shireen today had been final.

That night, the Internet became unreliable. Relaying phone messages between landlines got tough too. In their hands, people held small plastic boxes that were phones once. Now, they became little toys that could neither make nor receive calls. The phone and Internet services were shut off. Curfew was being enforced over the Valley.

The hotel manager told Shireen that the situation in Kashmir was fast deteriorating, by which he meant that civilians and protestors were being killed and security forces were being attacked. He also told her that a Mr Fayaz had arranged for her flight the next day and she should grab the opportunity and make haste to leave, unless she wanted to remain stuck here for an indefinite amount of time.

Burhan Wani[41] had been killed.

The young militant who had inspired a generation online had been gunned down by the Indian forces. Shivers ran down people's spines, young and old; men and women wept and spilled out on to the streets in a spontaneous outburst of sorrow. Shireen caught some of this on the news before she left.

The next day, Shireen was on the plane, feeling like a zombie, surrounded by people who chattered excitedly as they exchanged the news on what was happening. An earthquake had shattered her being. She did not feel the pain of the people she was leaving behind; she was not beating her chest in desperate anguish, facing the guns.

She searched her thoughts again, but there truly was no way she could emotionally hear the news of the killing, except as the tragedy of a young man who had been killed extrajudicially while fighting for his beliefs. What did it mean to be Kashmiri in the present? What did it mean to be Kashmiri in the past? Was the tale of Kashmir from the past to the present basically one of the continuous attrition of shared allusions, shared emotions, shared love and shared hate? And was the question she had been searching for about the past really going to be a question about the future: What would it mean to be Kashmiri in the future?

She was thinking about these questions when the elderly woman sitting next to her addressed Shireen.

She was Indian and appeared to be affluent. She was lamenting the state of the Valley.

'I have been coming here over the years,' she said. 'I have many friends here. These Kashmiris are very nice people, but they never liked India. It's Burhan Wani today, something else tomorrow.'

Shireen reflected on how Indians used the word 'Kashmiris' to refer to Hindus or Muslims depending on what they were saying.

As if divining her thoughts, the woman clarified, 'Kashmiri Muslims, of course. They've never been loyal to us, regardless of what we do for them.'

'Why do you say that?' Shireen asked, trying to think of a way of avoiding a protracted discussion.

'I'll tell you. You're too young to know all this. Our family does well, business-wise. We have visited many elite households here in the past. As a child, once I was playing with a child of one of the relatives of Sheikh Abdullah. We were in their garden. Then, the small boy, he was about the same age as me, invited me indoors and started to show me their photo albums...'

The woman picked up a glass of water from the tray held out by the airline steward. After taking a sip, she continued, 'You won't believe it, but in that entire album – which had pictures of many historical figures, since these were important people – in every picture, they used to be black and white in those days, the eyes of Nehru and other Indians had been poked out.'

Shireen uttered the one word: 'Strange'.

The woman continued to speak for a long time afterwards, changing topics, but stopping only when the plane landed in Delhi.

Shireen could not erase from her mind the image of the black-and-white pictures with the selectively poked-out eyes. Little did she know that in the weeks and months that followed that fateful Friday, the eyes of so many real living Kashmiris would be blinded by the pellets fired at them.

Part Three

What Comes Next

10

LATE AFTERNOON ON a sultry autumn day, the bus to Goa rolled out of the ISBT[42] station near Kashmere Gate in Delhi.

At the back of the bus sat three Kashmiri young men, or rather, two men and a boy with a crutch and a wooden leg. Imran asked Rafiq why the area was called 'Kashmere Gate' and was told that one of the Mughal emperors in the past had made a road that led to Kashmir from here. Everything always came back to the Mughals, the ones who made this country, and whom this country was trying its best to forget. Imran thought it was a strange name for a crowded place which had nary a mountain nor a stream in sight. How could places like this be called Kashmiri? On the other hand, the historical stone arch of a gate they had passed did remind him of the stone archway near the Pathar Saheb Gurudwara in Srinagar.

After a lot of deliberation with Rafiq and Bichor in their downtown basement hideout, Imran had decided to join their 'scheme' of doing something spectacular in order to exact revenge for what the Valley had seen during the summer of 2016. It was really Rafiq's scheme, and the other two had been led by his vision to become accomplices.

Rafiq and Bichor had become Imran's closest friends over the last few months. He had never brought them to Gul's home, nor had he mentioned his association with them to anyone, not even to Ifra. It was better that way. The three had developed a bond based on their unwillingness to adopt a stance of resignation in the face of what was happening around them. They were indignant and wanted to do something which did not follow the usual route of running away to join the fighters, train in using weapons, live in the jungle and be caught and killed within the maximum seven-year lifespan of an average Kashmiri militant.

Rafiq was a Class X dropout. He was caustic in his disdain for education, a system that produced dummies to serve the occupation, as he said. 'You tell me, if you are in school or college, do you get time to care about our struggle? Don't the parents who pay your fees want to see a return in terms of you getting a job? And what job are you going to get in a place like Kashmir unless you keep your head down and follow the rules? And who makes the rules, ultimately? Delhi? And who's our enemy? Delhi.' His logic was hard to reason with. It was true that all the dreams offered by education were cut to the size of an individual, not meant for the liberation of a society. How could a society break through its chains if it spent all its time learning how to make and fit those same chains on people around them? 'Once we have our freedom, we will know how to educate ourselves,' he would say, and sombrely add, 'But before that some upheavals need to happen. People need to see that Kashmiri puppets controlled by India cost us our lives.'

Rafiq had approached Imran that spring in a cafe where he was sitting with his friends. Rafiq hung around there and seemed to know the waiters well. Later, Imran had come to know that Rafiq had once worked there. In fact, he had apparently tried his hand at numerous professions and left them one by one. Somehow, Rafiq had sensed Imran's lack of ease with the posh college crowd and addressed him when he had gone out for a solitary cigarette. 'They're not your kind, brother,' he had stated. Imran had been taken aback and asked him what he meant. Their very first conversation had led to an exchange of phone numbers and an uncovering of mutually shared feelings of resentment and helplessness about the state of Kashmir and its people. 'You and I are not like them,' Rafiq had reminded Imran several times afterwards. 'We are not dead from selfishness inside; we have a fire and it will burn.' His zeal had reminded Imran of his friends from the village, except that Rafiq was more articulate and clearer with his vision of what he wanted to achieve.

He had invited Imran to play cricket with him and some others he knew. Although the same age as him, Rafiq made Imran feel that he needed to learn much from his friend. He noticed how many of Rafiq's friends hero-worshipped him. These cricket sessions were followed by long chats outdoors and then more intense political conversations in a basement that Rafiq had the exclusive use of. He had a home in the city with his cousin brother, but usually hung about in the run-down area by the graves, playing cricket overground and planning schemes underground.

When Rafiq's other friends would all leave, he would invite Imran and Bichor to have tea and break bread with him in his hideout. Bichor was the closest to Rafiq and gave one the impression that he would follow Rafiq off the edge of a cliff if needed. Bichor's real name was Mehraj, but no one ever called him that. As per his nickname, he was simply referred to as Bichor, the poor, the helpless, the unblessed. Bichor would place his crutch to one side and sit on a rock beside the wire fence to watch them play cricket, clapping enthusiastically every time a batsman scored well, especially if it was Rafiq. Many a time, Imran had felt sorry for Bichor, the disabled teenager who could neither run nor play; but as he had befriended the fellow, he had realized that Bichor's ability to laugh and joke and share in other people's dreams, merited not pity but applause. Back down in the basement, Bichor would be the one cheering them up with salacious jokes and an irreverent manner.

Right then, Bichor was snoring gently on the overnight bus to Goa, his head resting on Imran's shoulder. Rafiq was fiddling with his phone, changing sim cards, trying to find the one he needed from a small plastic box where they jiggled like mint-drops. Imran was not sleepy, thinking of how Uncle Fayaz and Uncle Gul's family all imagined him in Pahalgam at the time. After agreeing to accompany Rafiq on his mission, Imran had been required to be inventive with a catalogue of lies that involved spinning tales about going trekking for a few days with his friends to Pahalgam so that he could get permission to be away as well as cadge a few thousand rupees from his parents.

Of the three of them, Imran had the toughest time trying to persuade his parents and guardians to allow him to go away for a few days. He had to convince them that this was a rare opportunity to go trekking and network with the sons of 'important people'. He assured them that there were no girls involved in any part of this trip. He made them feel sorry for all those days when he had been indoors in a curfewed city and reminded them of how the heavenly environs of Pahalgam would lift his spirits. For good measure, he had also added that he would visit and pray for everyone's well-being at every shrine they passed along the way. The prospect of networking with the right kind of people – who could pull a string or two, or who could make a job interview possible – is what seemed to have finally swayed the decision in his favour.

In contrast, Bichor didn't need to say much; just that he was going with Rafiq to the latter's village for a few days. His parents had accepted that Rafiq – who occasionally helped them financially – had taken their son under his wing. Bichor's family was desperately poor. His eldest brother had been a victim of enforced disappearance seventeen years ago. The last anyone knew of his whereabouts was that he had been near a baker's shop in Batamaloo. After that had followed years of searching, writing of letters and filing of police complaints, but neither the young man nor his body had ever been found. This was not unusual in those times; tens of thousands of young men had vanished from the Valley. When she could, Bichor's mother too joined the families of the disappeared as they held their vigil every month in the city, holding the photographs of their dead sons, asking the same question over and over again: 'India, where is my son?' Bichor's second eldest brother had joined a mosque as an attendant and rarely came home. His elder sister had been married at a young age and lived with her farmer husband far from the city. In a mud-walled room with bedsheets for curtains, his mother tailored clothes to eke out a living. His father was employed as a casual labourer in the role of a gardener in one of the city's forgotten and ill-maintained archaeological monuments. The case for the regularization of his employment had been in court since the late 1990s with no end in sight. The number of days in his yearly employment had been reduced to two hundred and forty under an illogical rule that disproportionately affected the poor Muslims of the Valley. It is true that he didn't have to do much work, but on the other hand, he was paid his salary irregularly too. The old man now often spent his days counting his prayer beads. When anyone asked him about the state of affairs concerning his job or his pay, he replied with the acerbic taunt, 'Hindustan ka kanoon, Hindustan ko mubarak' – Let India be blessed with its Indian laws!

When Rafiq had sorted out his phone, Imran asked him to lend a hotspot Internet connection. The journey was long and Imran was wrestling with a confused mass of sensations. Rafiq gave him the password and also sent along the links to a couple of YouTube videos of Gaza and Syria. Imran fished out his battered headphones and plugged in. The Internet speed was good. As he saw the bombs dropping on the cities, the screaming women, the dead children in the rubble, he realized that around him in the overnight bus were people heading for a holiday by the coast, oblivious to any of these concerns. Outside the tinted windows of the speeding night bus, glinted the steady procession of passing neon lights and signs. How different all these worlds were! An Indian newspaper lay beside another passenger; its headlines could not be farther from Kashmir. Here in India, the Internet worked, the phones worked, people were not curfewed and pellets were never fired to blind young men. The miserable thought re-entered his head that no matter what happened to people like him in the Valley, the world here would hardly know or care. This thought had been the main reason why he had been persuaded that Rafiq's scheme could change the game.

Rafiq had explained to him the futility of going on doing what had been done before. It didn't matter how many stones were pelted, how many constables were targeted with grenades; the Indians would bring out more bullets, pellets and soon, probably their drones. The Indian media controlled the narrative; the Indians only heard of the Kashmiris being a nuisance, protesting and being killed. Rafiq dreamed big. He didn't want to be one of the men who crossed the border and sold their souls to Pakistanis, who in turn used the disgruntled men to serve their own ends against Indians. He wanted to create a ripple, a big event that would upset the Indians and teach the Kashmiri collaborators a lesson. He had in mind carrying out a string of political assassinations. This obviously needed a lot of planning. In response to Imran's queries, he said that he worked with a militant cell that had been trying to actualize this for many years now. He had built contacts among Kashmiris in the Valley and elsewhere, and now it was a question of arranging the funding before moving on to the later stages. When Bichor got impatient with the wait, Rafiq would pat him on the back and say, it will take some time, but it will be done, Inshallah.

'Why Goa?' Imran had asked. Goa, because it is where a lot of unchannelled money lies. The Russians, the Nigerians, the Indians, everyone had made their way through the shady dealings behind the beautiful postcard pictures of the beaches and the partying lanes. Some of it was drugs, but it wasn't just the drug money, he said. There are discontented Bangladeshi men in Goa, there are prosperous Kashmiri businessmen in Goa, the trio would find a way to money there. Acquiring the chemicals and the nails and weapons was easy. He knew boys who could arrange that back home. What was tough was to create untraceable trails in Kashmir where people's loyalties were being bought and sold by all sides every other week. He needed to meet a few people in Goa. Imran and Bichor being with him would give the impression of a vacation in case anyone was prying.

Imran and Bichor did have clean records. Neither had been arrested before. Bichor, in fact, had been hit in his leg during the 2010 protests, but he had not been taken to a hospital so that he could be saved from criminalization. His elder brother had asked a medical student to treat him at his home, visiting from the mosque to bring supplies whenever he could. Bichor had lain on a bed in excruciating pain, drained and drugged for months on end. The devout intern had tried his best, but the boy had lost his leg. Nobody ever expressed a regret about him not being rushed to a hospital after the injury. Even if his limb was saved, he would have spent the years afterwards being taken in and out of prisons, framed on false charges or forced to turn into an informer.

Imran was the cleanest of them all. He went to college, had an uncle in state service and lived in the home of a policeman. He could be charming and polite, knew how to interact with those ranked above him, and had relatively unfettered access to at least one police station and potentially a CRPF office next door. Imran had seen young boys his age drip despair as they sat on the rusted metal rafters under the bridges on the Jhelum, their heads hung low in a drugged daze, manically watching the piles of rubbish float by. Imran didn't want to be one of those men; he didn't want to be like the shiny people of the cafes either. He liked the combination of defiant resistance and spirited dreams that Rafiq offered him.

Rafiq and Imran had something else in common. They had both been witness to the mind-bending cynicism of those serving the state as its tools. Rafiq's elder brother was a driver for the politicians. He had worked for fifteen years, driving the politicians to and fro, ferrying their visitors and relatives. He was a peculiar man who spoke little and always wore a deerstalker cap. He had never married either. He spent all his days in the driving seat of a bulletproof jeep with a small CCTV camera pinned to its rear-view mirror. Over the years, he had been assigned to various politicians, of one party and then the other. What he had observed was that it was all rotten, completely rotten. This kernel of his wisdom he had managed to convey to his younger cousin, who had then taken it away and created his own schemes for revenge around that incontrovertible reality. In Gul's household, Imran too had been privy to many overheard exchanges about Kashmir between the policeman and his many friends and acquaintances. These conversations regarding the goings-on in Kashmir were replete with gallows humour. Imran observed a kind of laughably absurd submission to long-term irrationality for the sake of petty short-run benefits.

The three of them reached Goa the next afternoon. Imran felt exhausted and was confounded by the sight of a place that was utterly alien. At his first sight of the sea, he felt trepidation instead of excitement. He was overcome with a feeling of missing home, which hit him like a huge wave. He began to wonder what he was doing here. Bichor said he was drained and hungry. Rafiq chided them for being weaklings and confidently led them to the room where they would all be staying. It was a forlorn and cramped space with a barred window and three charpoys laid out in a row. The small building had a carpentry workroom on the ground floor and a stairway around the side that led up to their accommodation. Soon after they sat down, Rafiq instructed them to turn off their phones. If they needed to contact anyone, they could use a SIM from his phone. They followed his instructions and then the three had a meal in a cheap and dingy eatery nearby, where a bulky woman served them large portions of overcooked rice and spicy beef stew.

'Tomorrow, I get busy,' announced Rafiq. 'You come with me wherever possible, but there are people I need to meet alone.' They nodded. Imran was pondering how he might go out separately to buy a proper meal with his own money – something tasty, with juicy bits of meat.

That night, they went to a beach in the main touristy area. Rafiq pointed out the shops run by Kashmiris here and there, pointing out that for all the hysteria in Hindu India, Pandits weren't the only people to be driven out of Kashmir. 'These Kashmiri men, so many Muslims like us, had to flee Kashmir in the 1990s too. They went everywhere.'

Bichor was trying his best to keep up with the other two and, when they slowed down to wait for him, the numerous peddlers of toys and souvenirs pestered them. Rafiq brushed them aside authoritatively in a way that made Imran wonder how his friend had matured beyond his years. Notwithstanding his education, in front of Rafiq, Imran felt green and callow.

Sitting on the sand in front of the dark roaring waves, they relaxed. Gazing at the frothy crests, Bichor announced they made him think of detergent foam. He laughed suddenly and didn't stop till he felt a cough coming on, thinking of the endless clothes being washed at the centre of the ocean. The others indulged him; the boy was obviously excited. When the mirth subsided, Rafiq said the sea waves were like beer froth. Imran didn't compare them to anything; he was preoccupied with all kinds of thoughts. Now thinking of his mother's food, now of the floods back home. Then, he fell to thinking of Ifra. He wondered how it would feel to be in a place like this with a girlfriend. Around them were the tourists, mostly Indian but some foreigners too. They walked hand in hand on the wet sands or chased their squealing children away from the waves. Some distance behind them were large numbers of people seated on plastic chairs and tables under the starry skies, feeling the cool breeze, hearing the whooshing waves, eating food in the flickering light of glassy table-lanterns. Goa felt like a place of freedom. The people around him appeared to be cheerful and carefree. Was this what freedom felt like? To be able to do what you wanted?

Rafiq was telling Bichor a potted history of Goa. It was Portuguese and then it became Indian a few decades ago. As time went by, the place changed. Newer crowds came. Fewer foreigners, more Indians. Kashmir was never Portuguese, but like Goa, Indians came as tourists there too. 'Soon they will try to limit beef in restaurants and try to make people vegetarian here!' Rafiq concluded. A thin, white-skinned man approached them, offering drugs. 'No, brother,' said Rafiq, decisively. Imran didn't know where Rafiq got his money from. He had heard a whisper or two that he did some dealing, but if he did, he certainly would never have tried his own merchandise. He was always sober and in control.

Back in their room, Rafiq told them of future scenarios where everyone would sit up and take notice when the bombs would blow up the former torture centres along with the politicians now living in them. Bichor closed his eyes and prayed for the day when every missing man like his brother, every wound, and every broken limb and torn eye would be avenged. Imran stared into the darkness, thinking, thinking. He was here, he had opted to be an accomplice. He didn't know what lay ahead. Doing something was better than doing nothing. That's what it was. Something spectacular would make a difference. Rafiq made him believe that it was possible, that it could be done.

The next two days, they met a few people, sometimes in tea stalls, at other times in the backs of shops. Rafiq's main contact was a guy called Zulfiqar. Zulfi, as he was called, worked in one of the Kashmiri stores that sold shawls, dresses, embroidered jackets and bags. The large store had initially stocked Kashmiri garments, handicrafts and woodwork but over time had expanded into general garments and knick-knacks to adapt to the varied preferences of their expanding tourist clientele. The owner of the store was a rich businessman by the name of Amin who had investments in various places all over Goa. He had a villa in

Goa, associates in Pakistan and Bangladesh, and prime properties in Delhi and Dubai.

Zulfi took the three of them out for a hearty meal where he drank alcohol in large quantities and told them of his love for a Goan girl. 'There's no future, of course. My mother would consume poison if I married a Christian.' Rafiq paid attention to Zulfi's woes only after he extracted a definite promise from the latter that he would soon introduce them to Ehsan, the adoptive son of Amin. Imran felt sorry for Zulfi, but his prime focus was the food. He had gone for a while without a good meal and this mutton vindaloo was quite something. Bichor listened to Zulfi intently and later mimicked him back in their own room, pulling funny faces to depict his anguish: 'Can't marry a Christian girl! What a Majnu! If you can't take the pain, don't try loving! When I love a girl, I'll really love her, no matter what. I'll show her what bliss is like.' Rafiq and Imran had laughed at the kid with a wooden leg pontificating about romance. Who was he going to love! Who would fall for a poor limp kid like him! And still he dreamt!

In the morning, Rafiq was up and ready before the other two were jolted out of slumber by the sounds of scraping of wood and the whirring of machines from the workshop below them. It was a Monday. They were lucky to have avoided the continuous noise over the weekend. Rafiq shouted that he was going to meet someone alone. Imran hasped the door after Rafiq left, and slumped back into his charpoy, covering his ears with a spare pillow. Around noon, sometime after the noise from below abated, Bichor awoke and roused Imran. Rafiq was not back yet. Should they go and eat breakfast? Let us have brunch, replied Imran, checking for his wallet under his pillow. Bichor didn't know what brunch was, and when they crossed the busy dusty street to find a restaurant with a thatched roof and a proper menu, Bichor asked him what kind of food a 'brunch' was. 'What meat is it? I'm going to try it today,' said Bichor as they called for the menu. This was the first time that the two of them were out in Goa without Rafiq and they felt a little liberated. 'A brunch is a fish native to Goa; it's really tasty, let me order it for you,' said Imran, hiding his joke beneath a straight face. Imran asked the waiter for chicken lollipop starters, a meal of fried rice for himself and rice with curried squid for Bichor.

As Imran placed the order in English, Bichor, whose grasp of the language was poor, felt proud that he had accomplished friends like Rafiq and Imran who treated him so well. He rubbed his hands in excitement before beginning his meal. 'Okay, brunch fish, here you come into my mouth!' They laughed and joked in Kashmiri throughout the meal. Bichor said he loved the brunch and asked for a second helping. Imran light-heartedly made fun of Bichor eating more today because Rafiq wasn't paying. After the meal, Imran bought a single cigarette from a roadside vendor and allowed Bichor to take a drag. Bichor coughed and said he had had enough. He couldn't understand why anyone would want to smoke. Imran replied that he was a kid after all.

Hardly had they been back in their room when Bichor knocked loudly on the door of the bathroom. Imran, who was inside, was trying to bring up in his mind the images of all the sexy women he had ever seen, in an attempt to please himself. When Bichor started knocking, he had just commenced zooming in on foreign women wrestlers from a show that was popular among men. Imran himself had first seen it on the TV at the back of a roadside stall on a village road. Annoyed at the interruption, he decided to forgo the activity and opened the door. 'Sultan! What's the rush?' he mocked, making way for Bichor. Bichor's urgency did not permit a reply.

In the following hours, Bichor used the toilet multiple times. He also started to sweat profusely, complained of a stomach ache and showed signs of a developing fever. The continuous noise from downstairs added to his fraying nerves. When Rafiq returned, he was angry at both of them. Why did they not wait for him? It was clear that they had no idea of what to eat and where. Imran tried to explain that they had gone to a good place; that it hadn't been cheap either. 'It's not about the price!' he exclaimed in frustration. 'You guys look like fools. People will cheat you and poison you here in India, even in Goa.' Imran controlled his temper and lay down, facing the ceiling fan. In Imran's defense, Bichor weakly said that the brunch fish had been tasty, even if it had not agreed with his stomach. 'What fish?' asked Rafiq. 'The brunch fish,' Bichor repeated. 'Imran treated me to it. He said it's a fish native to Goa.' At this, Imran turned around to face them and said, 'Bichor, there's no such thing as a brunch fish. What you ate was a squid. Brunch is a word made up of breakfast and lunch. I was kidding you.' Bichor's face contorted as if he was about to burst into tears. Seeing this, Rafiq and Imran exploded into laughter at his gullible innocence and soon Bichor too joined them in laughing, in-between bouts of cough.

While the tension dissipated, Bichor's health continued to worsen. Imran called up a community health clinic doctor from the yellow pages and discussed his friend's condition over the phone. Rafiq consulted a pharmacist at a shop in the market. Bichor stayed shivering in bed under multiple covers. Rafiq gave him the medicines and Imran held ice to his forehead. That night, Rafiq said to Imran that the two of them should head back as soon as Bichor felt a little better. He could not afford to be distracted by all this. He was going to finally meet Ehsan and he needed to deal with a lot of other things in order to make the trip worthwhile.

The next day, Rafiq got food for them before going out. Bichor drifted in and out of sleep under the influence of the medicines. Imran sat by him, thinking of a myriad things, wanting to be back home as soon as possible. When Bichor was awake and the workers below took their breaks, the two of them discussed cricket, the better series, the classic shots, the best matches, their favourite players. Imran told him about his village life and his crushed dreams of playing cricket professionally. When he asked Bichor what he would have liked to do if life had been kinder, he was surprised by the answer: 'I would have been an engineer.' 'Engineer, why?' queried an amazed Imran. Who would have thought that this poor kid had such an ambition? Bichor revealed he wanted to build. 'I want to make real things happen out of my thoughts. I love the way engineers can build bridges and machines. I would have liked to build Kashmir, build things in Kashmir with my own hands. Marvellous things that could make life easier for everyone.' As he finished speaking, they sighed. It was an impossible dream for a disabled child from a penurious family in Kashmir. Studying anything cost money, engineering and medicine especially. And what could he have built anyway? He would have been swamped by the corrupt officials, the contemptible politicians. 'You study some more and, who knows, one of these days, your dreams may come true,' lied Imran, thinking of his own college exams next semester. Bichor knew his friend was lying, but the lie gave him satisfaction. 'Brother, I love you,' he said, holding Imran's hand in his sweat-soaked palm.

When Bichor's fever subsided, Rafiq came to see the two of them off at the bus stand. It was a long journey and he shared their anxiety about their ability to cope with the travel on their own. He handed Imran bags of food and shoved a packet into Bichor's light shoulder bag. 'This is for your parents. Give them my salaams and good wishes.' Bichor knew that it was money. When the bus started moving, he checked the envelope inside the packet, and sure enough, it contained several 500-rupee notes. He thanked the heavens for the blessing that would make the winter pass better for his family.

The next twenty-four hours would have been the most boring time of their life, had it not been for the sudden chatter that ran through the tired tourists around them. With a quizzical glance, Bichor prodded Imran to find out what was happening. Imran reached forward and tapped the shoulder of the man sitting on the seat in front of them. 'Excuse me, bhaisaheb, looks like there's some news everyone is getting worked up about. Do you mind telling me what it is?' Imran was using his most polite voice and adopting an Indian idiom of address. The man looked at him, frowning, 'Don't you have a mobile phone? Check for yourself.' Then before Imran could reply, in a voice betraying agitation, he added, 'Our currency has become toilet paper! Mera Bharat Mahaan.[43] From tonight, all 500- and 1000-rupee notes will become invalid. The PM has announced it.' 'What!' exclaimed Imran, unable to believe the man. But, phones were ringing on all sides; people were jabbering nervously. Bichor was aghast upon hearing these words. Tears welled up in his eyes as he thought to himself that he ought not to have checked what was inside the envelope before reaching home. This is what being too happy leads to!

Over the next several hours in the bus, every passenger became familiar with a word called 'demonetization'. One man was loudly proclaiming in anger that the country had gone to the dogs. His wife was trying to placate him by saying that the old notes could still be exchanged for new ones over the next few weeks. Hearing this brought some relief to Bichor, who thought that the world had caved in on him for a while. Imran did not want to flout Rafiq's instructions about not using the phone in case it led to any trouble; so he and Bichor patiently eavesdropped on every conversation within earshot. Gradually, piece-by-piece, they formed a picture of what was happening. The PM had dropped a bombshell on the country by announcing that most of the country's paper currency would now be worth nothing. The government would put new paper notes of 2000 rupees into circulation after some time. While this was all put into place, people could exchange the old notes for new ones at the banks, but in restricted quantities.

'Why?' Bichor asked Imran. 'Why would he do that?'

'Because he wants everyone to use digital money and because he says this will take care of black money,' replied Imran in a hushed tone.

'Money isn't black or white,' said Bichor. 'Money is money. It is people who use it for black or white purposes. Can't they do that with the 2000-rupee notes?'

Imran had no answer to this. Neither did many others on the bus.

Then, a man began to speak in Hindi, turning around to address the people in the bus. 'Brothers and sisters, I have friends who work for this party. They have been messaging me on WhatsApp to explain. Our PM has done the right thing. This will make the smugglers and criminals quake in their boots. The new 2000-rupee notes, it is said, will have a special microchip embedded in them and they can be traced anywhere when used for evil purposes ... even if they are buried under the ground.'

'Is that possible?' queried the frustrated man sitting in front of Imran.

'Of course it is. We live in the twenty-first century. It is the era of technology, and our PM will do everything to make India the greatest country in the world,' replied the mustachioed orator with a tilak on his forehead. He gave the impression of a man who should not be messed with.

'I hope it is. My daughter's wedding is in two months and I hope this chaos will be sorted by then.'

'You worry too much,' rebuked the orator.

People began to ask him other questions as if he were the official representative of the plan. Though the orator took his seat after a few minutes, for a long while afterwards, the question-and-answer session continued. The last thing the orator said before sitting down was that everyone on the bus had a duty to support the government in its endeavours. It was a patriotic duty to stand by the PM in his policies. After all, the PM had said that this was a 'surgical strike' on black money, just like the surgical strike against Pakistan on our borders a few months ago. He concluded with a vigorous 'Bharat mata ki jai'.

Imran and Bichor had heard of the 'surgical strikes', but this was their first realization that India really was arbitrary and cruel even in India! Living in Kashmir, they had been used to illogical Indian dictates, but now they saw that India could be wildly unpredictable anywhere and to anyone, including to its own poor people.

'What about those who don't have bank accounts?' asked Bichor softly. 'How will they eat? What if someone saves money, like my mother does, in a kitchen jar?'

'It is not our problem. Let them Indians go to hell. We will exchange those few notes as soon as we can and that will be it,' said Imran in his ears, barely audible.

'What about Rafiq? What will happen to him?' Bichor persevered.

This hadn't occurred to Imran, and his face fell at the question. 'May God take care of him.'

'I will pray for him,' whispered Bichor and closed his eyes. Imran didn't know if he had fallen asleep, but he stayed with his eyes closed for a long time.

Imran had been disturbed by the whole trip. He couldn't escape the feeling that he and Bichor had been liabilities to Rafiq at best. But, how could he have known any of this beforehand? In any case, he reasoned, soon they would be back home where he would have to give an impression of having returned fresh and invigorated from Pahalgam.

After his friends left, Rafiq dressed up in his cleanest clothes and set out for the meeting with Ehsan. Zulfi accompanied him to the room, which was an office of one of Ehsan's associates whom he was visiting that afternoon. Rafiq calmed his nerves and went in with a grin, greeting Ehsan warmly. Ehsan sat on a leather-backed chair behind a big table. He looked every inch the businessman. Beside him was another man who was introduced to Rafiq as Shamsul. Before they began any serious conversation, Zulfi brought in cups of saffron kehwa and biscuits, then took his leave.

'Shamsul is my partner; an investor I work with. His family is originally from Bangladesh,' explained Ehsan. 'As you probably know, my father is a well-accomplished industrialist who likes to keep a low profile in politics despite all his successes in various businesses spread over several cities.'

This was only partly correct, Rafiq reflected. He knew from several sources that Ehsan's father Amin had a finger on the pulse of politics. However, he had been assured of his sympathies for Kashmir. It was rumoured in Rafiq's cell that in the past, Amin had paid for weapons for militants through several convoluted channels. He was hoping to present a business plan for political assassination as a strategy. As he thought these words, Rafiq stifled his laughter, converting it into a suppressed smile. What a world! Routes to the fight for justice were being forced into business plans for funding, just as the injustice of state oppression was trying to buy up silence! What else were those relief packages in the aftermath of what they called 'human rights violations'. As if there was any concept of human rights for Kashmiris!

When Ehsan finished speaking in general terms, Shamsul began. He was a short bald man with an oily pate. Between his ten fingers, he wore four or five gemstone rings, mostly square. He was dressed in an expensive suit and leaned forward to rest his hands on the table with his fingers interlaced.

'I am an investor. I care for Kashmiris, of course. You are one of my fellow Muslim brethren. But I am principally an investor. What's in it for me?'

The slick selfishness that he embodied made Rafiq want to spit in his face and walk out of the room right then. What's in it for me, the bald slippery man wants to know. Have you seen the dead bodies of my brothers shot and blinded like animals and then dumped into mass graves? Rafiq wanted to ask. But he maintained his cool and said, 'I hope this room is secure ...'

'No need to worry about that,' assured Ehsan.

'Here's the thing, you know what I ... I mean we ... intend to do. We want to blow up the big figures locally so that things are shaken up. Then they can't continue doing what they do. If you help us do it, you are helping Kashmiris. In addition, your money will buy you shares in a future scenario led by different people.'

'So you want me to blow up my money ... or our money,' he said, looking at Ehsan, 'in the hope that we will be able to make deals with your guys later.'

'Actually ... we will get ammunition from people who are into other businesses, including real estate across the border.'

Shamsul laughed cruelly in Rafiq's face, 'You aren't really a businessman, are you? Our boys in Bangladesh do it better with simpler tools.'

Rafiq remained silent.

Ehsan spoke up. 'Rafiq, we know all about your plan. We did before we agreed to meet you. We have our channels too. Here's what we will do. We need to offload some cash that is a burden on us right now. So, when you walk out of that door, take the bag on the side table. It has cash that should keep you going for a while.'

Rafiq couldn't believe what he had heard. This was a success. He felt light-headed as he said 'Khuda Hafiz' and left.

At the bottom of the stairs, he checked the bag to make sure of the currency inside.

That night, he and Zulfi had a big meal, where he listened with genuine sympathy to the man's woes in love. He finally said, 'The Christian woman is like alcohol. You hide one from your mother, you hide the other too. Marry her here and if you can't help it, get a woman back home to keep your parents company. Until Kashmir is free, you don't need to choose a passport or a wife.'

Zulfi hung his head, murmuring, 'You don't understand love.'

'Who does?' said Rafiq before he called for the bill.

The next afternoon came the bombshell news of the demonetization. Rafiq was at a loss. Was it mere coincidence that Shamsul and Ehsan had offloaded a bag full of 500- and 1000-rupee notes on him just the previous day? Of course, it had to be. Nobody knew that this was going to be announced. No one except the PM. And he obviously would not let this leak to a Goa businessman. So, then, it was a coincidence. What now? Well, he had to somehow get back to the Valley so he could find the means to make legitimate cash out of the paper notes. Taking an airplane was out of the question. Even the train was risky. He booked a bus and got on it straightaway. On the way, when he was not watching the news on the web, he kept staring out of the window, thinking that if he had known that things would be wrapped up so quickly, he would not have sent his friends just a day ahead of him. Then those poor fellows could have travelled with him without having to deal with any anxiety.

Two days later, when the bus from Jammu reached the Srinagar station and he got off, he knew the game was over. Policemen appeared out of nowhere and surrounded him. They handcuffed him and, though he didn't resist, one of them slapped his face and kicked him in the shin for good measure.

The next day, the newspaper carried a small item: 'One man who uses the alias of Mr Rafiq Butt, twenty-three years old, has been arrested for smuggling illicit drugs and black currency. The police interrogated him and believe that he is a terrorist and a crook.'

'That was all the item said?' asked Imran when Gul was reading it aloud. Imran was trying to hide his shock and worry.

'Yes. Why?' Gul looked at him.

'Nothing,' replied Imran, sounding casual.

At the first opportunity, Imran met Bichor in their basement. Bichor was wailing. Imran was downcast and quiet. They knew that they might never see Rafiq again. The boys who played cricket with them didn't read newspapers. Nobody would dare to enquire, unless his elder brother did. But who knew where he lived? They had only ever heard of him from Rafiq, never seen him.

~

Ehsan shook hands with Shamsul. 'Well done! And luck favoured us. I was hoping that we would plant the money on him and report to the authorities, but look how fate favoured us! The demonetization was the icing on the cake.'

'You know, they were lax enough not to know of his being here till we told them. What I can't understand is that I reported him to the commissioner that very night. Why did they let him get as far as Kashmir?' wondered Shamsul.

Ehsan replied, 'There are layers of things that needed to be taken care of. It was better to nab him there. If they had arrested him here, many things would need to be proven. In Kashmir, you can do more to, and with, someone, with much less worry about the consequences.'

Shamsul nodded. 'Yes, of course. Now, what about that deal?'

Ehsan smiled. 'Consider it done. The commissioner is on our side now. He has the ear of the man who signs the approval for the land. There's no way that our chain of restaurants will not sparkle in Goa soon.'

Pausing as he headed to his car, Shamsul turned around and said, 'That drop-out militant who wanted to cut a deal with us, how cutely Kashmiri. By the way, don't forget to tip Zulfi.'

'I won't. These people are fools,' replied Ehsan, adding, 'why don't you join my father and me for dinner tonight? Let us celebrate the venture.'

'Superb. I won't miss it,' waved Shamsul before urging his chauffeur to drive off.

11

IN THE WEEKS that followed, Bichor spent much of his time at the graveyard that had for years been the stomping ground for him and Rafiq. He would limp over to his preferred rock and sit there for hours on end, watching the other boys play cricket. Everything was as before – the other boys cheered for the runs and shouted foul now and again. Bichor rarely clapped now. When they ruffled his hair to cheer him up, he would stare at them, managing a feeble smile. When the days grew colder and shorter, he would leave earlier in the evenings. Imran often came to meet him here and play cricket, but he too felt a cloud hanging over his head.

Then the day came when Imran said he was going to his village. The year was coming to a close and life in Kashmir was winding down its gears gradually at the approach of winter. Bichor started to spend more time indoors, sitting by his mother as she mended clothes for customers on her sewing machine. From one to the other, Bichor looked at his parents; his father praying, his mother forever stitching. One turned the rosary beads in his knobby hands, the other moved her sock-clad feet on a pedal as she turned the handle of the machine and slid the cloth forward with her hands. It was soporific to stare at the rosary beads being turned one by one alongside the circular motion of the round silver machine wheel rotated by the crank handle. Bichor wished his parents had not given birth to him. What joy, after all, had he brought to their lives?

One morning, as he went out to throw the rubbish at the end of the alley, he saw that a local clothes shop was closing down. He ambled over to the yard where a few boys were warming their hands over a fire made by setting light to raw wood planks from broken fruit cartons. They were laughing and joking. When Bichor approached, they gestured to him to come closer to the fire and warm himself too. Not too close, though, they warned, we don't want to see your wooden leg catch fire! The boy who said this winked at Bichor and he smiled back. He was used to this insulting brand of friendliness; he knew they didn't mean ill. After a few minutes, he asked them about the shop. Yes, it was boarded up now. The man was moving to Jammu for business and taking his parents along. 'So, nobody wants the dummies lying outside?' Bichor asked. 'Of course not, he's thrown the dummies away. Probably too much effort to take those plastic and clay bodies,' they replied.

For the first time in a while, Bichor's eyes lit up. He had an idea, but he needed assistance to act on it. With his most winsome teenager's smile, he asked the boys if they would help him carry a few of those dummies to his house further down the lane. The boys felt sorry for the lame kid and a couple of them immediately agreed to help. 'Enjoy, brother. We'll do it right now. Tell us which ones you would like, and where you want them.' Saying this, the bigger boys started out with Bichor towards the discarded pile of cardboard boxes and the mangle of distorted dummies lying face-down on the ground. As they moved away, the cheeky boy who had teased him earlier, shouted out after Bichor, saying that he should not do anything indecent with them. 'Don't worry. I'm not like you,' he turned back and replied with a laugh.

When the boys had left the dummies at his door, Bichor went in and got a pail of water and a strip of cloth. The water was cold to the touch, but Bichor folded up his pheran sleeves and wiped the dummies all over before dragging them inside with some difficulty. 'What are you doing?' cried out his mother when she spotted him. 'I'll tell you. Give me a minute' was all he said. When he had brought them all indoors and shut the door against the cold, he went up to his mother and told her about his brainwave. She mended clothes, didn't she? She also stitched new clothes for people now and again, didn't she? Well, if she made a few interesting garments and put them on these dummies, then they could hang them in a window along with a sign and maybe more people would give her orders for stitching! The readymade clothes shop had closed down, and who knew, people might think of a few new clothes if they saw some good ones. Plus, while the dummies were discarded and free, they were in a reasonably good condition; he could mend the broken nose and the crack in the arm. When he finished speaking, his mother came up to him and enveloped him in a bear hug. 'My little baby!' she said, 'you are so thoughtful and you come up with the strangest ideas.' As he broke away from the embrace, Bichor said with a serious face, 'It's not a strange idea at all. You'll see. I'll even make some handwritten flyers and drop them here and there in the neighbourhood houses.'

That winter, Bichor was radiant with hope. He felt he was being useful around the home. He cut up strips of cloth, he folded the clothes, pulled the thread through the eye of the needle when it slipped, and he sang songs of prayer with his father while his mother worked. She made a blue-and-pink salwar kameez for a female dummy, a green shirt and black trousers for the male one. Bichor requested that his mother make a white kurta-pyjama with a golden collar for the child dummy. He kept in touch with Imran on the phone and asked him for well-written text in English and Urdu for the flyers. 'Put the English one on top,' he said, 'and none of those brunch fish jokes, okay? This is for my mother's tailoring.' He copied out the text that Imran sent him on sheets of coloured paper and slid these under many doors. Several women came to see what his mother was up to; they gossiped and drank cups of tea, and some left with requests for a small kurta or a shirt. How happy Bichor felt! 'See, now anytime they pass by our window, they will remember the talent you have.' His mother loved the purposeful and excited manner of her son and did not tell him that there weren't that many extra orders.

Bichor kept a spare mannequin propped up by the wall near where his mother worked. It was a female draped in an old pheran and salwar, her head covered by a red scarf. 'She will give you company when I am not around,' he said. 'Your father is mostly at home. I have company. I want you to grow up and bring me a real wife. And don't marry someone as old as her,' she said with a chuckle, pointing to the mannequin as she took the pressure cooker off the stove. 'I must have inherited my impatience from you,' said Bichor as he strode off, red-faced. Joking among friends was another matter, but he couldn't take such humour at home as well.

Imran, meanwhile, had become immersed in the village household after his return there. His parents were always asking him to do things – read the holy verses to his grandmother, go fetch the medicines for an aunt, help a cousin with filling a form at the bank, deliver food at a neighbour's house, help the workers mend the shed before it snows, he had even chopped onions in the kitchen. Being an only child meant that his days at home could be more hectic than his days in the city. Whenever he had spare time in the afternoons, he logged online to a war game where he had to build his virtual village and defend his clan against invaders. In spite of the work, the best part about being home was, without a doubt, the food. His mother spoilt him rotten by making his favourite meat dishes and showering him with hugs and kisses at every opportunity. Imran acted the young son's part, scolding her for being such a demonstrative mother while at the same time loving the attention and the preferential treatment.

Ifra was also spending the winter with family in her village. She had stayed on in Srinagar with her elder sister, departing the city long after Imran had left. She had definite plans for the holidays – she would study a lot, read the articles she had saved from facebook links and books downloaded as pdfs from the websites that circulated links for free. However, regardless of how hard she tried, she found herself struggling to find the time to do any of these things. Her mother needed her in the kitchen or wanted her to take care of the younger children for most of the day. Ifra's mother was of the opinion that the girl's father had spoilt her with leniency and love. No matter how she lived in Srinagar, when in the village, her mother insisted that she cover her head and do as the other women do. Her parents lived in a joint family with other uncles and aunts, and the women were expected to take on all the responsibilites of care. It was usually in the evenings and at night when the others watched television that she found time for herself. This was also the hour when she could reply to her college girlfriends and chat with Imran. Her brother Abid in Dubai was really the only one she could open up to about her life, even if they didn't always see eye to eye on life choices. Abid was two years older than Ifra. After finishing his schooling, he had been sent to Dubai to live with an uncle who worked there. He was now a newly qualified engineer who often advised her to forget about politics and focus on her career. 'Try to become a lecturer or something,' he said. He thought that his sister was wasting her energies and talents on pointless causes.

'What do you want to be? A politician? Lol!' he would write.

'Maybe, but mostly, a good human being. What about you? Mr Engineer, don't you miss Kashmir? Don't you want to see us all have a better life?'

'But you've got to worry about yourself first. If you don't have money or power, no one will care about what you think.'

'It's important, Abu. It's my duty to fight for the rights of all.'

'Okay, so what's next in the struggle over there? Slaving in the kitchen with mom?'

'Ya. Missing her food, aren't you? ;)'

'Tell her I miss her. I spoke to Dad also today.'

Ifra wrote back: 'Dad's a star <3'. Then, after a pause, 'So, this summer I'm thinking of doing some work for APDP or JKCCS or some social service organization.'[44]

'Is it a paid job?'

'I'll be an intern. The experience will be worth it.'

'I wonder what social and service means back home.'

'Hey!!! Don't be such a wet blanket. I heard from an Indian girl who was here last year as a volunteer in human rights work that it's very meaningful. They document stories, collect evidence, etc.'

'Good on you, sis. Hope your studies are going well too.'

'It's easy. We're just doing more theories about the dead white English people we already studied in school. Any plans of visiting?'

'I'm thinking spring or autumn. Who knows what the summer will bring? I don't want to be stuck indoors with poor connectivity for weeks if there's another uprising.'

'We are all used to it. At least, if offices close, Dad will get to be at home for a few days. Remember those days when we were children?'

'How can I forget! Those endless summers of being locked indoors, the only news being of deaths and funerals. It was so damn claustrophic!'

'*Claustrophobic,' he typed the correction.

'Yes, the unending curfews – claustrophobic. Catastrophic. Abu, I sometimes wish we were born somewhere other than Kashmir. Can you imagine what childhoods we would have had, what free choices? No dark weight of conflict.'

'Tell me about it. I feel like I've escaped and tbh[45] I like it.'

'I really want to see you again. Hope you come soon. Don't forget to get me a good wristwatch this time.'

'Sure. Btw,[46] how's that boyfriend of yours, Imran?'

'Shush, don't tease me now. He's okay.'

'Lol!'[47]

'I'll give him your wishes, don't worry ;) You found anyone there?'

'Here?! No time, sis. Work and male socializing, mostly. Life's online. Which reminds me, why haven't you been posting on Facebook lately?'

'Too much effort. I'll return, don't worry. Was just feeling a bit low after all the depressing political news lately. Trump and all that.'

'I suppose. That's why I don't follow politics. If you didn't, you'd feel better too.'

'Doesn't work like that, bro. But this is an old argument.'

'Indeed, alright, I gtg[48] now. Give everyone my wishes. I'll be calling soon.'

'Goodnight and Allah hafiz, Abu.'

'To you too. And remember, there's nothing to worry about. All will be well. Just take care of yourself.'

'Will do. You stay blessed, bye.'

'Bye for now.'

One night, after a chat conversation with her brother on Skype, Ifra sent Imran a message conveying her brother's greetings, and remembered to ask after his aunt, Zeenat. She had heard from her sister who had heard from Gul's wife that Zeenat had left Fayaz. Imran didn't reply at first. He could guess that Ifra knew through Gul's family, but he was still smarting from the hurt that Fayaz had not discussed any of it with him. His parents also pretended as if none of this concerned Imran in any way. This made him feel like a child. If they could include him in everything that needed doing around the household and in connection with the relatives, surely they could have discussed Fayaz with him.

His reply to Ifra's question was honest: he didn't know how his aunt was doing. He mused to himself that he didn't even know what really broke up their marriage or whether there were any chances of reconciliation. He had observed that the relations between the two households had gone cold and he was never asked to go over to Zeenat's place. He wondered if he should broach the topic at home. Fayaz had not visited them for a while and maybe he could find a way of starting the conversation from this fact.

He first approached his grandmother, thinking rightly that since she was related to Zeenat's father, she might be the one most willing to talk about what had happened.

'It was God's wish,' she sighed, trying to close the conversation before it had even begun.

'If everyone knows what happened, why can't I be made aware of it too?' Imran ploughed on.

'What has got into you? No one knows what happened. She had made up some stories, that's all,' replied the old woman.

'But what stories are they? I know Uncle Fayaz is not coming home because of what happened.'

'Such a tragedy. That poor boy loved to be here and hated the city and this year he has stubbornly decided to stay in the city and not come here to us. I pray for him every day,' she exhaled noisily.

'So, he's not coming home because...'

'What good will it do to you to know lies?' she answered his questions with hers. 'Haven't you got anything better to do?'

'No, I haven't. If I know the lies, I can at least refute them when I hear them, as I will, eventually ... Unless you want me to find an excuse to go to their place and find out for myself.'

'You will do no such thing. I don't know what she has been telling her aunts and cousins, but some of the gossip has spread around ...' Imran's grandmother paused before continuing, 'Fayaz's wife has been saying that he treated her badly, that he had an affair with someone, and who knows what else.'

Imran was quiet for a moment, then he spoke up in defense of his uncle: 'I cannot imagine Uncle is a wife-beater, and he never seemed to be the type to have an affair.'

'That's what I said. It's all nonsense. I don't know why her parents are not asking her to go and try to make it up with Fayaz. Surely, they cannot imagine that their daughter, who was older than Fayaz anyway, will find another husband again.'

'Have you spoken to Uncle about it?' he asked.

'Why should I? The poor child already has so many responsibilities at work and now I hear that he has had to hire a servant to cook for him. I feel bad that his wife's father is my cousin. It was not a match I was wholly in favour of. But your grandfather was in an almighty rush to solemnize Fayaz's marriage as soon as the boy got a job and we chose badly.'

'Maybe someone should bring them together to talk to each other and try to resolve their differences,' Imran reasoned.

'You know how stubborn your uncle is. He will not listen to anyone else in such matters. He probably already feels bad that he didn't have any children by that wife of his ... Don't you worry about it. Allah watches over us all. Those who are wrong will get punished.'

Imran was not surprised by the harsh verdict his grandmother had passed upon Zeenat. She was a conservative old woman from another age. It was hardly fair to expect her to think like Ifra when she had received none of the education or the exposure that the girls of today had. Imran was aware of the story that when his grandfather had been a militant, he had asked his future father-in-law to hand the daughter over to him as his wife or be killed along with his family. There had been little choice but to agree to bond the girl into the marriage. The new bride had accepted her fate and been an exemplary wife and mother, enduring their long separations without so much as a murmur of discontent.

Later, when his grandmother settled for her afternoon nap and Imran was by himself, he could not drive what he had heard out of his mind: Fayaz had treated his wife badly and had an affair. Could it be possible? On the one hand, he could not come up with any good reasons why Zeenat would make all this up; on the other hand, after having lost some of the affection he had for Fayaz, he didn't want to further believe that he was capable of cruelty in the manner that Zeenat had alleged.

While his family members missed Fayaz that winter, Fayaz himself stayed in the city and drowned himself in work. He had put on weight and was taking anti-depressants. He would often find himself thinking of running away, but he had nowhere to go to. After repressing his dreams for much of his adult life, he didn't even know where to begin looking in order to discover them again.

In the initial months after the parting with Shireen, he had coped much better than how he felt now. Zeenat had wept daily, but she had been around. The summer had been overwhelming with its misery, and the news bulletins had hit everyone with a different tragedy every day – the girl blinded in her home, the boys killed, the lecturer beaten to death, the ATM guard pumped with pellets in all his organs, the woman who died in the crossfire – leaving little time to think about the small concerns of daily life, a life which was mostly curfewed anyhow. When Zeenat left, Fayaz's friends had been there to take care of him. Then, there was the backlog of files to be cleared and the task of dealing with the repercussions of demonetization for his department. Between one thing and another, the autumn too had slipped past. It was when nature's gold had turned dark and white that he had been inundated with memories.

How long ago everything seemed! Yet, it had only been last winter that he and Shireen had shared the snowy city. Now, there was no Zeenat left to hate and no Shireen left to love. His friends too had been busy lately, Gul with his family and Rehan with Saima. Thinking of

Rehan and Saima gave him flashbacks of the times the four of them had spent together too. He felt that just when the tree trunk of his soul had begun to sprout a beautiful new branch, it had been wilted at that selfsame spot. All that was left was the hurt, the misery, the guilt, the pain.

Shireen had written to him several times that summer after going back to Delhi, but he had never replied. What could he say? They were two different people who were too different for each other. He had been a fool to dream of anything in the first place. In his depths, he wasn't even sure he had dreamt anything properly at all. He had merely let himself live the moments as they had come, in order to escape the misery of his life.

He didn't know what Shireen did these days, nor whom to ask, how, or why. Rehan had told him that Saima had cleared her exams and was in Delhi, preparing for the civil services interview in February.

As it was, Saima was engrossed in devouring the latest on current affairs. So much was going on in the world – 'Syria factions, Iraq turmoil, Brexit, USA elections, Venezuelan chaos, North Korean strategy, China's ambitions, state of Pakistan, and of course, India, and this is just the contemporary politics section' – she complained to Shireen, 'and I have to be up to date with all of it for this archaic bureaucratic personality test and interview.' Shireen knew that when her friend moaned, her job was to remind her to focus on the goal and tell her to imagine the nameplate that would read: 'Saima Sultan, Sub-divisional Magistrate'. She did as she was supposed to, even if she herself could not understand why someone would put themselves through such a gruelling series of exams and tests and interviews in order to land a job as a glorified bureaucrat. She knew that Saima was Saima, and once she had set her mind to doing something, nothing in heaven and earth could dissuade her. Well, except perhaps Rehan, but thankfully for her friend, he didn't want to. On the contrary, Rehan sent her forwarded links to articles and encouraged her to make it successfully through those hellish times.

Shireen divided her time between working on a PhD proposal about the history and future of Kashmir, and scouring university websites in Hong Kong for admissions and funding. Neither of these wearisome tasks was easy to accomplish. She had discussed her proposal with a few professors at JNU, and everyone she spoke with said the same thing: 'It is too general and needs sharpening into specific research questions and a hypothesis.' She had written fifty heavily footnoted double-spaced pages, and was nowhere close to finalizing the five pages that she needed. Finding opportunities in Hong Kong was proving to be difficult too. In addition to finding a scholarship and bursaries, there was the hurdle of language requirements. She had bought elementary Chinese learning books and purchased the subscription to an app that spoke the characters aloud and let her practise writing them on her Android phone screen. Even so, when she went to bed thinking that she had mastered a few characters, the next morning, her mind was blank again. In spite of this, she derived pleasure out of trying to learn the language.

She would forget about all her other worries when practising the pattern of the strokes. Her favourite characters so far had been the different variations of the sound 'shi'. Depending on the tone and context, it could be written or combined to mean time, being, things, ten, fact, life, teacher, start, soldier, history, meal, execute, verse, corpse, and much more. She especially loved 'shì' in the form 是 'to be, being'. It was a perfectly elegant ideogram, the mysterious little box with a closed lid placed on a black table propped up by ornamental curving strokes. Shireen loved to invent her own ways of seeing the Chinese characters. As she pronounced 'shi' with the rolling trilling rrrrr sound at the end, it was almost as if 'to be' in Chinese was an incomplete version of her own name – Shireen.

By the time the snow began to thaw in the Kashmir Valley, other things had changed in Delhi too. One spring afternoon, Saima closed her door, turned off her phone and wept for hours on end. She had returned from her personality test and interview, and she was sure that she would not achieve the rank she had been hoping for. In her mind, the scenario of that room in Dholpur House in central Delhi flashed over and over again. The people opposite her had asked her questions and she had replied comprehensively and confidently. But judging from their reactions to her responses, she just knew that she was not going to make it. Which answer was it that had sealed her fate? The one about the pros and cons of widely implementing biometric technology to provide citizen entitlements in a democracy? Or the one about the place of environmental conservation in educational curricula in rising power nations? Had her answer to the former question been too critical? She didn't think so. Maybe she had not said enough about the rising power aspect of the nations and focused too much on the environmental issue without differentiating between developed and developing nations. Or had she not projected confidence in the way that she had supposed? What did any of it matter now? She knew what lay ahead – the consolations of family and friends that at least she had come this far and done her best. When she collected herself, she first called her parents and then Rehan. They said to her what she expected them to say, and also that she might not know if she had actually not done well; let the results come out, they counselled. When Shireen returned to their flat that evening, she gave Saima two doses of the twenty second hugs, made their college hostel time favourite eggy cheesy maggi noodles for her friend and they watched a DVD of *The Boss Baby* together, passing microwaved popcorn to each other across the bed. Rehan sent her some flowers the next day. 'He's a keeper, isn't he?' Saima sparkled at the sight of the gift. From the other side of the room, Shireen gave her a thumbs-up in between sorting the clothes for laundry. Saima and Rehan had briefly broken up during the summer last year over Fayaz's treatment of Shireen. Both of them had wanted to be loyal to their friends. Upset at being the cause of their distancing, Shireen had tried to get Saima to understand that Fayaz's white lies were not his friend's fault. It was Shireen's own mistake that she had kept her connexion with Fayaz a secret from Saima. The couple had eventually made up, communicating more than before after the enforced drought of the estrangement and the connectivity restrictions over the summer.

Saima's focus on her career aspirations had given Rehan an impetus as well. As the Valley had creaked back to the hum of a busier daily life after a winter of heavy snowfall, he had laboured hard at writing more. He spent days hunched over his computer, typing furiously, with intermissions for tea and cigarettes. One of his recent pieces had attracted considerable attention. It had been plainspeak on a new stage of evolution in the occupation and the resistance to it. He had been driven to write it after hearing the remarks on Kashmir made by the newly appointed Indian Army general. The man at the top had said that he would be happier if the Kashmiri protestors used guns instead of stones, since that would make it easier to open fire on them. He had also said that any civilian Kashmiris who come out chanting slogans or raising Pakistani flags in support of the militants were, by default, terrorists too, and should be treated as such. On the other side, villagers had begun to surround the sites of encounters with the militants, throwing stones at the army. This had led to the shooting dead of several civilian boys. Rehan had eloquently asked the question of where this logic of escalating rhetoric and action would eventually lead. On the day that his article had gone viral, one of his journalist friends had asked him to name his favourite meal. Assuming that he was intending for them to go out and eat, Rehan had said, 'Mutton biryani, why?' The guy had winked and said with a laugh, 'I just needed to know what to bring you in prison when they put you there.'

Of late, whenever he had spoken to Fayaz, Rehan had encouraged him to start exercising. He was worried at the despondency and lethargy of his friend. They had tried to go jogging together – the discipline was hard to maintain, but it was at least a start. He hoped that the brightening days would also dispel some of the gloom. Once or twice, he had tried to discuss Zeenat with Fayaz, but had hit a brick wall. His friend did not want to open up on the topic of his marriage. Nonetheless, he tried to meet up with Fayaz whenever possible.

One time, they had been sitting in a restaurant where a television mounted on the wall was playing an old Hindi movie. Fayaz was telling him about the growing disenchantment he felt at his job.

'It could be worse,' said Rehan. 'Look at Gul. That guy's job is a total nightmare.'

'It could be better too. Your writing ruffles feathers. That recent piece, for example,' replied Fayaz.

'Brother, you must have seen the explosions on my Facebook. Let people like me write; that's all we are capable of. Why don't you consider taking some leave and...'

Breaking off his thought in the middle, he called the waiter and asked him to change the channel or switch the TV off.

Fayaz had not been paying attention to the background noise. At this instruction by Rehan, he turned around to see what was playing.

It was an Indian patriotic song from an old Hindi movie starring Manoj Kumar.[49]

Before waiting for Fayaz to ask him, Rehan explained, 'I can't forget the way they played these Manoj Kumar songs from the loudspeakers at the army camps last summer while the people were being killed in the violence.'

'It's propaganda,' said Fayaz.

'So much of it on all sides,' agreed Rehan.

He forgot about what he was saying to Fayaz earlier and went on to tell him about some of the other articles he had been commissioned to write. Then, he got a call on his phone and excused himself to answer. How usual it was in Kashmir for people to have these patchworks of multiple conversations on phones, texts, and in person simultaneously. Fayaz checked his email while waiting for his friend to hang up.

'To whom were you being so courteous?'

'Ifra,' Rehan told him. 'You remember when all of us – you, me, Gul – went on that picnic last year.'

Fayaz did not immediately register whom he was referring to, so Rehan continued, 'Come on, it was only a few months ago. That cottage of Gul's we went to. That girl who was in the car with us, the feminist student from KU.'

'So now you are carrying on with her,' Fayaz stated tonelessly.

'No, man. I am not a teenager any more. She has been writing some pieces on her blog that she would like me to read and offer feedback on.'

'I didn't listen to her much that time. I only recall how she ate a lot.'

Rehan laughed at this odd bit of observation. He also wondered if Ifra was still Imran's girlfriend. In any event, Fayaz had not known then and wouldn't be told now.

'How's Imran these days?' he asked.

'Good. He went home for the winter break. He's back now and, from what he told me, concentrating on his studies. At least, I hope that's what he's up to,' said Fayaz, frowning a little.

'And Gul, what does he say?'

'Gul is Gul. What does he ever say except what people want to hear. He too says that the boy is doing fine. He went on a trek to Pahalgam late last autumn with his friends from college; so I suppose he's having fun too.'

Fayaz was silent for a while. When he spoke up, he asked, 'What about you? Gul hinted that you have been avoiding him for the past few weeks.'

'Maybe. As you said, Gul is Gul. If I can't take one call from him, he'll conclude that I am avoiding him. However, there may be some truth in his feeling on this occasion...'

'Why? What's up?'

'Yaar, you know how the journalist grapevine is full of stories ferreted out from dark places. I've heard some things about Gul that I don't want to believe in.'

'Like what?' asked Fayaz, as the image of the locked shed with the guns passed before his eyes.

'He's been a friend. We've all shared some times together. But I've heard he works for both sides. A middleman in uniform. I'll tell you the specific things I've heard later at home tonight. I know he's not the only one. It's probably a survival thing, or maybe they've got something on him. Whatever. I just don't want to be any closer to that stuff than I need to be. Writers are cowards, isn't it?' Rehan resorted to a laugh as he uttered these last few words, attempting to soften the impact of what he had just said.

'I can't say I'm totally surprised. I saw men with guns in the locked shed at the back of his cottage that time.'

'Really? Well, that might mean many things here in Kashmir.'

'It might. But I'm thinking of Imran now. I need to get him to move in with me.'

'Why did you not have him live with you to begin with?'

'Zeenat didn't want it,' lied Fayaz. He didn't want to explain how the boy had never forgiven him for talking him out of a career in cricket; how the boy didn't want to live in that tension-filled household of theirs.

Soon after this conversation, Fayaz spoke to his brother Junaid who ordered his son to move in with Fayaz forthwith. Given the command had come from the top, Imran had no choice but to pack up and shift to Fayaz's flat. Moving to the newer part of the city meant that he was much further away from the graveyard where he and Bichor had continued to meet regularly that spring.

In fact, Bichor had started clapping again when the boys scored big runs, applauding loudest for Imran now. They had spent time in the basement too, looking at the dim squares of light shift across the rough floor as they talked of Rafiq. There wasn't that searing pain in their words now, for they knew what had occurred was irreversible. Rather, they spoke of their bittersweet memories with a fondly shared nostalgia. Before moving away, Imran promised Bichor that he would make every effort to come back and spend time with him. Bichor didn't want to believe in words any more, so he embraced Imran and merely said, 'Inshallah.'

The bounty of a beautiful spring never left the Valley unblessed. When April came, it brought along the colourful riot of flowers in tow. People came from far and wide to marvel at the rows of tulips in the Srinagar gardens named after them, hardly any of them aware that the choreography of blossoms had been constructed over a rumoured graveyard of the past. Roses sprang up, boldly declaring their charms beside the most humble pavements. Cherry trees submitted their pale pink petitions to the chancy breezes. There were daisies for the taking, sprays of narcissi nodded their heads shyly, while the bees consorted with the carnations, jasmines and peonies. In the countryside too, yellow mustard fields mimicked the yellow of the sun, almonds and apples bloomed beside gushing streams on the fabulous magic green carpet of the earth that made space for everything, even the wildest and nameless little weed and its flower.

Bichor's graveyard haunt boasted some of these, but he couldn't take his eyes off the red poppies with their papery petals. When he limped towards their makeshift cricket pitch, the distant sight of poppies made him think of sprinkled drops of blood. He was beginning to get used to a life without his most cherished friends when something happened that shook him, and many others around, to their fragile core.

One April afternoon, the news from Kashmir became a louder ripple in the world at large. From the newspapers to the television channels, in the Valley and in India and in the rest of the world, were splashed the images of a Kashmiri man tied to the front of a jeep that led an Indian Army convoy. People pieced together the details over the coming days. There were by-elections in progress in a constituency where a paltry single-digit percentage of people who were eligible to vote had come out to cast their ballots. This was not unusual in itself since the arithmetic of Indian democracy could be a cruel joke in Kashmir. But something else transpired that day, which made it through the noise of world affairs and demonstrated to the world that there was an infinitely elastic range of things that could now be compatible with a place still being referred to as democratically governed. The Kashmiri people had known this all along, but now many Indians and others around the world were forced to take notice too.

When he saw the images and the video of the use of his fellow Kashmiri as a human shield, Imran wanted to go out and pelt every stone he could lay his hands on. Fayaz and Rehan were chillingly reminded of their childhood nightmares. Gul told his terrified family that this was nothing new. Like many other young boys, he himself had been used as a civilian human shield during the search operations years ago. Many men remembered how, back in the early years of the uprising, they were forced by the army to go into buildings that were to be checked for the presence of militants. Zeenat prayed, reaching the resolve that she would atone for her inability to fight the oppression by saving a life. Ifra composed letters to newspapers. Rehan wrote poetry in a drunken haze after his conversation with Saima about how miserable it was to be born a helpless Kashmiri. Saima went online to battle the xenophobic Indian trolls who could see nothing wrong with what had happened. Shireen realized that this was not an abstract tragedy for her either. This was the display of vile inhumanity that should offend a human being regardless of their identity. Men could be dolls too. She wondered how the soldiers could follow orders that made them do such things. Then, she realized that humanity lived in a world where the holocaust was not even a hundred years old.

Bichor lay on the floor at home, wishing Rafiq was around to blow up the tyrants. He stared at the backs of the dummies hanging in the window in front of him. Tied with plastic threads, the three silhouettes were suspended from the curtain rail above. Bichor's mother was at the neighbour's house and his father was sleeping nearby. He had heard that the clashes between the police and the protestors were spreading across the Valley. The images from the television reports played in slow motion inside his head.

A young civilian Kashmiri man goes out to vote, risking the disapproval of many around him who would die before confirming Indian rule in Kashmir through the visit to a polling booth. He casts his ballot and comes out. The soldiers of the Indian Army pick him up and truss him to a jeep. He is affixed to a spare tyre at the front. He wears a grey pheran over blue jeans, and his shoes are brown. Two lines of ropes are tied around his body to secure a white sheet of paper that warns other Kashmiri people not to protest. A triangular red flag flutters at the side of the vehicle. An Indian soldier stands imposingly behind the tied man, the upper half of his body visible through the sunroof. In a supposed spectacle of unabashed might, the soldier towers over a man who cannot move. Behind that jeep is a convoy of armoured and weaponized trucks. The Kashmiri man sits with his legs parted; he's tied to the jeep at the very front and has the look of a stone on his face. The entire horrific procession passes the shuttered shops on muddy roads lined with long corrugated tin sheets on either side.

We wanted to defend our lives and pass safely through the troubled area, said the army major in charge. The man was fomenting trouble and directing stone-pelters, they added.

Bichor could not sleep that night. He was clear that it was better for Kashmiri men to die with honour than to be tied to the fronts of jeeps. Whatever difference did education make? Didn't those Indian Army people go to schools and colleges? And had it taught them humanity?

'Human shield,' what a word in what a world!

How could human beings be treated like objects? He could not get this question out of his mind. How could it be possible not to see the difference between people and things? Even the most illiterate person could tell you what a thing was and how it was different from a person. Even a child could tell you that. What was it about a uniform that made people become unable to see something as obvious as that? When the powerful saw the powerless, maybe they saw them simply as human outlines – as dummies – to be used and discarded.

At the thought of dummies, his eyes automatically reverted to the figures hanging in the window. Dummies are shaped like humans to make other humans imagine themselves in their place when they look at the dummies. Dummies invite a gaze; they don't return it. Dummies are ... dummies are...

Like a shot, Bichor sat up. It was as if he had been struck by a thunderbolt. He knew exactly what he needed to do, and became impatient for the next morning to dawn so that he could start doing it. Now, he could not sleep for a very different reason; not because he was submerged in grief, but because he was possessed by an urge to exact his revenge.

The next morning, Bichor set about his task methodically. He got a paper and pencil, and made a list of all the things he would need. He asked Imran to come over at the first possible instance. When Imran came to their basement on the following evening, Bichor told him that he needed his friend's help with two things. He had devised a plan to create a spectacle of revenge, but he was short of money and wanted to know when the next big function with politicians in attendance was going to be held in the city.

Three weeks later, the big day arrived.

Pratap Park near Lal Chowk was festooned with strings of posters for a youth cultural event. Cushioned chairs were laid out for the dignitaries in the front row. Behind them were hundreds of chairs for school and college students. A covered stage had been erected at one end. Loudspeakers announced that security had been tightened for the event and anything suspicious must be reported immediately.

As the place filled up, the students were the first to be bussed in. They were all Class XI students from various schools in the city. Some were dressed in white uniforms, others in pink, grey and green. The boys and girls sat on separate sides of the park. Their teachers hovered over them, constantly putting index fingers to their own lips to encourage silence. When their teachers passed by, the young people lowered the volume of their chatter to a whisper, but as soon as the teacher was a few rows down, they would start buzzing again. They had left their bags and other belongings on the buses. Though they had been instructed to turn off their phones, many of them had simply switched off the volume and continued to secretly check the screens. They had been brought there an hour ahead of the official time of the programme. It was a warm morning and they made for a restless crowd. After a while, other young men and women joined them. These were the college students, some of whom were involved in organizing the function. They ran to and fro from the backstage to various people in the park, apprising their lecturers of what needed to be fixed. Everyone in the area had a laminated pass around his or her neck, without which it was impossible to come near Lal Chowk that day. Several photographers, journalists and members of the state broadcasting TV crew also milled around, now talking to the supervisors, now taking zoom shots of the students. More time passed before the administrative officials began to arrive and at last the politicians showed up in their cars. When an official car stopped, their security detail fussed all over the place before letting them set foot on the red carpet that stretched from the front row seats to a heavily guarded park entrance marked with the words: 'VIPs (Very Important Persons) and Honoured Dignitaries Only. All others prohibited.' When the most important VIP had taken her seat with a gracious smile, the programme leaflets were distributed and the show was inaugurated with a delay of a mere forty-five minutes past the original schedule.

The young people behind the marquee were palpitating with nervousness. The girls in elaborate regional costumes checked their earrings were in place as they adjusted their sequined dresses, the boys patted their hair, and everyone revised their lines. Each one of them wanted to perform to the satisfaction of their parents who would watch them on a video and in the news clip on the evening news. 'The Culture of Kashmir' programme was being held to showcase the music and dance from the different regions of Jammu & Kashmir; Ladakh was historically included in the nomenclature of Kashmir. Between every segment, instruments would need to be placed at their designated spots and the performers had to be careful to keep within the boundary lines marked on the stage during their dances. At the end of the hour-long programme and before the refreshments were to be served, the head of education would give a short speech, thanking the students for their effort and involvement. He would also express profound gratitude to the distinguished VIP for taking the time out to attend the function and invite her to offer a few closing remarks with a view to encouraging the students. Then she and the other dignitaries would leave and the students would get their tea and snacks.

The function commenced; the young people sang and danced; the audience showered fervent applause on the entertainment. Surrounding this extravagant display of creative arts were numerous soldiers and policemen, most of them uniformed but a few in plain clothes too. Holding their guns, they stood dotting the park. All of them were human beings. All except the one that stood all the way across at the very back of the park at a ninety-degree angle from where the microphone was placed on the middle of the stage. This soldier was dressed in an Indian uniform, but he was quite visibly a dummy.

An impeccably dressed boy had dragged the dummy along on a wheeled platform from the backstage end of the park. At this time, the dignitaries had not arrived and there had been the general commotion of the student organizers from various schools and colleges who were rushing around to put things in place for their own segments. The boy had been stopped more than once by different security persons. In every case, he had shown them his pass that said 'Imran Ashraf, BA Student'. When they asked him where he was headed and what the dummy was doing there, he replied in the affected English accent that upper-middle–class residents of a capital city like Srinagar use to impress clerks and constables, 'This soldier needs to be placed over there for the duration of the programme. I'm merely following instructions.' With a combination of the beatific look on his face, his posh clothes, the badge hanging around his neck, the English language, an abundance of courteous gestures, and the limp in his leg – and of course, the fact that he was carrying a supremely confident patriotic Indian soldier in order to put him on proud display – Bichor made it through the stops.

The Kashmiri constables standing a few feet away from the dummy surveyed it from head to toe and muttered to each other: Hindustani tamasha – the Indian charade. Nobody dared to go up and touch even the lifeless dummy of an Indian armyman. They imagined this to be a patriotic prop brought in to please the Indians and remind the Kashmiris of who was in charge.

In the days preceding the big event, Bichor had been busier than at any other time in his short life. Even so, he had never once felt weary, so fired up was he with the zeal of seeing his thoughts turn into public action. He had asked Imran to teach him a few English phrases and practised saying them in front of the rust-flecked mirror above the sink in the bathroom: 'I'm merely following instructions ... duration of the programme ... I'm merely following instructions.' His mother had stitched the uniform in a hurry as per the specified design, believing that she was doing so for a customer in return for a handsome payment. Imran had helped him turn the traditional South Asian garment shop dummy with its Western-inspired fair skin, blue eyes and blonde hair into one that would be more befitting of an Indian soldier. Together, they had repaired the male form of the dummy and painted it in a shade of brown with black for eyes and hair. Bichor had acquired everything else that he needed on his own. With his work on inventively filling the inside of the dummy, he had shown himself to be every inch the engineer that in his heart he had once aspired to become.

When the hour was over and the students had been thanked, the distinguished VIP climbed up to the stage with poise. She adjusted the covering on her head and began a rousing oratorical speech in praise of the diversity of Kashmir and the unity of all Kashmiris. 'India is known for its unity in diversity and we are an important part of this vision,' she proclaimed. She prompted the youth to follow good examples of success and create a future of jobs and growth for Kashmir: 'Together, we will develop Kashmir.'

There was pin-drop silence as she spoke. No one would have dared to cause an interruption, even that of a phone vibration, when someone as important as her was addressing a crowd of students.

Then, in the middle of her sentence, came a loud call: 'Azaadi!' And once the chanting of that lone loud voice started booming, it didn't stop. It rang with the force of a historic chant for Kashmiri freedom that was familiar to generations. The voice was deafeningly loud and passionately sibilant. It repeated over and over again:

Azaadi!
Jis Kashmir ko khoon se seencha, woh Kashmir hamara hai!
Hum kya chahtey?
Azaadi!
Zor se Bolo!

Azaadi!
Phoolon wali azaadi!
Woh aayi aayi azaadi![50]

At the first sound, the crowds were paralyzed by a shocked surprise. Then came the confusion and terror of not knowing what was happening. Who was shouting these slogans?

In the unfolding drama, it was quickly realized that the voice was coming from inside the dummy Indian soldier. The sight was unforgettable; the oppressor standing in front of the oppressed, chanting for their freedom, his voice a stark contrast to his erect and uniformed body. Some of the students fished out their phones and started repeating the chants, adding to the utter humiliation of the authorities in full view of the camera lens.

The dummy was shot.

His voice ceased as several bullets pierced his head and body. It was not blood that came out of his form, but fantastical confetti of small green pieces of paper that flew wildly about the air over his gunned-down body.

On each was written the one word in Urdu: 'Azaadi' آزادی

The green fragments rained over the students and the soldiers; a few pirouetted over everyone's heads and reached the houses and offices. They drifted inside open windows and slipped past barbed wire cordons to land anywhere that the wind took them. One found its place at the tip of a gun, another in a child's hand. The word for freedom had turned from sound into alphabet. It would be impossible to find and censor everywhere that it had been borne.

The security men immediately rushed to provide cover to the distinguished guest, who stumbled down the stage helped by them, her hands shaking.

Split seconds afterwards, Bichor was recognized as the boy who had brought the dummy. He was shot too. Warm blood gushed out over the cleanest and most expensive clothes he had ever worn. His body twitched as the bullets were pumped into it in quick succession, then all of him became as still as his wooden leg. Photographers who were taking pictures captured his last moment. He had a smile on his face as he fell.

During his life, those who had met Bichor after he lost his leg had unfailingly assumed that he was nicknamed 'helpless' because he didn't have both legs. Bichor told the real story behind his name only to those closest to him. Before losing his leg, once during a period of turmoil, several young protesters had been hospitalized as a result of the brutal retaliatory force used upon them by the security forces. Bichor had rushed to the hospital to donate blood. As he was a minor, they refused him. He had begged and pleaded with them to take his blood. But they were steadfast in their stance. Bichor could not understand why the blood of minors could not be taken to save minors who could be shot. He had wept helplessly. People laughed bitter laughs upon hearing about his disappointment. They had called him Bichor – 'poor' 'helpless,' and 'unblessed' – and the name had stuck.

Bichor's body lay in a bloodied pool beside the cracked fragments of the dummy soldier.

The man who was used as a human shield went to the state human rights commission asking for justice.

The army major was rewarded by the government with a medal for his bravery even before an investigation into his actions was concluded.

Not a single stone had been thrown in Lal Chowk that afternoon, but the disruptive spectacle of freedom that Bichor had engineered would not be forgotten. Perhaps many of those green drops of the rain of papery freedom are still in Srinagar: you could try looking for them in the centre of the city and further afield in the crevices on the walls by the clock tower, behind the crumbling Shiraz Cinema, on the ruined houses of wood, stuck in chinars, maybe even saved in the pencil boxes of some of the students who were there that day.

12

FAYAZ WAS AT work when he received the call informing him that Imran was in police custody. Junaid was rushing to the city from the village. Fayaz left immediately for the police station. He called Gul, asking him to help. As soon as he heard about the situation, Rehan too made his way to join Fayaz.

The concerned authorities were trying to play down the incident. The news said that a student-organized cultural function in the city had been disrupted by a young, mentally-unstable Kashmiri boy who had succumbed to death in the ensuing chaos. There were several posts online about the chants that came from the dummy of an Indian soldier, but as soon as any images were posted on social media, they tended to disappear. The VIP dignitary's office issued a statement conveying deep sadness at the way there had been an attempt to sabotage a cultural event meant to showcase the rich diversity of the Kashmiri people. The statement further expressed the hope that such unfortunate instances would not discourage the youth of Kashmir from aiming to create a better future for their society.

Fayaz could not believe what he heard from the police about Imran's role in the matter. When he had left for office in the morning, his nephew had been asleep in bed. He was sure there must have been a mistake on their part. When they showed him a laminated pass with Imran's name and a photograph of Bichor next to it, he insisted that Imran's access permit for the area on the day must have been stolen and tampered with. When they asked him why Imran had not reported this theft or turned up for the event on the day, he didn't know what to say. Moreover, they maintained that although they didn't have conclusive proof of it yet, they were actively seeking more information on the evidence of a friendship between the boys. There were numerous people who had seen them in each other's company at cricket matches not far from the locality where Imran had previously resided.

Imran himself would not say a single word to confirm or deny anything, making his uncle and father furious. In the presence of several people at the police station, his father slapped him hard more than once, stopping only when he was prevailed upon to desist by his brother and the other men. Imran did not even resist the beating that turned his face a blistering red. He merely stood with his head hung low, staring at the ground below him. His father abused him continually, throwing at him the questions: Is this what I sent you to the city for? I gave you money for food, clothes, education, everything, and you repay me with this? How dare you get involved in trouble after everything our family has been through? How can you be silent now, you insolent wretch?

Fayaz spoke with Gul in private outside the station.

'Gul, you must help me. The boy is too young. He must not get a criminal record; otherwise it will ruin his life. He is probably scared into silence, that's why he isn't denying anything.'

'I am not the commissioner. I cannot do much in a case where the chaos was witnessed by senior administration and people with power.'

'What kind of a friend are you?' asked Fayaz in a fit of frustration.

'Don't take it out on me. I'm here because of your phone call. I'm trying to explain the state of affairs to you.'

'I don't want explanations. I want my nephew out of prison,' Fayaz spat out.

'In that case, you should have taken more interest in what he was up to.'

This sentence stung Fayaz in every nerve. He hit his head in exasperation, hoarsely exclaiming, 'It's my fault, all right. But you are a policeman and he lived with you in your home where he supposedly forged a friendship with that mad criminal.'

Gul was calm. 'I let him stay with me as a favour to you because you are an old friend of mine. While he was at my home, none of this happened. He did not bring that boy to my home even once. I am an officer who has a job. I cannot spend my time supervising your nephew or vetting the boys he plays cricket with.'

Fayaz knew that Gul was right. Imran was not Gul's responsibility.

'Also, as I told you, I've helped numerous kids before, kids who get into trouble of all kinds. But this case is more vexed because of the people who were present at the scene,' Gul continued.

Fayaz was quiet for a long while. He was a picture of pain as conflicting feelings registered sequentially on his face.

'Shall I ask someone to get water for you?' Gul asked at last, placing a hand on his friend's shoulder.

Fayaz brushed off his hand and, with a steely stare, looked directly into Gul's eyes as he pronounced each sentence slowly: 'Gul, I know what you do. I have pictures of men with guns from that shed on your premises. I also have other evidence from trusted sources that could seriously implicate you in a mess if I shared it publicly. I may not have police contacts that rank as high as yours, but I know people who can make things difficult for you. You get Imran released somehow. If you do this for me, I will never bother you again.'

Gul had not expected this. He pursed his lips and let out a long sigh. Then, he said, 'Fayaz, our friendship is over. I never want to see your face again. I will manage the boy's release, but you should know that it would mean framing an innocent boy instead. It may still cause me trouble. I will probably be transferred away and will have to change my bearings anyhow. But from now on, you and I are strangers.'

When he finished, Gul turned around and walked away with swift strides.

Over the next forty-eight hours, an intricate web of telephone calls transpired. At the centre of this maze was Gul. He was not a high-ranking policeman, but knew a world of people who controlled the trade in many things, most important of which was information. Another boy was picked up from a locality known for stone pelting and it was agreed that this boy had known Bichor and met Imran. He had stolen and tampered with Imran's pass to fulfil his role as an accomplice of the insane plan carried out by Bichor. Imran had not realized that his identity had been stolen and as he was feeling unwell on the day of the event, he could not get up in time to inform anyone there. The boy who was framed was dirt-poor and without any close relatives. He had been in and out of police stations previously on charges of petty theft and public disorder. Some records needed to be falsified and a fair amount of money exchanged hands to get the required signatures. The media, administrative authorities and the VIP dignitary's office were assured that the boy they had caught now was the real culprit. Imran was released with the advice to be more careful in safeguarding his identity. Shortly afterwards, Gul applied to be transferred, cancelled the plans for the construction on the upper part of their house, and asked his family to start packing. The members of his household were delighted that they would finally move out of this rundown area and into a newer place.

Judging by his demeanour, Imran had aged years in the span of a few days. Unless it was imperative that he speak, he continued to be quiet. On the first day back at Fayaz's flat, he ate little, hardly looked at his phone, and spent most of his time sleeping or lying on his side staring at the walls. First Rafiq and then Bichor – they had both gone. Nothing could be changed. He thought of Bichor's family, his old parents who must be suffering abominably. They had lost another son. He thought of how he could have chosen to be a different person, educated and employed. But he couldn't, could he? Or could he have? He imagined Bichor's bullet-ridden body; the next minute, the image of an excited Bichor came up before him. The boy had sacrificed himself knowingly, and happily too. Imran himself had helped him without knowing that he was going to stay on to be deliberately caught. Bichor had told him that he would leave the scene and escape before the spectacle. Why had he not done as he had said? Maybe he had wanted to remain there and witness the humiliating effect of his daring upon the faces of so many people there, even if it meant dying in the bargain.

Rehan had been at Fayaz's side unfailingly through the entire nightmare. He was there during the discussions between Fayaz and Junaid, where it was decided that Imran's studies would be suspended for the foreseeable future and he would be sent back to the village. He put up an argument or two about why this may not be the best course of action, but the members of Imran's family were certain that the boy would be better off back home for a few months. Rehan wondered if Ifra knew what was unfolding, though he refrained from calling her. When he spoke to Saima, he told her what had happened. Saima and Shireen had never met Fayaz's nephew, but the tragedies of young men in the Valley didn't surprise them.

As soon as Imran reached home, the women showered their wrath on him too. His mother reminded him of all the times he had caused trouble right from his childhood. Alternating between rage and sorrow, she broke down as she reflected on how close Imran had been to being jailed or worse. His grandmother asked him what else he was going to inflict upon her in her fading years. Imran did not reply to either of them. Later, his mother brought him meat and rice and implored him to eat, sitting beside him, wiping her tears with the edge of her kurta. Imran looked at the plate as if he could not recognize what it was. He told her several times that he had no appetite, but she threatened to sit there forever if he did not eat. So, he ate. He could not taste anything he chewed. He felt that in spite of trying to follow his instincts at every step in doing the right thing, everything in his life had been a huge mistake. He had brought a deep disgrace upon those very people who had sacrificed so much to bring him up. He wanted to atone for all he had done to cause them pain, but he didn't know how.

It rained continually that night. Imran could not sleep; he lay in the darkness, running his finger on the scar on his face over and over again. There was no way out. He saw his father's face as he hit his son; he saw Fayaz's face outside the window of the police station, talking to Gul; he saw Bichor's dead body; he saw Rafiq from the window of the bus; he saw his grandmother sleeping, his mother weeping. At last, he saw Ifra's face. It was an old memory: that first sight of her on the staircase of Gul's home. He wanted to cry in her arms. He knew that it may never be possible now. Black thunderous clouds started to rain a black snow inside his heart. He felt as if his body was turning into heavy lead. He did not know what to do. The shame would never leave him.

He got up and bolted the door. Creeping about quietly, he opened the almirah and took out the longest fabrics he could find and knotted them together. Then, he placed the chair underneath the ceiling fan. After a few minutes, he texted a single word – 'Goodbye' – to Ifra and wrote a note addressed to his family asking them to forgive him for everything he had done to bring them trouble and shame. Finally, he fell down on his knees and prayed for a long time, asking for forgiveness for what he was about to do. Then, before dawn, he hanged himself.

When the sun broke through the sky, it brought an immense grief crashing down upon the household. Imran had taken his life. His mother had knocked the door and upon receiving no answer, started shouting frantically for her husband. Junaid had broken the door and his wife had fallen to the ground unconscious at the sight of her son's hanging body. Within the hour, several people had gathered. Imran's grandmother wept inconsolably, unable to stop blaming everyone and everything for this cursed spell that had been cast upon their household. Women of the village had assembled to wail and lament the loss. The men were making the arrangements for the funeral. It was a sin to commit suicide, an act expressly forbidden in Islam. The boy had asked for forgiveness in writing and prayers of dua must be made for his eventual peace. The corpse needed to be washed by the men of the family. The coffin and the shroud had to be procured. Fayaz wanted to throw himself against the walls in a grief that he felt as irredeemable guilt. More than anyone else, it was his fault. He had been the one who had failed his nephew. He had been the one who had let the boy fade out of his life. Now he was no more. The young cheerful Imran, the Imran whose scar he had nursed, the Imran who had looked up to him. Today, he was helping to scrub and perfume the corpse of that same boy. Would Fayaz ever be able to forgive himself for all the people he had wronged? Imran, most of all?

Zeenat's family came to offer condolences too. Her mother wept as she addressed her late cousin's son and consoled him for their tremendous loss. Imran had been her grandson too. Zeenat's own cousin and aunt and father were there as well. Zeenat herself tried to stay in the background as much as possible. She was right in doing so because as soon as Imran's grandmother saw her, she cried louder that an evil spell cast by a witch had cursed their family. She did not name Zeenat, but a few women whispered and directed hostile stares in Zeenat's direction. Fayaz saw Zeenat and felt that he was seeing a ghost. He could not believe that the two of them had been a couple. He could hardly recognize Zeenat with her gaunt body and blanched face. Fayaz could not escape the thought that whomever he had touched, he had broken. He did not dare contradict his mother when she asked the women mourning alongside her to see that Zeenat leave. She left with the rest of her family. However, Zeenat's mother stayed behind since Junaid would not agree to his aunt leaving along with everyone else.

He requested that his mother respect his aunt and let her grieve. So, the wailing continued, the procession went to the graveyard. Imran became the earth.

When Ifra saw Imran's text the next morning, she tried his number repeatedly. Then, she saw online that his friends were mourning his demise. Her head spun. They had not been in much contact lately, but she would receive his messages occasionally. They had met two weeks ago at an ice-cream parlour in the city. At that time, he had gifted her a small key ring shaped like a cricket bat on which was a sticker with the word 'freedom'. Last week, he had written her a long and lovely message on the morning of the Lal Chowk incident. When he didn't return her calls in the days afterwards, she didn't persist. She knew that he now lived with his uncle and had less freedom to do as he wished. She couldn't believe that Imran had taken his life. She broke down to her brother Abid on the phone. He told her not to punish herself by being depressed. She had no control over others. If she didn't know what was ailing him, then he was evidently not reaching out to her and that could only mean that he didn't want to. Her grief was a natural reaction but she must not let it overpower her emotions. There was no way Ifra could mention her loss to anyone else, even to her own sister, let alone anyone in Imran's household. Rehan came to mind and she rang him. He knew what had happened and was heading to Imran's house to be with Fayaz that evening. In fact, he said, he was hoping she would call since he did not want to bring her the news himself in case she was not aware of what had happened. Ifra sobbed into her phone, telling him how she would miss Imran and regretting all the times that she didn't go out with him and his friends. Rehan stopped by to meet her before leaving for Fayaz's village. They spoke for an hour and he told her about the troubles Imran had been involved in, how he had to be released from custody. Ifra understood that her boyfriend had lost his life to the chaotic cycle of humiliation, revenge and shame that was Kashmir. She could do nothing now, but one day, she wanted to play a part in politics and change things. If she were to be blessed with a long life, she would spend every day trying to create hope in that despairing place.

When Zeenat returned home from the mourning, she felt strangely liberated of her sorrows. She had seen Fayaz and read every alphabet of guilt and misery that was written on his face. She did not wish for revenge any longer. What is more, she prayed for forgiveness that she had ever wished ill upon him. Every human being is destined to live their fate. Compassion is the least of the virtues that one could offer to others, even those who have caused us hurt and harm. In her heart, she forgave Fayaz that day. She would not forget the way he had treated her, nor how he had made her feel like a worthless ugly object, a doll that he could rape and to whose tears he could respond to with indifference, but she forgave him for being himself, for having to be the person that he was. She looked at the massive green chinar tree in her yard and thought of her intent to save a life – the resolve she had made on the day she had seen the humiliation of her people in that picture of the human shield. She did not need to decide on the human being she wanted to shield most from the pains of this world. It had to be the mute child from whom she had withheld her kindness. The image of that pheran-clad child counting leaves patiently last autumn had never left her mind. It was not going to be easy to obtain the consent of her family, but she would not back down till they agreed to her bringing up that child as her own.

In the following months, Zeenat found every reason to persuade her family members one by one about why she needed to adopt that boy. It would give her a reason to live again, she told her cousin. It would fulfil her dreams of motherhood, she said to her mother. To her father, she mentioned how caring for an unfortunate person is a virtuous act that had religious grace. She convinced her aunt that if she adopted the child and lived with him in the city where he could go to a school for differently-abled children, she would be away from this village where the bitter sentiments of Fayaz's mother were causing some to see her as a woman who could wreck curses upon others. Eventually, they agreed.

Later that summer, days before the month of Ramzan, Zeenat's father accompanied her to the house of the village gravedigger. The child was shy and did not want to come near the strangers. The old man and his wife had been taking care of the deaf-mute orphan, but they knew how uncertain a future he had with them. Zeenat's father finalized the terms with the gravedigger. He had buried corpses all his adult life and his eyes were hollow with melancholy from the sights he had seen in that conflict zone. The man was happy to let go of the child. Before leaving, Zeenat secretly pressed a pair of beautiful gold earrings into the old woman's hands. She blessed Zeenat repeatedly. Zeenat no longer wanted the earrings Fayaz had bought for her, and which she had cherished for so long. Her parents knew that their daughter was not a young unmarried girl any more; she was scarred by a bad marriage and her reputation in their orthodox village had now been besmirched. Perhaps her living in the city with the child would be better for everyone. They could certainly afford to support their daughter; after all, she was bringing light to another life with her deeds.

As Zeenat moved to the city, Fayaz left it.

Fayaz applied for leave from his job for a few months and went to stay with his family. When the tides of visitors bringing sympathies abated, the family members were left to share their anguish and sorrow. Fayaz had kept away from his family for too long, he felt. He had not even come with Imran over the winter. Now he tried to be there for them all. He helped Junaid with his business; they spent days together at work, sharing their loss with a quiet brotherly understanding. He listened to his sister-in-law reminisce about her dead son, sharing his memories of his nephew with her. He sat with his mother for hours on end, massaging her arthritic legs to relieve her of the pains, while she repeated the same things to him in a growing fog of senility.

When his leave was about to expire, he asked for it to be extended on compassionate grounds. He steered clear of any contact with the people he knew from the city and tried not to bother with hearing the news whenever possible. The singular exception was Rehan, who dropped by a few times, and on such occasions, they would go on drives through the countryside to sit by a stream or take a walk in the forests together. During these outings, Rehan would often recite his poetry.

Light and dark at the edge defined:
Your shadow like a shawl
Drapes my being,
Then gathers a crease;
A furrow sown with that morning's thoughts,
When you and I had never met,
And our shadows still free,
Had freely roamed.

Fayaz would close his eyes to hear every word as it became gently infused with the sounds of nature around them. The gurgle and murmur of the waters as they purled their way around the boulders and the chirping of numerous birds added a sonorous texture to the lines.

He spoke to Rehan of many things: his guilt and sorrow over Imran, his feelings towards his dead father, his frustrations at his life choices, but even when he tried, he could not explain to his friend what his relationships with Zeenat or Shireen had meant to him. With the intense reflection afforded by the aftermath of deep suffering in his now-changed surroundings, he admitted that he had probably neither loved nor hated either of them. What he could not make sense of was why he had been cruel to them. He knew so many men, Rehan himself being an example, who had been able to conduct their relationships with women succesfully, but he didn't know why he himself could not do so. He wasn't just confused, he said. He had spent a lot of time thinking about it and he was sure he hadn't been able to let himself relate to them as people. Between the rights he thought he should have in a bond and the responsibilities that he felt he must own up to, he felt caged. He could tell what he wanted from women, whether it was the comfort of their body or the warmth of their affection, but he did not know how to commit to the sharing of dreams. When he had tried to simulate shared dreams, his own had become increasingly blank. Rehan listened to his friend, but had no wise words to offer. Perhaps not as intensely as Fayaz, but who had not felt so at some point in their life? It was terribly hard to love other people after a while, unless one could share dreams; but dreams were evanescent and changing. The hardest thing always was to know one's own self.

Midway through the summer that Zeenat moved back to Srinagar with her deaf-mute son, Saima's and Shireen's life changed too. When the interview results were declared at the end of May, Saima found out just how wrong she had been about being unsuccessful at the interview. She was one of the candidates in the final list. She screamed in joy so loudly that the neighbours banged on the walls in consternation. She jumped on the sofa and hugged Shireen for what seemed an eternity. She rang everyone she knew, not just her family and Rehan and friends, but her school and college friends whom she had not spoken to for years. She thought of the many ways in which she would pamper herself; she made lists of the gifts she wanted from her brother, her sister, her father and mother. The next morning, she still could not believe that she wasn't living in an exquisite dream. Rehan came down to Delhi for the weekend and she kissed him in public at the airport.

Shireen was waiting to hear back from the universities in Hong Kong where she had applied for a PhD. She had begun corresponding with some potential supervisors who were hopeful of her chances of winning funding for the first year, after which she could apply to become a teaching assistant in order to support herself. Her doctoral proposal, when it had finally been submitted, had not been about the history of Kashmir after all. The canvas of history with all its constitutional complications was too large. The question she had wanted to ask about the past had led her to eventually recognize that the histories she had pored over with a scholarly diligence had, in fact, been his-stories. Where were the Kashmiri women?

She wanted to speak about the her-stories – the trauma of her grandmother and others like her who had suffered violence during the invasion. And if that was the past, the present too was rife with stories of sexual violence and mass rapes. Kashmiri Muslim women in Kunan and Poshpora villages had been mass raped by the army; the uniformed men had not been brought to account. When Kashmir was being communally divided in the 1990s under Governor's Rule, Kashmiri Pandit women had been threatened and raped. Stories of women being raped were hushed up across the border on the other side of Kashmir. The military and the militants had both been men. Shireen remembered how she had felt upon reading her grandfather's diaries – she often had to remind herself that he was, and also wasn't, her grandfather – the men did not fight over women and property, they fought over property and women as property. Building upon the work done by others, her question about Kashmir's future was about investigating sexual violence against women during the war and non-war situations, but further, it was about understanding how the occupation of Kashmir by the different regimes had seen Kashmir itself as a feminized place. When she had shown her final five-page draft to a professor at JNU, she had found it so persuasive that she had asked Shireen why she didn't want to pursue her PhD at JNU itself. 'Because here my work might end up being too anti-national and thus censored,' she replied. These were fraught times in the country and especially at universities with a critical tradition, so the professor had merely replied with an 'of course'.

Saima was excitedly preparing for her impending time at the Officers' Training Academy in the hills of Mussoorie, where she would attend a residential school with her batchmates. Shireen was sitting on the bed with her Chinese books and a laptop in front of her, advising Saima on how she could possibly narrow down her selection of clothes from the masses that she had originally intended to take. An email pinged as it landed in her inbox. Assuming it was just another promotional offer or a listserve forward, Shireen casually typed in her password to wake the screen. When she read the email, she involuntarily drew a breath and froze. Thinking it was something serious, Saima asked her: 'What's it? Tell me.' Shireen turned the screen around for her friend to see, but did not move or utter a word. She was still as a statue until her friend clapped her hands repeating, 'Wow, wow, wow!' Her application had been successful and she had been offered a funded place at a Hong Kong university. Shireen thought of the childhood slides that said 'Kowloon' and 'Pearl Harbour'. Alongside them, however, now came up the image of another one, not the one with the dainty umbrellas, but one where she's by the window of a library that overlooks the sea. Underneath, it says: Shireen Raina, PhD scholar.

Later, over Shireen's favourite pizza, Saima teased her friend, saying, 'So, I go to Uttarakhand and you go to Hong Kong. The vagaries of fate!'

'Look at it this way; we both go to the colonial haunts of the British,' Shireen answered.

'Hey, jigar, I wasn't being serious. I'd rather be an officer than a student. And anyhow, much of the world would qualify as ex-British colonized.'

'I know ... but I'm being serious now; we'll both be in different places this autumn. So when do we meet next?'

'Summer. Kashmir. Promise,' Saima said these three words, reaching out for a handshake to confirm their agreement.

Shireen took Saima's hand in hers, replying, 'Promise.'

The friendship between the women had been a precious gift to both. It had allowed them to grow without letting the world close in on either of them.

An entire year passed.

The lustrous summery sky of a late afternoon had polished Srinagar into a painting that Shireen wished she could one day hope to imitate. The two women had kept their promise and met up in the city where Saima was now posted. Saima had parked her car and they were walking past the 14th Avenue cafe by the banks of the Jhelum. They looked at the glass-fronted upper floor where a pair of lovers was having their rendezvous. When they came upon the new SPS Museum – a purpose-built structure where the artefacts had been eventually relocated after the floods – Shireen recalled how she had visited the older building with a sleep-deprived Fayaz two winters ago.

'I had come here with Fayaz once. With a ballpoint pen, I had corrected the spelling of a 9th-century ~~Trible Diety~~ to Tribal Deity. As if the divinity would mind being referred to with a mistaken spelling! I would never do that now, given how foolish I have felt over the last one year in Hong Kong, trying to cope in a different language environment, making so many mistakes.'

Shireen had sent her commiserations in a message to Fayaz after Imran's death, and received a polite thanks. Saima had on occasion been in touch with him over the phone.

'I'm sure your Chinese is much better now,' said Saima. 'Living in another language can be the hardest thing to do.'

'The languages of others, how we try to make them our own ...' Shireen did not complete the sentence she had begun.

They had talked of their experiences in the intervening year. Saima enjoyed the challenges of her job. Shireen had struggled with her studies, forming the opinion that anyone who said education in India was demanding should try studying in Hong Kong! She was now back for her fieldwork in the Valley.

The two women crossed the road and stood looking out over the slow-drifting ripples on the tourmaline-green waters of the tranquil river. At that hour, only a couple of shikaras were floating by.

They would have liked to sit down on the grassy slope, but their clothes would not permit it. Saima was wearing her lilac-and-black kurta that Shireen had admired in Leh. Shireen was dressed in a white cotton salwar kameez. As they continued standing there, waiting for Rehan to turn up, Saima told Shireen how her job meant taking care of so many urgent needs of the people.

'It's about creating opportunities for people while the juggernaut of conflict rolls on, but it is vital too. I'm trying my best anyway.'

'I'm sure you are,' said Shireen. 'But, tell me, where are you going to take me that I haven't seen already?'

They went over a long list of places named by Saima, each of which Shireen had already been to, either by herself, or with Rehan or Fayaz.

At last, Saima said, 'What about the botanical gardens?'

'So we *do* have a place to explore on our own!'

Saima told her friend how she had first heard of the beautiful rolling green gardens from a European woman whom she and Rehan had spoken to years ago at a function in Delhi where Agha Shahid Ali's poetry was being celebrated.

'She married a Kashmiri man and has lived here since. She told me that there is a colossal chinar tree at the very back of the extensive gardens, which she calls the Mouj Chinar for the way it provides an encompassing canopy.'

'Mother Chinar. How beautiful! Like Mouj Kasheer.'[51]

'At the time I heard about the place from her, I hadn't been here much. And somehow I have still not managed to see that tree,' said Saima.

'Because we were meant to see it together,' answered Shireen with a smile.

Rehan was walking towards them from a distance. Their radiant outlines delighted him. He was happy to be seeing Shireen after a long time. Her hair seemed to be a curly reddish mass above her white clothes. She was turning towards Saima as she said something. Since Saima had moved to the city, she and Rehan had been able to meet more often and he was beginning to think that he might finally have to speak to his parents about their marriage. Saima made him happy and that, above all, was what it meant to love and be loved.

When Shireen and Saima did go to the botanical gardens, they made sure to wear clothes that would allow them to explore the green woodland. Driving down from Brein where Saima was living, they first passed the tulip gardens where the tulips had withered in the heat by now. Outside the botanical gardens were the sellers of souvenirs and Indian snacks for the tourists. At one such stall, bleached wood pen stands engraved with the words 'Jannat & Kashmir'[52] were being sold. Shireen was again reminded of the significance of the ampersand there. Kashmir was heaven, but it also wasn't, for what heaven is caged and conflicted? Did omitting 'Jammu' from that naming signify a more heavenly Kashmir by Jammu's absence? Or did the naming paradoxically try to claim all heaven for itself, but then which heaven teems with intolerant nationalism? With her camera pressed against the diagonal wire frame of the fence, Saima took pictures of the rainbow created by the spray of a tall fountain inside. Shireen was mesmerised by the seven-coloured arch that was magically suspended above the mist that engulfed the red roses lining the perimeter.

At the entrance, they were given lingering glances of appreciation by the young boys who sold them the tickets through the semicircular hatch carved out to serve as a window of the green wooden booth. Inside the initial stretch were the Indian families joyously paddling in boats in a small pool. As they went further into the landscape, the people thinned out. Middle-aged women gardeners were cutting the grass, moving step by step as they sat on their haunches with sickles in their hennaed hands. Two beautiful yellow-breasted, black-crowned birds flitted under a horse chestnut tree. A large bee buzzed. Dry leaves drifted down to nestle among the sun-dappled blades of grass.

After a long walk through tree-lined paths, at the far end, they espied the breathtakingly magnificent chinar tree. A gentle breeze threaded its way through the million shimmering green leaves held up by an ancient and massive trunk.

'If we were children, we would carve our names here!' said Shireen.

'The Mother Chinar in Mother Kashmir. This is our home in all its infinite opulent unriddled ... us-ness ... I can't find a word.'

'I know what you mean, jigar. I'll remember this place as a monument to our friendship.'

'I love you, Saima. You have been the one beautiful constant through these difficult and transitional years.'

'I love you too,' said Saima.

'Can you imagine what it would be like if people could see this place in the light of the full moon? What a painting it would be!'

Saima let out a soft sigh. 'We will never know. Anyone who dares that will not see the following dawn. This is Kashmir, after all.'

Settling down under the Mother Chinar tree, they spoke for a long time. They had made other friends in the past year, Saima might be married before too long, life would create obstructions, but they decided to never give up on each other, come what may.

The shikara that had drifted past Saima and Shireen on the summer afternoon was being rowed for its two passengers, Zeenat and Nayeem.

Zeenat had named her deaf-mute son Nayeem. The paperwork for adoption and official registration had taken several months, but while this was being finalized, Zeenat was able to move to a neighbourhood in Srinagar with her son. They lived in a small house in Solina, not far from where there was a school for deaf, mute and blind children run by an NGO. The two of them had been attending that charitable institution for the differently abled for the last year, assiduously learning sign language in order to break their prisons of silence. Their previous lives had been mournful, but together they found a reason to be happy.

Nayeem was a child gifted with prodigious patience and a unique skill for being fascinated by the most mundane of things. He looked at everything long and hard, as if silently building a tally of the universe in his head. From the broken to the inanimate, nothing was insignificant enough not to merit his careful attention; he observed the overgrown grass, the leaking roof, the tear in the bedsheet, a basket handle, shards of glass. There was the time last year when Zeenat had found him eyeing the rubbish dump. Pinching his nose with his fingers, he had stood staring at the pile of garbage: leftovers, peels, pieces of wood, twigs, fragments of discarded things. As she pulled him away from the overpowering smell, she realized that he was watching with rapt attention a fly that was buzzing in a circle of eight over the container. A few days afterwards, when she made a paper plane for him and showed him how it flew through the air, he soon took it and started running in a circle of eight, perhaps pretending that he were, simultaneously, both a fly and a plane.

Similarly, the boy's mind was a hive of activity as he saw the rectangle where a windowpane had been broken. As a temporary measure, Zeenat had taped the wooden frame from end to end with a thick cardboard on the outside and stuck a wad of old newspapers from the inside for extra support. Sitting on the floor, Nayeem turned his head to his left and cast a panoramic glance around the room's line of windows, tracing an arc with his eyes from left to right. Light light light dark light light. Five rectangles of blue sky that made five sunny squares on the floor, and one dark, no ... absent sunny square. An interruption. He focused on the darkened window and tried to make out the pictures on the newspapers, but from his height, he could not see this clearly. Five sunny pieces, if only he could have marbles in that colour! Sunny marbles that glowed warm in his hands. When his mother was busy cooking in the kitchen, he would count the tables, chairs, pots and pans, lines on the curtains, the number of steps on the stairs.

Living with him, Zeenat felt surrounded by a beautiful tangibility. Her wondrous child made everything more bearable. It had been hard to settle into the city where the memories of her painful marriage could assail her at any time. The first autumn back last year was particularly tough. This had been the season of her leaving then. Autumn was that period of time when entire stretches of walkway are thickly carpeted by the dry golden chinar leaves; these five-pointed leaves encompass more directions than one could imagine. As the trees gradually bare their branches and the weather brings moisture, the fiery crackling expanse becomes mulch. The ground is a soggy rug for days before it hardens and is embellished by the frosts of late autumn and early winter. Several times outdoors, Zeenat felt that she was stepping again into the quagmire of the wet chinar leaves that lined the long straight boulevard of her memories. She went forward carefully. Even so, the coordinates around her would move, as if guided by the crazed compass of a chinar leaf dancing in the wind, and the scene would begin to dissolve before her very eyes. At such times, she would feel herself shrinking; it was not her body that was being diminished in size, it was her eyeline that fell closer and closer to the ground. She would be sinking into the wet carpet of the watery leaves. Then, she would blink away her tears, and Nayeem's hand in hers would save her.

The child, her son, had grown closer to her over the last year. He had shown a reluctance to leave the gravedigger's family and had continued to be morose for a while after they moved to the city last summer. But, now, he clung to her, often smiling, wanting to be picked up in her arms, pointing to the things he liked. At his school, the teachers mentioned how he was a bright and quick-learning pupil. Zeenat worked as a volunteer at the school that needed all the help that it could get. The floods of 2014 had destroyed much of the technical audio and visual equipment that had been collected over the years in order to help the students. In a city and a country with so many competing demands and such a measure of conflict, few cared for the precarious lives of the differently-abled young Kashmiris. After all, when people drunk on power had blinded the young wilfully, what else could one expect? Nonetheless, the school, with all its limitations, was a citadel of hope where Nayeem and numerous others aspired to dream beyond anyone's wildest expectations.

Lately, the mother and son had begun to use some of their new language amongst themselves, communing with each other through the use of their palms, lips and facial expressions. They mimed gestures with the kinesthetics of their arms, making sound seem redundant in an already noisy world.

The shikara ride was Nayeem's birthday present. Nobody knew the exact day the child had been born. So a date of 14 June was made up to fill in his birthdate in the documents last summer. Now, a year later, Zeenat wanted her boy to see the city from a boat on his birthday. She herself had been on such a ride on the river only once before in her life. As they approached the concrete steps of a ghat by the river that meandered through the city, Nayeem excitedly pointed to a battered old vessel, yellow on the outside, fading blue inside, with a white-painted tin casing over the wooden roof. Unlike the fancy shikaras kitted out for the tourists, this one had no English name pinned to the front. In any case, the tourists liked being ferried on the Dal lake much more than on the Jhelum River. Zeenat negotiated the price with the blue-eyed boatman whose browned skin matched his trousers and his dyed hair. It was an entirely memorable experience for the mother and child. Zeenat adjusted her head covering and helped Nayeem into the seat at the centre, which was covered by a tattered old white Kashmiri shawl embroidered with orange and yellow flowers. Once she herself stepped on board and Nayeem was ensconced in her lap, the boatman pushed away from the ghat with his blue-tipped oar and they set out on the birthday adventure.

Nayeem looked up into Zeenat's eyes and gave her a smile that made her feel that she had truly lived. She kissed the boy's hair and muttered a prayer as they set sail. Under the azure skies, stray clouds topped the green mountains in the distance. Nayeem pointed to the reflection of the scene in the waters. In spite of knowing that he would not understand what she said, she softly told him about the places they passed. The boy patiently listened with the touch of his skin against his mother's arms. 'That, my heart, is a wooden shrine that is rare and beautiful.' 'Those are the houseboats. People live on them; visitors come from around the world to stay in these marvellous dwellings that are moored to the banks of the waters of Srinagar.' 'See that utterly crushed structure opposite? That was caused by the floods that almost ate up this city's history.'

The currents were in their favour and the lay of the land there meant that the boat tenderly drifted along the surface of the river. They passed by immaculate long yellow and gold houseboats covered with freshly painted green roofs. Anchored next to such boats were the smaller, older ones with the frayed wood panels and gas cylinders attached on the outside. Inside the pulled-apart shutters, they saw women peeling onions and men watching television.

The boatman asked her son if he liked the ride. He cannot speak, but he is happy, she had answered for him while he, of course, was oblivious to all sound and engrossed in studying the visual echo of everything on the gently gliding waters. 'Oh, oh. Poor child,' replied the boatman. 'He's happy,' Zeenat repeated again. 'Where's your husband? His father? Did he not want to come along?' the boatman asked out of a genuine curiosity. Zeenat answered without a pause for reflection, 'He's afraid of the water.' She had said this instinctively. Hadn't Fayaz really been afraid of everything, after all? Also, she wanted to stem the questions from the boatman.

The boatman thought about her answer seriously for a while and then replied in a long monologue: 'I can understand, some people fear the water. The water did bring the havoc of a deluge to us not long ago. But I can assure you that us boatmen will do anything before the slightest harm could possibly befall a passenger. It is our duty to put our lives on the line before risking anyone else's. Two years ago, one of my friends drowned in this very river. His boat overturned and he saved the three Indian tourists without caring for his own life. After being rescued by him, they sent him back to fetch their bags from the river. By this time, the boatman – his name was Ghulam – was exhausted. So the poor sixty-year–old died on the final dive, but only after he had saved everyone else. We will sacrifice our life before we let anything happen to anyone in our care.' He took a long breath and then concluded: 'You should tell your husband that he must trust us. Next time, inshallah, he will accompany his wife and son.'

Their shikara passed underneath a pale green metal bridge. Nayeem was absorbed in counting the rafters. Zeenat did not interrupt him for a while. She liked the poetic older wooden bridges made of wood; the newer ones had been fashioned out of metal beams and drab concrete. As they went further at a turning of the river, the current became stronger, and the light on the water was a shifting trail of gold. Temple domes came into view on the banks, as did the many newly constructed houses. Every stairway on the riverbank read 'Go India, Go Back' and 'Election Boycott'. Colourful clothes were hung out to dry over metal railings beyond the upward slope. Soon, they were approaching the Amira Kadal bridge. Nayeem registered no difference in the sound, but the volume of the bustling, congested city in front was jarring for Zeenat. Hawkers cried out their wares, men fished from the bridge with makeshift gear made of strings tied to bait in plastic buckets, mosque and antenna towers came into view, garbage lined the edges of the water.

'Let us go back,' she told the boatman. He deftly turned the boat around. Nayeem wanted to stand up for a while, so she let him, but held fast to both his hands. He indicated to her that he was hungry and she gave him a piece of soft cake rusk from her purse. Settling into her lap again, he nibbled at the slice. When navigating the bend in the river again, the boat became mired in wet mud. As the boatman used his energy to break the vessel free, Nayeem pointed out to his mother a kangri lying on the riverbank. He mimed a huddle in its glowing warmth. She laughed, and he joined her. 'My heart,' she said to him again.

How paltry is the language of spoken words! Anyone who could see the strenghtening bond of deep love between Zeenat and her son would not fail to notice the way in which finding each other had been a renaissance for them both.

A world without spoken words, where verbal language did not exist, might not only be more beautiful, but also more peaceful, she thought. When interacting with each other, people would not be able to hide behind the artifice of words; neither would they be able to disguise their own intentions to themselves by attributing them to the fallacy of what words indicated but hardly ever meant in practice. It would be a world for people like her and Nayeem, a world in which eyes, skins, hands and deeds made sense of everything. In such a world, it would not be possible to communicate to large masses in ways to create consent for the hateful ideas of inflicting violence upon others. It would be a sublime world.

Nayeem had finished eating his piece of rusk and pointed to an unfinished scaffolding of another bridge that lay far ahead, well past where they were to dock. Zeenat nodded. Better worlds will be built out of this one, even in Kashmir. K-a-s-h-m-i-r, she said to him, uttering the word slowly and with an exaggerated lip movement. His eyes twinkled and he clapped his hands in joy. Did he understand?

Or had he cheered at the fact that they were reaching land soon? She pulled up his tiny fist in hers and kissed it.

When she was taking the money out of her purse to pay the boatman, he tugged at her salwar, wanting another slice of the cake rusk. Zeenat took out the packet, gave a few slices to the boatman and one to him. When she turned around, having paid and thanked the boatman, she saw Nayeem crumbling a corner of the bread to feed a swarm of ants near the edge of the stone steps. Her son was preoccupied in feeding the little black ants. She held back and waited for him to finish scattering the crumbs for them, recalling that first meeting of theirs two years ago. It was as if she was running her fingers against the grain on the velvety texture of lost time. When her son turned back, he was smiling contentedly. He ran towards her and she held her arms wide open to lift him, pressing him lovingly against her bosom.

~

At this time, Fayaz had just finished a draft of his resignation letter in his village home. He was going to embark on a journey whose destination he would not know for a while. In his mind was the image of a walnut tree that buckled under its weight in a storm and then rose up again.

~

That evening, a marching line of clouds formed to filter the sun's angel rays upon the Valley at sunset. A subaltern Indian soldier was rebuked by his officer for looking at a motorbike gleaming in the showcase of a shop instead of being vigilant about his surroundings when on duty. Another young man's funeral was held after a protest in south Kashmir. When night fell, stars mapped the dark black fields of the sky, but they were invisible above the neon and fluorescent patchwork of lights over the deserted city streets. Beside the blue roofs of the UN Office in

Srinagar, amber traffic signals blinked ceaselessly for ghost traffic. Tall trees stood proudly above the necklaces of barbed wire; the ornaments of nightmare that Kashmir has worn too long. Dogs barked into the vast empty bowl of a chilly night. Children crossed over into the lands of dreams, and their daily tasks done, women looked out from behind dusty windows, finding reasons to hope for the irrepressible life of freedom in a fugitive city.

Notes

1 Salted pink Kashmiri tea.

2 The destination is her. The road is her. Let yourself drown, prompts the depth of my love. Else, learn to live with the pain in your heart.

3 The poem 'Bol' ('Speak') by the eminent Urdu poet and intellectual Faiz Ahmed Faiz (1911-1984).

4 'My Darling,' it literally means, My Life or My Loved One.

5 Cloth spread on the carpeted floor upon which the dishes are kept during a meal.

6 Strike.

7 The slogan: Kashmir will be/become Pakistan.

8 Oppression.

9 Cafe Coffee Day in Sonawar, a posh area of the city near Gupkar Road.

10 Delhi Public School and Tyndale Biscoe School are elite educational establishments in Srinagar.

11 Chequered Palestinian version of the traditional Middle Eastern/West Asian scarf.

12 Sunnah refers to the exemplary traditions, customs and practices of the Prophet in Islam.

13 In addition to the J&K (Jammu and Kashmir) Police, the various security forces in the Kashmir Valley include various units of the Indian Army, the BSF or Border Security Force, and CRPF or Central Reserve Police Force.

14 Misspelling of 'Fuck Indians' and 'Fauji [army-serving] Indians.'

15 Station Head Officer.

16 Kashmiri term for male family elders, often used for grandfather.

17 Clean India Campaign.

18 Song title: '*What a strange story this is*'.

19 Movie title, which could be rendered as: 'The heart belongs to me, but its love doesn't' (1960).

20 Jigar is a term of endearment (literally meaning 'my liver').

21 My entire world lies captured in your closed fist,
My heaven is locked in your eyes,
Were you to give me refuge in your heart,
I would come face to face with my desired love.

22 This building of our shared memories, under whose shelter we have spent so many nights...

23 Kanger is Kashmiri for Kangri, or a clay fire-pot with coal embers inside a portable wicker basket that is used for warmth in the winters.

24 Pheran is a well-recognized, loose-fitting Kashmiri outer garment.

25 Shravan is the fifth month of the traditional Hindu calendar (usually in late July/August). Purnamashi or Purnima is the full moon of that month. It is a holy day dedicated to Lord Shiva, and significant for Kashmiri Pandits who are Shaivites.

26 Elongated lamb meatballs in spicy red gravy, a dish in Kashmiri Pandit cuisine.

27 Kohl Rabi pickle, a Kashmiri speciality.

28 Kashmiri brinjal dish.

29 Yogurt.

30 Baten/Batni is a generic Kashmiri term used to refer to a Kashmiri Pandit woman.

31 Mujahid (plural Mujahideen) is a term for a religious warrior engaged in Jihad, often used for, and by, Islamic militants.

32 Pakistan, Afghanistan, these are graveyards for communists.

33 Hak is a leafy green Kashmiri vegetable, batta is rice in Kashmiri, kangri is a Kashmiri firepot used for warmth in the winters, pheran is a loose Kashmiri outer garment worn by all genders.

34 Kashmiri (Koshur), implying, 'Listen to me'.

35 Victory to Mother India.

36 Sehri is the meal before the break of dawn during Ramzan fasting.

37 Iftaar is the meal after sunset during Ramzan fasting.

38 A refreshing Kashmiri drink made of basil seeds soaked in milk, typically consumed when breaking the fast in the evening.

39 Kashmiri for 'rice-devouring djinn.' It is a colloquial Kashmiri phrase used to humorously refer to (and self-refer among) Kashmiris as voracious rice eaters.

40 The burning heart of a flame too has / the restless desires of a circling moth / else, without reason, relations cannot form / in the depths of lonely nights.

41 Burhan Wani was a rebel commander belonging to Hizbul Mujahideen who was killed by the Indian security forces on 8 July 2016. His death was followed by massive displays of public grief and a violent uprising against Indian rule during which pellet guns were used on protestors leading to severe casualties, especially relating to blindings.

42 ISBT: Inter State Bus Terminus.

43 'My India is Great!': a patriotic slogan, sometimes also used sarcastically.

44 APDP is Association for the Parents of Disappeared Persons, JKCCS is Jammu & Kashmir Coalition of Civil Society.

45 To Be Honest.

46 By The Way.

47 Laugh Out Loud.

48 Got To Go.

49 A male Hindi movie actor famous for depicting Indian patriotic/nationalist characters in several films of the 1960s and 1970s.

50 These phrases comprise of several Kashmiri freedom chants:
Freedom!
The Kashmir that we have fed with blood, that Kashmir is ours!
What do we want?
We want freedom!
Say it louder!
Freedom!
See that flowering freedom!
Here it comes now, our freedom!

51 Mouj is mother in Kashmiri. Mouj Kasheer means Mother Kashmir and is an evocative term for the homeland of Kashmiris.

52 Jannat is an Urdu word for heaven. So, Jannat & Kashmir would translate as 'Heaven & Kashmir'; the abbreviation J&K usually stands for Jammu & Kashmir.